THE ADJUSTMENT LEAGUE

THE ADJUSTMENT LEAGUE

File 1: The Boiled Child

MIKE BARNES

BIBLIOASIS
windsor, ontario

FIRST EDITION

Library and Archives Canada Cataloguing in Publication

Barnes, Mike, 1955-, author
        The Adjustment League / Mike Barnes.

Issued in print and electronic formats.
ISBN 978-1-77196-082-3 (paperback).--ISBN 978-1-77196-083-0 (ebook)

        I. Title.

PS8553.A7633A35 2016   C813'.54   C2016-900904-1
                                                 C2016-900905-X

Edited by Daniel Wells
Copy-edited by Natalie Hamilton
Typeset by Chris Andrechek
Cover designed by Gordon Robertson

Published with the generous assistance of the Canada Council for the Arts and the Ontario Arts Council. Biblioasis also acknowledges the support of the Government of Canada through the Canada Book Fund and the Government of Ontario through the Ontario Book Publishing Tax Credit.

PRINTED AND BOUND IN CANADA

for Heather

19.10.13
—
02.11.13

1

SATURDAY MORNING, EARLY. Sweeping up broken glass and litter on the lobby stairs, I catch a peep of white from the mailbox below. Inside, a line in blue ink on a folded sheet of paper. Handwriting I don't recognize, though a wobble in the letters tugs at me. An address up on Highway 7.

Then the three block capitals: TAL. Which I do know.

An hour later, up in Markham, I pull over on the long drive opposite the covered entranceway. Sitting in the Honda, I take it in. The sign flanked by junipers behind a low rock garden: **VIVERA: A Helping Community**. Below, in smaller letters: **With Special Assistance For The Memory Impaired**. Words to hang on City Hall.

Two stories in brick and wood, spacious, with long side wings. Fresh white trim around picture windows. Shrubs and flowers rising from raked wood chips beside the walkway. Gourds and ornamental grasses in big ceramic urns leading to the double wooden doors.

Vibe of an old-time farmhouse or plantation manor. Rambling as generations add on wings. The gray McHomes stretching to either side a jarring note. Ditto the four lanes of traffic. But the low-lying woods to the north, aflame now with scarlets and yellows, work perfectly.

Inside, old people. Women, mostly. In armchairs, on couches. Two in wheelchairs helping an Asian girl put creamers in bowls. A woman gripping her walker, another inching hers ahead. A ginger-spice smell that's hard to place. Apple cake? Sunday pot roast? Slow, savoury hours. A gray terrier and a calico cat mooching about.

"Judy Wyvern," I tell the young black receptionist. She looks up from her magazine, frowning at what she sees.

Remembering, she gentles her face. "Family?" The phone rings and she holds up a finger. Behind me, I hear "Just a minute," but am halfway across a livingroom-like space towards the door marked Director.

Older than the receptionist, mid-thirties, palely pretty with long black hair. Gray business suit and slacks over a ruffled white blouse. She extends a hand at Judy's name. "Family?"

I give her the slip of paper. "I'm sorry," she says. Her eyes stray up me without a flicker. Why she's not answering phones. She pulls a file over the form she'd been filling in. "Come with me."

People's assumptions will carry you a long way. If you don't force a scene, their own hunger to find one will take you a few steps further than you were meant to go.

§

First, see it plain.

The soldier and the bride, bodiless costumes facing each other across the shallow alcove. Sunlight slicing between pulled drapes, pooling on the stained carpet. The soldier hanging on one wall, low, the cuffs of his dress khakis almost touching the floor. Spikes under his shoulders, elbows and wrists make his arms seem to rise in a welcoming embrace. Opposite him, the bride in her white gown, pegged and cinched to a wooden frame. A corner of her veil tacked loosely above one shoulder, as if swept there by an errant breeze. Between them, on walls and tables, pictures of the times they lived through. The War and After.

The bubble woman following us steps cautiously toward the soldier. Stops, turns, approaches the bride. Her hand rising to touch the fabric. Down. Then up again to take a bit of the silk between thumb and forefinger. Rubbing gently as if to test it. She opens and closes her mouth several times. Finds her bubble sound of surprise. *Puh.*

"Does she see that she's headless?" I say.

"Maybe, maybe not," says the Director. Studying my face, the side I'm giving her. "Touch means most to them at this stage."

"They don't frighten her?" The alcove seems stretched just then with a terrible vulnerability, a skin of ultimate exposure that a glance might shatter.

"Does she look frightened?"

No. Or no more so than when the elevator doors opened between us. Pale creature in a flowered house-dress, dandelion fluff hair. Her eyes a thin, brilliant blue, magnified by thick glasses. Open as wide as eyes can be and stay that way. As if witnessing a tremendous and unending marvel. She stays at my side, and halfway to the alcove, I feel her touch my sleeve. A graze like a moth's wing. Stop, look her in the face. Same wide, unblinking

11

blue. The high sky just before space. And her lips part to make her wonder sound, a puff of air.

Puh.

"Where's Judy?"

"It's down the hall." The Director's voice cooling, spine stiffening as she leads me on. Who or what I might be a growing question. Wrong scene, voices are whispering to her. But how to change or end it?

Lamps, warm yellow, in sconces spaced above the carpet. Movie posters: *Rebecca. High Noon.* And pictures, pictures, pictures. Landscapes, pleasant scenes, in oil and watercolour. Photographs. A smiling man. Two women. Sisters? Families.

No sounds. None at all.

A man standing before one grouping. Fit-looking, short brown hair, dark pants, check shirt. Looking. Seeing?

And then the Director is opening a door, and for the second time in twenty years, Judy and I face each other on a locked ward.

Only this time you can leave.

§

The Director hangs back, lets me go in first. Respectful. And wanting to see what kind of greeting Judy gives… whoever I might be.

Not much. A look up from the bedside, a tiny lengthening of her lips that is the faintest smile. Twenty years twenty minutes perhaps in the spooky theater of her mind. Her strange agelessness. A child-crone then. A crone-child now. Fine, dry, center-parted hair, gray-brown, falling to her shoulders. Fine lines in her small-featured face, cracking like a doll's in an attic.

What she sees in my face as much a mystery as ever. Her eyes don't linger on the most obvious changes. Other people no more real to her than in those days, it seems. Or fitfully real. As real as she can let them be, as they need to be, in her private drama.

"I got your message."

"Yes." And goes back to what she was doing. Placing something near the feet of the other person in the room. The one who not only can leave, but has. Death has unlocked the door. "This is a crossing ceremony." Soft wonder colouring her hollow voice.

A small mound under the orange blanket. Sprigs of silver hair on the pillow.

"I thought you were…" The Director comes round to face me. "I assumed you were family. If you're not, I'm going to have to ask—"

"Leave," I say quietly. A scene ends when you take sides. And she's the one with the keys. Or codes now—numbers that unlock doors and elevators. That much has changed in twenty years.

"There's a protocol we follow. Friends are welcome at the family's invitation, but until all the family's been notified—"

"Out." In the hush of final notice.

"I'll be right back."

"I know you will."

§

I watch as Judy proceeds with her crossing ceremony, which she now calls a protection ring. Or a protection ring is part of a crossing ceremony. She doesn't say. She told me once her head was half-glass, half-brick.

"You're looking for the next object in the series," I say, as she opens bureau drawers. My voice-over part of our old ward style.

"The talisman, yes."

I step closer to the single bed. See a bit more of Mrs. Wyvern. Age-spotted brow, closed eye, curving nose. A wrinkled, sunken cheek. Curled on her side under the orange blanket, as if seeking warmth at the end. Propped against her back, a single monarch butterfly wing float-mounted in a dark frame. By her feet, the talisman Judy was placing when I arrived. Black and white photo in a gilt frame of a pretty young woman at a desk. Eighteen, nineteen.

Judy brings a soft green sweater with big buttons. More warmth. "Up by her face, please." I reach across to place it. Judy five foot nothing.

I stay beside the bed. Judy behind me rummaging in the drawers and closet. Murmuring. The sense, uncanny, that the woman in the bed is not dead. How can she be since the three of us are performing her crossing ceremony?

Madness is contagious. Something in sanity wants to undo itself. Drop free and scatter.

She brings things, places them. Sometimes takes one back. As always, her rites proceed by secret rules but falter even at those. Placing one object at her mother's feet and one at her head, one midway the far side, but as I'm thinking now this side, the cardinal directions, the next one goes below her knees, too close to the one at her feet and too far from anything else, destroying the symmetry. As if she loses sight of, or interest in, her own guiding stars. Tunes out the angels she said advised her. Though she never had a deaf ear for the devils.

She stops without warning. Breaks off the crossing ceremony—which even I can see is unfinished—and sits in the plush armchair by the curtained windows. Hands folded in her lap, looking about at the photographs on the walls. More than anything so far, it takes me back to the ward. Back to the dozens of people I met there. And the hundreds of outpatients since. People forever battening down hatches against a flood, but never completing the job, as if to prove that some waters won't be stayed.

The furniture, this place. Snaps of home and cottage. *Judy comes from money.*

A thought to shock, since I never saw the ghost of it in her life.

§

Two young guys from the funeral home in the doorway. Their collapsible cart discreetly between them. Who let them up? Judy at her most wraith-like slips sideways past them, they don't even seem to notice.

Stocky, crew cuts, suits. Like Mormons. God's marines. And sounding a bit like them, too. The softly brazen tones of young men schooled to make nice when they want to mix it up.

"How are you, sir?" The front guy extending his hand.

"I'm all right. But I'm not the one you're picking up."

The face darkening before it summons a sad smile.

"You might want to wait outside, sir. It's not usually recommended that the family watch the removal."

"I've seen it before. More than once."

"Well, it's up to you, sir, of course. But I just want to caution you that, depending on the time of passing, it's possible we might have to…" Trailing off to let me imagine what I've just told him I've seen. "And there are fluids in the remains that, not always, but quite often—"

"Get on with it."

I won't leave the weak with strangers. And there's nothing weaker than the dead. And nothing stranger than the young with too much muscle for their task.

"It's certainly your decision."

"That's certainly true."

With a glance back at his buddy, he comes on, hoping to give me some of his shoulder in the narrow hallway. Me wanting it too. This far into hyper-black, it will taste like a kiss.

"Stop right there. Hold up, everybody."

A cop. The Director beside him. Suddenly the death scene is crowded, almost lively. Five of us in or near the doorway.

"You." Cocking a finger at me. "Out here with me." Jerking a thumb backwards. "You guys." Two fingers. "This lady needs a word."

I don't like cops, it would be strange if I did, but I have to admire the way he clears the snarl. I've done the same, not so neatly, with tenants squabbling in the halls.

§

The cop and I sheer opposites. Him: short and pumped and smooth-skinned, cropped fair hair, spotless uniform. Staring up through clear gray eyes at six and a half feet of bone and swollen joints, Reaper skin stretched over them, the topmost foot an El Greco egg, bald and pitted and lushly scarred. Wearing a shapeless knee-length trench coat, frayed jeans and sneakers—about right for late October, though it doesn't change in July or January. The coat dark-splotched and wrinkled, like a giant old dishcloth, but fronted with four big pockets with brass buttons that snap shut—useful, like wearing four carry-cases on your chest. Standing by the bureau—where I've backed to monitor the scene around the bed—we make a comedy duo. Fuzz and Scuzz.

"I've asked you politely to leave, sir. Don't make me ask you again."

"No, don't. Because I'll only give you the same reply." Which was nothing. The worst thing you can say to a cop.

His jawline hardens. I look away from him, through the crowd of three, at the mound under the covers with its splayed sprigs of silver.

"Taser me or cuff me or frog-march me out—whatever your next move is, get on with it. It'll upset some of the residents, but most of them won't remember it long."

In silence he considers it. A care facility. A death scene. The Director's voice comes back. She's placed herself between the bed and the funeral heavies, hands flat in the air. I like that. Her.

"As I said, I *understand* the family's made arrangements."

"Pre-arrangements."

"Yes. Which you can follow as soon as you leave the property. But this is… a different kind of residence." She might be explaining to children, though the boys seem oblivious. "And we have a protocol whenever possible for daytime removals."

"When the family notifies us, we check the instructions on file—"

"Shh. You can watch the whole thing. Help if you want. Asmita, Meru."

Two East Indian women come out from behind the cop, the younger brushing at her eyes. Move silent as deer to the bed.

Shh. The word we were missing.

Such silence and stillness, a suspension, in rooms with the dead. Even with this crowd the aura of it lingers. A feeling that superfluities have been carved away and, for a moment, a door is ajar between the worlds of the present and the gone, a crack that reveals them to have been one world all along, separated by no more than a filmy membrane. Dual sense of a hollowing of the everyday, a going out of some part of it, and at the same time a sense that something new and formerly missing and powerful is rushing in—or no, not rushing, but coming in steadily as on a tide. The crack, or door, will only stay open a short time, since people will rush, with forms and ceremonies, to close it tight and pretend it never existed. A privilege to stand near it, dare yourself to go where it beckons.

§

"How'd you get that? Looks like somebody did a number on you, bud."

Cop's eyes at my temple, the particularly nasty webbing around my left eye.

"It's one thing you can always count on. Numbers."

A low sound. "I'm guessing he got what was coming to him."

"He did. Most definitely."

And then Maude Wyvern is making her last trip down the hallway of her home. On her back on the stretcher, her head on her pillow and her orange blanket tucked around her. Her slightly parted eyelids emit moist gleams. She looks deathly ill, not dead. Her caregivers walk on either side, one hand guiding the stretcher, one hand on her. The Director going ahead to run interference. *Maude's not well. We're taking her to the hospital.* Not even a lie required.

The funeral boys and I trail behind. Along with the cop, looking bored. A shit call.

No interference needed, as it turns out. Breakfast is over and the residents are gathered in a large room for morning stretches. Sitting on chairs, or in wheelchairs, in a circle. A show tune bounces from the ghetto blaster. The physio, a young Asian man, stands in the middle and, turning, exhorts the residents to follow his movements. Lift your right arm. Now your left. Now waggle your fingers, give a good shake. Like this. That's it! Some try to follow. Caregivers bend to offer encouragement, start a hand upward. The caregivers all dark-skinned: African, East Indian, Filipino.

The nighttime drapes are open and October light blooms through the sheers in a fuzzy cloud. Luminous drifting dust makes the physio and the torsos of the residents seem to float, swaying like stalks in a current. The bubble woman, standing at one side, never takes her eyes off the leader. Sometimes brings an arm up partway, regardless of what he is doing. The eddying light dissolves her filaments of hair, makes her round scalp glow a profound pearl. She opens and closes her mouth. Over the warble of the music, I hear it deep inside.

Puh.

§

After her mother's been taken away, I go in search of Judy. The Director let the funeral boys have their zippered bag at the end, checking first that the van doors screened all sight lines to the windows. Like throwing kibble to snarling dogs. Toss them something so they don't take it out on her on the ride. And after.

A glassed-in veranda curves to either side of the front doors. Midway along it I find her. Sitting in a cushioned wicker chair, hands folded in her lap. I'd never seen anyone who could maintain such stillness. The orange-and-white cat pads up and rubs against her leg. Hops up onto her and pushes with its face at her hands, which she lifts and settles again on its curved back.

"Do you want to go somewhere? Maybe get a coffee?"

"Yes, that would be very nice. Thank you."

Formal and absent as ever. As if taught early—and this lesson stayed—that the world is a kind of Sunday School fronting terrible denominations.

Even at her most extreme she'd enunciated primly. Standing by my bed in the ward's gloom, a shock sight in her bloody nightgown.

The Devil raped me. No, this time He was alone.

§

Driving west a few minutes, we come to Markville Mall. Another Super-something fronted by Walmart. Parking around back, we enter a more upscale assortment of shops, new names along with the regulars. A bigger, cleaner-looking food court, with more varied options. Amaya closed, though. The Thai place too.

"Do you want me to see if I can find a sandwich?" I say, looking around at the unlit kiosks.

"Not lunchtime yet," Judy says, sounding for a moment like a mother.

Checking my watch, I see it's just after nine. For a moment I can hardly believe it. Death's come and gone and I've been up for hours. Cooking, cleaning. Reading half a book. After all these years, hyper-time still astounds. Like living a couple of extra lives.

Judy heads toward a table in the empty center—exactly opposite to the perimeter perches everyone else stakes out—while I go for coffees and donuts at the Timmie's down the way. When I get back she has a plastic pill case out in front of her. **9 AM** in black on the flip top.

"Could you get me a glass of water, please?"

Her hands shake, a fine constant tremor. Not as spastically as I remember, but more constant. Like a tuned, idling motor. She takes bee sips of the water, a lurch in her throat to get it down. Same with the coffee. Nibbles, with small beige pointy teeth, at the sides of her donut. I've never known a longtime mental patient with good teeth. Occasionally, decent muscle tone—gym rats who keep at it, at least in the early years. But healthy white teeth—never.

I sip my coffee, waiting to see where Judy will take it. TAL gives me a good guess.

"Do you still perform adjustments?" A wicked gleam in her eyes. She was always a bit of a flirt. With funhouse fractures, to be sure, but you could see the ghost of someone's darling doll—a lot of people's probably—who must have picked at hearts through childhood and a bit beyond.

"Do you still do them?"

Do them? They're what I live for practically. "When they're needed. And I can," I say. Trading dangerous hints, just like in the dear old days of derangement.

"The Adjustment League," she says dreamily.

"I can't believe you remember that." Though of the two people I'd imagined writing TAL, I picked Judy straight off. A mystery how she found my mailbox, though perhaps not much of one. Judy, when not in lockdown, slipping invisibly along the streets, and me hardly inconspicuous. A mystery that will wait.

"I remember it." She picks up her nibbled-at donut. "Brad. Lynette. What was his name?"

"The nurse?"

"The big fat one."

"I don't remember." Then I do. "Fresca. Moaning like a speared beluga as they strapped him to the stretcher."

Judy grins. A real grin—sickness trashed again. With those pointy brown teeth. Feral, like a squirrel's.

And for a few minutes we just remember together. Filling in each other's blanks. Judy talkative, engaged. She switches on and off. Like anyone. Except her on is not far on. And her off is way, way off.

§

Brad, fat and oily-skinned, balding at thirty, tuned to Radio Moscow in the wee hours on the shortwave his father built. A decent Brezhnev when he isn't weeping. Lynette, a buxom farm girl—honey pigtails, big breasts and hips anyone with traces of a sex drive wants to nuzzle. Sniffling softly, sleeping with a stuffed giraffe. But yells sometimes too—what gets her into trouble with Fresca. A couple of Bubble Room stints, which frighten the bejesus out of the poor kid, Fresca ogling her through the plexi nipple while she cowers in a corner, hugging her knees. Or it's nothing to do with her rare out-bursts, which are standard wardstuff after all, just that Fresca hates not sleeping with her, and for sure has tried… among his other slurs, petty rants, power trips…

Fine. An adjustment is clearly indicated.

What's that? Brad and Lynette, excited. Easy to forget they're younger. We've all paid a cover charge of violence to be here. Still, this stuff ages you.

When you see something wildly out of whack. Something that needs straightening. Now.

Which is everything. Hugging the giraffe. Sniffles starting.

No. Most things take major bangs. And even then. But there are times—places—when a few good raps, sometimes just a tap, will set the whole thing tumbling.

More words than I've spoken in weeks. Not tiring, though. And Judy doing a little bobble-head of *yup* atop her catatonia. If only mad would stay mad. The most disconcerting thing the way it can slide away suddenly, never with any warning and seldom for longer than a moment, and a sly knowing face peeps out at you—at a table, in a mirror—as if an alert little squirrel is nesting within the sticks and leaves of symptoms. It shows itself for a second every so often, testing the weather perhaps.

Easy once you decide. *Just bring him the world.* Save a pill each, pot luck. Palm them when Becky, lazy and nice, is on meds. And fun, the meeting in *the lab*—whispers, evil giggles. The heavy tranks from Judy and me, real brain bombs, for the main load. But throw in the little upper from Lynette—a kind of jolter, jerky spiker, not a regular anti-D. Our shot of tabasco. Catch him in cross-currents.

The pop he drains in noisy gulps a good dissolver. And Brad thundering from the Duma beside Lynette in a thin nightie almost overkill as distraction.

Then just wait. Bedded down, like good nuts. And not for long.

Flopping around the station like a flabby fish. Slurring, grunting wacko riffs. Drooling into his *Maclean's*. His partner—Rodney?—back from patrol. *Jesus, man! Here, lie down. Can you breathe? Fucking hell. No, stay—*

Good fun. And sets the ward chattering for a long time. New army on the march: The Adjustment League. Codename TAL. Wink it over putrid coffee.

Not me, though. It disappears in my rearview and I go back to being bombed. Like Dresden after the soldiers leave. Slate days, weeks. And then—Lynette's mom bringing apple cake in Tupperware. *Thank you for our daughter. She says you've helped her a lot.* Tearing up. Husband with big rough hands shifting behind her. Cupcakes, another time. Brownies. Mouthing slow sugars in a chair by the window. Snow melting on blackened brick beyond the mesh. Nothing.

Or—way down deep—a dawning sense of adjustments adjusting beyond themselves. Adjustments becoming arrangements, even. Sometimes anyway…

§

"Do you still keep in touch with Brad?"

"No. Brad killed himself a long time ago." *Attempted it from a balcony, then an overpass. Got it done under a subway train. St. George Station.*

"I know that he did."

"And Lynette I lost track of completely. No idea where she might be."

"I understand." She's phasing out again.

The ward talk takes my eyes down to her neck, her denim shirt buttoned to the top. A natural drop, which started at Vivera, but now my eyes get locked there. Natural when you've seen her naked as many times as I have. The bloody nightgown optional on her nighttime crawls. Her cuttings rampant but exact, stopping precisely at her shoulders and knees. Someone—herself, even?—wanting her in short skirts sometimes. With glass, with knives, with needles and pins. But never on her face, never below her knees. Nor her hands—not there, below the elbows, either. Barbie's head—button nose, waterfall hair—and shapely calves, tapering fingers, jointed to a trunk spiderwebbed with scars and scabs, radiating and intersecting, like glass after multiple impacts. A mad monk's vision of a ruined Eve. That horny-hateful.

"Do you mind if I go to the bathroom?"

And puts you in the position of minder. Gatekeeper. Always has. "Of course not. I'll be right here. I'm not going anywhere."

"Thank you. I know that."

§

Ward memories. So sparse and fragmentary, but the strangest and most haunting are of visitors, outsiders flaring like comets through black space, vanishing just as mysteriously. Could the lady with oozing butter tarts have been Maude, Judy's mom? I see amber syrup, similarly coloured hair— nothing in between. And *noses*. My last foster parents, the ones I ditched mid-high-school, as monkishly persistent as gumshoes. Tracking me to rooms years apart, donating to the abortive stab at university. I know they made a couple of stupefied, awkward visits... but what I *see*, all I see, are noses. Pink fleshy organs of delicate sense, grimy grains settling on them. Made for better scents than Ajax and unwashed bodies.

You two, staff said, and roomed us across the hall from each other. But Judy and I never more than bio-doppels. Ward grunts, two decades into our tours, with lookalike rap sheets: classic first breaks with reality, hallucinations, ideas of reference, violence and paralysis, the whole shooting match of florid madness, which in Judy's case spelled schizophrenia, and in mine—less confidently—severe mania followed by equally severe and far more prolonged catatonic depression. Hyper-time, then Stone. How else for plump, indulged Brad to see us but as grizzled gurus? Tutelary berserkers. Even more so Lynette: in her twenties, but recently shucking corn with Dad, while Judy and I'd been on the streets since fifteen.

I wondered with Judy, as with all of us, if her diagnosis did more than graze what ailed her, gesture at it with a medico-syllabic wave. Acumen what you keep hoping will rear its head. But far rarer than compassion: smart, sustained noticing.

Not mere doped looking—Food Court pack sniffing difference over its chicken nuggets. Ogling singularity, judging it. Which makes me want to shove in their faces, as in earlier and less wily incarnations I've done.

Psych rez in one of the tiny conference rooms, pre-Fresca. You touched knees in those closets, soul-moths sharing a jar. Tantalizing, or pure torment—depending on the other moth. A big guy, burly, with a drooping Nietzschean moustache. Mulish enough to ignore protocol and suss me out alone. A former millwright, he informed me gruffly—part of a "real-world" trial in some med school, presumably—and I certainly must have resembled a pile of scrap iron.

Which he proceeded to tinker with aloud, undistracted by my silence.

One name for your down phase. Stone. Right, I get it. Chained to the rock. But all these terms for your other pole—hairy sausage fingers in the file—windows, hyper-time, hyper-black. Not names, I notice. Things. States. Makes sense maybe. Too much happening to settle on one name. We are legion.

"I am…" Scriptural correction a fly's whisper.

Huh? I get it. Course, another possibility might be: no names! Avoid 'em. Why, I wonder. Was it always like that? Or just since this last time, when your daughter, when Me—

Got to him before he got her name out. Someone must've heard the bang when he hit the wall. Multiple hands scrabbling with his to pry mine from his throat. The neck brace he wore for a few days gave him more gravitas, an unslouched gait and flaring jowls that reddened when we passed. Keep it, I might have advised him, if I'd had a voice.

§

What is it about the mentally ill that tells you they're off? Watching Judy walk towards me, I know that no one seeing her—and heads do turn, holding their stares for longer than curiosity permits—would mistake her for whatever they call normal. What is it, though? The unnaturally stiff spine and stately, mincing steps? A queen forced to walk a narrow ice bridge in armour. The child-like size and sex-toy hairstyle—but with puffy, mealy skin… aged doll, child crone. Her seeming obliviousness of, utter disengagement from, the other customers—which yet conveys an animal's tense, secret-sense monitoring of their exact positions and potential movements. A general sense—weirdest of all, this —of being scooped out, hollow, at her center, with all that's left standing sentry at the periphery. Guards around a pit operation. Is it just me seeing this? No, the other heads, young moms especially, their eyes narrowing as they track her, then turning back with renewed patience to mind their children, shushing their ruckus, helping them eat. *There be monsters.*

§

Without sanity dictating the script, you can start anywhere. The relaxation of lockstep bathes you in a mild euphoria. Seductive. And addictive. And dangerous: you can drift so

27

far out on warm currents of dissociation, it's a hard desperate flounder to get back to programmed encounters when you need them.

"What did your father do? As a career, I mean." Thinking of the wedding photo on Maude's bedside table. The groom already silver-haired, his black-haired bride beaming up at him. A long absence of widowhood, followed by the progressive absence of dementia. Long years of emptying. "He looked... distinguished. A professional, I assume."

"He put people to sleep."

Poetry or prose? The primal question with Judy.

"An anaesthetist?"

"Yes. The Sandman."

We work down more of our donuts with coffee.

"How long did your mom live at Vivera?"

"Two years and two months. Two and two, very true. She moved in in August."

"Who took care of her?"

"I take care of my mother."

"You do?" I can't keep all the surprise from my voice. "Where do your brothers live?"

"In Toronto."

In Toronto, but AWOL. Letting their damaged sister shoulder the load. At least in Judy's version. An adjustment is beginning to take shape. Or the outline, the need for one—a dull ache somewhere behind my eyes, like the first intimations of a pressure headache.

I push it back, like cramming a gelatinous genie back into its bottle. There isn't time, for one thing. Stone would be the first to remind me. Four weeks ago, perhaps. But this window's closing. And I pick them more carefully than I used to. Conserving energy with age. And what's here, after all? Asshole families nothing new. The rule, except in Dreamville. If you find these things remarkable, have another coffee.

Which I do. So does Judy.

"Do you still see Stone?" Out of left field again. But this time I don't wonder at her memory. Or her telepathy. All our wardspeak's coming back. All the invisible antennae fluttering, the warders blundering about with nets.

"I'll always need to see Stone."

"When is your next appointment?"

"Two weeks, maybe three. In about two weeks. The schedule varies, but we always start in early November. Then I'm his till at least the New Year."

Nothing wrong with her memory. Horrible to contemplate, given the splinters of her mind.

Does she remember seeing snowflakes behind me, as I remember seeing them over her shoulder beyond a window reinforced with heavy wire diamonds?

"That is not what killed my mother," Judy says. Bringing me out of a long spell of singling out faces and evaporating them. The food court filling like a sink. With only the very young and very old looking content, settled in their lives. Everyone else, especially those with kids, looking more or less like murder. Not for the first time, I'm glad to have a face that sends stares packing.

"That is not in fact what kills her."

"What isn't?"

"Tch." A teacher's frown. "Heavenly choirs."

So strange, these formal and tangential memos, without contractions and with small clear spaces sheltering them. As if she never found a home in English, though she has no other address.

Or is self-absorption all the key that's needed? Living in an all-consuming drama that only occasionally needs to be spoken aloud. Another is part audience, part bit player—part neither, just someone left out in the lobby, catching stray bits of dialogue when an usher opens the door. You haven't begun to fathom mental illness until you grasp the monstrous self-absorption it inflicts on its victims—like a giant snake, it forces us to swallow ourselves whole, digesting every facet of what we were in slow coils of peristaltic rumination.

"I am glad to see you feeling better. Someone said you stopped treatment."

An accusation, clearly. And beyond that: a judgement and a sentence.

Either way, not requiring an answer.

We leave when Judy begins checking her watch repeatedly, murmuring of "lunch" and "noontime pills." Clocks, meals, meds: treatment. But she spurns my offer of a drive to her group home off Danforth.

"My brother bought me a GO pass. So I could visit her."

One way of making sure someone does.

"Fine, but that works like tickets. You won't lose anything if I drop you off this time."

"Max told me to use the pass."

Max. With that prickle of adjustment asking to be scratched.

Yet, when I drop her at the Kennedy GO station, she walks in her slow stately way around to my side of the car. I roll down the window.

"Could you pick me up tomorrow morning? They told me I have to clear her room."

"What time?" No reaction. "How about ten o'clock?"

"That would be very nice."

And sails like a little queen into the dead sea of the station.

2

BARELY MENTIONED IN the food court and Judy's eyes bone dry, yet Maude Wyvern walking beside her daughter, sitting beside me in the front seat of the Honda. Everywhere now. The mortuary goofs ferrying an empty bag.

I almost take the 407 ramp, then remember and jump a lane over to continue down Kennedy.

Tempting, that clear dash to the 404, down to the 401. Home in thirty minutes this time Saturday. But too many dollars to the Spanish-Australian owners watching the video cams. And grime or snow smearing the plate doesn't fool them. A ninety-dollar fine to learn that lesson.

So take the slow way home, again. *Pennies saved...*

That's the discipline. Not one grand self-denial, but a thousand little ones. Just say No. And No again, a dozen times a day. The price of eking out an atrocity windfall. The price of living off the treatment reservation.

The car labouring a bit. Not grinding or knocking, but heavy somehow. The engine stroking in a thickened medium. Nine and a half years, but more than that. Talk to Lucius.

Glad to see you feeling better. Somebody said you stopped treatment.

Somebody should pay closer attention. Treatment stopped me long before I stopped it. Stopped me time and time again. Shaking, drooling, mini-seizures. Shuffling zombie fogs. Muscle twitches, knots, spasms. Pimples head to toe, another drug. Stomach cramps, nausea, diarrhea. And the worst: all-over inner itching, fire ants along the nerves. Lose twenty pounds in two weeks trying to stalk it off.

What choice—or guts—in chucking that? The wonder that you stuck with it so long. On, off, on. Back on. What kind of micro-toilet view of yourself? Stare into it like a cloud of knives. Asbestos breaths of self-erasure. Never forget it.

Or forget you're sick and need treatment. *Somebody said.* But your own, not theirs.

Adjustments and arrangements. Building a platform out of this and that, collecting cast-off boards and piss-stained styrofoam and balls of twine and tugging them into a shelter. Jerry-rigging a new windbreak after each storm.

No more recovery porn. Swear off the stuff. Live within the sickness. Own your shit.

Be a management monk.

No picnic, Judy, living off the reservation. Nothing to envy. Or—

See the little waif, orphaned girl-crone, mincing stiffly through the wilds of Markville Mall.

Not standing by my bed in a bloodied nightgown, no, the lines of her latest work seeping through white cotton. Not recounting in tape-drone voice her latest rape by the Devil, many devils, the angels' futile resistance and slaughter. Nor boasting, in a dybbuk's roar rent by shrill barks of laughter, of an isolated victory. Routing the Red Raper, snapping the wings ·

He flailed like broken umbrella struts, raking her worse than His talons ever did. None of her old forms of violence seems likely now. Twenty years of treatment—drugs and talk and drugs and forms and rooms and drugs and group homes and drugs drugs drugs—have done that much. But done what else? New things, or else exaggerations of the old. Around dull eyes, her face mask-like, waxen. Was it always? I remember more mobility: sly smiles, fierce sudden grins at a joke no one else could catch, pale light flickering sometimes through the glaze, like the flashlight beam of someone trapped deep inside a plastic labyrinth. Still that small churchy voice, just above a whisper. But more spaces than ever between the words, gaps where she waits and searches, hunting pages in a gutted library. Her shaking hands. They always shook—she'd been on top-grade mind-melters for twenty years by her thirties, we both had—and she used to hold them up to her face, watch them tremble, and tell how her own had been lopped off and these quivering things attached to the stumps. The tremor less obvious now but more constant, a checked force. Which sometimes shoots up her wrists and through her body in a spasm, a small intense seizure lasting half a second. And yet here she is. Living off-ward. Looking after her mom. Eating an apple fritter—in nibbles chewed to paste, her chin jerking with each gulp. Answering questions more or less sensibly. Remembering things no one would expect her to—my adjustment? TAL? Stone, weirdest of all. She seems diminished, yet sane. Ailing on multiple fronts, but in acceptable ways. A little shuffling person capable of joining the other snackers in the brash mall. A victory, then?

If so, why do they still stare? Flee their mundane misery with the kids to ogle the more blatantly undone?

Humping down Kennedy, picking up speed between self-storage places and fenced waste lots fronted with condo graphics, hitting every green until a red stops me at Steeles. **Welcome To Toronto**. But it's all Toronto now. From lapping lake to halfway to Barrie. Bowmanville around to Hamilton Harbour. You can drive and drive and never leave the zone.

Stopped behind a bus by Tam O'Shanter Golf Course, I catch a glimpse of fabric strips, maybe a pant leg and a sleeve, gray long undies, all draped over a flaming red bush by a water hazard. Litter to the untrained eye—but someone's made himself a den and it's laundry day. Stretched out inside an igloo of bent branches, lined with Glad against the rain, dozing while the pastel duffers loiter nearby, chuckling and cursing and dropping a dimpled new ball.

Enveloped by a blue fart of bus exhaust, I'm off with it. Introduce real hazard to the comatose game. Shank your drive and do a stint living rough. Sleep in a bush with flies and mice and garbage-mad coons pissing eviction on you. Spirit-cowing emissaries. Hack out your time or take a stroke and twitch on Haldol. It's fun to run with.

But that sludgy drag again when I turn into Agincourt Mall. Some kind of resistance flowing up from the tires to my palms over the wheel.

Circling for a spot, I place a palm on my forehead. Not burning, but warm. Not like fever yet, brains boiling. Just the churning inside, throwing off heat.

A Mr. Stone on the line? Something about confirming an appointment? Yes, he says he'll wait.

§

No Frills has a good deal on bok choy and gai lan, I bag several bundles of each. Also a five-pound bag of chicken backs and necks that an older butcher fills for me. They seldom put them out anymore, they don't move even in a discount store. Twelve packs of Mr. Noodle, on sale three for two dollars, and I'm set up for dinner for two weeks. Top-ups of breakfast stuff—coffee, milk, peanut butter, bread—push the tab to thirty bucks. Maintenance on two dollars a day.

§

Lucius, Lucy and Jared have been out grocery shopping too. They're unpacking the Landscaping & Home Repairs pickup when I pull into the garage on Eglinton. Big smiles from all three. My favourite tenants, no question. Lucius and Lucy almost identical, down to Levi's and ball caps. Small, strong people. White teeth in round brown faces. Soft, obliging voices.

But tough. Built for long-haul punishment, which no doubt they've seen plenty of. Lucius hustling, hustling—Lucy helping when she's not cleaning houses—yet they stay in 304, a one-bedroom, screening off a corner of the living room for Jared's bed and desk. Send whatever they can scrimp down south. Ecuador, Peru—the family dispersed. We don't inquire too closely into each other's arrangements. The bond is having them. Tight leash recognition.

"Meeting on Monday night?" Jared says, coming halfway to the Honda.

"You got it."

"Seven o'clock."

"Yup. Same as always."

What he knows but has to hear. His frown lines relax a little. A strange little guy, nine but looks seven, paler than his parents, with pointy elfin ears. Teased and bullied to hell and back.

I mention the heavy feeling in the Honda to Lucius.

"Still drive okay? Start up?"

"Yeah. Just… heavy. Sticky, almost. Like someone coated it with tar."

Looking like he wants to put down his bag of brown bananas and get under the hood now, he tells me he could be a day or two getting to it. Frown of apology. His busy season. Grass still growing and leaves to rake up, flower beds to cut back. Some nervous types already wanting burlap around their dwarf evergreens. Things slack off after the first heavy frosts, when he puts on the blade and prays for a big dump. That or frozen pipes. Both, in a good year.

"Sure, no rush. It's just a heads-up."

§

Up in 501, I get the big stock pot of chicken parts simmering, vegetables washed and draining. Plastic containers lined up, lids behind them, on the counter. Rinsed bread bags for the chopped vegetables. Check my watch: not quite 12:00. Still two hours before I show 305.

Nothing takes long enough. The trouble with speed-up. The hours stretch, or there are more of them. Minutes multiply like mushrooms, and lost for wholesome ways to fill them, you start looking elsewhere. Everywhere.

I make a cup of green tea and take it to the armchair by the living-room window. Lean forward, hands around the warm. The new EMS station across the street below. Next to it, old fire station 135 with the red door. Cars and buses cutting and gunning along Eglinton, two lanes either way. Slamming for the lights at Chaplin. Condo tower on the southwest corner, high and plush. Chaplin slicing diagonally down into the cake of Forest Hill.

A good view, still. Well worth the top-up to the Owner.

I take care of my mother.

Sipping Luck Yu, I can feel myself drifting toward an adjustment. And feel myself pushing against the drift, since I don't know if an adjustment's called for, or, if it is, if I'm the person—the person with the time—to make it.

Adjustment. Such an easy word to say. Like tapping a loose part into place, or straightening a crooked picture. Except that people, especially the loose and crooked, seldom sit still for their tapping. Or resist the urge to tap back.

It's wise to recall first principles.

An adjustment occurs when a deserving target intersects with a mood of black fuckitness. But be careful. In a world howling for adjustments, you can't make all of them. And you can't make even one unless you have the window—time and means (especially mental means)—you need.

So—go carefully at the start. Move slowly across the ice of status quo, pushing your poles ahead of you. Is there a crevasse demanding your attention? A spot the snow pokes through and tumbles into, a place of nothing, darkness under white skin. And can you find the deep black crack inside yourself that matches it?

Nothing to undertake without due thought. Without due caution.

§

Sometimes an adjustment leads to an arrangement, though it's never cause to take one on. Lucius and the Honda, Jared and my lessons: two adjustments and a few arrangements hiding behind our little exchange in the garage, though you have to peel it back to see them.

The Civic a gift from a woman whose husband had been banging her around for years, then harassing her when she finally walked. She didn't want him banged back, preferred a gentler eye for eye. Swore she didn't love him, was over that long plague, but was sick of hurt and had found a kind of religion too.

I took my time with him. Fixed it so his locks wouldn't work, at home or in his office. Not all of them, just some. Then his car wouldn't start. Then it fixed itself. The computers in his start-up crashed. Then his life settled down for a while. I let him breathe easy. Then pieces of his mail went missing. Three different religious cults got it into their heads he was a lapsed member dying to return to the fold.

I'd put him down for a while, then remember and pick him up again. Like a hobby duck, whittled at in the garage over a winter. He must have thought the gods were taking random pisses on him. But he was too consumed with self-regard to imagine that they wanted to take long bloody shits and were being restrained.

The Civic, just a year old when she gave it to me, a kiss-up gift the time he broke two ribs. Bruises not in visible spots just got roses. Gross red bunches of them—two dozen, three dozen. It still had two years on the warranty.

And ran well, needing only basic maintenance, for two years after that. It wasn't until four years ago that the heftier bills began. The same time Jared was starting school. And already struggling, as I learned from his parents in the halls and garage. Bullying from the other students. Taunting, teasing. In class, in the yard.

I'm no teacher. Which Lucius saw, but Lucy couldn't or wouldn't. "Many books… all the time books," she said about my library armloads. And useless to tell a desperate mother how, unless a complete dolt, any time-server collects a magpie learning from the landfill hours.

Until one day she's at my door, peering up through slitted eyes. Too zeroed-in for tears. "What means *identified*?"

Handing me the form, with its boxed summaries. Keywords in Bold: **dyslexia,** probable **ADHD**... **processing**... **2nd percentile**. Sign-offs in three different pens.

What means identified? What you never want to be. By anyone or anything, especially a school. Spotted and slotted and sidelined before you're past the starting gate.

What Jared and I do, twice a week, is too pleasant to be called instruction. Which is no doubt why it's working—slowly, with many flatlines and fallbacks. We read together, me the left-hand page, him the right. Shy, shit-eating grin from him when he draws a page with just a picture or a two-line chapter end. Then we turn to writing. He tells me things and I record them, printing without capitals or punctuation. He takes them home to copy and correct.

Lucius keeps the Honda running. And Lucy stays in my kitchen for the hour I'm with Jared, making something spicy that will freeze. Just because I'm Socrates doesn't mean she's willing to leave me with her son. A wise woman.

Keeps her focus. Wide lens and small. Whereas Lucius—like most men, he can get stuck on a mower blade or grease pan, forgetting the whole for the part. They make a good team.

People ask for adjustments all the time—it's practically all they talk about, if you listen—but just the asking isn't reason enough. In fact, sometimes the adjustment needed is opposite to what the asker wants. Like the student pleading for rescue from a persecuting TA. A jealous terror dyke, sabotaging her GPA, derailing her law school plans. When I found out this student had been plagiarizing her essays, I dug through library stacks for two days to find her sources, then made sure copies with highlighted sections got to the TA. No payment on that one, other than the satisfaction of hearing she'd been hauled before the Dean and bounced from the faculty. Her family would buy her a second chance—they'd bought her the first—but the price would climb. And it wasn't the plagiarism that wound me up. It was the teary self-pity she'd played me with, running me around inside, wasting my energies. That awoke the anger I needed to make an adjustment. It stoked the fire that had scorched the inner terrain, exhausting combustible materials, so it had to locate the right class of fuel outside.

Though fire a flawed analogy, since fire always produces ash, and ash always has its uses—as fertilizer, as insulation to bank the next fire. *Metaphors teach the eye nothing*. Still, they point as far as can be seen and help you conjure what's around the bend.

How did I get into them? When? I can hardly remember, and don't entirely trust the dates and events that do come to mind. It felt like a drift, but an inevitable one. Fresca left me with intimations of something dim and ancient—old patterns, old ways of being in the world—rising into sharper focus, becoming more acute and willed. The more I learned about an area, or areas, of myself that were beyond adjustment, the more I sought out outer adjustments that could still be made. That sounds simplistic, like a formula. But sometimes the simple is simply true, or the start of truth. And plenty of formulas describe a certain class of events with perfect clarity.

§

The stock's ready, I turn it off to cool. A rich fug of poultry permeates the space. The smell of home, some would say. Though the smells of long-term rental are the smells I trust, the ones most likely to let me sleep.

I turn on the counter radio, tuned to CJRT, while I chop the vegetables and measure them into two-cup bags. I'm not a jazz buff, though I've become a moderate fan. The pop stations drove me there, a refugee from groove-paralysis. At 91.1 the DJs actually love the music, which gives them a sense of adventure. Dust off the backlist, play the new bands live. Here's a quirky new take on an eighty-year-old standard. Whereas Classic Rock—the soundtrack of my childhood—is dead and stuffed and mounted on the rec-room wall. Hendrix fronting mindless cinder block. A hundred decent tracks by the Stones, yet they punch the same five out at you. New Rock's not much better. Different bands, same handful of hits. Tire hum of given up.

So listen to the jazzheads. A quartet now—who knows who—ticking and thrumming and tinkling and beeping time into its atomic elements.

Listen and stir. Skin detaches from flesh, flesh from bone. Carrot bits, onion. Stir, stir. Stir to stretch two hundred grand into a lifetime. *Stir because you'll never work again and psychosis doesn't come with a pension plan.*

§

The phone rings as a voice is telling me the sun is shining. I buzz them up.

"Are you the super?"

"So the Owner keeps reminding me."

Stiff smiles, hers fading first. Late twenties, cookie-cut from Condo Life. Their visit not off to a good start: slice of nameless gray between the Favorite and the Latimer, lurching ancient elevator box. And now me. But you have to see a scope-out through. *You never know.*

A few minutes later, they're glad they did. 305, like the other units, looks better inside than out. No Name Towers reverses the norm, that way. Gray slab of door, but behind it three large bedrooms and wide windows, parquet floors, passable appliances and plumbing. Experienced hunters, they have no trouble mentally erasing the tacky furnishings and installing their own. I leave them to explore, burbling in low voices about space and light, while I hang back by the door.

After a few minutes, the guy comes back to confirm the rent I gave him over the phone.

"That seems... reasonable." Trying out his trading floor voice.

"In this neighbourhood it's a lot better than that. Ask the Owner."

He nods, scoots back to her. My mouth, like my face, will be a carrying cost.

The Owner can't do math. He can't even do basic arithmetic, since he won't put a minus sign on any side but yours. He yowled at the hundred bucks the Old Man knocked off my rent for the help I gave him: shovelling snow, cleaning and painting vacated apartments, caulking, unplugging toilets, showing units when he was sick or just too tired. We worked in speechless synchrony, super and protegé. I'd reached an eerie, afterlife-ish calm, where I knew I'd never be Admitted and wear a plastic bracelet again, because the ward was something I carried wherever I went. I just needed to rack up living arrangements. When I took over from the Old Man—still in ICU, but headed for a home—I was told by the voice on the phone I was only entitled to free rent in the dinky first-floor unit. For the two-bedroom I was occupying, I'd have to settle for half off. But half off doesn't equal the one-bedroom rent, I said. And eventually got him to see, or agree at least, though I had to rub his face in it awhile.

We do the same dance with every vacancy. The Owner hyped to jack the rent, it's his only redress for the socialist crime of rent controls. And I have to explain, each time, that the "market value" rents he's barking down the line won't bring in the "better class of tenants" he's dreaming of—with these halls? that vertical coffin lift?—they'll just force the unit-sharing, two students, two waiters and a cook, divvying up the rent. Which means more parties. Which means more noise. And which also means more vacancies, since sooner or later one finds a girlfriend, or a boyfriend, or they argue. And they leave.

Or don't leave. And I have to make them. Like the cruise ship musicians in 305. Nice when they're gone, but when they aren't, they think midnight is a good time to start wailing. Off key, too. Though quality hardly matters when you're punching a 6 a.m. clock—the guy in 205—or nursing nerves so tender an elf fart wakes you—either of the couple in 405.

The Owner's all for evictions. But though he may rule Bay Street, he can't see that rent jacked two hundred dollars will mean eight months to recoup his losses if the unit stands empty a month. Almost a year and a half if it stretches to two. He can't do math.

So he grumbles and fulminates and finally sticks a dial tone in my ear.

The couple comes back. She leads with the line they've decided on. "It seems to be in... *fairly* decent shape. The apartment, at least. We do have some questions about the building. But we like the neighbourhood."

"We all do. We're poaching on Forest Hill, basically. This row dates from the forties. North of the mansions then. Then the second-tier burghers caught up and built in around them. You can use the services they require—good restaurants, cafés, all kinds of shops—without paying their property taxes. Or their mortgages." They exchange a glance they think I don't catch. Who in their right mind would delay buying a house a second longer than they had to? No need to hype them to my view. *To rent is to live a little longer. To own is to die. A baby rents its patch of flesh. A corpse owns it.*

"You may be wondering"—the guy again—"why we need three bedrooms, since we don't have kids and aren't planning on any for a while."

I wasn't wondering. They *need* house space while they're saving house cash. No downbeat scrimping like their parents did. But I stare above them at a blazing maple while he lays out how she needs a studio for her painting, watercolours mostly, and he, he's developing a software project, early days of course, but some promising offers...

They're almost touching, this new breed of birds. *Us*-triches, with plans so long-range subtle they assume they're invisible to the guy slicing their sashimi or unclogging their drain.

"It's long-term rental we're thinking of." She cuts into his rap, which has gone meandery. "Three or four years minimum. Five, maybe."

A lie, clearly. These two will treadmill toonies into their mutual fund. But they'll be quiet at least. Sipping fair trade lattes while they split the *Post* Financial.

"Short-term's what I'm thinking of. It'll be vacant at midnight on the thirty-first, occupied at 12:01 on the first. Right now, that minute's up for grabs."

As they leave clutching the Owner's application, I can hear the dilemma that will envelop them two steps out the door. *Decent place, lotsa' room. Great location! Not a bad rent. But that guy!*

Well, everything comes at a price, my dears. But I hope they take it, they're not bad little strivers compared to some. And will inherit what's left of the earth, no question.

§

The soup down, the jazz still ticking. *Nothing takes long enough.* Not in hyper.

3 p.m. Not a time of day for reading. Not morning, not night. Halfway House.

I move around the premises. The faded IKEA furniture Lois's father bought us. Her parents playing house, fixing it up for the kids who would give them grandkids. After twenty years, it looks like the Goodwill gear they wanted to save us from. They did save *us*. It's just me using it. Living room. Bedroom.

Building a life from other people's lack of imagination. Jordan and Melanie unable to picture their twenty-three-year-old daughter living in a shitty apartment. "Starving artist," all right, but please, at least a decent sofa, Queen bed... And when pregnancy surprised, utterly unable and unwilling— no wiggle here—to imagine their grandchild living much past infancy in rented rooms. Gifting us the house down payment. And all predicated on their greatest failure of vision: to see no reason why a thirty-five-year-old shipper-receiver with "brains to burn" couldn't scale the heights belatedly. Lois, smart as she was, inherited this blindness—or love dimmed her sight, made her a dreamy myope. Because she'd met me in a quiescent phase that might be mistaken for the ups and downs of a "moody" person, calm of the Island she helped create, she heard my stories of the Hurricane Years as just that, stories. And she loved stories. *Imagination feeding lack of imagination. Murmuring to Terror, "It's only a dream..."*

I avoid opening the second bedroom door until avoiding it's all I'm aware of doing.

Absence, empty space, has its own life stages. Like a series of ugly worms that can become a butterfly—given enough time and the right conditions.

Starting as sheer torture, as it must, absence modulates to a trial. That's when most people rush to fill it, stupidly, since the filling is often worse than the hole. Hang on through that, though, and *gone*—the clinging, hanging sense of *un*—can become a habit. A nagging one, to start with, then just habit: mindless *non*.

From there—in special cases—it may evolve into positive need, a nutrient approaching pleasure.

Vacuum become oxygen. Black space spreading and drying its wings in your lungs.

Big Empty looks like it did twenty-three years ago. The Old Man gave us the ten days before move-in to clean and paint. It was the first room we did.

Windexed the big, south-facing panes. Patched and painted the white walls and ceiling. I give them a fresh coat every few years, otherwise just wipe them down with a damp cloth when they look dull, maybe four times a year. Mr. Cleaned the parquet squares up to shine. I still do that at least once a month, oftener than they need. Liking the pine-honey gleams.

Sanctum. Sitting room. And many nights—every night as a window closes—my lying room. The last place I can chase sleep.

Smelling the subtle aromas of time and space in a vacant room. Scents that never cloy or tire.

It brings you things, Big Empty. Never what, or when, you expect. News on its own schedule.

Today, just two memories. Lois and I making it on the bare wood floor. Laughing afterwards. Lying on our backs, seeing a spot we'd missed. Late August. Traffic sounds in the claggy air.

Her father handing me the cheque in Sunnybrook. Not quite twenty-eight months—lifetimes—later. Waiting there—how long?—in the lounge outside ICU, to make sure I got no further. A shock to realize that. With conditions and lawyer-drawn papers—going to his partner, no less—to make sure they stuck.

A shock in stages: the elevator, the parking lot. The bus, going home. No snow yet, but lights on trees and window frames.

Someone willing to spend a fifth of a million dollars to keep you clear of Lois. Clear of Megan.

Of all the names you called him down the years, bad father never among them.

§

That is not what killed my mother.

Force it down. *Not now, not now, no time.* Stone saying it to me, or me saying it to Stone? Does it even matter anymore?

Adjustment more than drooping blood sugar. Afternoon sag of sleep-poor nights. Four hours, five—how many weeks now?

Open Mr. Noodle, pitch the chemical flavour pack. Boil three minutes, drain. Warm up a container of the fresh stock. Four more in the fridge, the rest in the freezer, two older to the front. Discipline. Add a baggie of vegetables. The noodles.

4 p.m.

Nothing takes long enough.

Though speed the perfect weight-loss regimen. Twenty waking hours to burn off calories, ten hours between meals.

Look around. Too early to leave. Too late not to.
  Out the door.

Killing time, I walk books up the hill to the library, pick out another stack from the shelves. Sitting by the windows with the pensioners and a pair of teen snugglers, I flip through the weekend papers. Freak pics of the Big Man crowding wars and famine off the front page. When the branch closes at five, I walk the books back down to the car. Still nowhere near dark. I head up Chaplin to Memorial Park and make slow circuits of the track, joggers lapping me, a soccer team passing and booting on the inner grass. Finally the sun, long gone behind the wide apartment blocks, surrounds their bases with orange flame. The air begins to gray and clot with grainy flecks, and I feel the vampire's relief at the turn into dusk.

I never imagine I'll find what I'm looking for by day, but despite all history, I sense it around every corner in the dark.

§

A taxi driver's grid on my brain, squares and zones I troll up and down. Two weeks ago, in Indian summer, I made a rare daylight sortie out to Woodbine Beach. Cruising the strolling latte sippers north and south of Queen, then along the boardwalk of saunterers, power walkers flexing arm weights, joggers, volleyball players, even a few charred sunbathers, a fireball turning the lake to blood. I watched through mesh as the slender ones in tennis whites thocked lime balls across the nets. It all felt rich and low percentage even as I did it—but who knows what a kid becomes in twenty years?

Megan, my undone child. Where and who—and what—are you now?

Tonight's route a more regular one. Down through the glass canyons of Bay, layer-lit by cleaners, then back up and down the streets through the university, ending at Queen. Her grandparents rich and smart, her mother talented and funky-chic. And well-fixed now, too—Jordan would see to that. Grumbling, she'd buy in. Past their twenties few spurn what they're used to.

I take it slow, ignoring the honks and pissy swerves, peering ahead, to either side. Swivelling sharply at a wisp-haired forehead asleep on a shoulder. Then again, ten blocks on, at a profile with fine blonde hair brushed to her waist. *Time mirages.* I know it and keep looking. Sighting what I knew and is gone, sighting what I can't know and is here. Black hair? Brown? Red? Purple-yellow? It only takes bottles of dye.

A face half melted, graft-helped and wig-sheltered? Or skin new-grown, a triumph of resilience and state-of-the-art scalpels—leaving just faint lines, a mosaic of seams? I can't decide, and opt for half-views in profile. Unnerved by full face scans.

Halfway up the east side of Trinity Bellwoods, I pull over and cut through the park to Queen. A district primed for ghost encounters with Judy and myself. Brad. Lynette. But I don't meet them, not as more than normal memories. *Why would you?* Sickness starts anywhere, but its essence is roaming. Station to station.

Group homes. Rooms. The basement apartment. Offices: doctor, social worker, Manpower counsellor. Parole officer, when it takes that turn. Riding the TTC to subsidized jobs here, there. Here again.

"Hey, buddy. Spare some change?"

A group—four, five—around a bench. Approaching them, I open the pocket with the rolls of loonies. Hand a coin each around.

"Thanks, man." "God bless." "Got another to go with it, any chance?"

"Hey, man, any of those little jobs kicking around?" Snag. His huge hairless dog curled shivering on the bench, taking up most of it. Nervous, with bulging wet black eyes, it shivers through all seasons.

"Not right now. Soon, maybe."

"Gettin' chilly, man. Winter's coming. Ask Sammy, you don't believe me."

Wet, phlegmy laughter at the cur's expense.

"Like I said, soon."

I walk a few blocks up the strip, slowly, handing out a loonie or two a block. Call it a tithe. Everything going, an autumn Saturday night.

Oyster Boy. The Drake. Beaconsfield. Beaver Café. The Gladstone. Hipsters near each door, smoking, being seen. Tipping beers, waggling glasses. Young, warm-blooded— even the ones in shirt sleeves or skirts shiver less than Sammy.

I want to hit something. Someone. Not to do damage, though it will. More just to make contact.

But not with these. Would be like hitting air.

Not the way it works anyway. You don't look for opportunities. You realize you need one, and wait to see what's delivered.

Curling down Sudbury. The Center for Mindfulness Studies. Nothing to hit there.

Sighting up Abell, some kind of blockage, something half-built rearing to the side. Up Lisgar back to Queen. Over to Abell and down the short side.

Where I find it.

Across a space of churned-up mud, rutted by big treads, brown-water puddles jagged with wire, broken pipes and brick. Refuse from the condo pit behind the hoardings and bent mesh.

Two of them going at it hard. Her on the ground, swinging wildly. Him aiming short, sharp kicks everywhere he can.

Just beyond a zone of heavy dark, a lighted cube with paintings, people clustered near the doors with drinks.

Maybe they think it's a performance piece. Maybe it is.

I pat the coat's pockets, then decide against it. *Need to feel it.*

Wade into it bare-handed.

§

He's tall and skinny, rigged as a taller dead man. Dark suit from the forties or fifties dragging past his heels in the mud. Hard sinew through the cloth when I grab his upper arms from behind and shove him at the hoarding. His weight surprises. Fire shoots through my shoulder joints. High-pitched yelp and he hits the plywood and falls, crumpled.

I bend to help the one he was kicking, but she's still flailing wildly from her tuck, screaming hoarse bloody murder. "Fucking bitch cunt I'll kill you cocksucker!" Lover boy took all the style, she's left with shapeless khaki and a plaid jacket her bushy hair's tucked into.

One of her paws catches my left knee—another wrecked joint, another fiery stab. And then a much more searing pain across the backs of both knees and as I fall and twist back, bringing my arm up over my face, I see the bar backswung over his head like a golfer. Cackling through a spittle-strung black hole, dark stringy hair trailing into her suit collar.

Her. Not his. Thin hairless ruin of a woman's face.

Too far to kick. And no time. Just enough to tuck and start to roll away from the swing, which comes down on my upper arm, trying for my head. I hear the *crack* inside the *whump* a microsecond before I feel it.

And see, my eyes and mouth shocked wide, the flailing in front of me stop and a bushy brown beard come up out of its turtle tuck, sunk eyes glittering.

A hand comes up out of the mud with surprising speed and pushes a jagged stone or brick into my cheek. A back tooth gives, spurting blood. My eyes fasten on a milky skin of congealed plastic leaked from the construction site, a tumour of glowing white leather.

After that it's just tuck and take it. Twisting side to side to confuse the bar's aim, then throwing out a lucky kick that sends it ringing off somewhere. Kicks from either side, from everywhere. Gleeful curses, united now. Catching a foot and upending someone with a heavy crash. Afterward the sharp stone driving down into my forearms, trying to get at my face.

Then the other—*she*—drops to her knees to join in the close work.

Snorts and grunts, high-pitched and low, like pigs closing on truffles.

It feels like years before the artists from the opening jog shouting across the black space to pull us apart.

§

On the balcony, one of the frozen soup containers against my face. Forehead, cheek, chin—they caught me everywhere. Back of the neck. Goose eggs coming up like tumours. Crusted mud and blood melt and drip in red-brown rivulets off the soup container when I hold it away. *Wait to try the mirror.*

Stabbing in the joints. Knees, shoulders, elbows. Hips. Ankles. Like a doll with gone stitching. Wide darkening stripe across the upper arm, doesn't feel broken.

Three slabs down, the girls in 504 passing an orange glowing tip. Cupping hands for each other, a wind coming up. They see me and scoot inside. A buzzkill if they knew how little I care.

Straight south over the fire station, the CN needle, blinking a programmed pink, lime, red.

The street so dead. Saturday, not much past midnight. One car, another, then a long gap before the next. Presbyterian speedway.

Sunday my least favourite day and this one starting early. Sabbaths, Days of Rest: a feel like choking, someone holding a pillow over the world's face. The deadness builds through fifty-two weeks to bottom out at Christmas. Super-Sunday.

Yet just across a slice of air, the wall of the Latimer. Chipped red brick, no windows. *That helps you breathe, loosens your chest.* There are blanks and blanks.

§

Christ, the joints. The two Advils from an hour ago aren't touching it, I drop another pair on top of them. Throbs and needle spikes—wherever bone meets bone.

The cause a cold case. Presumed fractures and dislocations, long before memory. An early pair of foster parents—dogged, dim moon faces—took me round to doctors, trying to explain the gaps and cracks on X-rays. Right baby finger skewed to an angle, years before it became an alien tip-off on *The Invaders*. "Unspecified early trauma" the most any of them would say.

Which doesn't age well. As tonight's shit-kicking reminds. A throwback to Hurricane force, before the brief spell of the Island, and before the long years of adjustments and arrangements that have shaped Off Island time. Flailing years, throwing punches, kicks, spitting teeth and laughing at the sight of blood, your own and others. Lashing out with bone, glass, blades. With anything. Rusted pipes, nail-studded boards. Trying to make outer weather match the inner, so the world and you inside it could make a little sense at least, a conjoined chaos.

Before the time of adjustments, when you learned how a little wrench to the larger wheel could ease the small wheels' spinnings…

Pacing slow circles, waiting on the Advil, I see, just inside the door, the slip of paper I missed when I stumbled in.

The best tenants bitch the least. Take it past all reason, then ask with an apology.

Sorry for desturb but its waking Jared.

The shoulder screams, but I pound to get over the din and start us off. 305 pops the door breezily, ready for it. What the hell. *An eviction party*, we used to call it.

Nothing to lose. Except there always is.

"Tell Skeletor it's Saturday night," shouts a voice from down the hall. Sounding like one of the funeral home boys, brash on a double shot of ginger ale. "Tell him to fuck—"

Then comes up far enough to see the Face. Sometimes it does half my work for me. All of it when it's been alley-painted with war.

"Turn it down a coupla notches?"

"Turn it *off*."

I close the door for them. Slow-motion to the click.

Halfway to the elevator—two flights too much just now—the drug dealer in 303 cracks his door, smirking. Wisps of peat and dirty socks float out at me.

"Same deft touch with humanity, I see."

"As long as humanity keeps using the same deft touch on me."

3

JUDY'S GROUP HOME on Selkirk Street east of Pape. The number hard to see from the street, or else missing. Then I realize I don't need it. At the dead end of the street is a straggle of people, six or eight, outside a weather-beaten two-story house. Standing on the lawn, sitting on the curb. One guy slumped on an overturned milk crate beside a rusted bike missing its chain. As if the rest of the street, trim and Lord's-Day-void, is tilted to flow down to this drain.

Judy's waiting at the end of the walk, dressed as if for Grade Eight graduation. Red jumper with a frilly white blouse that flutters like a sea animal at her throat. Feet in black pumps primly together, nylons. Red lipstick, dark eyeshadow. Yesterday's gray jacket over her arm, though the wind's gone raw and blustery, blowing scraps about. And a little gold-strapped turquoise handbag that goes with none of it.

While she's buckling up and I'm three-pointing us the other way, her landlady comes out the front door with a broom. Doesn't sweep the porch or steps with it, but descends halfway and points at the loiterers in turn, jerking the bristles sharply sideways. *Move on!* The pair on the lawn shift to the sidewalk. The one on the sidewalk shuffles a few feet farther along it.

Now she advances on the car, peering in at us with an ugly scowl. Broom still semi-rampant. She's peering past Judy to get a look at me, which takes me back a thousand years—a thousand seconds—to a conversation in the rotunda's sagging fart-catchers.

Judy telling me—calmly and clearly, her head all glass for once—of the tricks she sometimes turned to supplement her disability cheques. Me asking about her scars. The ward a place where, if you could talk at all, you might talk about anything.

I just use my hand. Or my mouth. They are usually in a hurry.

We might have been any two workers discussing an occupational drawback and remedy.

All glass—or all brick? Glass lets anyone see in—or out—but shatters easily. Bricks are solid facts you can build with, if you don't mind living in a bunker. Judy's half-glass, half-brick gets it better. As some of her pronouncements do, turned over patiently enough. Curious pebbles. Wave-worn.

Today's make-up a pulp moll muddle. Lips a perfect cherry pout, despite her shaky hands. Mauve eyeshadow the colour of last night's bruises. Orangey blush patched in, mostly in two cheek circles.

Her moving day rig. For the funeral she might find dirty overalls and gardening gloves.

She's chattery as we make our way onto the DVP and join the stream north. Mostly making good sense, too—though sometimes you have to peer around a moony murmuring to see the truth it's shining on. Which strikes me—and always has—as exactly opposite to the case with most people. Where lunatic bullshit lurks behind the supposed straight facts they're peddling.

Mrs. Rasmussen a decent house mother, one of the best she's had. She rousts them between meals to clean the place, but lets them stay on the porch in bad weather. Won't tolerate bad language. Calls it streetmouth. Or barnyard humour.

"How many people are living there now?"

"Six in the basement. Six on the first floor. Mrs. Rasmussen lives on top. She calls it her egg carton."

A nicer name than fire trap.

Judy stares straight ahead out the windshield, hands folded in her lap. Yet I never lose the sense that she's watching me closely. Glancing at her, I see how faded the jumper is, scuff marks on the bag and pumps. Goodwill gear. But her tiny size gives her more choice, able to pick from the kids' racks and the ladies' petite.

"Half-packs stack better if you are feeding one."

§

A break at Vivera—a different receptionist on the desk and the Director not in either. I make a mental note that she'll probably be off tomorrow too, having worked Saturday. *Something to try Monday, my last chance here.* I don't know what it is yet and don't need to wonder. It's out a little ways ahead of me, preparing itself. The way it happens this deep in hyper.

In the lounge, staff and a couple of volunteers are bringing chairs from the dining room to augment the sofa and armchairs. Lectern in place in front of the flatscreen TV, youngish white-collared priest arranging his papers on it. An old man opening a hymn book at the piano. A few residents already in their places. Not talking, hands in their laps. A lesson locked in for eighty years, since the first knuckle raps—*hands folded!*

not a peep!—which might outlast memories of homes, families, careers, selves. Might outlast speech and movement.

Hands folded. Not a peep.

Yesterday's savoury smell sweeter today. Oranges and cloves? Nut bread? Something twigs, and I look up into the high corners for air fresheners. Vents exhaling a comforting chemical mist. Nothing. Nor, sniffing under it, the odours of stale bodies and incontinence that need masking. Vivera very good. Right up to the mark. Details.

A pointed glance from one staffer as we head to the elevator, but nothing more. Plenty of scenes to witness— plenty to keep shut about.

Judy punches in the code to the secure floor: 1111. Which seems cruelly simple. Insulting, too, as it always is when you stop believing people can surprise you. For a few seconds, I envision a mass breakout. Tunnels, shorted alarms, ropes of knotted sheets, night staff duct-taped. Just the cat and dog wandering free when day shift arrives. I watch it all, an ultra-absorbing ten-second movie, and then the screen goes black and it's gone, the celluloid crisped.

§

Flattened moving boxes are already in the room, leaning against the wall in the hallway and stacked in the bedroom. **STRONGBACKS... Lets YOU Relax!** over a graphic of what appear to be two gorillas in jumpsuits hoisting a sofa beside a pencil-necked guy in a La-Z-Boy.

Someone in a big hurry. Someone organized. Nailing down who my first priority.

Which takes all of twenty seconds. The phone on a small, marble-topped table in the corner rings. I'm closest to it.

"Yes?"

"Who is this?"

"Judy's friend."

"Hello, Judy's friend. Would you put my sister on?"

No, that's your job. Judy watches the receiver approach her through the air as if she's tracking a super-slow-motion missile. "For you," I say while it's between us. "A telemarketer, I think. Maybe someone who bothered your mom."

Then watch while Judy gets the earful meant for me. Nothing new to her, I'm sure, or I'd feel more guilty. She listens in silence, nothing in her face, then starts saying "Yes" at intervals to what I assume is a list of instructions. "Yes. Yes. Two o'clock. Yes." After listening again for a long time, a minute or two, she passes the phone back to me. "Max wants to talk to you."

Lubberly. I hold the receiver at my side, like a lunchbox handle. Max already someone I want to wind up. Someone maybe worth winding up. The crisp, prep school voice— *Hello, Judy's friend.* The tickety-boo Strongbacks arrangements. I dangle the phone over the cradle, let him listen while he checks his watch, then drop it clattering down. Unplug the jack before he can redial.

Judy is sitting on the bed. Not looking sad. Looking lost. Hands flat on a rose-patterned duvet where the orange blanket was yesterday.

Turning my head slowly, I breathe in the slightly stale smells mixed with sweeter scents of lotions and floral detergents, until I'm sure of it. *Three of us.* That relief, each time you learn it, that whatever the soul might be, it won't be bum's-rushed like the body.

§

Judy dithers about, picking things up and putting them down, assembling little piles and then abandoning them. *I take care of my mother.* Meanwhile I take out my X-Acto knife, slice the plastic strapping and set up the first box.

The normal contents of the coat pockets: two cutters, a Classic Fine Point and a heavier blade, a short-handled finishing hammer, multi-head screwdriver, three rolls of loonies, duct tape and clear tape, paper pad and pen. Special circumstances sometimes require another tool, but these cover almost any everyday situation. *My everydays anyway.*

I start with the photos on the walls, planning to work down to the floor. Lots of pictures of the whole family in the early years—cottage, home, beach getaways—but none of Judy past her mid-teens. What I noticed yesterday. As if she died at sixteen. And notice something else today, like a bookend: nothing of Maude beyond about age seventy. One of the last a group photo in a restaurant, leaning in with her husband to blow out candles. Anniversary? Maude still with a little dark in her hair, Dr. Wyvern white-haired, trim but in his eighties. No Judy, but a brother to either side, smiling and clapping. Both good-looking, but in opposite ways. The thin, fine-featured one with round glasses, a fluff of fair hair—that would be Max. The other burly, with a strong large nose, long rock star ringlets of dark hair—Sandor, Judy said the youngest was. And then Maude's photo record goes as blank as her first child's.

Rough times not welcome in the family. *Non in absentia or dementia.*

Looking around at the photographs, even hung out of sequence as they are, I can easily see the formation and cresting and devolution of a family in time. Husband and wife meeting in black and white, the mid- to late-forties from the car they're standing beside. Him a good ten years older: handsome, assured, angular intelligent face. His arm encircling the waist of the petite, pretty young woman looking up at him adoringly. What would he think of the hash presumably made of caring for her after he'd gone? The promises, deathbed ones perhaps, broken every day? Then the years of kids. A Christmas portrait in front of the tree: Judy in a green dress, green-bowtied brother to either side. Vacations: tropical rentals, the family cottage. A graduation picture for the second child, the first son, at a fancy restaurant—Judy absent now, her career as a mental patient underway. A gap then, curious—no pictures of the Wyverns' middle years, their children grown and out in careers. *We don't play with the kids away?*

I try again to remember Judy's visitors on the ward, if she had them. *Butter tarts.* And fleeting images of a woman walking the halls with her—but it's no good, it could have been anyone. Or no one at all. It's like trying to pin down details in a blender filled with fog.

It's not until I've got most of the pictures in boxes that I identify another blank, another absence tugging at me. No third generation. No grandkids. *Not breeders either.*

Strange for money. Which sometimes breeds more slowly, but usually more surely. Making sure to send fresh roots down into the dark.

Amrita, the young caregiver who teared up for Maude yesterday, comes in and starts taking out Maude's clothes from the closet and folding them on the bed for us to pack. Her sure, gentle movements tell she knows these clothes, knew the woman she dressed in them. Judy states, her voice loud in the silence, that her mother does not like her clothes folded like that. But offers no other way, so Amrita, after a pause, keeps on folding. It's so rare to hear an unambiguous emotion from Judy—jealousy in this case, possessiveness—that I watch her for a bit, taking down the last photographs. Same painted statuette standing by the window. As if the Easter Islanders turned in the end to doing little girls in jumpers and frills staring out at sixty.

Amrita leaves and shortly after a maintenance man with a wispy moustache arrives. Again, that sense of a well-oiled operation: help arriving in small, unobtrusive doses. "How you folks doin'? Not so good, I guess. I'm sorry for your troubles."

A young guy, early thirties at most, yet sounding wise and old-timey, the way the simple-minded can.

"There's no hurry, you know. I just want to make sure you know that. This place has a five-day compassion window. Longer than some places, that's for sure."

Longer than Max's. "Thanks," I say. "Do you need to do some work?"

He raises and lowers his tool box. A blush seeping out from his ginger hair, as if an old scalp wound has opened. "Well, I just thought I'd see if I can get her toilet moving better. I had it on my list for yesterday, before…"

"It's all right. Go ahead."

I follow him into the bathroom and, while he's down on his knees opening up the tool box, ask him what the problem is. His hands sunk in tools and oddments, he speaks more comfortably.

"Well. It happens sometimes around here. The ladies—not the men that I've seen—they start putting a lot of things down it. Papers, socks. Underwear. Even slacks and blouses. Sometimes cut up some, if they get ahold of some scissors or a knife. Confused, I guess. You can't blame them. But you don't want to be putting those things down pipes, do you?"

You might if you couldn't fit yourself.

He's got a big wrench out and is reaching behind for the valves. "You folks okay without this for a bit? There's the little sink by her fridge, that still works. And there's a bathroom down the hall if you need it."

"We'll be fine."

On the metal frame of the mirror above the sink, two photos under butterfly and beetle magnets. Pictures of Maude, unlike any I've seen. Tousle-haired, a wind pushing her perm around, broad smile. The sun full in her face, sparking off her glasses as she turns up into it. *Who took these?* Just behind her, thick autumn colours: tall white flowers, blue ones, yellow goldenrod, big purple thistles, milkweed—a wild beauty in the disordered clump, bumblebees sunk in blooms or fat blurs lifting off or landing. *This time of year*—though not this year, surely. Water in the background, blurry dots that might be ducks or geese. The same day. Reaching out a hand toward a bumblebee on a purple thistle—smiling, unafraid. Alone again with nature, the photographer forgotten—the miracles of growing things and small animals she reached out to first, sitting on the ground, before she could walk. *Who?* Someone she trusted. Probably the same person who added tape behind the magnets. *These ones should stay. These ones she should see, morning, night.* I slide the magnets aside and peel off the shots. Pocket them.

§

1:00. Small as the room is, we're going to have to pick up the pace to be ready for Strongbacks in an hour. I decide to break down the bed to give us more room. I look around for Judy, thinking this part might be difficult for her to watch, but she's gone.

Bathroom break? She always seemed to recall the needs of her body suddenly, as if it were a mostly silent companion who sometimes tapped her on the shoulder to make a request. There's no telling. She's always taken powders. Ghosting in and out of rooms and scenes. *Not her rooms, not her scenes.* Drug itch? Drug bladder? Beyond those, just an inability to situate herself anywhere for very long. A psychic vagrant. Long before she was a physical one.

Strange, how work goes faster when the one not working leaves. Non-help not just failing to add but subtracting from what's there. Sinkhole of inaction...

Five minutes and the bed's apart and leaning against the wall. Bedclothes folded, box spring, mattress. Scarred and sticky wooden frame unscrewed and wrenched free—headboard, foot, metal side slats. Scrubbed-at rust and ochre stains splotching the mattress, both sides. Faint in places—caregivers and cleaners doing their best, plus the rubber sheets and incontinence pads shelved in the closet—but multiple and dark in the central combat zones, rising to the eyes like aerial views of an ancient battlefield, nightly skirmishes with Bladder and Bowel spilling ineradicably into the ground.

A heavy black woman, Jade on her name tag, comes in with garbage bags. Puts them in places around the room. "Things too old, no good anymore, or broken maybe"—she leans close and says in a low voice, Maude nearby but still hard of hearing—"or things that are too dirty, who can wear them now? Just throw them quietly"—with a downward pushing of her big hands to show me. "It's not disrespect. Is what she wants."

My head is woozy, soaked in sense. It's late in the window to be sorting so much.

Her garbage bags around, and a few items swept into them to get me started, Jade plants herself in front of me and speaks with deep feeling, with expansive hand gestures and without expectation of reply.

"Oh, oh, oh, I'm missing this gal. Lovely lady. Always such a big, bright smile. Never temper. Almost never. Oh, she can fool me. Fool me! The tricks she can play sometimes! She makes me think, Why are you here? I'm so tired, I should be here, you go home, Mama, and take care of my own kids. Nice voice, she has. Singalong, we always get her first. 'Where's Maude?' Anyone will say that. Baking activity. Movie night. 'Maude, c'mon girl, this is not your nap time. Sleep later. We *need* you!' And she'll be feisty too. Some lady she doesn't like, make her fist up at her. I love her, this lady. How is her daughter?"

It takes me a second to realize I've been asked a question, and I have to backtrack to find the four words. When I do, the lack of a first name, even if she simply doesn't know it, seems strangely respectful. I raise my palms. *How is Judy?*

Jade nods, tight-lipped. "Not easy for that girl, wake up like that. But I'm happy for Maude. Not to be alone when her time is come. When the Lord calls her home."

"She wasn't alone?"

Jade rears back, wide-eyed. Speaks to the room at large. Half-deaf or not, Maude needs to hear this. "Sometimes she likes to, we call her landlady. Against the rules, but on weekends sometimes I allow. Sleep with Mama, why not? What harm? Good for Mama, good for daughter too."

Which explains how Judy beat me up here yesterday, though I hadn't wondered, assuming GO started running early even on weekends. But another unasked question tugs at me now, distantly, I can't place it or slow it down to look at it. It wings past in a blur. Last night's sleep no worse than the others lately, a patchy four hours, but the accumulation of them beginning to take its toll. I ask instead about Maude's recent health.

"Pretty good on her last review. August, I think. Summer sometime. Physical, not bad. Little heart problem, but with her pill and puffer, she's okay. But her brain"—she puts her hands up beside her own head and mimes a falling motion, little waterfalls out both ears. "She has it many years, the Lord gives her a long trial." Good-natured scowl at the ceiling. "But these old ones—they go when they have to. They know best."

She steps away from me, turns her back, and makes what seems a ceremonial facing of the window, the wall with the call string dangling, the short wall the headboard abutted.

"Ohhhh," she says, a deep groan, and strides out the door.

Silence. Deeper without Jade, as if she took something with her.

For an absurd moment—if it is absurd—I want to move into Vivera. Right now. Drive home and get my things. Have Jade and Amrita and Meru look in on me. Remind me of mealtimes and activities. Help me dress on the worst days. I can't see the punishment I've taken letting me reach that stage, but who knows? Sometimes it's the most spindly, grub-hollowed tree that hangs on through the storm, bushy-leaved saplings blown down around it...

Wishing Judy would come back, I get busy on the bureau to liven up the room. Jade's advice helps. Old cards and torn-off calendar pages, balled-up single socks, the detached blades of a pair of scissors, sweets wrappers of all kinds—gums, chocolates, mints, caramels, half a rock-hard cookie, papers torn from notepads, many with cross-outs or illegible scrawls. Playing cards, some with a third ripped away, a half.

And a scrap that stops me cold. On a square of white paper, a series of lines that look like the birth of language. Squiggles at the top, a bumpy graph from some primeval experiment. Which separates in the next line into four bumpy strands, like cells dividing. Loops protruding above and below, scrawny, crabbed—trying to become limbs. Then a couple of cross-outs, aborted words. *Feel*, clearly— but a heavy stroke through it. Then a small word with a tail—*mud? rod?* And then, after a space, the tiny, wobbling sentence, terrible and achieved:

I am feeling sad.

Everything I know about Alzheimer's, which is not much, upended by this. People speaking of it with a terror almost fond, the loss of memory, of self—but peaceful, like a cloud dissolving, a slate wiping itself clean. Which is nothing like what I'm seeing here, nothing at all. Everything ripped, broken. All this evidence of a pitched battle filled with violence and pain. Chaos, yes—but not raw chaos, pure. Dirty, sorrowful chaos. *A person steering through it.*

It stokes me with a cold fury, puts me on notice that there may not be any choice about an adjustment. Maybe there never is.

Which only intensifies drawer by drawer.

Judy come back. The bureau is a pure bitch.

Pictures in a jumble in the third drawer. Eras mixed and overlapping, snaps taken from many albums. Many folded, torn at the corners. Pieces of photos, torn to bits. But plenty to see Jade's lovely lady—smiling, smiling under a changing hairstyle. Pictures of friends, classmates. Husband and children through decades. Parents—sun-dark couple in a field.

Others who might be siblings, nieces, nephews. *So where are they? Why are you alone in the room with me?*

Some pictures with notations beside the faces, or above or below them. Names legible in a couple of cases. But usually the ink blurry, flaking off, registering poorly on the photo plastic despite repeated shaky over-pressings.

One photo, though. A class reunion, looks like. Late-middle-aged ladies, arranged in rows. X's through some of the faces, check marks over the rest. *The living and the dead.* X means *dead*. X means *gone*. Her own face—middle row, left of center—the only one without a sign.

Cards scattered throughout the drawers. Christmas, Valentine's Day, Easter, Mother's Day, Birthday. The message half torn off many of them, leaving just pictures: a wagon approaching a log cabin on a frosty night, a basket of coloured eggs tied with a pink ribbon, a Beatrix Potter rabbit wiping her baby's muzzle with a cloth—a lot of flowers. Here and there, a card left whole—from Sandor, from Max, even a couple from Judy. From others too, notes from friends, though none more recent than two years back, when Judy said she'd moved to Vivera.

One in the bottom drawer still in its envelope. A Mother's Day card with embossed roses, rhyming sentiments inside. *Love, Max* in a quick hand. But a different hand, a woman's, entering the name and address on the envelope. In the top left corner, a tony address sticker, black italics on gold: *Dr. Max Wyvern*, with an address at Yonge and Eglinton. Franked stamp on the right.

A story in a card. Mother's Day, but he mails it from the same city. Gets his secretary to fill it out, present it to him for signing. She would have bought it too, hitting the lobby pharmacy on her way back from lunch. *The doctor my son.*

A keeper. I put it in a coat pocket.

Another keeper a photo of mother and father and sons. The family minus Judy. Maybe ten years old, but the most recent group shot I can find. In the white border under each person, an identification in the shaky blue over-pressings. *My husband   me (Maude) son Max   son)Sandor* The *dead*-X firmly through the husband's face.

There's one more object that, on instinct, I pocket. A little box of unfinished wood, maybe two inches by three, with a plastic top window and a cheap clasp, I've seen them in Dollarama. "Precious Things" printed neatly in blue ink above the window—not in Maude's hand anytime lately, and probably not ever. Something mannish, almost Roman, in the firm strokes. *Though the quote marks an odd touch.* Whimsical? A bit fey?

Inside the box, a balled-up nylon whose cheesy smell wafts out when I open it. It's stuffed in, almost filling the small box. Uncoil it, though, a limp snakeskin, and underneath are a pair of nail clippers, two bobby pins, and a USB stick with a self-adhesive label cut to fit on the side, titled "Christmas Music." Same quote marks and near blue letters, though perhaps a different hand. It can be hard to tell with printing.

With a silent apology to Maude, I stow her "Precious Things" in a pocket too.

Standing in the stripped room, boxes around me. Bureau, bed, chairs. A couple of small tables. Feeling tired by it. And feeling the other presence fainter now. The parts left in her things detaching, beginning to float free.

What did you do to earn this neglect? The answer not far to find. Staring anyone who looks in the face. *You got sick.*

§

The Strongbacks men waiting by their truck, outside. Why, I have no idea. Do they need our permission to do their job? Judy with them. The square-bodied young guy leaning against the passenger door, smoking. The seedy older guy chatting Judy up, smiles and gestures. Judy nodding. Flirting? Nothing's impossible—she must cycle through every drama eventually—though it's a vice with men to mistake vacant for coy.

Are they wrong? She can't object if she's left the premises.

After we're loaded up, I tell them I need to go back for a minute, one last thing I need to take care of. The young guy has his pack out before I've turned.

§

1111.

A skeleton confronts me a few steps from the elevator. Socket eyes, lips skinned back from yellow teeth, a thin glaze of skin over planes and scarps of bone. The instant I return his gaze, he drops his eyes, fusses with the ties of his housecoat. Turns away.

Some kind of baking activity at a long table in the kitchen. A staffer passing the mixing bowl to a resident, lifting his fingers to the handle of the wooden spoon. A bridal dress, even earlier, it seems to come from Depression films, hanging on the wall in another alcove. A WWI soldier's uniform. *Fathers, uncles could be that old.* More photographs, war medals. A tuxedo and an emerald dress on adjacent dressmakers' dummies. Like stiffened ghost dancers. While I stand there, waiting for I don't know what, two residents shuffle over and touch the fabrics. The bubble lady stands by a window near the uniform, blowing her slow soundless pops. With each generation, they'll have to update the memory aids. Twenty years from now, it'll be jeans and peasant blouses and an Abbey Road poster. Then what? An iPhone and a Gap T-shirt? Time not only moving more swiftly, but also becoming more insubstantial. Leaving flimsier traces. For those losing their minds in the Information Age, there'll be few spars to cling to. You'll just eddy in the data, dissolving in bits.

In the middle of the torn-down room, head cocked. On alert. Hungry for orientation, scoping the human terrain. *Are you on an adjustment?* Tinglings of a familiar space opening up between my brain and the top of my head, a fizzing lightness that in time will turn murky, as if a swamp is releasing bubbles of gas that have nowhere to go and so build up in pressure. And the sense, basic—*something wrong here. Something not right.* Itchy, pre-twitch crawlings between my shoulder blades, the muscles there preparing to announce their need to lash out and hit something, grab it and shake hard. Rage heralds.

Which yield to, or become, a feeling of utter peace. Cool fingers cupping my skull. Hand cap of calm.

At moments it makes me wonder about myself, this peace I feel with the dead, with empty rooms. It isn't morbidity, or not just, because at moments I'll find it with the living and with fully furnished spaces as well. That's rarer, though, more elusive. Usually the living are like the mall seething around Judy and me yesterday—an insane noise and welter of aimless movement, a ceaseless surf of scams, fool's errands, and skulduggery.

Opening the sheers, I stand with Maude at my side—her head coming to just below my shoulder—staring a last time at the trees rising from the swamp, half bare, stretches of dark bark between their coloured flags.

Searing endless blue. Ash heaps of cloud.

§

At the storage place off Laird in Leaside, Max has left "oral instructions" that "family only" are to accompany the movers inside. *Not a man slow to avenge a dial tone.* "Sorry, sir, but direct authorization is part of our security package," says the balding, Brit-accented manager, his voice strong for the stacked receptionist he goes back to ogling. Who by her revolving gum and glazed eyes couldn't possibly be interested in any package he might produce.

It's fine by me. Over their shoulders, I see, on the first of a row of black-and-white screens, Judy and the Strongbacks men unloading the elevator. Tiny Judy float-walking ahead of the two men pushing dollies as they exit through the edge of one screen and appear on the next, walking in light towards carpeted dark, ceiling strip lights coming on ahead of them. Turning corners, more corridors, dark doors to either side, the lights quivering on. Like a girl in a spacecraft's corridors, her beefy astronaut sidekicks. Like something from *2001*. Or *Solaris*, the mind-planet plucking people from memory and setting them to run down corridors, sit weeping in metal compartments.

And takes me back, too, to my four months at U of T. The similar lights in the stacks of Robarts Library. Fort Book. Automated cameras, light strips going on as sensors pick up your approach. All that knowledge sitting waiting in deep dusk the rest of the time. *Just four months. September to December.* Time enough to awe Lois's parents, nourishing wild dreams. Lois a bit awed too by the A+ papers and tests coming in on schedule, though she'd never admit it, went catfish-jawed and shook her head, insisting she'd known it all along. Time enough to awe, time enough to appall. *What goes up must come down.* At least at certain velocities.

The camera can't quite see into the Wyvern unit they unlock, roll up the door and start unloading into. Just corners of boxes and totes, a lamp. Probably waiting many years now in the dark, presumably from when the family home was dissolved.

Alzheimer's, old age by any name, a retreat under fire, finding smaller and smaller refuges as the enemy advances. Until the last cave, where they find you with your back to the wall, out of ammunition. *Butch and Sundance.* But Newman and Redford white-haired, supported by walkers? Would never work.

A better fantasy starts to form but pops when the manager says into the phone, "Another thing you need to know, it's in our contract, is that all units are for storage purposes only. No business can be conducted from them." Chuckles at something the caller says. "No, that's right, you'll need a proper office for that. And of course" he waits until he's got the girl's eye—"no living in one either." Gets a skimpy smile and raised eyebrow for the hundredth time.

I fish-hook us over to Laird via the faux-fronted shops of a new Village. The usual suspects: Home Depot, Best Buy, Starbucks, LCBO. A "retail community" that went from hoardings to gala opening inside six months, thrown up like a Hollywood wild west set, minus the wildness and the west. Immense yawning asphalt instead of a muddy street between the town's opposing storefronts, so huge it makes even Home Depot look dinky. Everything looking like the first November blow will knock it down.

"Who is your mother's Power of Attorney?" I say, waiting for the light. A slump-shouldered man wearing an ad board doing a faint shuffle in front of Five Guys Burgers and Fries, moving his arms back and forth in slow passes that obscure the words on his chest. Either from the chill or from some profounder misunderstanding of his role.

"Max," Judy says.

"And Max pays you to look after your mom." Chancing it a bit, following it as it arranges itself out ahead of me like the strip lights in the storage vessel.

"Yes. I look after her."

She lapses back into silence. Hasn't said much since leaving Vivera, when I asked her for a basic rundown on her brothers.

"I hope Sandor mentions that in her obituary. Probably no one will think of it," she says just before we reach Selkirk.

The comment reminds me why, for all we went through together, living across the hall through months of siege, I haven't looked her up in twenty years or ever felt inclined to. No one else can ever really be real to her. And such a person is an active danger to one aspiring to escape the ghost world and put on solid flesh again. Who prayer-folds actions like a thousand paper cranes to that end.

4

WHAT HAVE YOU GOT?

Sitting in the armchair overlooking Eglinton, I consider it. Money-man Max, his chequebook grieving. The place to start, but no dentist reachable on a Sunday. Playing golf or watching it. Sandor, a retired English teacher and "a kind of writer"—a sly jab in another mouth, but Judy's flattens it to a ledger entry. Sandor the youngest, fifty or thereabouts—retired? Can be found, according to Judy, most nights at the Queen's Arms. *Show her arms, hide her charms.* Which, unless she's got it wrong, is only a few blocks away, a five-minute walk to just past Avenue. Max, when I get to him, pulling teeth at Yonge-Eg. What started way up in Markham shaping up as a local job after all.

The last thought pulls me up like a pinch. *You're not considering an adjustment, you're in one already.* Well in. I could feel it watching the grainy floating scenes on the storage monitors. The two goons pushing piled dollies behind their ethereal little captain. Wanting to pull what I was seeing apart. Rearrange it.

At dusk I head out, after leaving messages on four machines. I like setting them out like bait after business hours, plug in my own phone in the morning and see what's in the net. I've never felt the need to be more closely connected. Hours already seem a fast turnaround, I don't need seconds. And there are enough people camped out inside my skin.

The Owner: *305's rented. They dropped off the lease and first and last. You're going to love these two. They'll never bounce a cheque or make a peep. Maybe the occasional muffled scream when the markets fall. But only during business hours.*

Nicole, the Move-in Coordinator from Vivera's menu: *Hello, I'm wondering if I could arrange a tour. I don't know if you have any vacancies, but I have a family member who needs, uh, placement—it's my wife actually—and, well, I'm afraid we've hobbled along until things have become urgent. If you have no space available, I understand. We've got a short list we're working through. But if by luck I've caught you at the right time, is there any chance we could meet tomorrow morning?*

Ken, my advisor at CIBC: *Hi, Ken. I'm into something here that's going to need a few extra funds. Not a lot, I don't think. And, yes, I do want you to do the drill. Standard operating procedure.*

The office of Dr. Max Wyvern, though I almost give up at the interminable preamble that's designed to make me do just that. Hello, you've reached… and then later, We are located… and Our business hours are… and only then, We are presently closed and will reopen at… and then, with sadistically slow enunciation, an advisory that any emergency situation should be dealt with at a hospital… until finally, after a minute that feels like a day, the voice conceding to any masochist still on the line, If you would like to leave a brief message and your number, please do so after the beep. *Um. I don't know if you're accepting new patients, but one of my teeth broke apart just now. When I was eating some nuts. Lower tooth, on the left side. I'm not in pain, it just sort of crumbled away around the fillings. There's a back tooth loose too.*

Wiggling. Neither is an emergency, but, um, it doesn't seem like something I should wait on. Could you phone me at this number if you have any openings? Thank you very much.

Lure of crowns, extractions, likely canal work. Like dangling a square of red rag on a hook in front of a bullfrog. The huge mouth drops open and the great legs uncoil in a coordinated lunge. One foster dad an outdoorsman. Not with them long.

§

"Green tea or black?"

A new question. Black, I decide.

"What kind?"

Also new. Previously it was just Red Rose on offer, stale bags in a jar beside the till.

"Do you have Earl Grey?"

"We have. With milk?"

"Just black, thanks."

Other than expanding the tea selection, the new Korean owners haven't messed with the Queen's Arms' modestly winning formula. Same TV screens with sports and news so nobody has to feel they've left home. Pool table at the back. Just enough stains on the carpet and faint fumes of draft and puke to keep it real. Our dingy, grotty local.

Family run, at least this time on a Sunday. Mother behind the bar. Daughter in hot pants handling the three guys in sports jerseys at a table. Kidding with her as they wait for a game, any game. Father's role at the moment working through a stack of Scratch 'n Win at the end of the bar.

"Straight to the hard stuff, eh?" says the guy two stools over when Mother brings my tea.

"Straight to the source," I say, weirding him back to his pint.

But he's a talker, wants contact, and a couple of minutes later he taps the *Star* on the bar between us. Hizzoner spread over it in close-up, pig-eyed, ranting at a scrum. The mics black bulrushes he's peering over.

"The Big Man's quite the distraction, isn't he?" says my neighbour.

"He is that."

"Distracting us from the city's business."

"Distracting us from himself."

"How's that work? You can't get away from him. He's everywhere."

"Exactly. He is. Not his policies. Listen to these stories enough and you might start to believe he's a civic-minded gent whose outsize appetites led him astray. But he couldn't be civic-minded if you dried him out and slimmed him down and locked him in a room with Thomas Merton for a year. An alligator doesn't lose his taste for meat if you starve him."

That restores the silence between us. He pulls the paper over and starts leafing to find more the kind of thing he's looking for.

A UFC cage match takes place on the main TV. A two-minute flurry capping a half hour of build-up, clips and commentary by three talking heads. The jerseys at the table cheer the jabs and kicks that connect, then, when the wiry fighter trips the bulky one, they pound on the table in sync with the face punches to the tap out. Father doesn't pause in his lottery mining, rubbing just enough with his dime to verify a loser then dropping it in the trash and starting on another. As bloody and brutal as the mayhem in the octagon is, it's also far more graceful and choreographed than

any real-life fight I've seen. And far briefer and more deci-
sive than what must be occurring in kitchens and bedrooms
within a short walk of us.

Public horrors. Never as raw and terrible as the private kind.
But only a gruesome enough spectacle lets us forget that.

"When's Sandor usually show up?" I say to Mother
Barkeep. "I'm supposed to be meeting him here."

After a deft Face-over, almost delicate, she says, "If you
sit where you're sitting, you'll see anyone who arrives."

Which sounds close enough to a perfect koan that I
order another tea to keep my seat.

§

Sandor's party sweeps in on a gust of talk—seven of them,
different conversations going—and take their seats around
two tables pushed together near the pool table. The pretty
brunette beside Sandor not saying much, concentrating on
smiling at the right lines, especially his. Another couple,
longer-term, beside her: the blonde a stunner, her husband,
balding over wireframe glasses, looking like polished intel-
ligence has lifted him somewhere high. The other three singles, a man and two women, younger outriders—students
or assistants maybe. I've seen some of them at Shoppers,
where all of the neighbourhood shows up eventually. The
blonde for sure. Her fluffy white dog waiting chained to the
railing, gray streaks in its fur like a dirty snowbank.

Watching them through the first round, sipping my tea.
Sandor not loud or pushy. But commanding without effort.
Getting the biggest laughs. *Oh you!* pokes from the ladies.

My neighbour tries a last time. He can't be alone.

"I gotta ask about the tea. Curiosity and the cat, I know.
But I don't see someone sitting here as long as you have

81

if they were in 12-step, really following the program. Or being in here at all, really. So?" He gestures at his tall glass of yellow, gliding a hand alongside it like a salesman in a showroom.

"It makes me see things I can't see."

"Heh heh. Why we invented the stuff, wasn't it?"

Which sounds so stupid that I decide to let him have it. Though probably it has nothing to do with him at all. Locking onto his eyes, I stare through them at a kitchen six long blocks away.

"One drop and I see a crazy man grabbing a woman boiling water for spaghetti, trying to get her to dance. She just wants to cook, see. But he's a dancing fool. Grabbing at her waist, trying to twirl her. Her pushing him away. Their little girl with her face raised, laughing at them."

The guy has his beer up—mouth open, ready to laugh at the punchline, puzzled when it doesn't come. I go back to my tea and leave him with it.

After a bit I hear him chuckling softly—now he's got it, so subtle he missed it before. Then falls silent. There's just no stopper like the truth. Hand it to people and they'll never believe it. Will pronounce you a clown, a raving lunatic, or a complete shit—will do anything except sit still and look at it.

Though who in hell could look at the fright-pic you're peddling? Toddler scalded head to hips because her lunatic dad just had to boogie.

Eventually he says, "What happened to the little girl?" Not sure how he should deliver it, straight-man-firm or sombre-gently. It comes out an awkward mix.

Sip of the Earl's black.

"Just because I invited you in for a kiss doesn't mean I'm going to let you fuck me ragged."

Instantly, Father pauses in his dime-rubbing and Mother in her counter-wiping—their heads come up and they look at each other, not at me. Perhaps as much notice as they ever have to give in the place, it's a pretty placid neighbourhood for all the posturing. My Grand Inquisitor settles up and leaves.

§

The daughter flinches at my touch on her arm. For all the skill a barmaid—any maid—hones at forcing down distaste, she can't keep all of it out of her face.

"This round is on me." I give her three twenties. All I got out of the ABM on the way here, all I was sure the account would cover. Ken will have to come through tomorrow. "Be sure to tell them it's for the Wyvern wake."

When she heads back with their tray of pints and wine glasses, I order my third tea. Mother sets this one down with a clatter. Looking up, I see a shaven-headed monk whose *zazen* is dime-rubbing, regarding me with mild regret.

Strange how just being in a bar induces drunkenness. Prepares the way for it—opens some kind of loose-hinged door and invites it in. Even on a string of teas. Memories, of course, but not just. Something more like spectral auras housed in wood, glass, upholstery, carpets, cushions. Even in sinks and toilet bowls. Spirit armies fighting to leave the body, face-punch free of its good sense.

When the touch on my shoulder comes, it's light, almost apologetic. So is the voice—deep, but quiet. "Look, I don't know what the idea is exactly. We're just trying to have a few drinks and a conversation."

I let him finish before I turn. Then we both see what there is to see. From my side: thick, curly hair tumbling to broad

83

shoulders. Only a little silver in it yet. Fleshy, well-formed nose. But reddening with alcohol use, hairline red vines scrolling out into the cheeks. Not yet the ruddy blasts of the lifelong drinker—but a start on them. Dark, sad eyes which would attract many women, some kinds anyway. A taller, darker Roger Daltrey gone to seed. The kind of guy women, if they go for him, don't say *I like him* or *I'm attracted to him*. They say *I'm smitten*, maybe with a girlish hand twirl recalled from Drama Club. He's honey to that kind of fly.

"There's no idea," I say. Oddly enough, it's the truth. There isn't. The procedure is to toss out actions in advance of the idea, see if you can tempt it to show itself. It passed this way, you sense, too swiftly to catch. Bits of its own scent may bring it back around.

"That's good, because when the round came with a mention of a wake I wondered—"

"Oh, no need, no need. Never wonder. It's exactly the way to do it, I think. And what Maude would have wanted. Celebrate the life, don't dwell on the passing."

Something turbid comes twisting up slowly in his dark eyes. Really dark, brown where it verges on black. Something muddy, something glum, something heavy and inertly strong and barbed, comes spiralling up slowly from its home, like a catfish dragged up from the bottom of a pond. It wants to thrash at something. Which isn't me, though I may have to do.

"Whatever it is you're implying... Who are you anyway?"

"Nobody. A friend of Judy's."

The thing at the surface sinks back down, not all the way. Hovers at a depth. The blue cable-knit sweater he's wearing makes him look huge.

"A friend of Judy's. That would explain a lot. My brother said she had a new one sniffing around."

"You can't help it when you catch some smells."

And go back to sipping my tea. Trying not to tense my neck, though I see it through those black eyes, a pale twig at the end of big arms and shoulders.

And then I feel him leave.

From the door, two minutes later, I look back and see him sitting on the other side of the table, his back to where I was, his head down, the blonde woman sitting beside him rubbing his sweatered back in slow circles. Her husband and Sandor's date, the brunette, shooting death rays at me from the other side of the table. The other three clueless but obscurely roused, busily settling jackets and drinks in their new seats. *Musical chairs.*

§

A mangy mood blows me further east, down the hill past Sleep Country to Shoeless Joe's. The air around the Oriole intersection always heavy and tainted, Burger Shack venting soggy charred fumes, doused carcass breaths the morning after the slaughterhouse fire. Some of it oozes in with me through the door. Some of it always inside Shoeless Joe's, where it hovers rancidly amid the TVs bringing us football, hockey, soccer across continents and time zones. Not so dead on a Sunday. More screens.

I order a three-dollar cup of Red Rose to claim a seat. Food for a day and a half. Ken groaning in his sleep somewhere. Leave it untouched. I've had enough for one night.

Before long another lonely guy barnacles to me. The Face draws some types like a centerfold's. Someone who's been there. Or with no choice but to listen. Starts right in on the atrocities of his ex-wife, this super-bitch, not divorced yet but she's lawyered up, separation papers coming out his ass already... continuous war crimes of this cunt, sorry but no other word for some of them, not the girl I married or maybe it was hell we were both kids... working my balls off for her and the boys, ten years fifteen twenty, and all of a sudden it's sheer neglect if I relax for a few hours gaming, it's fucking adultery, *psychic* adultery I guess, when she finds an online porn payment on the card... little titty site, tame, I drop in at the end of the day who'm I sposed to get it from, *HER?*... but no, her skinny ass is stomping up and down stairs at the thought of it, suitcases, clothes in Glad bags, screaming and crying the twins trying to do their geography project... but wait, here's the punchline, it turns out—she's so fucking over the top she can't stop herself from screaming it—she's *fucking this guy*... so lonely I *drove* her to it... *right*... she's out banging a live asshole while I'm at home in the office one hand on my mouse and *she's* the one being *neglected?*... keeps telling me I need to get a lawyer, apparently they're Siamese twins one can't talk unless it's attached to another... greedy whining selfish supercunt, she'll be sorry when I do...

It takes a long time to get through, and we never leave the one chapter. A man spinning in a small whirlpool of shit, reporting all he sees. But relaying it slow, jerky, piecemeal—it comes at me in variable chunks and speeds, depending on the screens. Full-face Uzi bursts when they go to commercial, dribbling out the side of his mouth when the play sputters midfield or between the blue lines, stopping entirely for a big play or goal, roaring and slamming his hand on the table, his home life incinerated in his joy. Then back to me after the replay...

"How about you?" He juggles half a beer down his throat. "You got a warm one waiting to welcome you home tonight? What's your story, man?"

Some ear-benders, the cannier kind, will share the stage at strategic moments when a sixth sense tells them it's time. Surrender a quarter of the airtime to hog the rest and make it last longer. His shit eddy will still be there.

The tea has little whorls of gray oil on its surface, roughly concentric spirals as if droplets of the burger grease have settled and aligned to simulate a Caribbean storm forming on the Weather Channel. I pick it up, it smells like a gym bag. Set it back down.

"What's my story?"

Let him have it. Has worked so far tonight.

"I've no idea who or what my parents were. I went from home to home as a kid. Foster parents coping as long as they could or would, then passing me on. Some good people. Some the other kind.

"I dropped out of school halfway through Grade Eleven. About two years too late probably. Bad moods, fights. The first of what I called spells—what shrinks call fugue states, I learned later. Being someplace and not knowing how I'd got there. Minutes missing at first. Then hours. All the storms I conjured as a kid—people shouting and screaming and crying, me among them—were sideshows to what was really brewing. I only realized a long time later. Maybe ways to let a bit of it out, maybe just ways to forget for a few thrashing moments—who knows? After school I lived on the streets and people's couches where I could find them. Lots of drugs, it goes without saying. Stints in detention, hospitals. The first treatments: A to L, let's say. I don't really remember that much. A couple of dozen scenes standing in for several years. The spells getting longer. Plus the drugs. The last of my foster parents finally packed it in. Good people, who wouldn't let themselves off the hook. I was twenty-one, a legal adult. Childhood was over."

Marital Breakdown is staring at me with a stunned, solemn expression. Like a beef cow grazed by the bolt. Maybe it's my flat delivery that's throwing him, so different from the melodrama he's spewing. Deadpan synoptic swathes to his shitspin. But they're made for different purposes, our stories. I settled on my five-stage potted bio a long time ago. Five paragraphs that don't change, lashed together to make a raft in heavy seas. Like someone charged with crafting an encyclopedia entry, I assembled what I knew beyond question in my head. Cut out anything extraneous or debatable. Just the facts, Jack. I don't need to hype my story, just keep it straight. I give him till the end of the next chapter to make his exit.

"Next came the Hurricane Years. Fifteen years, or one minute repeated over and over. The same scenes looping—different actors, different sets. Longer lock-ups, no longer a juvenile. And hospitals: M to Z, then start from A again. Every kind of temporary room. Short-term jobs as janitor, dishwasher, coat-check attendant. Then subsidized positions, Goodwill the longest. Then full disability—the 5 circled at the top of the list. A lot of travel mixed in at times. To Europe, parts of Asia, Mexico, Costa Rica. Big enough winds blow you everywhere. Sometimes on a girlfriend's dime. But I'd learned to save like a demon—my most unquestioned skill to this day. And most places are cheap if you're willing to live rough."

"Hold that thought, can you?" he says, right on cue. Soft pink palm up, gold wedding band. "I've got to take a wicked shit."

And he's gone, hitching up his cords, for the back stairs. He got fixated during the Hurricane Years on a particular patch of my right forehead. The scars are a palimpsest, one coming forward from the mix one time, another time another, but I knew what was trapping his gaze just now, it used to trap mine when I still did mirrors, before I learned to shave and brush seeing just the patch under repair. A hashtag, faint but deep, once you spot it it keeps coming at you. Like a tic-tac-toe grid cut on a diagonal into flesh. Though the truth is far stranger.

The table peaceful, spacious, with the departure of my woman-hating wanker. Bobbing beneath the colours and the roar. And relief to know his wicked shit will be long if not eternal. Otherwise I'd have to edit the next, the shortest-softest-strangest of my phases. And prepared texts don't take to editing, they buck and buckle at it.

I prefer telling it to the oil atop the rocking tea. Taking all the time I need.

The Island. A place of magic and stability, as all islands first appear. Looming from choppy seas. Settling some. Age? Finding—and keeping—a shipper-receiver job at an art store. Lois the weekend framer, a painter finishing OCAD. Twelve years younger. Her family old money—old and new. And smart. Smart enough not to kick at the connection, figuring it would run its course. A nice enough guy, rough edges but treats her well I guess—still, I mean... Give her time... A solid plan. But then Megan came along. Unplanned, unprevented. Lois weathering the blunt force advisories at family dinners, chin set. And then the turnaround: deposit on the apartment. A year later, Megan almost walking, the down payment on the house. Smart again, midnight discussions: we're not going to lose our only child and grandchild. *All sealed with a kind of party trick. Jordan bringing out his old LSAT prep books after a dinner—a running joke, a ghost plan, that one day Lois would pack up the easel and join him in the firm. Megan gurgling, Lois tending to her, while I—subbing in, a good sport—run through the sections without a miss. Pop-eyed stares from Jordan, Melanie. The schooled with no conception of what omnivorous constant reading—in freight elevators stopped between floors, in coffee shops, in cells—can accomplish. Cut to first semester at U of T's Bridging Program. Everything holding steady on the Island. Bringing home the A+s with only a modicum of effort. Rather relishing my status as a find, a project, Jordan's outright merriment, like the guy who pried up an old floorboard out of boredom and found the jewels. Infectious, the delight. Like a speed habit gaining. By October, less prep and less sleep necessary for the same results. Amazement all around. By November, almost no sleep and definitely no prep or attendance needed—all energy redirected to much more pressing private research in the stacks. Independent initiatives. Which both subsume and trivialize the mandated syllabus. Don't worry, be happy! Bridge? I'll show you a bridge. And poor Lois with not much better luck with the parents—too ensconced in the fantasy train to feel the bump to another track.*

And out, into the chill and burger fug, before he can return.

§

Back at the ranch.

Fuddling around the living room. On the couch, off. Reading. Checking out the window, Eglinton still there. Stretches on the floor—keep the joints usable, maybe tire out the body. One of those nights. Sleep not coming soon if at all.

That is not what killed my mother. Not who. What. Talking about a suspicious death in the usual sense, the police sense? Judy gone everyday-procedural?

No, it won't be that simple.

So you hope and pray.

In Big Empty, I arrange the artifacts from Maude's room along the front wall, propping them at intervals against the baseboard below the window. Photos—fall walk, family dinner. Bobby pins, clippers. "Christmas Music" on the USB. The box itself.

You should have brought the balled-up nylon. Not part of the picture.

Wrong. How can you know until you see it?

Max's card. Also, the box-framed single monarch wing. Fished out of a carton just before Strongbacks started loading. An unconventional memento. And the first of Judy's talismans. *A single wing.* Half a migration? Half a metamorphosis?

I sit cross-legged in the middle of the room. Not a posture I can maintain long. Back, knees. Letting the objects fill the space and say what they have to say.

Which is nothing yet. They don't have anything to say. Or voice to say it with.

I lie down on my back and try it that way. Eyes closed. Same result. Nothing yet.

Your mission, Mr. Phelps, should you decide to accept it—

My teammates: a brainsick girl and her dead mother. *You've had worse.*

As usual, this tape will self-destruct in five seconds…

§

Joy the enemy. Joy the culprit.

It happened in a moment of wild dancing. A burst of savage euphoria that just had to share itself.

And did.

By next afternoon the apartment half cleaned out, their presences amputated cleanly, the stump disinfected with a note. *I don't blame you, but what you are is too dangerous to be close to. I wish you well. Please don't try to contact us.*

I have to run very fast to stay ahead of it. Slowing or stopping, softness of any kind, brings it a step nearer. Images start to crowd me, splicings of memory and nightmare. Things that must have happened, could never have happened.

Shrivelled screaming instants.

§

The views. From the balcony, the good brick wall and dark flashing of the Latimer. The blinking, giant's playnib beside the lake, flicking neon at the clouds. From the window, fire station 135, the bus shelter, EMS. Lights on, doors closed. Good, but not the best. Best is knowing beyond doubt that people are on the job. That they've got your back, even without knowing who you are, and stand ready to make adjustments. And, flipside, the worst: the comatose Sunday mornings, Christmas, Easter, and all Civic Holidays—all those artificial lulls when the city lies on the couch like someone pretending to sleep while keeping one eye open. That's when green tea longs for its departed betters of tequila shots and acid tabs and I stare until my eyes ache at the red doors of the fire station, praying for them to fly open, men in helmets scrambling, praying for the deliverance of a siren and the grill of the big truck in motion.

The discipline. To work in six-to-eight-week windows of gathering rage and speed, followed by a wordless crash. To know the personnel and the conditions of the job site.

Stone: *Learn your windows.*

Mixed states my specialty. Acute, jittery alertness combined with steadily darkening mood. Turbid, seething energies: a rage recipe. A car chase on black ice, which ends, as it must, in a crash.

In the aftermath of hyper-black, standard protocol mandates a return to base. That is when I'm most in need of a prolonged debriefing with Stone. And get one, always. The man reliably strange, strangely reliable.

Ah, Stone. Healer, taskmaster, known enemy, surprising friend. His place of work a confessional crossed with a torture chamber. Hospice fronting a leper colony. I dread my unavoidable visits to him as a man with twisted limbs dreads his visit to the surgeon who must break each bone in order to reset it.

And if the assignment arrives five weeks into the window? Maybe six. Inconvenient—very. A timing problem. Maybe serious.

But a problem. Not a dilemma.

You're *on* the adjustment.

§

On the couch under a blanket. Close my eyes, then open them and watch the gleams from headlights and streetlights flutter up by the glass. The bed a mockery once insomnia sets in to stay. Better odds at surprising sleep out here.

Grind-thoughts of a girl. How old now? With a half-melted face, standing at the edge of a classroom or recess yard— *no, age her dammit*—seminar room, employee lounge. Or girl—*woman!*—with a graft-smoothed face, talking and laughing in a group, knowing that underneath the work of a dozen surgeries she is still half-melted, will always be half-melted.

And Lois. Really, forgiveness in her heart? Is there? Could there be?

Stirred in with thoughts of the city.

Something wrong, the streets unnaturally still.

Can't sleep.

And then, the first light spooling into dark, I hear the sirens and I can.

5

"**WHAT KIND OF** funds are we talking about?"

"Nine hundred dollars will do it, I think."

A tiny pause. "Same as last time, then," Ken says. Less gets by him than he pretends. *Anything over a thousand, make me itemize it.* What I insisted on at the start.

"Different situation. But yes, about the same costs."

"And you feel yourself to be of sound mind?" Ken getting it out quickly, not comfortable even after all these years with asking such a thing, though the question is my own and I wouldn't give him my business unless he agreed to it.

"I do."

"And it's something you've considered carefully. Reviewed over a period of time."

A short time. "I have."

"All right, then."

I now pronounce you manic and funds.

The money will be in my bank tomorrow, Wednesday morning at the latest. Same account my regular remit goes into—$800, two days before the end of each month. Half for rent, the Owner's top-up, and half for food, gas and other sundries. A maintenance dose. Money methadone, to keep the cells this side of screaming. And coverable, on average, from a conservative investment portfolio, not touching the principal. Leaving aside a little extra *for the unforeseen*. Ken double-checking on his calculator that first meeting, but doing most of it in his head.

"Keep well," he says before hanging up.

"Sorry, that suite's taken. Hanging in might still be available."

No dry chuckle this time. "Stay safe, my friend."

Stay safe, my friend. Making another coffee in the French press snagged at Goodwill, I consider it. Banker's bonhomie in another mouth, but not in Ken's I don't think. Not just that. Though we meet barely once a year, neither of us could forget our first encounter. Lifting the lid on my life to let him peep at the roiling. I needed to scare him to gain his full attention. Let him know exactly what he was dealing with. His eyes widened, the MBA part of his soul wanted to run. But the concern he added, then and now, seemed his own. Seems genuine.

Two months after discharge, still lying about the half-empty apartment. Mind blank as sand, hours passing without event, as I moved from chair to bed to chair again. Spring happening unnoticed beyond the windows. Bringing myself slowly off the haze of ward drugs, halving the dosages, quartering them a few days later. Jordan's cheque still uncashed. Anxious messages from him, mutterings of "expiry dates," the danger of funds "in limbo." Even an icy reminder from Lois, Jordan looming inaudibly behind her. But I needed to know. Or needed to be sure of what I already knew. I wouldn't work again. The hodgepodge of half-jobs and charity placements that had sustained me for two decades was done. At a stroke on a December evening, real winter had begun, and I was no longer work material. That was beyond question. The only question was how to live the time that remained on Jordan's payout.

Stretching a sum that was huge if life was a day, a week, a month. Modest if it was years. But if the life dragged on for decades—as even impossible lives were known to do? *Live on two hundred grand a year—hey! Live off it forty years—oh oh.* The only alternative would be declaring—or trying unsuccessfully to hide—my atrocity windfall, Social Services suspending my disability pension (with clawbacks for the assets hidden), then burning through the whole amount, leaving me, one fine day, a broke mental patient in his mid- to late-forties. No job, no income, no hope—a perfect zero.

Psychosis doesn't come with a pension plan. And death's the only mandatory retirement.

"You need to know everything to be of use to me. I'm a pretty strange case," I said, that first day in Ken's office.

"Every person's situation is unique," he replied. I let that go. Ken was better than that. He'd better be. What I'd told him so far simply wasn't dire enough. An edited version that would sober him without frightening him off. An ex paid by wealthy in-laws to vanish couldn't shock a banker. Megan might, but she would never come into it.

"I'm severely ill, Ken. I've worked in the past, but I'm unemployable now. That door's closed."

"You seem pretty lucid to me." Straightening his tie, then bringing his eyes back up to mine. A suspicion that I might be able to trust him after all beginning to germinate. I could feel its tendrils, thin as hairs, somewhere under my breastbone.

"Seeming lucid is what I do. And can almost always do. It's how I get by."

"Surely there must be some treatments... I've known people who... ... depression makes a poor advisor..." I let him go on murmuring these bromides, which in ninety of a hundred cases might be true or partly true, because I knew he needed to get them out of his system.

"Ken, I wouldn't be sitting here if I hadn't tried everything. Riding a broken merry-go-round and dreaming of the high plains isn't hopeful, it's dumb. Especially if the plastic ponies are booby-trapped." *Just confusing him now. No metaphor.* "Now, I need you to tell me what, on average, you can make two hundred thousand dollars bring in a month."

"I can do that. But I'll tell you before I do, it won't be enough to live on. Not even close. Especially not in Toronto."

"I'll make it be enough." *Arrangements.* And hitting me, belatedly, like cold rain after clouds, the surprise that I wanted to make it last. Wanted to live. Just what I'd denied, time after toneless time, to the heads without faces, smooth ovals, on the ward.

"And the principal stays put for a rainy day? For an eventual retirement?"

Stays put for a tsunami. But don't hit Ken with your world all at once. He's done well. Better than well.

"For retirement. You got it."

§

Just after 8:00. Ken starts early. So do I. Up at 6:00, after a few hours on the couch that are less like sleep than like mildly sedated wrestling. Eyes open, closed, open—there's not much difference, the same coiled thrashing. *So tired, so fucking bloody tired, so so...* and yet. Tired's only what you're supposed to be, all you're supposed to be. Only part of what you are. What's this now? Like a three-hundred-pound doorman heaving a whiny drunk, energy bounces the drain. Force that surges from within, blooms bursting from your chest and limbs like the Hulk exploding the natural boundaries of Bruce Banner. You're *here*.

Not calm and rested, heavy-feeling. You've had the occasional solid shut-eye, eight hours of nourishing oblivion, and there's no mistaking the difference. This is adrenaline laid over exhaustion. A snort of meth or coke jacking a steady drop.

Tingling with energy you know should not be there, but still it feels so good, better and better with each second, depletion a cranky neighbour whose moans grow steadily fainter.

With just that nagging sense of guilt, shitbird cawing erratically from your shoulder—warning that the surge is wrong, to be other than flat-out wrecked is wrong, a violation against input-output regs reliable as gravity.

Which the first sip of coffee shoots you past, far out into *there* and neutron star doing. Fatigue and hesitation falling out of view, lifeless planetoids not worth recalling.

No lobby glass today. This morning's harvest is tipped recycle bins. Blue maws spilling cans, bottles, newspapers, pizza boxes, takeout cartons, and untied bags of trash passersby chuck in rather than wait till the next city bin. Tenants do, too, some of them. Flip it where it doesn't belong on their way out, save the ten steps down the hall to the garbage room.

The other nightwork's a huge black tag sprayed onto the concrete beside the garage door. A huge square, maybe eight by eight feet, it makes the perfect canvas. Primed by Owner-ordered attempts with wire brush and soapy water to remove previous tags—arm-wasting hours that smoothed the bumpy surface and sealed it with an all-over mottled gray.

This tag interesting. Black bulbous curves, surging and overlapping. Some dipping down, an overall rising. Too insistent to be called loops. Power coils thrusting against a pressure trying to contain them. A local breakthrough on Eglinton Avenue, kraken to the Owner's gray goo.

Upstairs, the phone machine tells me two fish have wandered into last night's net. Blinks of phosphorescent green as they dart inside the electronic mesh. The Owner won't be one of them. He sulks at every rental, glaring at the gouge he missed. *Yes* and *thanks* Sanskrit to him.

Nicole, Vivera's Move-In Coordinator, will be pleased to give me a tour any time before noon. And luckily, as it happens, Dr. Wyvern can fit me in at 3:15. The same middle-aged female voice as on the answering machine. But cheerful now, not droning. Needing to welcome, not dissuade.

Day is forming. Horse and wooden cart and hunched-over driver have taken shape out of thin air and are moving, clip clop, down a fogbound street. Hop on the back and see what comes out of the mist.

Feeding time. You've let the stomach grumble long enough. Top it up and tell it you'll be back in ten hours, outside. It's less likely to pound on the door if it knows the stint ahead.

Two slices of toast with peanut butter. A banana. Glass of soy milk. A complete protein, a vegan in a line smiled approvingly. And the bigger miracle that you don't get tired of it, day after day. Still a tasty blend, three hundred and sixty-five mornings a year.

Chew it slowly by the window. Small sips. Make it last.

...luckily... as it happens... can fit. The art of medical reception to always let the patient know his less-than-urgent complaint is being shoehorned into the healer's crammed queue, a crumb of attention strictly on compassionate grounds. Starts you off craven-grateful, a workable footing.

But we know better, don't we? A broken tooth, a loose one... faltering, out-of-it-sounding voice. What're we looking at here? A crown, a likely extraction, at a minimum. Three grand to start, with every likelihood of more from the crumbling, middle-aged mouth. Compared with a good oral soldier, wanting a check-up and cleaning, what dentist could resist?

8:50. *Nothing takes long enough.* By 9:05 I've got the sign made. Front and back panels cut from someone's flatscreen box left outside the garbage room. A steady supply of cardboard and styrofoam, all sizes. Folks will scrimp on food and clothes before they deny themselves electro-fun. Collar from some plastic strapping. Upstairs, the words are waiting for me. Written on the air in front of my eyes. I take them down in black magic marker.

§

Over on Laird, the sign carrier's in position outside Five Guys. Not shuffling with his sign, though. Sitting cross-legged on the curb, slumped and dishevelled. Collapsed Buddha needing a shave. Topknot wild and woolly, unenlightened frizz.

"They said 9:00. 9:00 to 2:00... five hours. Now they say... 11:30. 11:30, 1:30. Maybe that."

His speech glomps like cold ketchup.

"There's no minimum shift?"

"Minimum?"

"I'll pick you up here when you're done. 1:45, say. I've got a one-hour job for you. One hour tops. But you get paid for four, no matter what. Forty bucks minimum."

No way to tell what gets through the glaze of his eyes. Gray-green gel, like aquarium build-up.

"New rules?" he says finally, squinting up at me.

"Old ones. You'll like them better than the new."

§

"This is nice. I can picture her here, I think."

"Good, good. Visualizing them in the new space is always the first step." Nicole sounds bored, sleepy even on the verge of a sale. "Take your time. I'll just be over here if you have any questions."

She moves halfway down the corridor and stands with her head lowered, hands flat out in front of her, thumbs almost touching. Blonde hair falling forward as she checks her nails. Then swivels one hand out to the side and, with a deft ankle turn, cocks a high-heeled pump below it. Same shade exactly. Creamy purple, lilac stirred with milk. Shapes of people moving about Reception in the space beyond the door. A central location, as promised. *They tend to go fast.*

At seven grand a month to start—the bottom of the rate schedule she slid across in the office—probably not so fast. It's the Basic Rooms in government-regulated homes that get snapped up, that have three-year waiting lists. And no need for saleswomen.

Turn back to the window. Bird feeder on a nearly leaf-less sapling. Sparrows and finches darting between it and a large blue spruce. Stocking up under a pewter sky. Blue carpet, stains driven deep. Cream walls, the nail holes gone. A bigger, cleaner room than Maude's upstairs. But same basic layout.

Single bed. Pine table and chair. Water glass, coffee mug. No pictures.

Vivera's Mad Monk. A strange case, but our easiest resident ever, no question. Seldom speaks. No, not a vow of silence exactly, but yeah, mostly mute. Don't knock except for meals.

Right. With Jordan's payoff lasting what, two years? Ken screaming holy ass-rape with each month's auto-withdrawal. Doing his blue-suited best to prevent nest-egg suicide.

Closing window thoughts, chum. Hear them and pick up the pace.

"I think it's time to see upstairs. The... secure ward, I think you called it."

Opens and closes her eyes two times, slowly, like someone roused from sleep. Lashes coated black and knobbed like tulip anthers. "Our Memory Gardens, the second *floor*, is always part of the tour. But, I'm sorry, didn't you say your mother—"

"My wife."

"I'm sorry, your wife." Touching my arm. "Didn't you say your wife was still living with you? For someone still capable of semi-independent living, it would be very unusual to graduate directly to Memory Gardens. Unless she's..."

"She's very advanced, yes. Very far gone."

Another touch on the arm, this time lingering. "In that case you must be a saint."

"Maybe a slow-moving sinner."

"Oh! Right! Ha ha. You definitely need a sense of humour, that's for sure."

"Use it or lose it."

She doesn't do a Face-fuck, I'll give her that. Stays vaguely on my eyes, no flicks to the scar map they're sunk in.

"Let's go and make our visit."

1112.

Someone must have slipped out. Probably by accident. Four pushes on the 1.

Down the corridor opposite Maude's. Opens into an alcove with three sofas around a coffee table. Nobody. Against the wall opposite, a creepy big black rocking cradle, slatted sides, baby blankets and clothes, stuffed animals. "...of our Life Stations." Near it, on a wooden table, two old black typewriters and a Burroughs adding machine. *William Burroughs? Wasn't he a remit man from an ancestor's invention?* Old Bill of *The Western Lands* and *The Ticket That Exploded* right at home here. Less so—or else just differently—the three Hopper-esque paintings on the wall. Like someone trying in watercolour to give a Hallmark glow to empty streets and solitary diners, a gas station with cracked asphalt. A bizarre project. The more so given how well they're executed. Like staring down tubes of lunacy.

"We call it the ever-forgiving."

"What?"

"Here. Where we are. The Memory Gardens neighbourhood."

Beautiful heft and clunkiness of the machines. Big round keys, solid for striking. Raised numbers and letters in plain, no-nonsense fonts. That sense, in old movies, that the rotary dial phone, the clacking typewriter are of a piece, can hold their own, with the decanters on the sideboard, the oak desk, the heavy pulled drapes. And the utter visual collapse whenever someone whips out a cellphone in a modern movie, which directors, aping verisimilitude, have them do constantly. The weightless thing: pure function, free of gravity. Gravity of form, of beauty. The sense of being racked during close-ups on computer screens. Pixel dance torment. Why we hunger to get back to the serial guy. Real steel. Real throats.

"I assume there are sign-in, sign-out protocols. For residents and visitors."

"Oh, yes, of course. For safety and for security. Both. There's a book on this floor and one down on Assisted."

"And you keep the pages, I guess?"

"Keep?" She cocks her head, smiles sweetly. "Honestly, I've never been asked that. But it's a good question."

"But you see the previous pages if you flip back through."

Glance down the hall, then back. She doesn't have a clue. "I'm pretty sure it's just the day's page. Keep it simple for everybody."

"Where do the old records go?"

She frowns, perplexed by my persistence on this niggle. "Let's start back, shall we?" Good idea. *Rosemary's Baby* and Burroughs and Hopper Lite and the vaporized cocktail party aren't helping either of us. "They must go somewhere. To the Director of Care, I assume. Or maybe to the Executive Director, since they're not really a care issue. It's a good question. I'll find out for you. I'm glad you asked, actually." Liar.

Halfway back, we pass a caregiver pushing a woman in a wheelchair. The resident cranes up at me. "Would you come here, please?" In a high, pained voice. I do. She's got a doll in her lap, a blanket tucked around it. "Give me your hand, will you?" I do. She presses it against her cheek—cool and soft, like her hand—and then brings it to her lips and kisses my palm, slowly. "I love you," she says. A smell of soiled diapers surrounds the words. They bloom in the stink, swamp lily. "Who's this little one?" I say. "That's my Jackie." Lifting him by the hair to stand on her thigh. "Don't go," she whines as I withdraw my hand.

Behind me, I catch a look on Nicole's face like she's opened her refrigerator door and seen earthworms crawling her lettuce. She'll never make it in sales. Or maybe will shoot straight to the top. I know more about Mars.

"What do you do if you can't forgive?"

"Excuse me?"

"You said ever-forgiving. I know you meant because they forget so quickly. But as long as there's mental activity at all, there may be things you can't forget and can't forgive."

"Join them on the journey," she says tonelessly. Looks behind her at a loud voice near Reception. We're back in the first floor room. "Whatever journey they're on, join them on it," she recites.

I can't blame her. A shit start to her week. Grief-addled husband parsing straws, when she could have drawn a couple of well-lubed offspring eager to offload Dad and just needing the dotted line. I'm sagging too. I'm not going to find out anything more about Maude here. Gone is gone, and gone here is gone quick. Two days ago—Saturday— might as well be two years. All I've really learned is that Vivera—maybe any private care home—works like a kind of processing plant. Intake is downstairs, where you can still walk outside. From there you "graduate" to the locked unit, where vacancies are as brief as possible. Maude's room is already taken. Final graduation as per Maude's.

The owner of the loud voice outside comes into the room. Walks past Nicole, past me, without a greeting. Square, mannish shape, broad shoulders. Short brown hair. Sensible navy slacks, cream shirt. Like Jade, she claims the space too naturally to offend, asserting herself in it like a rock. Stands with her hands on her hips and her back to us, looking out the window.

"Is this your wife? Or another family member?" Poor Nicole. I hope she brought a good lunch.

The woman turns without haste. A gaze strong and direct, this side steely. Could tear up, but she won't let it happen. Not here, not with us.

"She was my friend. I looked after her."

"Who? Where?"

A hint of condescension in the smile. A capable person, used to handling fumblers.

"Lots of places. This room was the last."

As I realize with a shock that this room, too, was Maude's. Her first at Vivera, before she got shipped upstairs.

§

The woman, whose name is Danika, shrugs when I invite her to lunch. Doesn't ask for details when I tell her Judy's my connection to the family. Saying I want to talk about Maude enough for her, it seems.

Danika was with Maude seven years. Working more hours each year, doing more for her. Like helping someone down a very long staircase into the dark, giving them more of your arm with each flight, taking more of the weight as their legs weaken. First, Rosewell Retirement Residence for three years. Then Rosewell's Enrichment Floor for two years, as Maude became more disoriented and, increasingly, incontinent. When Rosewell couldn't meet her escalating needs, the move to Vivera's Assisted Living, the first floor room we met in. Six months ago, the move upstairs.

"And after that she didn't need your help?"

"She needs more than ever. And I keep helping. I told you, we are friends. I work for her and she's my friend. But... we run into a problem. Lots of problems, of course. All the time. We always find a way to solve. This time a big one, though. She starts to think I'm someone who wants to hurt her. Very upset when she sees me. This happens. Lots of times, it happens. Maybe she thinks I'm a stranger, a bad person. Or maybe someone she knows. We try it for a while, try different things, different times of day, see if it changes again. Then I talk it over with the nursing director, we agree I should stay away. I call two, three times a week, see how she's doing. This morning I called."

We're sitting in the food court at Markville Mall. At a table tucked against a divider near the elevator. There's hardly an empty seat. Just after noon. Somewhere, Judy just took a pill. Each of us has Amaya's samosa platter— warmed and chopped open with hot sauce drizzled over, chick pea salad on the side—and a mango lassi. Danika's treat. And she insisted on driving me over in her new Ford Escape. She's proud of what she's made of herself in twenty years in Canada. Works three-quarter time at a care facility, plus for several private clients, a waiting list just from word-of-mouth. Her second day in Canada, she sat down with pen and paper and figured out how many work hours there are in a week, minus six hours for sleeping each night and an allowance for travel time and unavoidable physical necessities. Later, with her private list growing, she found she could cut back sleep to four hours. "Hard at first, then not so hard. The body adjusts." That big-shouldered shrug.

"What do you think Maude died of?" We're sitting over coffees now. Danika's treat again, though I cleared our table and fetched them.

She looks around at the people eating, sitting down, leaving. "She has it six years almost. Some people last a little longer, not too many. Lots of people not so long."

Back at Vivera, standing by Danika's car, I show her one of the photos of Maude by the autumn flowers, the water behind. I put it in my coat pocket this morning.

"Did you take this?"

"I don't take pictures. That's what this is for." Tapping her head hard, like a woodpecker's knock. "To look and keep."

An odd comment from someone so versed in dementia. Or maybe not. What use is a picture if there's nothing in your head to match it with?

She studies the photo. "I know where it is, though. Toogood Pond. Ten minutes from here. Just west of Kennedy, in Unionville. We used to go sometimes. Nature she likes very much. Plants, birds. She remembered some of the names a long time. Me, I'm a city person. Cars, stores, lots of jobs. My family lived outside a village in my country. That's enough. But Maude—she always talks about the farm. Even when she can't remember anything else. Feeding the chickens. She was afraid of the cows, even when she's big. Made her dad laugh. Eating peas in the garden. Before she came here and got married."

"Who do you think took it? Judy?"

"The daughter? If the camera's pointing at herself, maybe."

"You don't like Judy?"

"Like, don't like. What's the difference? I never see."

"Max, then, I guess. He's the POA."

She gives me a look. Seriously? Max? Goes back to looking at the photo.

"Sandor, it must be." She shrugs, but her eyes soften. She smiles at something. Sandor and the ladies. Even the toughest ready to cut him slack.

"So Sandor hired you?"

The quit-jiving look again. "Max hires everyone. POA, like you said. But Sandor brings my pay. Or mails it, the last year. When he couldn't come. I give him a receipt, or send it."

"Why couldn't he come last year?"

She answers without taking her eyes off the picture. "Taking care's like this." She puts a hand up by her head and makes a rapid series of gestures with it: fluttering her fingers, shaking them in a fine quiver, spreading them out straight and stiff, then closing them into an abrupt fist and tugging down, like someone yanking an alarm or stop lever. "It's hard. Hard for anybody. Too hard sometimes."

"You've done it for twenty years."

"I'm strong. And they're my friends. Not my mother. Not my father."

She starts to give me the picture, then pulls it back. Brings it close to her face and looks at it a few long moments—the eye-seal to lock something in place. She hands it to me and, as I'm snapping the pocket shut over it, she wraps me in a hug, hard. It's hard to breathe inside her iron arms, my ribs still sore from Saturday's kicking. Looking down, I see the top of her head, tight against my chest. When she steps back, there's no sign in her face of what just happened. It's as if I dreamed it.

We head up the walk together, I'm not sure why. Little pumpkins are beside the other gourds in the urns, tucked like large coloured eggs below the dried grasses.

"Danika, you said Maude had Alzheimer's for six years. But you said you were with her for seven. From when she started living at Rosewell."

She nods. "I was with her when the doctor told her. I drove her to the appointment. Went for dinner afterwards. My treat, I said, but she won't let me pay. She said she felt relieved. She knew something was wrong in her head a long time, many years. Not Alzheimer's, something else—bad ideas, pictures—dark things, but she can't say. 'At least this has a name,' she said. Brave lady."

"Why was she already living in Rosewell then?"

Even as I ask the question, a cold oozy sense comes over me that I'm beginning to recognize as Wyvern slime. Things under rocks that eat each other in the dark.

Danika stops. Seems to take her first good look at me. "She tried to kill herself." *If you don't know that, who are you?* "Stepped in front of a car on Bloor Street."

"And her injuries were that…"

"Broken arm, broken pelvis. Physically, she healed all right. Little limp, but okay. But after, the family decided she can't live at home anymore."

"Meaning Max?" *The hard-on I'm getting for this guy.*

"Max was already POA. But even Maude agrees. Most of the time anyway. Gets mad about it sometimes. Mad and sad."

Just inside the doors, on a shelf opposite the sign-in book, a memorial's gone up while we were at lunch. A circle of Inukshuks an inch high. Each with a clear tapered bulb on top, a light inside, like the mini-bulbs on Christmas strings. Little wooden easel in the center, a silver-framed photo on it. Maude in a straw hat, yellow gloves with dirt on them. Big smile. A planting activity. *In Memoriam Maude Wyvern*.

We stand in front of it a few moments.

Without saying goodbye, Danika walks across the lobby and lounge, hugs a caregiver she meets just outside Maude's old door, enters the vacant room, and shuts the door behind her.

I take a few steps into the lobby, not knowing why. *You're done here*. And then I see it, on the corner of the bistro counter. A white slow-cooker with the top off. I go over to it, though I know, more or less, what I'll find. Onions, cloves, cinnamon sticks in taffy-coloured water. A brownish ball that might be an apple. The spicy smell strong close-up. Vivera's command of details. Why pipe in the fake when the real's so easy? Cheaper, too.

§

Danika, Jade, Amrita. Meeting people who loved and cared for Maude Wyvern, held her close right till the end, but none of them related to her by blood. Unless I make an exception for Judy, and, as always with Judy, I'm not sure I can.

Hand on the car door handle, I turn for a last look up at the window I—we—looked out of. Just yesterday. The curtains move, and then two people *are* looking out. A third shape behind them.

Not a wasted day for Nicole after all. Unless it's an internal move, which would presumably kill her commission.

6

WHAT'RE YOU DICKING *around like this for?*

Sometimes you have to dick around while you're waiting for instructions.

Stone and I have this little exchange while I watch the sign carrier at work across the street, humping the sign from the lights at Eglinton to up past Indigo and back again. Holding down my window seat in the Duke of Kent, first with a meditative glass of water, and now, since the waitress planted herself with her arms folded, with a three-dollar Tropical Green Tea. Mid-afternoon, the place is dead, and I'll be gone long before the cocktail crowd.

He's doing well. Attracting little knots of people who poke each other and point and laugh, snap a photo with their phones. An added bonus I hadn't foreseen. Get it up on social media where a friend or foe—a busybody, any link in the chain—might send it back to the office. He's perfect. Everything that made him wrong as a burger shill—the hangdog face, slump-shouldered shuffle, the random hand passes over his knees like a brain-damaged Charleston dancer—makes him perfect as a disaffected dental client. Someone pissed and crazy enough to schlep a homemade sign below the office tower where he got screwed. He's even got a gold front tooth, black spaces behind it.

An Indigo manager comes out, hands on hips. Relaxes when he sees it's nothing to do with scented candles or meditation pebbles. Snaps a shot with his phone.

It's basically the same message coming and going, in my black magic marker.

Looking for PAIN?
HIGH PRICES?
COLD IMPERSONAL SERVICE?
See Max Wyvern, Dentist to the Daft, Suite 1203 above

When it comes to your MOUTH
why skimp on TORMENT? Go to
Dr. Maxwell Wyvern, Oral Sadist Extraordinaire
"You'll beg for dentures or your money back."

After twenty minutes someone from the office appears. I wasn't sure it would happen at all. What's the point of a tower if you can't disconnect from streetside? Facebook and the rest must have helped.

Middle-aged, short. Glasses and a cap of gray hair. She berates him, growing red-faced when he won't stop shuffling. Heckling just bad weather to him. More people gather. Start taking shots of the two of them. Street theater. Maybe a ninety-second bit on YouTube, "Signs of Stress." When she realizes, she advances on the camera-wielders. Face cherry, hands pressed together in a weird wedge, like she means to dive into the little lens and yank her image back. Which is already flying around the world. They step back expertly, keep snapping. Everyone a half-assed Arbus now.

After a last blast, long, fifteen or twenty seconds, she throws up her hands and stalks back to the glass doors of the office tower. As soon as she's gone, the pedestrians start dividing around him in a smooth stream, only a few looking back to read his other side. Solo and duo shots, he's done. Used up as a subject.

Go on, I'm thinking. Scram. Just ditch the sign and vanish. What I told him on the drive over. *You'll have a couple of minutes before they arrive.*

But he just keeps walking. Slower, bent lower, like he's carrying bricks instead of weightless Samsung panels. And those maddening hand passes, dream-like crossovers. *A weird power, the senseless. A brainworm once you let it in.*

The cruiser arrives. Pulls over going south and the passenger-side cop gets out. Says something and waits while he takes the sign off. Clumsily, half-strangling himself with the plastic collar. Cop opens the back door of the cruiser, slides the sign inside. Motions the carrier in after it. In less than a minute, they're off downhill, catching the green light.

A drive and dump, most likely. Barring a super-slow day or super-bad mood, just take him to some distant neighbourhood off the bus routes, keep the sign and cut him loose. But they'll talk a bit along the way. By habit cops are info-hounds. Tapping any walls to find the spaces between the studs.

Not much to find, probably. On the way over, I asked him if he could describe who had hired him. Out came the perfect phrases, no coaching required.

"Never said his name. But little guy, short. Kind of little bit fat. Lotsa' hair. On his head, on his face. Monkey man."

I looked over at him, surprised. Morning meds wearing off?

§

Up in the office. The usual smell of Listerine and boiled rubber. Gwen, her nameplate says, still looking flustered, staring at her computer screen without tapping or mousing. Pinpricks of pink at the base of her neck, a slowly vanishing collar.

"How's Monday treating you?" Hands on her counter, wall of coloured files behind her. Tooth-shaped fridge magnets with the office info beside her keyboard, washroom keys attached to pink and blue toothbrushes.

"Have a seat. You're a few minutes early."

Sorry. Next time I'll come an hour late.

"Fill out one of the new patient forms. Please."

In a plastic basket on a corner table are several clipboards, each with a pen on a string tied to it, a paper under the clip. An empty basket labelled **Completed Patient Forms** beside it. I take a clipboard to a seat, check every box on the double-sided questionnaire and write N.A. beside every question without a box. On the lines under Additional Comments, I write the first two verses of "Sittin' in the Sun," which Satchmo was singing on CJRT recently:

> *Sittin' in the sun, countin' my money*
> *Fanned by a summer breeze*
> *Sweeter than the honey*
> *Is countin' my money*
> *Those greenbacks on the trees*

Comes a summer shower, drops o' rain falling
Sweeter than Christmas chimes
Hearing those jingles upon the roof shingles
Like pennies, nickels and dimes

After returning it to the basket, I follow the next step indicated. An office a deaf-mute would have no trouble in. **Please Select a Video to Watch During Your Appointment** on the cover of a big three-ring binder, DVD covers under plastic on each page. Tabs to help you find TV Series, Movies, Concerts. In Documentaries I find *No Direction Home*, a Scorsese Dylan bio. Bob in shades and wild hair, looking skinny and fierce, on the side of a road in bare flatlands. A ways behind him, a guy leaning against a sixties-era car with the driver's door open.

Perfect. Pit stop on the way to nowhere.

3:14, the door opens and the previous patient comes out, goes to the counter to be processed. The dental assistant comes through the door to Gwen's space with the file. Then opens the door to the waiting room and calls my name. 3:15 on the dot. Why there was no one else waiting. The place runs like a Rolex.

She motions me into one of the rooms, into the chair. Clips the bib on. A strip of caramel skin, almond eyes and fringe of black hair between her cap and mask. Starts setting out instruments on a tray. A nice figure, slight but curvy, even in the baggy greens. **Vivian**, says the bar above her left breast. "It's your first time with us, I know," she says. "When was the last time you saw a dentist?"

"Years ago, I'm afraid. Maybe decades. My mouth and I are barely on speaking terms."

Two-note chuckle behind her mask. She pauses, half-turns to glance at me. "Well, relax. You're in good hands

117

here." Not giving it much, but pleasantly enough. Having a face like the Face makes you something of a connoisseur of the economies of human warmth. Banter, mild flirtation, a part of medical sedation. Some assistants exude it naturally, democratically. People persons. Others have an instinct for exactly how much, and on whom, to spend.

Max comes in. Dr. Wyvern. I hear him behind me first. No greeting. He comes around to where I can see him, still no eye contact. "Did you pick your video?"

I tell him. He looks at Vivian and she leaves the room. Above me the TV screen waits on a hinged arm, earphones on a cord embracing it.

Max moves in the small space around me, readying his things. No cap, his mask down around his neck. He looks like his photos, but different too. Maybe just life-size. I'd probably think the same meeting Dylan. Short fluff of hair, fine and thinning in the gentlest way, a golden cloud dissolving on his scalp. Round, gold-framed glasses. Long thin nose, thin lips—*Swedish* comes into my head—but all well-shaped, this side severe. Doesn't look at all like Sandor and not much like Judy. Like they were hatched from three different nests. Little hole in one earlobe, I notice. Takes it out at work. Cream pants, pale blue shirt, gray loafers.

"Does it feel like rain out there?" he says with his back to me.

"It feels like hell."

"Well, they were calling for showers, not typhoons." Mr. Smooth. *Dr.* Smooth. Who cares what kind of nut case you've got in the chair, as long as his teeth are falling apart and his plastic still goes through?

"Open your mouth." Turning, mask up now, and bending with a pick in his hand.

"That's funny. I was about to say the same thing to you."

It never gets old, never loses its lustre—finding the phrase that stops smooth in its tracks. Makes the quick, assured eyes go blank and swimmy.

"Ex-cuse me?"

"I don't see how. But I would like to hear about your family."

"My…?" The eyes above the mask flicking at the door, they don't settle on me again after that first frozen stare. "You called about your breaking and loosening teeth. I imagine you're in a fair bit of discomfort. As soon as I do a preliminary—"

"Fuck my teeth. And jam that nose-picker sideways up your ass."

His eyes all over the empty door. Where's Vivian??!! She's supposed to hand him what he needs, suction up messes.

"You can start with your mom. You're obviously not taking a bereavement day. I'm sure your patients appreciate that. But if that subject's too raw, I'm interested in Sandor too. Judy. I'm all ears for any of—"

He's gone. From the hall come the sounds of the tantrum he's pitching. Chewing out Gwen and Vivian—these women whose job it is, like the videos, to deliver acquiescent mouths detached from the heads they're stuck in. The voice a high-pressure hiss, outraged but trying to keep it low, inaudible to the ears in other chairs. "…totally unacceptable…" all I catch clearly.

Seems we got typhoons after all.

And then Vivian is standing beside me, her body still and quite unafraid. A deadness in those choice almond eyes that would do a loan shark proud.

§

Hanging around the Yonge-Eg corner for a while. No reason to linger, but unwilling to quit the scene where my sign carrier and I poked two sticks into smoothly spinning Wyvern wheels. *Strange, how he didn't recognize your voice from yesterday. Not even with the Judy reference.* No, not strange. People see what they expect to see. Today, a customer with a bad mouth. Yesterday, just another piece of Judy's lunatic baggage, forgotten once disposed of.

Hello, Judy's brother.

I cross the street, head up towards the Duke of Kent. Retracing my steps, knowing where I need to go without thinking about it. It's the usual cure after close proximity with Indigo and the mall. Three little holdouts of personal retail facing the conglomerate, crowded dens where you can find a much deeper and more varied collection of music, films and books without ever having to look at a placemat or candle snuffer. The first two are up long, creaky flights of stairs. Vortex Records: vinyl and CDs in all genres, DVDs too, though no cassette tapes any more. I flip through the New Arrivals, see some amazing stuff. Wish for a moment a management monk's audio system might be upgraded a little. But only for a moment. I know the radio on the counter is perfect. One tuning dial, one volume dial, one ON/OFF switch. And I listen to other people's choices, not run my own rat-wheel of favourites.

Two doors south, Upstairs Video. I was never a frequent renter, even with Lois—she was usually painting and I was reading, and latterly studying. When we did rent, in that window between Nirvana and the Internet that seems much more than twenty years ago, we liked movies most people didn't: *Barfly. Naked Lunch. Bitter Moon. Jacob's Ladder.* Along with the ones everyone loved: *Reservoir Dogs. Terminator Two.* Surprisingly, for a rich man's daughter, Lois never succumbed to snobbery or a willed anti-snobbery. She liked what she liked, and never tried to be different. The different don't have to. I always knew our choice before dropping in, but liked picking up the various boxes, moving slowly along the display wall. Later, the VCR and TV gone with the rest, I knew why. The box with cover graphics, actors' names and faces, back summary and blurbs—each one half graphic novel, half celebrity mag. A little Hollywood vignette. A minimalist Sunset koan.

BMV is the last bead on my retail rosary. Just a few doors north of Eglinton. Street level entry, sci-fi and comics and textbooks on the second floor. At BMV I started as a seller, not a buyer. Bringing in the box of books Lois had left inexplicably, I learned a little about the used book trade. Most of the high-end art books the counterman refused, except for a couple of standard overviews, which he flipped through rapidly to make sure they were pristine. Nor did he want any of the hardback novels, even the award-winners by famous authors. "Once the paperback comes out, I can't move them." What he took at a glance—which I'd been least confident about, since they were in fair but not mint condition—were her paperback memoirs and thrillers. The rest I took to Goodwill.

I got into a habit for a while of visiting two or three times a week, even after Ken and I had worked out my remit schedule and I was learning to live within a budget that I knew these visits violated. Not that my BMV purchases were large—but anything not bone and sinew was fat. I treated the shop as a kind of lending library charging a nominal members' fee. BMV would buy back its own books for half the price you'd paid—once the hawk-eyed clerks had ascertained you hadn't abused it overnight. Buy a book for four bucks, return it for two. Buy another for six, return it for three. It wasn't much, all the books I wanted for ten to twelve bucks a week—but Ken's face hovered wincing over every transaction, however small, and if I was looking to pare expenses to the minimum, this was one that could go—especially since, on top of the forty to fifty bucks a month for books I read and returned, there were occasional purchases outright, books I couldn't part with. Céline's *Journey to the End of the Night*. Knut Hamsun's *Pan* and *Hunger*. Lichtenberg's *Waste Books*. *Gray's Anatomy* (hardbound, but discounted for a page ripped out of Urology). Luria's two great studies: *The Mind of a Mnemonist* and *The Man with the Shattered World*. Unable to choose from among them, I sold them all back and started going to the library. Since then, I've been a pure browser. The bane of the book trade, though on slow days your sequential book in hand simulates traffic.

Today, though, I see a book on the front table of publishers' overruns. *More Than Memory: What We Don't Talk About When We Talk About Alzheimer's*. Hardbound, new. Sixteen bucks, even at half price. Another phantom groan from Ken.

Still, I have to pick it up. Have to know just what it is—besides suicidal urges that make you step in front of cars—that the Wyverns can't stand looking at.

"Not to pry, but I hope it helps." The guy behind me at the cash, fiftyish, fit-looking. "Despite all the talk, it's hard to get straight information. But I've heard good things about that one."

"You're going through this?"

"I was until last March. It took five years to see Dad through to the end, but it aged me fifteen. I'd catch sight of myself in slivers of glass and think, 'Who's that poor old bastard?'"

"It's not for me. It's for a family I know."

"Let me guess. They just got the word."

"That's right. Just yesterday."

"On a Sunday? Well, they've got a decent doctor, that's something. Do they have any idea what they're up against?"

"They're beginning to, I think."

"Well, good luck to them. They're going to need it."

"Yes they are."

§

I'm too full from lunch to bother with dinner. The stomach trained to do a ten-hour stretch, now bloated with samosas. One missed meal a sop at least to Ken, a toonie tossed back in the pot.

Sitting in the armchair with a mug of Luck Yu, hearing rush hour crest below, I think of the story of Diogenes breaking his last possession, his wooden begging bowl. "At last," he cries, "I'm free!" Probably apocryphal, though with good stories what does it matter?

The chair under my ass annoys me. The cushion behind my back. The sofa. The low, scratched table I set my mug on. Even the mug. I wish I could find a spring of lukewarm tea, cup my hands under it when thirst comes over me. To most people's eyes, the meagre furnishings here would look like someone just moving in or almost finished moving out. But sometimes—often—I look at them and see the crap heap of the world. An attic stuffed with clutter I can't move or think straight in. I long to make it all vanish. And come close to doing it sometimes, step right up to the edge of free, feel the cold rushing air I long to let go and topple into—when practical consideration, like a strong hand, grabs me by the belt and pulls me back, just as I'm closing my eyes and leaning.

What floor-sitting does to a body your age. To a body with multiply broken bones and dislocated joints...

The Diogenes itch. It gets stronger in hyper-time. Stronger still during an adjustment. I feel, like a pillow clamped over my face, the space taken up by the spoons in my drawer, the kettle crouching like a mutant mushroom on the counter, the box spring and the pegs that keep it off the floor, giving dust a home. By every concept and assumption heaped in my head, turning it into a sluggard's crammed garage. How the crap I'm hanging on to, buried under, makes me stupid. Makes me dull. Makes it that much harder to think a clear thought, feel a strong feeling. The crowdedness. The clutter. You don't live with it. You force a dribble of living through it.

How the mind mourns—the greedy whining child in it—but the chest expands, the spirit rinses off its crud, with each thing you break, lose, give away, dump overboard. The boat rises just that fraction. Divest, divest! And the practical proofs, every time. Feeling myself become a better reader without the fallback of books at hand, knowing I know only what I carry in my head. *So many proofs, so few solutions.*

And wanting to vaporize everything I see.

A half hour before Jared and Lucy arrive, I spend some time in Big Empty. I don't know what they make of the door that's always closed during their visit. I don't care, I wouldn't open it for the Chief of Police. It belonged to Megan, it belongs to me. Jared's never asked about it, which says a lot for a curious kid with poor impulse control. The mystery door is probably one of the reasons Lucy stays close by during the lesson, humming Andean melodies while she spices her stew.

I take a walk around Maude's talismans, but I don't need to sit or lie among them to know they're still mute, they haven't found their voice, or maybe their alphabet, their language, yet. Or they're chattering like magpies and I haven't grown ears to hear them.

Dumb objects.

Dumb animal staring at them.

It's weird, but even Big Empty feels cluttered tonight. Like the air isn't molecules of innocent gases, but a million cheesy hotel paintings, the contents of the world's Walmarts and Dollaramas, miniaturized and hanging in space, filling it without a crack to slide a hair through.

I can't make it empty enough to speak to me.

A thought that makes me weary to the bone, worse than a dozen sleepless nights. And makes my stomach coil around samosa vapours, a queasy wrench that has nothing to do with hunger.

I know—roughly—what happens next. That sense, as hyper-black accelerates and the window smears to close, of being pushed from room to room in search of progressively emptier space. From bedroom to couch—that's already happened. From couch to sleeping bag in Big Empty. Finally, to the place I give no name. Which is the final destination, but is by invitation only.

Terrible to know *almost* all of a trip. Better to know some, or little, or nothing. But to know the path to an inn, the inn, the innkeeper—everything but the innkeeper's face, which until the last second remains a fizzing white oval. No voice—since he has no mouth yet—just the possibility of sound, a spectrum from silence to screech. Until the lips begin to form.

"Is it… do you want to kill yourself?" An early psychiatrist—no, a school psychologist. One of the last, not long before you quit. Two chairs, a room behind Counselling.

A good question and you wanted to answer it, answer him, where seconds ago you'd burned to smash his face, your fists tingling with it. Thinking a long time with your head down, which must have primed him for the whispered *yes.*

"No. It's not nothing I want. It's just less. Much less."

"Less. I'm sorry, I'm not following. Less than... Can you...?" The poor bastard couldn't have looked more lost if they'd handed him the wrong exam and a broken pencil.

And no answer for him then. Not even the start of one for myself.

You reach a certain point where vagrancy is required. Since only a certain limited amount can be accomplished from a home. A fixed address.

But there's that tricky period before you can cancel your mail, dump your gear and shove off.

Isn't there, though?

§

Lucy squeezes past me with her bag of ingredients and the big, brown-stained pot she always cooks in. Says it's part of every recipe and "adds to the flavour." I hear her running water. Jared sets up his things—books and dictionary, notebook, pencils. We had a tense moment early on, which felt like it could go either way, when I told him I wouldn't read with him without a dictionary. He dug in his heels, ended up shedding a few tears. Later, Lucy came to my door to thank me. Her eyes were misty too. What the hell just happened? I thought as I closed the door.

Lucius has come too, for some reason. He stands outside the door, looking uneasy. Making no move to enter, though

I stand aside. A very meek, infinitely capable man who makes me wonder about the soul of a gardener. Merging through sundial hours with the plants he raises, transplants, and cuts. He must get short-changed a lot—soft fingers sliding late, light envelopes out back doors, along with another demand and *Thanks so much!* How much, exactly? When *thank you* bloats, look out.

"Is it 305?"

"No, no problem. Some bumps and bangs. Getting ready to move, I think. I'm just wonder... how is your car?"

My car. From the blank in my head, I realize I've been driving without being aware of it. It might be sluggish or it might not, I haven't paid any attention to it. It's still moving is all.

"No worse. About the same, I'd say. I'll keep a closer eye on it tomorrow."

Lucius frowns, the prelude to an apology. Today's gray chill has brought more calls for burlap. Wasp nest removals.

"Take your time."

§

Jared's a wonder reader. Same as I was. Maybe all kids are. I never felt enough connection to my peers to learn their normal, except to know it wasn't mine. But when I turned, early on, from kid to adult books, I skimmed to find the passages that would pummel me with awe. The sensation of being stunned, my head socked with disbelief as it would later be by fists, was my earliest delight. Delight, and the search for it, were divorced from moral judgement, from any judgement whatsoever. My foster-father when I became a serious reader was a history buff, at least in the rich field of World War II. And my first impression of *The Rise and*

Fall of the Third Reich was a squirmy relish at its sheer preposterousness. The homeless vet and ex-con clawing his way up to become absolute ruler in ten years. The idea of exterminating millions, drawing up the plans and carrying them out—the stupefying sickness of it, like a banquet of vomit, made my head swim. And the Bunker scenes: issuing crazed orders while Zhukov's giant guns pulverized Berlin, tantrums in the diesel-rank air, his appalling breath, single-vegetable dinners, unsleeping monologues on *King Kong* while even the faithful slipped away or discreetly dozed... What a fantastic story! *Ringworld*, a million miles wide and the area of three million Earths, was the natural next phase in my search for the incredible, and for several years I was a sci-fi freak. Then happened upon *The Mind of a Mnemonist* and came home to human beings who yielded nothing to the fantasists in the realms of the stupendous.

Jared, too, asks only to be thunderstruck. He's still got last week's *Planet Danger*, renewed a second time, along with *Extinct* and *The Amazing Body*, all of which deliver precisely what their titles promise. He flips to whatever's currently blowing his mind and we read the passage together, him stopping frequently to ask me questions. What I can't answer, he takes home as a research project, bringing back next week what he's found online. Lucy raises her eyebrows at some of the titles, but this haphazard tour of the spectacular has gone much better than *Charlotte's Web* or *Tuck Everlasting*, which only made him surly and wilfully obtuse.

"Mosquitoes!" he announces gleefully, when I fail several times to guess the world's deadliest animal. The omnipresent little shits carry off two million people a year, making sharks and cobras and tigers look like dilettantes.

Sitting side by side on the couch, bent over the coffee table studying a blow-up of the Ebola virus, we present almost comically contrasting body types to the casual eye. Jared short and slight for his age, with a little pot belly from the snack-food bingeing he does after bullying sessions, a child's smooth skin and careless flop of hair—and me, stretched and hollowed and inscribed by a Torquemada-Kafka machine. But look a little closer—Jared's worry creases, premature etchings around his eyes and down his forehead, and his small ears, pointed as if snipped at the vet's—and someone might get a sense they couldn't quite name, some shadow of shared deformity, oddness at least, deviation from the norm.

And shared orientations, similar skews of thought, would make the likeness sharper. With the passenger pigeon chapter in *Extinct*, Jared went, as I would, past the mass murder itself, or else inside it, to more speaking details. Miracle hunting. Audobon in 1813, riding through western Kentucky, recording a migrating flock that darkened the sky like an eclipse, dung falling from it like snow, and did not stop for three days—which the naturalist calculated at 1.1 billion members. "It passeth credit," a New Englander had written two hundred years earlier, "but the truth should be written." "Passeth" gives Jared no pause—to the stumbling reader, the alien-archaic no harder than the alien-contemporary. Other scenes he fastens on are of Martha, the last of her kind, trembling with old age in a zoo in Cincinnati. Zoogoers tossing sand at her to make her move. After her death, roughly coincident with the start of World War I, her fifteen-inch-long body frozen into a three-hundred-pound block of ice for shipment to the Smithsonian.

"Wow." It could be Jared. It could be me. *Wow* the essence of our hunt.

Lately he has begun touching me gently. With a glance back to make sure his mom is occupied, he puts out fingertips—so light I barely feel them—to the large, zigzagging veins on my hand and forearm. "Like snakes," he says. "I can feel something moving." And draws his fingers back. I search, but can't find a reason to oppose it. It is more than a child's appalled wonder at the aging body, turning itself inside out with such garish drama, all its inner workings rising to the surface to declare themselves. I sense he is also worried—a worry he can't name or acknowledge—that I will pass away. That I will be encased in a block of ice and shipped somewhere, his knocks on my door unanswered. When a recent digression led us to haemophilia—a paper cut that never stops bleeding, imagine!—he looked everywhere but at my face.

The writing part starts poorly. I pick up the pen, rest it on the Hilroy notebook. Jared perches on the edge of the couch, his body tense, almost quivering. Excited to think his weightless thoughts have a secretary waiting, an adult with no other purpose but to scribe his musings in blue ink.

"How was school?" I start—as per usual, probably stupidly. And listen to the usual misery chant: wanting to burn it down, wishing for a flood that would engulf it, overflowing toilets…"I'd like to put some people in a dungeon." His eyes intent, focused on something far away.

I open the book. "What kind of dungeon would it be?"

I perk up, we both perk up, an energy has entered the room, as the phrases come, slowly at first, born in funk but veering from it, making something of it. There's a "hollow tube," some kind of entrance below the roots of a "giant tree… so high it has leaves in space."

Something has definitely entered the room. Something real, something genuine. You know it because you do—there's no mistaking it—and because it speaks haltingly. It gulps, gasps, belches—testing its lungs (if it has any), trying to find a way to breathe. I feel a tingling in my stomach as something comes into being that didn't exist five seconds ago.

And then—poof! like that!—it's gone. The dungeon that was forming degenerates into borrowed trash, game-fed stuff about aliens, zombies, mutants, lasers, hit points, nuclears. It spools out of him so fast he doesn't even notice I've stopped writing and have closed the book over my thumb.

I feel sick. And pissed. In a split second, Jared's fantasy has left the room. Jared has left the room, leaving me to watch this jizzfest by a kid in Tokyo or Seattle.

"Jared, that's not your dungeon."

"Yes it is."

"It's from a game you played. Or watched. Or maybe a TV show."

"No, it isn't. I made it up."

Stalemate.

I give it some time, then say, "Jared, the tree with its top in space was interesting. And I'd like to know where the hollow tube goes."

"That was stupid."

"Well, I liked it. And you could always start another."

For a nervous little elf, he can sulk like a trucker at closing time. I have no idea whether I'm being a responsible teacher or a sadist. He could learn better sentence structure by punctuating his first-person-shooter scenario. But I'm simply unwilling to transcribe something so zillionth-hand lame.

Looking away, chin pushed out sullenly—behind us, Lucy has stopped cooking, there's no sound from the kitchen. After a time, he starts. Tonelessly, letting me know that what he's describing might be a dungeon meant for me. But at least it's his own.

There's a shack in the desert. Nothing else around. Sign on the front: For Bullies. It's a little thin shack with a pointed roof. "Like a poop shack." A single chair inside. I think of school when he says that. When the bully sits down, the chair flips over instantly, sending him down a chute. Then rights itself as if nothing has happened. If you blink you miss it.

"What's down the chute?"

But that's it. All I'm getting today. As we wrap up, I encourage him to bring more ideas Wednesday. What awaits the bully at the bottom of the chute? Is there any way out? How?

I might be advising myself, I think as I shut the door. But that is what teaching is, or what I take it to be: helping someone to go where you've gone, should go, will soon go, are still going...

§

After they leave, I do a drive-about. But know, before the garage door has quite rolled up to the ceiling, that it's hopeless. Not only do I know there'll be no sign of her, but I'm lacking any sense she even *could* appear. Not fear of failure: certainty of it. And on top of that: a confusion about whether I'm looking for Megan, or Lois, or someone else entirely. When there's no someone to find, you can only find everyone.

Down Avenue to St. Clair. East to Mt. Pleasant and down the hill. Turning east again above Branksome Hall, then up and down streets in the Rosedale maze. Lois's home turf.

Confusions spill from the first one, miniature spiders scattering from a split egg sac.

Why have you always assumed they'd still be in Toronto? That she was never more than a lucky car ride away?

The family would try to keep them close, no question. And would have succeeded in the short run, the safe nest needed. But Lois restless, strong-willed. And would meet someone, not right away, but before very long—that was easy, strangely comforting, to accept. And all the things that could take the new trio anywhere. Jobs. Exhibitions. Medical procedures. Christ, university by now. It's not 1813. The odds are powerfully against anyone staying where they begin.

Dandelion world. Filaments hanging by a thread, the winds gusty.

You just couldn't bear to think of them scattered by sheer chance. Blown beyond even the unlikeliest stroke of luck.

Not only can I not hear if the engine's sludgy, even the wheel beneath my hands feels like test pattern dots. The lawns beyond my headlights a mirage seen through binoculars.

Nothing. Nothing out here.

I stop beneath a shade tree, a big one still with its leaves, and turn everything off.

Silence. And then the something always there, behind it. A kind of whispering.

Wealth has locked its doors and turned off its lights but I seem to hear it all around me, a barely audible rustling like the quiet munching of silkworms in the dark.

7

PROLOGUE: THE STAIRS

The dreams come on schedule.
(The dreams are the schedule.)
The dreams lead down.
(The dreams lead to Stone.)

First, the Ugly Dreams. Lurid loops of filth and savagery. Burst sewers in a human abbatoir. Severed heads and limbs in watery sludge bobbing with turds. Not snapshots of carnage but endless coiling chases <u>through</u> it. Through corridors and up and down stairs in a house riddled with grimed passageways clogged with smashed belongings. A sense hanging in the fetid air of endless years of neglect, endless abandonment. Isolate decay.

Yet—something is moving. In the stillness of the ruined architecture, something moves without pause, wrecking all it finds. You sense it, always. Pursue it, flee it. It is just ahead and just behind. It needs no rest, so you can take none.

Finally, in a room fogged and reeking, you meet. The putrid chase ends abruptly. You see his back, hunched over his work, and feel the weight of steel in your hand. <u>You've always known this</u>. He won't pause to turn, now. Neither will you.

    <u>This is the bottom</u>.

And yet—it isn't.

    Incredibly, all the panting pursuit and stomach-churning finds, all the grinding repetitions of terror—they amount to a barrier you must cross. A shell, a membrane, you must tear through to reach a threshold. It is there, on the other side of the Ugly Dreams, that the stairs start.

    They are—the Ugly Dreams—a passage through to the landing.

    And a message, too. Stone's reminder that hyper-black is far along and won't hold much longer. Descend the stairs to learn what must be done. Descend the stairs to find Stone.

    The job is on the stairs, and Stone waits at the bottom.

The dreams come on schedule.
(The dreams are the schedule.)
The dreams lead down.
(The dreams lead to Stone.)

§

Amazing how little has changed. Twenty-three years since the page was typed on Lois's Smith-Corona, yet it captures perfectly what just jolted me awake on the couch. Bolt upright, shaking with terror and disgust. 3 a.m.? 4? Sooty gray through the uncurtained window, but the street dead silent.

    The dream already scuttling backwards into the black it came from. Even this dim too bright for it. Just traces, disappearing. A leg torn off below the hip, flesh oozing red around the splintered femur. Brown swipes on the wall. Sludge ankle-deep already. And the sense, hovering: whoever did this, is doing it, is close. Close by. *Just ahead and just behind.*

All here. On a page buried among other papers from that time, a box of them in a corner of the bedroom closet. What you set down, then. What just tore you out of sleep, now.

There is no now and then. You're in a loop. Round and round.

Aging. Not changing.

Out on the balcony, suck in air that's taken a wintry turn. Dark bricks ahead. Fenced slabs of concrete one way, blinking tower the other. Hizzoner underneath it with his pals, plotting and partying in his black-velvet cellar.

City Hall not the tower, nowhere near it. But geography broke for fantasy long ago. Where else for the Big Man's bunker but sunk deep below the pseudo-building? Flunkies bringing stacks of takeout 24/7 as, drunk and high, he screams and schemes how to keep his base, his Nation. Sucked wings and bottles smash against the walls, bellows of outrage stab the ears. How? HOW??!! Such pointless pain, when a tranked-out monkey could tell him his base is firmly in his sweaty palms, it always has been, he hit on the formula from the start. *No new taxes.* Save the guy with the three-car garage and the heated driveway two hundred bucks a year and he's yours. Whisper at the same time that what little he does pay won't find its way into the paws of the lazy breeding maggots in the roach towers, pregnant teen sluts sucking strangers for smokes—*not a fuckin' nickel, y'hear, I'm workin' on it*—and he's yours for life.

Him and all his mall-trawling, frappa-slurping, Bluetooth-bawling brood.

The Nation safe.

Night's done, no question. Sleep anyway. Back on the couch, I read again the piece from years ago. Calmer now. Hizzoner does that for me, I'll give him that. His dream plug-ugly, but mundane. *Fuck you I got mine* a credo old as office.

The description holds. So does its meaning. Stone putting me on notice. The window closing, our meeting can't be postponed much longer. As vile as the Ugly Dreams are, slayfests of gore and shit, what waits beyond them will be far more eerie and unsettling. Crushings of the birth canal nothing to the light and chill of Delivery.

With steps to a secret cellar, put the nastiest-looking guy you can find outside the unmarked door. Members Only says his hideous mug.

§

Lois's idea—

Remembering that as I unplug the toilet for the girls in 201. A monthly job at least, which I'm just as glad to have today. Morning shredded by that start. Odd-job some hours at No Name Towers, hope things gel by evening. Embarrassed, Alyssa's gone to make tea. Usually it's a toothbrush or make-up applier or disposable razor I fish out—things they always pop cute eyes at "how that got there." Though the real mystery to me is how you can brush your teeth or curl your lashes over a bowl of shit, yet be too dainty to dip a hand in to retrieve the fallen thing.

Try writing it down. Quick, before you forget it. Lois sounding sleepy, looking for a way to salvage some shut-eye herself. Said I thrashed and groaned, then whimpered before shouting myself awake. But believed in writing too. Kept various journals, one just for dreams. No recovery pimp—I couldn't have loved that—but believed in digging channels to connect above and below. A miner at heart. Psychically, artistically. And tough and brave enough for that work.

"This is good," she said next morning over coffee. "Creepy. Maybe a little too abstract, but it catches something. And makes me want to keep reading." And suggested—the thriller reader—that I add the title: <u>Prologue: The Stairs</u>. Got right away that it had to lead much further down.

"Well, it could hardly lead up."

We laughed. We laughed a lot. Even that last fall—though worry weighed on her—we could still crack each other up... right up to the moment past which we'd never laugh or even smile in each other's presence again.

A little tussle—Lois puzzled and put out somehow—when I didn't want to repeat the experience. Neither by extending this writing or trying another one. Someone not just talented but managing her talent, wringing every drop from it, parsing all its promptings—she couldn't fathom not following up on a win. But writing held no allure for me. I liked reading, was all. That, to her, was wasteful. Or self-deceiving.

"What about someone who visits art galleries? Buys art books. Buys pictures even. But never once sits down in front of an easel, or has any desire to."

That helped a little. She knew lots of those people, after all. Had sold pictures to a few.

Though she wouldn't quite surrender her sense that something—someone—was being squandered.

How do you not love that?

§

A toilet, a leaky faucet, some loose bathroom tiles. I head out at 3:45, catch the bank just before closing. No funds yet. "Tomorrow for sure." But my people don't work for tomorrow—not for me, they don't. "I'll be back first thing."

Pigeon Man sitting by an alley just east of Yonge. Back against the wall, legs straight out in front of him. The birds march up and down the narrow alley, mill around him, walk circles on his lap and up and down his outstretched legs. Shitting randomly, as birds do. Splotches of white coat his crotch and legs, wrists, hands. It looks like an act he's worked up, dedicated himself to. And the wide berth people give him, arcing to the curb as they pass, clears a neat semicircular stage. But he's relaxed, smiling, murmuring to his companions. In his own world, no hint of performance. He calls them by name as they peck at his half bagel. A stink comes off him—picked up where the detour to curbside starts, the pedestrians as choreographed as the birds. He's tall, bony, with a movie prophet's mane of graying hair. St. Jerome, devils by CGI. Face and hands a deep, leathery brown—he hasn't been inside since winter.

It's obvious the scene will have to be transplanted to Max's office, where it will just about fit. Plenty of room for traipsing and for short, shit-spilling flights. And no shortage in this crew of toothless bills needing fittings. Massively receded gums.

I just need the funds, Ken. Insta-everything the promise these days. And a lot does come that way. But then there are these pockets, way-stations. Info-bit spots an old pal on the circuit and holes up for a few hours over bad coffee, bitching and laughing about the binary grind.

Tomorrow for sure. I can't see any reason why it…

Presto-World. Everything guaranteed—in foam, not iron.

BMV is pleased to buy back the Alzheimer's book. Overnight read-and-sells nothing new to them—obsession is the bedrock of their business. The clerk, same guy as yesterday, skips the flip-through. Another virtue of the word freak: he's not on a page long enough to soil it.

On a parkette bench down the hill from the Queen's Arms, I empty my pockets and count coins. Besides the eight bucks from BMV, I've got another toonie, and the loonie and two quarters I found in a dryer drum in the third-floor laundry room. Just over eleven bucks. Reluctantly, I open one of the rolls in my jacket pocket and add another four loonies, crimp it shut again. They're supposed to be for emergency use only, but I need enough to stake me to the first round at least.

In my early days as a super, I thought the laundry room might serve as another bank for short-term loans. Along with the rent cheques at the first of the month, I deposit the rolls of coins I collect from the boxes on the Owner's two washers and two dryers. A source, I thought, of small tide-me-overs at lean month-ends. If I had to siphon too much, I could bump up next month's deposit. He could hardly miss such relatively small and random discrepancies.

Not so fast. The first time I shorted him by ten bucks—from a two-hundred-dollar take from the four machines—the Owner was on the phone before the end of the business day. Not accusing me—not directly—but wondering if a tenant had found a way to wash or dry without paying. Did I know if that was possible? It seems he'd actually had someone graph the receipts over years, factoring in the regular rises in fees for which I changed the coin slots accordingly, and he knew to a remarkable degree of accuracy what an average month of use should bring in. Even knew which months were heavy and lighter. Did I know that people washed their clothes much more often in the summer? Outside more, of course. Sweating. And seeing others and being seen. Much easier to let a wash go late in the winter, shiver in the comfy same a couple more days. Did I know that? I did now. It was January when we were speaking.

He'll be alone tonight. But not before 6:30. Most drinkers have braking devices in place, and start time is a common one. No wonder how I know these things, no guessing required. Prophecy common window coin. Five weeks ago, it might've been a shooting star sparking in black, a fizz of lime-white announcing a window opening… but not now. Cross the river in the dark and the next stone will be right where your foot needs it to be, shining in a spot of helpful moonlight.

No less natural than the squirrel tugging the Burger Shack bag out from under the juniper.

§

He's sitting at the very back this time, alone, at one of the round tables pushed against the wall around the pool table. He's on the side that catches some of the light over the baize and the racked balls. Facing me but hunched over, reading something intently.

The front room's boisterous already, though it's all coming from one long row of tables. A strange party. A bunch of boys, young men—one, two, three… seven of them—looking barely old enough to shave, directing overlapping stories and jokes at a massive, suet-faced woman sitting at one end of the table. They're dressed identically, in gray jackets and blue ties. She's wearing voluminous cloth, striped diagonally in primary colours. Marlon Brando in his muumuu in *The Island of Dr. Moreau*. The scene is hard to figure. Private school boys taking their teacher or headmistress for a pint? But these boys, though they look young enough to card, must be beyond high school. They've all got glasses of beer in front of them, including her, three pitchers on the table. Grad students, then, with their curmudgeonly advisor? But why the matching, prep school rigs?

"What's he drinking? Whatever it is, I'd like two of them."

The daughter puts her hands on her hips. She's very pretty, a different shade of hot pants tonight. Turns to her mother, who's already clocking me. Father nowhere in sight.

Mother approaches with a kindly expression. Puts a hand briefly on mine. Cool, soft—I wish she'd leave it there. The trouble with some people touching you. "No trouble please," she says.

"None. Word of honour." With my hands up like she's got a gun. "It'll end with a friendly handshake. Just watch. You'll see."

She shakes her head slowly, but nods at the daughter, who pulls the two half-pints. Sets them on the bar and reaches overhead for a tray. When I tell her I'll carry them over myself, she picks at my toonies and loonies like they're turds, leaves the extras, my tip, lying on the counter. My charms at work.

Now Mother, hands folded below her waist, is staring at me with a blank face in which I can't read even the hint of an emotion. *People are strangers to me. I know nothing of them.*

Absolutely the wrong thought to carry into an encounter.

I bring the glasses up towards my nose and inhale deeply. Toasted malt, strongly nutty, cradled by sweetly vegetal vapours with tangy strikes—rain-washed grass beside a pine tree. The trick, for me—which, with some close calls, has worked so far—is to experience the full allure of the travel brochure and decide not to embark. Avert your eyes and you may find yourself on board by mistake.

When I open my eyes, after a second that feels like a long time away, the scene of the cavorting boys and the unsmiling dowager reveals itself, tidepool-clear after my deep sniff. They all live together in a hut deep in the forest. Which is also the center of the city, disguised as a small apartment building. They serve her sexually, one per night, and at the end of a long, elaborate copulation she eats that night's partner. Not with a chomp, like a praying mantis, but delicately, savouringly, start-ing with his feet, leaving blue eyes in a pale white face, bangs of love-damp hair, till the end. Next morning, she gives birth to his replacement. Once a week they gather here, the eternal den mother and seven mates who didn't exist a week ago.

Above them, men in shorts and long underwear tear with raised sticks around an ice rink, unwatched by anyone.

Time to meet Sandor.

"Peace offering?" I say, setting down the beers. "We didn't exactly get off to a raging start the other night."

He comes up slowly out of his reading, emerging from a pool of deep absorption. A notebook, he closes it now over his pen. A well-worn paperback—George R.R. Martin's *A Dance With Dragons*, the last of the series so far—on the table also. He doesn't seem at all surprised to see me. Might have come expressly for that purpose, been waiting at our table.

"I'd say we got off to the start you planned. And, yes, rage was a big part of it." He says this as I'm settling into my seat, the dark side of the table. No meanness in his voice, just a rueful kind of levelling—a *let's at least be honest* that's a reasonable request. "No tea tonight?"

"No anything. But I have to buy my seat." I slide the glasses over.

He lifts and settles those big shoulders inside another sweater. "Sure, why not? Besides, how often does a bipolar detective deliver you your beer?"

No problem hiding my surprise. I've lived far behind my skin for longer than I can remember. But a strain to conceal how fast gears are turning in my head, trying to puzzle out who might've shown Sandor this funhouse version of me. Sipping the last of his beer placidly, no *gotcha* gleam winking out at me. I can't fit *detective* with any of the people who've seen me poking around since Saturday—Judy, Danika, the Vivera staff—or, more to the point, match it with someone who would convey her impressions to Sandor. Though it has been *her*, every time. And don't discount the loyalty, often desperate, a ladies' man inspires. Danika's secret smile at Sandor's name. But *bipolar*? It's only one of a grab bag of labels thrown at me early on—gaining over time, but seldom on its own. Usually a double or triple string of terms coined for my windows, or *episodes* as they called them. Along with, always, a double-duty qualifier to complete the picture. *Treatment-resistant. Non-compliant.* Four or five words to give a gist of me. And anyway it's been years, decades, since I got close enough to a shrink to get any name. So—a homemade diagnosis? A psychiatric hobbyist?

When in doubt, plunge in. Take the attack when the opponent succeeds in surprising you, abandoning your gradualist strategies in an instant. The moment itself is familiar, an occupational hazard. No matter the adjustment, there comes a time when someone—sometimes a principal, sometimes a side performer—offers you a glimpse of what you're doing as a stumble in midway dark, yourself a strobed caricature, Silly Putty strands and bulbs waving in rippled glass. It's absolutely the wrong time to pause and consider the vision, whose plausibility can only demoralize. And equally wrong to press on in the dark, groping in a labyrinth that has just shown its eagerness to repel you. It's axe time. Grab the nearest one and swing it at the wall of glass, the painted plywood behind it. Crash and splinter straight ahead to find open air.

"You're welcome, I think. But I'm way too crazy to be a real detective. And not nearly crazy enough to ignore things that smell off."

Which sounds, even to my ears, nothing like an axe. More like a toy hammer, tapping.

"What things?"

"Someone slipping away for no apparent cause."

"People do, you know. Especially at eighty-two." Staring into his glass. "My mother… she tried to end her life once. Maybe you know. It turns out all she had to do was wait." Drains the last of it. "Though nobody ever said waiting was easy."

"No one surprised, or even curious. Her last check-up clean. No doctor attending, just mortuary goons who arrive in double-time. A cop summoned at the first sign of anyone remotely interested in her death."

"Are you done?"

"Barely started. Sons who don't pause when their mother falls off the earth, they go on drinking with friends, pulling teeth. Sign-in pages like mayflies, they vanish at the end of the day. A daughter who sometimes sleeps over with her mom. Staff look the other way—but they keep looking that night? After that night? A daughter who always has pocketfuls of pills—any five of which would drop a linebacker into coma."

On cue at "sons," Sandor starts in on the next beer. Half of it goes down his throat before he pauses, glass near his chin. Takes down the rest.

"And you were on the scene because you know Judy?"

"Yes." TAL does a lazy flit through my head and out again. It might as well be me downing the beers, I'm so poor at keeping some things in view.

"And, knowing her, you know she has a history of violence. Extreme at times."

"Violence to herself. I've never known her to hurt someone else." *They'd have to become real to her first.*

"If you say so." Sipping. "Since you're implying there's something suspicious about my mother's death, I assume motive is the next consideration. That's how these conversations usually go, isn't it?"

"Usually, yes. And it's best to start with the obvious, no matter how far away from it you end up."

"Money."

"As far as I can see, Maude was the only thing standing between her children and it."

"You don't know anything, do you? Does Judy strike you as money hungry?"

"Money starved, not money hungry. And her family has certainly pulled together to make sure she never developed a taste for the stuff."

A deep draft, half the remaining.

"Teachers have creamy pensions, but you took yours early. And pension is as lifestyle does. Max should certainly be well-greased, at least by any normal standards. But even on first meeting he strikes me as someone with expensive tastes."

"Have you met Vivian?"

"I've had that pleasure."

"Well, you can cross money off your notepad. I own my house outright and have two condos I'm renting out. One I'm getting ready to sell for thirty percent profit. Max is much more diligent, he must have five or six going. Dad started flipping them as a retirement project and he gave us each a starter. That was thirty years ago, but he saw exactly where things were headed, housing-wise. As a graduation gift, it was pretty generous. Does that clear things up?"

"Not really. Not very many things. *Housing-wise*, I'm still left with a tiny woman curled in a single bed, her group home daughter arranging small objects in a crossing ceremony."

The bottom of the glass. Sandor raises two fingers to the bar. "This round's on me."

"That's good. Otherwise we're buying it with pocket lint."

"Sounds like you're the one with money motivations."

"And you're the one sounding like he doesn't know anything."

Claps his hands once. "Good. No sense drinking together if we're not equally out of it." Then remembers I'm not drinking. "Don't worry, we'll keep your phantom glass full. The Kims wouldn't like you nursing an empty." And then seems to deflate. "It's all academic anyway."

"What is?"

"The autopsy, toxicology screen—whatever you think is coming next. My mother was cremated this afternoon. I was writing about that in my journal. Trying to describe how strange it felt, not knowing the exact moment she turned to smoke."

§

"Two Double D's for my regular. Pint of hot air for Scarface."

Perfect delivery by Ella as she sets them down in front of Sandor and swings away. Sandor turns far enough to watch her in her hot pants and heels. He starts on a new beer, in a new rhythm. Frequent small sips, keeping it close to his lips.

It's awkward not having a drink. The body bobs like a helium balloon without plausible action. Napkin to tuck. Fork to jiggle. Cup to place, glass to grip. Nicotine choreography.

It's Sandor's turn to take us forward. Time for me to shut up and stop feeding him lines. Especially since he's out ahead of me in some way. I sense it without understanding what I sense. He seems to know me, know about me. From whom I can't imagine. Judy the only person that comes to mind. But she doesn't talk about real people—not in the info-trading way most people do. But who else? All I'm left with is the sense that he's primed somehow to meet me. A stakeout with Double D's and journal—and I'm the gumshoe?

Funny, though. I don't have the impulse to hurt him I feel with Max. Or I do, but it's hazy, complicated somehow.

Not a good sign in an adjustment—melting when you need to freeze solid. Max encased in so much metal I just want to bang on him with a pipe, break his eardrums at least. Sandor, for all his size and secrets—it would feel like stepping on a snail.

"So the premise you came in with is gone," he says finally.

I lace my fingers, lean forward to lay my arms on the table. Greater contact doesn't slow, though. Hyper-time closes off as many options as it opens. Silent waiting being one of them.

"Three days. There's a handy proof of not mattering. Not being able to become a suspicious death. You can't become a question, let alone a lingering one."

Sandor appears to consider it. Swishes the last of this glass in his mouth, like a taster.

"Are you finished?"

"Until I think of a new way to start."

There. That dark, determined thing rising in him again. What I saw surfacing the other night. Not grief exactly. Not just. Or not new grief. Maybe what grief becomes if it lingers, finds a silty habitat and fattens patiently, hugging the bottom, opening its mouth at what it needs.

"You really don't know anything, do you?" he says. For what, the third time? Not meanly, though. Ruefully, more like. More moxy on my end needed to grease—what?

"I wouldn't be much of a detective if I did, would I?"

An inspired non sequitur that arrives out of nowhere to save us. Sandor relaxes visibly. Inflates that big chest and gut, lets it out slowly. Lifts the fifth glass and fingers for the next two.

§

We're there. We've reached it: the infinite spigot of self-pity where your work is done, just sit back as it cranks wide, nod when necessary, and do nothing to impede the gush.

"You don't know what it's like. No one could who hasn't been through it. Max was POA, yes, but only for finances. Personal Care was me. Dad was cagey, see. Setting it up at the first signs, though he had most of it in place already. Dementia wasn't going to cramp his style any more than depression had. But he divvied it up. Didn't trust anybody. Or trusted bits of different people. Max handling the money end, me looking after her but submitting the receipts to Max. Except that Max was too lazy to keep tabs. Piles of little slips—PSW hours, incontinence pads, bras, sockettes— not his thing at all. So he worked it out with the banker, not sure how exactly, probably a stack of well-chosen samples, that since expenses averaged ten thousand a month, why not just transfer that regularly to her account, let me spend as needed. I came close to screaming when people said how lucky Mom was to have a POA who didn't scrimp, who trusted his brother, the stories they could tell... As it turned out, there was a surplus in the Rosewell years, it piled up steadily. And then went down just as steadily at Vivera, down to almost nothing by the end. Max was always great with numbers. Not so great at visiting. Maybe twice a year in the early years. Pop-ins on his way somewhere. Occasional meal out when she could still cut and chew a steak beside him. Not at all when the going got heavy. Judy about the same. Except she popped up for a few days at a time, then gone. Popped up most near the end. Which was a blessing really, because I'd hit a wall. Hit a series of them, but this one was the last. I could feel that. The weeping, the panic calls at 3 a.m.—*Where am I? How did I get here? Where*

is everybody? What am I supposed to do?... I can't describe it.
Every kind of breakage and loss. Memory's just the tip.
Who you knew just eaten, bit by bit. But the bits don't
smile vacantly, nod away. They scream. Accuse. Beg. Weep.
Concoct schemes while they're still able. Gouge their faces,
yank out their hair. I don't know why I'm telling you this,
and I don't care if you believe it, but it broke me. Broke me
many times and I kept patching myself together and going
on. My doctor said, 'What're you trying to be, the last caregiver standing?'"

"I'm sure there was never much danger of that."

"Could be you're underestimating me."

"Not much chance of that either." He's stopped drinking.

"It wears you down. Like a grinding machine. The other
visitors, the regular ones—we all looked old, older than
some of the residents. I did it until I couldn't any more. And
a little past that. My mistake. There was no one left who
knew me. No one I could talk to even a little. I was just a
nice man who brought chocolate bars. Often less than that.
And I stopped. And I guess, from the reports I got from
Vivera, that's when Judy started turning up. She always surfaced at weird times. Who knows why? Maybe she was after
something. She's cunning in her way. Has had to be, I guess.
Or maybe just more used to talking to someone who isn't
there. Pathetic, but that may have been the size of it. A job
she was actually trained for. So I sent her some of Danika's
pay. Not as much, of course—she was hardly Danika—but
I compensated her for whatever she was able to bring. Max
never knew. No reason for him to sweat these little payouts,
but he might've. He always hated Judy. Not just fed up, but
pissed. Always predicting the day she'd come 'sucking back
around,' and always standing guard to prevent it."

"Goo goo ga ga. Moo goo guy pan."

"What's that supposed to mean?"

"It means how scintillating a conversationalist were you your first three years?"

"Three...?"

"Of your life. Let me guess. For the first nine months you had as much to say as a tapeworm. And behaved pretty much like one, a barely moving parasite sucking the host dry. And then you spent a year shitting yourself and howling when you wanted food or felt the slightest discomfort. And then learned a few monosyllables so you could command more accurately and babble bad imitations of human speech."

"That's a pretty cruel parody of human infancy."

"Is it? We begin as bedridden invalids requiring total care. Don't you think a lot of people stuck in a room with this gibbering thing might want to stick a gun in their mouth?"

"You're the one who's babbling."

I am a bit. No question. But not as much as Sandor thinks. Adjustment radar is taking me somewhere, sensing what I need to find so I can blunder towards it.

"I knew my mother," he says. "Even as a child, I knew her."

"Did you? Knew her dreams and hopes? Her secret history?"

"Not as I came to later. But yes. She was always a person to me."

"You must've been a prodigy then. Most infants know a tit and a diaper changer. If those vanish, they won't lose any sleep, as long as the milk and fresh linen keep coming."

"You've got a dark view of things. An ugly view."

"It's been said. Many times."

"Look. There's no need to get all inhuman about this. We're not talking about abstractions, and we're not talking about infants. Every person—every adult person—needs to be recognized. Known for who they are. Or do you want to tear that down too?"

. I don't. Or I do, but only because it makes me see things—a little storm of pictures, like a paperweight blizzard—I can't stand to see.

"You're walking with a friend," I say. Channelling a philosophy TA I recall with sudden vividness, a bright figment from my nine weeks as an undergraduate. He liked to launch his thought experiments abruptly, though he marred the effect by smirking, a mistake I don't repeat. "Someone close to you, an intimate, who suddenly loses consciousness. Falls down from a stroke and just lies there. Not responding. Eyes rolled back, tongue lolling. Do you walk away because they're no longer aware of precious you?"

"Of course not. You're being silly again."

"Am I? You'll help someone in a coma if they get there suddenly. But your mom entered a coma gradually, over years. And there you draw the line."

The black eyes, and the thing that rises in them. Not anger so much as knowledge he absolutely can't accept, can't let close or look at even momentarily.

"No, I draw the line here. At talking to you anymore. That was my mistake."

I stand up. Stay with fingertips grazing the table until his eyes come up from his empties.

"It was, you know. For once we're in perfect agreement."

§

All the Kims mobilized for my departure. Ella looking past me at poor Sandor. Father off his stool, cards set aside for his sorrows-of-the-world face, fingers lightly curled, like he might have to dial up an early lesson and knock me on my ass. Mother out in front of the bar, between me and the door, reminding me of a promise not kept.

Back at the table, I extend my hand.

"What's this?" Sandor says.

"I promised we'd end amicably."

He shrugs, reaches across.

"Not like you're grabbing Ella's ass. I want to feel it."

He clamps down hard, I feel plenty, then tries to withdraw his hand. I hang on to it. He's strong all right. Shoulder. Chest. A lot of weight.

"That's enough now. We're done. I'm not playing—"

"Shut up and squeeze. Give it to me. And listen."

He does. The thing in his eyes comes up, actually swirls at the surface, rippling the black, and he crushes my hand in his, putting everything he's got behind it. Two, three seconds. Then we both hear it. Muffled pops, like sticks snapping in a wet sack. Not loud, but making it over the TV and voices in the front room. He drops my hand. "The hell was that?"

"My little finger. Maybe the one next to it too. You *are* strong, you know. Though they're pretty primed."

"You fucking lunatic." Slurring finally, drunk all at once as the reservoir floods his brain.

"Right. That's something to keep in mind. Along with this: Did you see my face, what it did?"

"I'm not blind. I didn't see a fucking thing."

"That's the other thing you need to remember."

Heading out, I sneak a peek at the hand. The fingers straight and normally aligned. I'll pop the baby one back to skew as soon as I get home, maybe tape its neighbour. The kitchen counter edge the usual popping station. Start the heat-ice cycle. A costly demonstration. Stupid probably, though it took shape faster than thought.

The old battle-axe has left with one of the boys, her first night's sacrifice. The six that remain, three on a side, are talking in low voices, subdued by his departure and the start of their short lives' ceremony. Above them, the hockey players have hit the showers and the Big Man is spinning slowly under splintered light, a pale sweating mass, maudlin as a hog's head scalded and oiled to hang swaying above the parsley. Headline margined by Hizzoner: *Mad Monk Rides Again*. "Next time po-lice," says the lotto-monk as I open the door left-handed.

8

5:30 A.M. ANOTHER complete protein breakfast after another shredded night. Courtesy of another Ugly Dream. Plus coffee. Call it a tie, Stomach versus Mind.

The Ugly Dreams get tedious fast. Such relentless variation within such a narrow range. A robot shuffling an endless pack of snuff pics.

Look closely! Be a miner. Study a rock face long enough and it'll show you its glints—copper, nickel. Aluminum. Iron. Silver, who knows? Whatever it's got. Fool's gold even.

Strange, how Lois's voice lives on in my head. Saying things she never said or could have, since they apply to circumstances I'm living now. Her voice *then*. Who knows what she sounds like now? Maybe her paints and easel are long gone and she lives for home decor, sharing a giggle with Megan as they stretch Daddy's Platinum at Au Lit followed by a sushi lunch. (Megan never got a voice I can hear, though her mouth flies open in what looks like a laugh and she leans to whisper in her mother's ear. Even the fluent prattle she'd worked up to is gone. Nothing before or after that last, earsplitting wail.)

My own voice, then. Lois-in-me.

Just because something's ugly doesn't make it interesting. Tedium's not a mask for meaning. (Though perhaps a privileged upbringing helps you believe so.) Sometimes it's just being stuck in someone's grotty TV room, watching looped torture trailers while he fiddles in the kitchen fixing something to eat.

No, stick with it. Look!

I start in on a second coffee. Feel its acids push breakfast on its way. 6:10. Stomach's got a long haul before the supper screw arrives with a bowl of veggie-noodle broth.

But then, after a while, dammit, I do begin to see. Lois smarter than me, always. Her parents just too dumb to realize it. Especially Jordan. Too impressed by Jeopardy-like mental stunts, prizing them over true insight. The flash of quick-draw over slow, bull's-eye aim.

Seeing comes gradually. Like the lightening of the fall sky. 504's dragging steps to the elevator, an early shift. But as I replay what I can retrieve from last night's dream—they're hard to recall as separate episodes, they blur into one über-spew like the *Saw* films—I begin to see a difference. Feel it, sense it, more than see. Not in the elements themselves, which are as repetitive and loathsome as ever. Body parts, turdwater sludge, wrecked and seeping passageways. Low-budget slasher set in derelict septic station, backup generator gloom.

The difference is in me. Pursuer and pursued. But neither diving through the blood and shit nor rising above it—instead, becoming one with it, dissolving my boundaries from it, realizing it was me all along. I was it. Or whether it was or wasn't me or I was or wasn't it makes no difference and never has.

Once I am part of it, then—*then*—the next thing can happen.

I will pass through.

That hair-thin glint shining in the rock face.

Before I leave, a short communion with Maude's artifacts in Big Empty. Not expecting much, which is exactly what I get. It feels like a duty call. Surely, since she is smoke and ash, these paltry things—all that is left of her—will want to speak to me. To someone.

I sit awhile on the floor in the middle of the room, where, with small shifts of my head and eyes, I can take them all in. Nothing. Then move closer, sliding along the floor. Pick up a couple of them. The butterfly wing. Max's card. The "Christmas Music" USB.

Nothing's changed. Which tells you something, I realize, heading down in the elevator. Whatever set you going wasn't affected by Maude's hasty cremation—no hastier than any other aspect of her death. Murder had only flickered as a possibility—one form, not the most likely, what you sensed might take. A shape, a face, it might wear.

What might wear?

The Wyvern bad smell. Something off. Which floated reeking on a breeze.

Found its way to my nose.

§

The white dog's in its usual spot, chained to the railing of the wheelchair ramp outside Shoppers. It's had a shampoo, its white hair brushed and silky, the gray streaks silvery. A Samoyed, I thought, the first time I saw it, though its tail is not so bushy and arched, it hangs down normally, and its eyes are not the black I'm used to in that breed. Icemelt eyes of palest blue gaze up at me. The Forest Hill crowd are "dog people," self-described—every kind of breed and size, except mutts, often pulling a Filipina maid who has two or three leashes wrapped around one hand, turned-out plastic bags at the ready in the other. A half hour later she'll pass going the other way walking the kids, again juggling multiples, maybe a toddler on a tether and twins in a double stroller. And the dogs' bright coats and milk-white teeth and shiny clipped nails—one little Scottie has its facial hair shaped once a month, beard and eyebrows trimmed, and wears tasselled vests in varied plaids at any hint of a chill—convince you that personal grooming has reached its acme with these pets. Until you meet their owners.

I go in to see what reaction I'll get from the blonde, Sandor's friend, after I left her consoling him Sunday in the Queen's Arms. *Rubbing his back in slow, practiced circles.*

Minutes after opening, the place is already packed. The neighbourhood's favourite store, no question. And since Tuesday is Seniors' Day, anyone under sixty-five makes up for it on Wednesday. Management recently enlarged the food section, which takes up four aisles, with a deli corner of pre-packaged trays where photo-processing used to be. One lady in the parking lot recently bubbling to another about how she buys all her food there, "I don't need to go anywhere else." Standing by a high-end Lexus, jazzed about drugstore groceries.

Money almost touching in its idiocy sometimes. It literally doesn't know what to do with itself.

Standing midway inside, where the line-ups snake and snark—outside of Walmart, no cashiers toil more miserably—wondering which aisle to try, when she comes straight up the one I'm facing. Gives me the Infinite Tunnel all the way. No change when I start towards her, none when we pass. She stares at a vanishing point on an imaginary horizon, betraying no awareness that Ichabod Crane after a razor brawl is bearing down on her. The same spooky freak she's seen haunting these premises before. The same one who hassled her friend three days ago.

The Infinite Tunnel is a learned human skill. More common—more needed—in urban environments, but especially prevalent in Toronto. In neighbourhoods like mine it's one of two default ways people meet, the other being cries and cheek brushes if they know each other. Still, it's quite a feat of avoidance when done perfectly, and the blonde is an artist. As we pass she peers down a canyon that goes on to forever, rock walls rearing up on either side, so she can't see someone right beside her even if she wanted to.

I'm not bound by the same rules, of course, so I check her out as we pass. Pale pink lipstick. Autumn's halfway tan between cottage and the Caribbean. Forty-five? Fifty, even. The work is that good. Some dulling and thickening of the skin that nothing can hide—the dew that burns away and is gone—but none of the lines, even faint, that should come with it. An effect a bit jarring. Double vision. Like the teenage teeth that gleam from old celebrity mouths, and would from hers if she smiled.

Gray skirt and blouse, darker gray pumps. Tasteful, but not hiding the curves. And able to hold her full shopping basket a steady six inches out from her side. Gym work, plus the skiing and swimming. Tennis. No concessions to gravity yet as she walks away unhurriedly.

I watch her until she turns the corner. I don't know why she catches my eye so often. God knows, there's no shortage of cryogenic cheerleaders in the neighbourhood. Yes, she rubbed Sandor's back after I upset him in the bar. But she's been trapping my gaze from the first time I spotted her. Two, three years ago? Something about her... It's not lust, certainly. Sex is a toy I stowed in the cellar ages ago. I remember clearly the joy it brought when I played with it, without ever feeling the impulse to retrieve it. Still, I stare down the aisle at the space where she was, trying to locate the faint itch I can't scratch.

Since I'm there, I pick up a pack of plain white envelopes on sale. Also more Advil for the hand Sandor rearranged. The fourth and fifth finger knuckles still red and swollen, throbbing slightly, though already headed back to normal. The trouble with multiple dislocations: things pop back into place almost as easily as they pop out, since the place they pop back into wasn't the right place to begin with. A twinge in my jaw reminds me to pick up a box of salt. Warm saltwater gargles to try to stave off the infection that's setting up camp at the base of Saturday's kicked-loose tooth. Giving me a real dental problem where I invented one.

The trouble with lies. There's no such thing really. Just dress rehearsals in parallel universes, waiting for their break in this one.

§

The funds are at the bank. The cashier apologizes for the delay, then makes a face when I ask for the first four hundred in ten-dollar bills. Says he has to get a key for "so many bills of one denomination." A trip of four steps to a cabinet behind him.

Banks. The less they do for you, the more they resent doing anything at all.

Though the cashiers are low rungs in the Great Chain of Less. Mixing surly cookies and Rice Krispie squares on their off hours, digging out musty paperbacks from closets for another laughable charity drive—there's one going today in the waiting area. For Hodgkin's Disease, this time. A loonie from my roll buys me bad coffee from the urn and a cupcake with sparkle frosting. Sign behind the donation bowl: *Scotiabank is pleased to match donations dollar for dollar.* Which should set them back about fifty bucks if the baked goods sell out. It's too bad the Hodgkin's people can't afford to throw it back in their face.

Books no one in their right mind wants. Personal finance guides—relax after work studying *Ready, Set, Retire!* Dog-eared airport thrillers. Astrology and personal healing. Various Dummie's Guides. Even a couple of high-school textbooks, for chrissakes—does no one even screen the stuff?

Around Toogood Pond. A thin, small-press paperback by Wun Wing. The author's name makes me think of Chinese poetry, but Toogood Pond was where Danika said she took Maude for walks. Where the photo of her was taken, though not by Danika.

For Grace, with fond memories inside the cover, above Wun Wing's scrawl.

I add two more loonies to the bowl—five of them there now—and button the book in a lower jacket pocket.

Apparently, Grace recalled things differently.

§

Snag's not far from where I left him Saturday, at a broken picnic table someone dragged into Trinity Bellwoods. The bench on one side is smashed. Wild swings with a crowbar, it looks like. Snag's straddling the other side. Sammy curled on the canted top, shivering in the warm sun.

"Who's he?" Nearby, a guy is lying face up on flattened cardboard, as still and straight as a body on an embalming table.

"Oh, that's Flatbread. He's no good to you. Total night owl. Prowls to here and gone all night, then does his coma thing all day. People step on him and he doesn't move. Coupla' kids were making a game of it until I set them straight."

"Well, you're the boss. Hire the crew you need."

Snag jerks his head at Sammy. "Even a scared-shitless pup?"

"Absolutely. Especially if you've fed him lots of fiber."

That gets a wet, rattly chuckle. I hand Snag his envelope first: sixty dollars—fifteen times four hours—as my foreman. Then three forty-dollar envelopes. Then, on second thought, two more. All have Max's name and office address on the front. "Three should get you started for today. But just in case."

"Any special instructions this time round?"

I think about it. Does it just feel different because I want it more?

"No. Be creative. Pour it on. Bring him the world."

"You got it."

At the sight of the white envelopes, denizens of the park have appeared and started towards us. One from behind a tree, one rolled out from under some bushes, another just walking across an open space. I can't help but think of zombie flicks, scenes of the undead shuffling and jerking toward the camera, faces raised on unnaturally stiff necks to catch scents of the living.

I point to the bush-man, linebacker-sized in a lumber jacket, swinging dirty yellow dreadlocks on a short thick neck. Like a bull working himself up to charge. "How about him? Can we put him in the picture? Any skills there we can use?"

"Christof? Skills, I don't know. Initiative for sure."

"Good. He's hired."

As I'm walking away, feeling good about things, a thought stops me and I go back. The undead are closing, tightening their ring. I've barely begun describing the pigeons and their prophet when Snag cuts me off.

"Birdy. Sure, I know Birdy."

"Birdy?"

"Yeah, Birdy. He's a little unpredictable. Unstable. Even by my standards."

"Perfect. He's hired." I start away, turn back yet again. The first arrival's reached the broken bench, a girl with raccoon eyes, wearing a stained pink halter top, a rose tattoo blooming up out of one large breast. She puts a hand on Sammy's shaking side. "Hey, he's actually warm, your dog. Seriously. Like toast."

"Sorry," I say to Snag. "I start off telling you it's your crew, then make your first two hires for you."

His grin is half wince. "No worries, bro. You forget, I worked in the real world too."

After a little walkabout, I get the car and go back home. I hadn't expected to return till dark, but forgot that putting something in motion isn't the same as letting it take effect. I strike a couple of tenant-requested repairs off the list in my notebook, change a hallway light bulb. Clean up a garbage can that someone tipped in the garage. That takes me to almost 4:00, two hours before my debrief with Snag.

§

Watching the sign carrier from the Duke was fun, but it's even better browsing in BMV and never looking out the window. Not having a clue what's happening nearby, but feeling sure that something is and whatever it is can't be wrong. Though the browsing stokes book-lust, testing a management monk's vows. Like a celibate strolling around a harem. Asking for trouble.

Upstairs, along with comics and sci-fi and textbooks and Shakespeare, are old magazines in plastic. **Vintage** says red marker on cardboard. Some are—others just old. The Kennedy assassination in *Life*. I try to remember where I might have been, with which family, in November 1963. Not a foggy. Then Nixon, that weird boneless wave before they coptered him out. That one I know. I was nineteen. On a psych ward for another evaluation before they processed me as an adult offender. My legal aid lawyer, young and keen, thought she had an angle after reviewing my file. But she didn't. Not a good enough one anyway. I move to Comics. Batman. Superman. The Thing. Always my favourite, hands down. The others just had too much going for them. Their various "dark shadows" just stains of plausibility to brand them as mass-market wet dreams. Which, even as a kid, never got me off.

It's clobberin' time!

Ten to six, coming out of BMV, I see Snag on the opposite corner of Yonge and Eglinton. Looking in all four directions, like he's lost. I cross over to him.

"Where's Sammy?"

"He ran off chasing a bitch down an alley a while ago. I bin lookin' for him."

I try to imagine Sammy surmounting his fear to chase anything. "Does that happen often?"

"Yeah, too often. Sometimes I lose that fucker for days at a time. He always turns up eventually. Sammy's not tellin', but I don't think it's usually a lady dog. Sammy's pretty old."

"What else would it be?"

"He's a dog, man. Ask *him*."

Snag gives me most of the report as we walk up the hill to Timmie's, pausing at every street and alley to look for Sammy. Birdy didn't make it past the security guard. "He tried to take too many of his flock. I told him to just tuck a couple under his jacket, but he wouldn't leave the rest behind. Like I said, he's independent-minded." Still, they brought plenty of world to the smooth-running office. Snag got Sammy past security—distracted by Birdy's flock, a bonus—and panhandled his way down the twelfth floor, settling in the Wyvern waiting room. Gwen rousted them, of course, but panicked when Sammy, right on cue, started circling on the rug, chasing his tail in search of a place to shit. She got him out in time—"scared his ass shut"—but while she was chasing them to the elevator, a couple came in from the staircase and took the washroom keys, "the ones on toothbrushes, pink and blue. Used the facilities thoroughly, if you know what I mean, and brought the keys back super-polite, thank you ma'am, leaning in over her counter, like that. Taking their time, letting the patients see they belonged. Leaving behind lots for her air fresheners to work on."

"His and hers. That was a nice touch."

"I thought so." They gave them a break after that, but kept it coming later. Bringing it on in waves that seemed random. Waiting for the blood pressure to come down, the guard to drop, before the next encounter. Making it seem not so much a special targeting as a case of the city's homeless having multiplied tenfold, so that they turned up everywhere. No escaping them. The dentist and his secretary having a quiet lunch at Starbucks when in comes another beggar, gripping their table, getting loud, until the manager comes over to evict him.

"His hygienist, you mean. Pretty, brown-skinned."

"No, the short old lady. With the toothbrush keys, on the front desk."

§

At Timmie's, I settle for a large Earl Grey, but order the Combo for Snag: spring vegetable soup, ham and Swiss on a croissant, donut, coffee. *Bits and pieces, Ken. It adds up.* I sip with the cup in my right hand, trying to bring the damaged fingers back into play. But it's still too soon, and I end up holding the handle with my thumb and first two fingers, the other two pointing outward in different directions. "Are we having high tea?" Snag says, starting in on his tray.

He scarfs down the soup and sandwich and is taking the donut more leisurely, when he remembers something and fishes it out of a pocket. "Oh hey, man. Don't know what this means, but Darlene grabbed it when she took the washroom key. From beside the computer."

Gwen's Post-It pad. *Friday 6 PM* and a phone number. A restaurant reservation is my first guess. An idea starts to form. Or it's waiting for me, and I start to see it.

I describe to Snag the couple on the construction site on Lisgar. A her that looks like him, a him that—

"Nicholas and Simone."

"Nicholas and Simone?"

"Why you repeating everyone's names, man? You did it earlier, with Birdy. Like you can't believe we have names. Or at least not the ones you're hearing."

"Come off it, Snag. How long've you known me?" *Why else, then?*

"Yeah. *Nich-o-las* and *Si-mone*. They give you that face?"

"The newer parts."

"I thought so. They like to roughhouse."

"I may have a job for them. Sort of a special assignment."

"I don't know. They're wack jobs when they're high."

"Sounds perfect. Could you find them, though?"

"Yeah, probably. Someone said they're working the 401 exit at Bayview. Downtown sorta chased them out. Good luck to them on getting roll-downs."

"Looking like he does, I kept Christof outside most of the day. Hitting people up for change as they came down from upstairs. Especially anyone working their jaws, or holding dental floss and a new toothbrush. He got into it at the end, though. Like I said, initiative. Went down into the parking garage and waited until the dentist and some babe got into his car, then squashed his face against the window asking for money."

"How's he talk with his face squashed against the glass?"

"It comes out pretty funny. But I guess the real point is the inside of his mouth and nose from up close. He does it all over the place. Cars, restaurant windows. Gets some coin too. Probably just to make him stop."

"What'd he get this time?"

"Said the dude just gripped his steering wheel. Super pissed, but too pussy to do anything about it. The lady, though. She got out her side right away and came around like she meant business. Christof ran off. He said she was pretty hot. Young, too. His girlfriend, you think?"

"Yup. One of them anyway."

That wet rattle, like he's gargling his coffee. "Money. Who says it can't buy you love?"

"The Beatles. But only after it was buying them plenty."

"Um." A server—a team member, they probably call her. A plump, pretty girl. White points in her blush where she removed her piercings for her shift. "I'm sorry, but. Someone complained to the manager about a sme—… about an unpleasant odour."

"I showered yesterday," I say.

"It wasn't, um… it's not…" Her eyes avoiding Snag. It isn't the kid's fault. Across the store, the manager is taking an exaggerated interest in a pyramid of coffee tins.

"Forget it, man. You too, hon. I got the meal into me, and it was good." Snag stands. "So here's a good juicy tip." He puts out his hands for balance and does a Chinese-y squat, his ass very low—for all his rough living he's strong, I realize; big too, even bigger with all his layers—and waits, his face tense, until it comes: a long, rumbling, very wet and involved fart that sounds a lot like his laugh, only with the voice box removed. Rises with a look of satisfaction and signs to me that he'll be outside.

I take what's left of my tea over to the counter, behind which the manager is standing with his arms folded, scowling. He's fortyish, husky, balding. A huge silver buckle with a Libra symbol centering his brown belt.

"If I dump this on your floor, you'll just make one of these minimum-wagers mop it up, won't you?"

"Yes, I will. So don't do it."

His high voice and the trace of a childhood lisp almost stop me.

I grab the buckle—it's solid as a doorknob—and in the split second before his body follows it, pour the tea down the inside of his pants.

"OWW!" he yowls. Clutches his drenched crotch with both hands. From shock, it must've been. The tea was just lukewarm.

Off to the side, the de-pierced girl has a hand over her mouth. "Tell him to stop groping you or you're going to the Labour Board," I advise her loudly, looking around the restaurant until the faces duck back down to their meals.

"See this street?" We're on the south-west corner, opposite Timmie's. I look the wrong way, see Best Buy, FedEx. Snag jabs his raised hand the other way. "No, man, *down* Yonge. Towards the lake. This is Montgomery, man. Montgomery? This Post Office right here, Station K. Montgomery Tavern?"

I shrug, palms out. In or out of school, History was always my worst subject.

Snag shakes his head in disbelief. "They fought a battle here, man. The rebels. 1837. Pitchforks, clubs, a few guns against the militia. They tried to take it to Bond Head and the Family Compact. Sir Francis Bond Head. Fucker deserved to be run out of town just for his name. They gathered here and marched down to City Hall, demanding representative government."

I look down the hill we just walked up, trying to imagine what it might've looked like a hundred-and-eighty years ago. A dirt road? Through sloping woods down to a shining blue lake? It's hard to block out the cars and jostling sidewalks. Hard to imagine anything very different.

"Did they get it?"

§

"Ukiyo-e. How may I help you?"

The girlish singsong, which some Japanese women keep well into middle age, mesmerizes me, it sounds like bird trills more than a telephone formula, so that I almost miss the name of the restaurant and lose the reason I dialled.

"Could you hold for a second?"

"Of course, sir."

Standing in my kitchen, hand over the receiver. Important to get this right. I'd hoped for a restaurant, but not the high-end sushi place four blocks up the street. *A local job.* More local by the day. I arrange it in my head.

"It's Dr. Max Wyvern calling. You've got a reservation for me this Friday?"

A moment's pause. "Yes, sir. This Friday, six o'clock. For two."

"I'd like to change that to four people, if it's possible."

"It's possible, of course. No problem. Four people, Friday six o'clock. See you—"

"Just a moment, please. The other couple will be arriving early, a half hour ahead of us. I hope that's no trouble. Their names are Nicholas and Simone. And, ah, there's one other thing. It's a little delicate."

"Delicate? If I can help…"

"Nicholas and Simone—they may try to pay in advance, but don't let them. This is my treat. And they may be a little shy about ordering ahead, on their own. So don't even ask. Just bring them some wonderful drinks and appetizers as soon as they sit down."

"Best drink! Best appetizer! No problem!" Her excitement flits like a swallow down the line. We might be arranging a prom dress for the poorest girl in class. "It will be our pleasure!"

Christ, will it ever.

9

"THE BONE DUNGEON," Jared says. And watches while I print it in capital letters, pressing firmly, at the top of a clean page in his writing book. I underline it with his ruler and turn it around to show him.

Lizard flick of tongue. He never looks more scared than when something's pleased him, like he's being set up.

Our joint title definitely the high point for him. Always. The idea he supplies, which an adult prints cleanly and boldly. Everything after that, even the best parts, are anticlimactic step-throughs to justify the name of his creation. He already knows it, he visits and lives there, so it's tedious to describe it in such halting, sketchy detail. Starting from the middle, wherever he finds himself, he moves forward tentatively, quickening if he spots something new. Backtracking reluctantly, usually at my request, to mark the trail for others.

But no way he'll start without the title. I learned that in an early session. Gave him all the reasons why it's sometimes wise to hold off on titles, or fill in a working one, let the real one emerge from the story itself. Otherwise you could find yourself filling out an order you didn't mean, programmed by your lead-off. He listened sullenly, skepticism thickening like a wall of scratched plexiglass that made his tiny, dock-eared, frown-lined face recede and grow indistinct.

Mutual stubbornnesses squared off. Thirty silent minutes later, Lucy, humming nervously, led him out the door.

the dungeon is made of old bones it has normal cave walls but long yellowish bones come down from the roof and up from the floor the bones in the dungeon turn to clear crystal over a long time eventually they become totally transparent when that happens the bones possess great powers someone who finds a clear bone and removes it carefully will possess great powers

It takes us a fair while to produce this start. Jared speaking slowly, musingly, his voice sounding as faraway as it is, relaying what he sees as he moves about the Bone Dungeon. Back on the couch in the apartment, I fashion the disjointed phrases he transmits into simple sentences, trying to give them shape and order without changing the content, removing the capital letters and punctuation for him to add as best he can. Introducing new words to his vocabulary when they seem to do no harm to his meaning. *Transparent. Possess.*

My hackles rise at *crystal* and *powers*. They seem game-fed. But Jared's slowly-going-clear bones reassure me. A gamer, I feel sure, would opt for bones that blaze luridly.

"How do you get out?"

Jared frowns. We're barely *in*.

"How do you get through the bones?" I'm picturing something like a calcium thicket.

"Follow the *birds*. The paths they make."

"What birds?"

Apparently, Jared informs me sighing, besides the prisoners sent there, there are birds who reside in the Bone

Dungeon, its only natural inhabitants. "Hollow" birds that can't fly.

"Do they have long necks?" I say, I don't know why. To say something.

"They don't have *any* necks. But they have big heads."

We don't get much further tonight. But I can feel the Bone Dungeon operating behind his worry lines. As usual, I wonder whether I'm teaching him or leading him down a garden path. I was the one who requested a dungeon. Decide, as always, it's bound to be a bit of both.

"Smells good, Lucy."

She looks up from the pot she's stirring. Steam has turned her brown face the colour of red brick. I pick up cumin, garlic, a curry blend.

"Is mainly chick peas. But I soak them myself. No cans. Tomato. Onion. Some eggplant."

"Is that tofu in it?"

"No tofu. Paneer."

"I like paneer. I get it in Indian restaurants." *Used to get.* "Matar paneer's my favourite—peas and cheese chunks. I always thought it would be tricky to make."

She shakes her head, stirring. "Milk. Lemon. Cheesecloth. Half an hour, cheese."

"Oh yeah?"

§

Patrick is the name on my drug dealer's mailbox and lease. And I've heard people buzzing up call him Skidder and Lump. But for some reason I can't associate him with those names or any other. So I call him nothing to his face—same thing he calls me—and 303 in my head.

He cracks his door. Pinkish eyes in peat puff.

"Time to earn your keep. It won't take long."

He scowls, but steps aside to let me in. Lingers a moment to check the hallway. What would he do if there was a uniform outside? Twizzler-thin, pallid and bleary-eyed, he has no words and only furtive glances for other tenants, puffs dope in the stairwell and even in the elevator, and buzzes in five-minute visitors day and night.

"If you want to stay out of jail," I said once, early on, "Why don't you start greeting people, get some sun and grow a paunch, and throw the occasional dinner party?"

"Why don't you wear a toupee and get some dermabrasion?" he shot back. Scoring some points with me.

Sweet rich funk inside. Caramel-coated straw on low banked embers. Hazy wisps and wraiths piddling about—morning mist on a pond. From speakers somewhere, a guy whining off-the-shelf rock. Electro-gear everywhere. In the living room, amid cushions, clothes, and takeout cartons, the largest screen, towers on either side of it but wired for the moment to a game console. Multi-armed alien frozen in mid-splatter, a shocked look on its face. An Obus chair in front of the screen, kidney-shaped supports at the lower back and between the shoulders. From his slouch down streets and corridors, 303 looks achey, semi-boneless. Like he's having trouble holding himself up. Yet he's in his twenties. What will he do at fifty-five? Seventy-five? Chiropractors might be the big winners in the wired world. A laptop on the only space not piled with dishes in the galley kitchen. Beyond, by the mattress on the bedroom floor, a larger model with the Apple logo.

"What do you use in the bathroom?"

"What is it you want?"

"Just an idea of what carols some people are listening to."

"Carols?" He stares at the USB stick I hand him. "I loathe Christmas."

"So do I. It's the Ebola of holidays."

"I'll use the laptop in the kitchen. You actually want to hear this shit?"

"Not if it's the usual. 'Silent Night,' 'Jingle Bell Rock.' Just give me an idea of the playlist."

He goes through the kitchen into the bedroom, rummages under some clothes and comes up with earphones. Keeps fishing for something else. As he crouches, his pants slide down his skinny hips, treating me to gamer's crack. He rises slowly, a hand on his lower back. Taking another step into the living room, I come to a telephone table. No telephone, but three large art books under a Finger Eleven T-shirt. *Assassin's Creed. World of Warcraft. Final Fantasy.* A flip-through of *Creed* confirms the cover blurb: glossy drawings exactly as they appear in the game. Strange. You sit and look at a book of what you sit and look at on a screen. "Hearing any reindeer yet?"

"Not going to," he calls back. "These are JPEGs, not audio files. I'm going to open them on the Mac. The graphics card on this is shot."

Adjustments, arrangements. 303 and I are an arrangement. Each an arrangement for the other.

I help you keep up with the wired world?

You help me any way I need.

I see. And for that you turn a blind eye.

My eyes are working fine. I'll tell the cops whatever they want to know when they knock on my door. When, not if.

So what do I get then?

I don't call them tonight and I don't evict you.

All in place after a first night's sniff. Easy as a one-handed download.

A cleared throat. I turn and see 303 in the kitchen doorway. He shrugs, palms up. "I don't get it. Someone's homemade porn. So what? The dental set's not my thing, but whatever. It's pretty soft—"

"Dental set? Let me see."

§

The first picture shows a girl in a dentist's chair. Twelve, maybe thirteen, with long blonde hair. Her eyes are closed, her mouth open slackly. Her head lolls to one side on the headrest. The photograph, rich and clear on the Apple, shows her from the waist up—her face and hair and the dental bib, her narrow shoulders, and her arms on the arms of the chair.

Max's chair. Dentist's offices are generic, but I'm sure of it. The USB buried in Maude's "Precious Things" box. *Buried by whom?*

"Like I said, pretty tame," says 303, somewhere to my right. "They get kinkier, but still. You want heavy, live-action shit, it's a mouse-click away."

"This is closer than a mouse-click. A dentist just down the street. I can introduce you if you want."

A pause.

"Like a real dentist, you mean? Real girls?"

I glance at 303. Even a ghost gets whiter when it's scared. He's blinking long blinks, like he's trying to wake up.

"Real girl. Real *minor* girl. Take a look at her face. Does she look like she volunteered?"

303 puts his hands up in a surrender-no-hassle combo. "Hey, man, your get-off is your business. Whatever. And our deal is what it is. But this sounds heavy maybe. I can't have my name anywhere near it." He's still muttering as I turn back to the screen and click ahead.

The next picture is of the same girl in close-up, her face filling the screen. Her head has been positioned to face the lens straight on. A plastic retractor has been inserted in her mouth, pushing her lips in four directions, exposing all of her teeth and gums. The rectangular grimace, wider than any natural laugh or scream could be, is reminiscent of Francis Bacon's screaming popes, hugely baring their teeth while immobilized in a high-backed chair. Her eyelids are open a crack in this second picture, showing a seam of white sclera.

It is the start of a long series of such photographs. Variations within the constant of a dentist's chair. *Is it the start?* It's the first picture encountered on this USB, but the pictures have no dates or titles, no indication of whether or how they might fit in a larger series of photographs. But the first two photos give the sense of something starting, a discovery made. A quick shot, perhaps on impulse, of an unconscious girl. And then—when no heavens fell, when no voice roared objection—a bolder and more deliberate arrangement of the same subject.

With a mixture of sick apprehension and compulsion, a sour reeling sense, I click on the mouse to advance the series. 303 doesn't say anything. Neither do I. What is there to say?

Each woman is in the dentist's chair. Since the chair reclines, the postures of the women range from halfway sitting up to lying almost flat. Most of the women have their eyes closed.

The eyes that are open look glazed, unfocused, sometimes rolled back to show mostly whites.

They range in age from pre-teen to late middle age. From girls as young as eleven or twelve to women who might be fifty-five or even sixty. The majority falls where it would with most men—between eighteen and forty, roughly. A few of the women are beautiful, most are pretty, and even the minority that would be considered plain have at least one feature that the photographer found attractive. It's obvious what the feature is because, about fifteen pictures in, he starts undoing and removing pieces of clothing to reveal it.

A blouse unbuttoned to reveal plump breasts in a bra. A skirt rucked up above shapely thighs. And then the same woman a few pictures later—with other girls and women in between—with a different skirt pushed up to her waist and her panties pulled down to above her knees, showing thighs and black pubic hair. A shot of slim ankles and bare feet with red toenails, the feet angled out and the legs parted. This shot of calves to toes fills the frame in clear focus, the plastic chair covering a blur behind them, but the photograph before showed the same woman reclining in the chair with her eyes closed, her red toenails peeping out from high-end sandals. *Like a director's establishing shot. So he can match the whole face and body with the fetish part.*

As the series goes on, the poses become more graphic, and the use of dental equipment props, occasional before, more frequent. A woman lying face down on her crossed arms, her slacks and panties pulled down and the middle of the chair raised, presenting her buttocks to the viewer. This is the shot that reminds me of what I should have realized earlier. The shots, like any photographs, are frozen moments, telling nothing about what went on before or after this staging.

The bizarre retractor grimace—a hideous smile or clinical scream—combined with an exposed breast, its nipple erect. A hand made to grip a flattish rubber thing and push it halfway into pubic hair in which it pauses, a pale gray slug. A metal examining pick like the one Max bent over me with, hooked into the hole of a zipper tab pulled down to reveal deep cleavage, a screaming female pope above.

"How many are there all together?"

303 does something with the mouse, brings up an information tab. "A hundred and fifty-three," he says.

A new hobby? Or a recent scrapbook of an old one?

"They could have been taken over years," I say, thinking out loud.

"Maybe." 303 shrugs. It's almost palpable, his effort to return to his base camp of blasé. "Every so often he meets someone willing to pose. A lot of chicks—"

"You're forgetting that none of these women volunteered."

"You don't know that."

"Look at the eyes. The limp bodies. They're drugged senseless."

303 is looking at me the way Danika did near the end of our meeting. As if just seeing me for the first time. Peering at me with a seriousness I wouldn't have thought him capable of.

I want to go on, don't want to let myself go on. End up clicking rapidly through what's left, seeing no changes except for an escalating intensity. The photographer getting bolder, following his urges more insistently.

Perhaps because he has a trusted assistant. Can work more safely and quickly.

Vivian appears the first time around the thirtieth image. Comes back every so often after that, the only woman to appear so regularly, though there are other repeaters. It's the first time I've seen her without her mask, but it's her. Wavy black hair, caramel skin, in a white or pink or blue uniform of slacks and top. Plus her mask. Up over her mouth in some shots, down around her neck in others. Tugged to one side like a bandana in the picture where she's wearing nothing else, sucking her thumb.

Woman? Vivian maybe fifteen, sixteen in the nude shot. It's hard to say exactly, she's wearing lots of make-up—but no, she's very young. And how old now? Twenty-five? A decade at this already. And the younger and older shots of her out of chronological order. Selections saved to this USB from a larger cache? Many caches?

The only total nudie in the bunch. And different for another reason too. Though her eyes are closed, her head lolling to one side, there's a suggestion of muscular tension in her body that the others lack. It's hard to go totally limp—all those gunshot victims in Hollywood movies who look like what they are, people who fell down and are waiting to get back up and hit the food truck. Bad acting. *Or perfect acting—depends on what the director wants.*

Awake? Hard to say for sure. But she had to be, didn't she?

"I need copies of these. Two. No, three."

"No, man." 303 takes a step back. "I told you, I'm not touching this shit. It sounds like it could get heavy."

I stand up. "For a cyber-wise dude, you seem a little disconnected. This *is* heavy. These are from a dentist in our neighbourhood, drugging his female patients and posing them in kink-freak shots. Posing them at least. I think the cops are going to be very interested."

303's eyes are rounder, more alert than I've ever seen them. "Fine. So make your own copies. It's not like I'm the only—"

"Three USBs. Or the cops visit you tonight." He gulps. I owe him something. Without a go-to computer guy, who knows when I would have heard the Wyverns' Christmas music? "But give me the three sticks and our agreement is over. I won't call on you again."

"What are you going to do with them?"

"Whatever it is, your name won't be mentioned. Ever."

He crouches down in the corner, muttering as he roots under another pile of clothes and crumpled bags.

"How many jerk-pics does one guy need?" I say, thinking aloud again.

"Who says they're for one guy?" says the salesman in 303.

§

Up in Big Empty, I pace before Maude's Precious Things, wanting to touch them but afraid for some reason. Several times my hand reaches for one and then I straighten again. Max's Mother's Day card. Why do I need to look at it when it's in my head? Along with his photo gallery. *No* little *kids in the pictures.* None under eleven or so. On the other hand, a parent often accompanies a little kid, talking, holding a frightened hand. No old people either. A question of taste? Or the uncertainty of drug reactions past a certain age? Fear approaches me like a speeding train, thoughts inside it I can't see yet, and just like that, I'm out the door, headed for the garage.

At the house on Selkirk Street, I walk across the front lawn and peer in the window. Bluish TV glow, backs of people in a semicircle, watching. Mrs. Rasmussen staring out at me from the other side of the glass, a dish rag in her hand.

Two seconds later she's on the front step. "What in the name of—"

My hands up, like 303's. Everyone with a gun trained on them nowadays. "Mrs. Rasmussen, please. I just need to talk to Judy for five minutes. Two minutes."

"Come back tomorrow if you have to. They're in their pajamas, having a snack. Front door closes at 10 p.m." Her eyes flat as nail heads. Would make a good bouncer in any bar.

But it's strange. I'm trying to think of a good reason— something more communicable than my fear train—when she relents on her own. Usually the Face frightens people, hardening their opposition. But once in a great while— never when I expect, and seldom when I need it to—it has the opposite effect. "Five minutes. I'll be right inside the door, timing them. And just in the porch. It's chilly out here, and she just had her bath."

Judy looks old and smaller than ever. Her hair wet and combed, in her pajamas and slippers.

"Can he have some cocoa, Mrs. R? He is a good friend."

"He can't stay long, sweetheart. He just has a message to deliver."

But as Judy sits in one of the rocking chairs, hands around her cocoa mug, any message that might have been forming skips out the door and down the wooden steps. Nearing sixty, asking for cocoa for her friend. I pull a rocker up beside hers and sit down in it, get it going slowly. *Forgot how good this feels, how relaxing. Back and forth.* The motion that goes nowhere takes my questions with it. There's no approaching Judy directly anyway, there never has been. It was only sudden panic made me forget that. Why did you leave home so early?

That is not what killed my mother—what did you mean by that?

We sit and rock like a couple of old ghosts atop a tower, looking out to sea.

"My mother went up the chimney," Judy says, bringing her mug to her lips.

"I know. Sandor told me she was cremated."

"She did not fly. She climbed." In oracular mode, Judy's voice goes toneless, flat as nothing. The wind through broken masonry. It's why the shrinks—most people probably—never considered her answers real replies. Kept asking the same questions.

"She climbed up."

Still no idea what to do with it. I wait.

"Do you like Sandor?" she says, a few sips later.

"I've met worse."

"He is my little brother."

"I know he is, Judy."

We sit and rock a while longer and gradually I become aware of a little sound, light and flicking, like the tip of a thin branch hitting a window, and realize it's Mrs. Rasmussen behind us, a small sharp sound, *tick tick tick*, she must be using her fingernail.

§

Back at No Name, the phone machine is blinking. Staring at it, I narrow the most likely possibilities down to two—a strange ritual, considering that I'll know as soon as I pick it up. It could be the Owner, ready, after a two-day sulk, to bitch about the "sweet deal" the new tenants are getting. When it suits him, he forgets my job is centered on mopping hallways and unplugging toilets, and talks as if I have suction with the higher-ups on the Landlord and Tenant Bureau who exist to screw an honest businessman out of his profits. He might also have seen the new tag on a drive-by and be needing to fulminate about his vandalised property.

Or it could be the new tenants themselves. Any chance they could begin setting up—cleaning and painting—a day or two early? They'd be willing to pay, pro-rated, for the advance. And will I get around to the repairs we discussed before or after they move in—just checking? Something like that.

I pick up the phone and push the button. A woman's voice. Someone between thirty and fifty probably, though voices can fool you. That and the fact that her voice is calm and pleasant, easy-sounding, is all I can be sure of, though I replay and listen to the message several times. Curious at first. Then just wanting the voice and what it says in my ear.

"Hello. I apologize, I misdialled the number. And I hope you have a blessed day."

10

SUNRISE. HAPPENING WHETHER *you see it or not...*

Night's a long time clearing, its shadows lurk and huddle in the pink-veined sky, daring daylight to disperse them. But night can't win an argument with day, or day with night—they're evenly matched, half-kings each—and it's day's turn now. Somewhere behind Shoppers, the sun has cleared the houses and is climbing steadily. Laying a lane of light down eastbound Eglinton, making the fire-hall's red door glow.

No sirens—not for a couple of hours, since they brought an abrupt end to dreaming. Breakfast time in the city, but no one yet has dropped a smoke into bedclothes and rolled over to catch a few more zees. Stood too close to the burner with housecoat ties dangling.

Light blooms steadily, a soft explosion. Undramatic, undeniable. Faced with a ball of flaming gas a million miles wide, those dark shifty punks scatter underground to regroup and wait for twilight's chances. All they leave, their calling card, is the sooty brick and dark brown flashing of the Latimer, an alley-width in front of me. It seems absurd that a five-story apartment building can block my view of the largest object in the local universe. *99.8% of the mass of the solar system, which might be termed the sun plus some debris.*

Yet it's true. The Latimer's enough. Day will have to climb a little higher before light reaches this balcony.

Making a third coffee. Two's the normal limit—like the first beer, the third coffee shows me things I can't afford to see. But today I know I'm going to see them no matter what precautions I take. Another notice from Stone last night, he's a broken record now. Besides, I need the caffeine to bring me fully awake. I'm not tired, not physically or mentally—I wish I was—but I'm deeply disoriented. Drifting somewhere above sleep but below waking. Or somewhere off to the side of both of them—in a spooky place with its own rules, not answerable to day or night.

"Waking dreams, uh huh," murmured an early assessor, "Fairly common in many pathological states, especially psychotic or dissociative ones." His bland, bored-sounding voice and the quiet rasp of his pen—which sounds like a cement mixer in my ears—telling me he's never had anything like a waking dream, it's a phrase in a textbook to him. And I want to jam that pen in his eye.

The water in the glass carafe goes past dark to black. Watching the coffee grains tumble in convection spirals below the plunger, zoning out on them, I return easily to the dream or waking vision I've never really left. Some kind of dim underground room, or set of rooms with doors and corridors connecting them, in which the dead and living mingled. Maude. Her late husband. Brad. A boy I roomed with, sharing the febrile intimacy of a cramped cube with cots. But also Judy. And myself of course. And Danika, weirdly. The faces dim, hard to recognize, as they shuffled in the grainy light—then glowing for an instant, as if lit by a candle from within, when I came close to them.

Don't use the past tense with dreams. They fade at narrative convention… keep the distance you're forcing on them. Stay present instead. Stay in them.

All right, Lois. Too wiped out to argue.

I'm working in a series of small, unfurnished rooms. Underground rooms, their walls and floors bare stone. Broken up in places by slender pillars, rough to the touch. Gray, grainy light seeps down slowly from above, as if filtered through layers of cotton gauze.

I go from room to room with a pair of heavy metal shears, like tin snips or secateurs. In the first room I meet Maude Wyvern's husband. Because he is the longest dead, I realize. I recognize his face from her photographs, but he's wearing some kind of long robe, a fancy housecoat maybe. He shows me the ornate fetters on his wrists and forearms. They are like sleeves of metal, elaborately patterned, through which his mottled skin shows in places. The metal catches what light there is, giving gleams of silver, of copper, of gold perhaps.

I work with the shears, pressing to get the heavy tip of the lower blade between his skin and the metal. He winces in a familiar way—the babyish, make-it-stop grimace of the chronically ill. The metal gives way finally, though I have to press hard, feeling the strain in my wrist and fingers. When the fetters fall away, he doesn't look up or say anything, but remains stooped over, rubbing the red marks the shears have left on his arms. This too is familiar.

In the next room, Maude stands waiting beside a pillar, looking vacant. Even in death she has dementia. I go to work the shears on her fetters, which are smaller than her husband's, a narrow band, as if they are still forming. I aim the tip carefully, but somehow, by a slip on her part or mine, when I close the grip the shears shift and I snip off her baby finger.

I exclaim in horror, and feel as if I might throw up, but Maude just looks at me calmly. She seems to be waiting for me to continue, or begin. There was no crunch of bone or spurt of blood. The finger felt like soft dough and the stump has already sealed over. I realize that I did not cry out, only wanted to. Down here there are no sounds at all.

Near Maude is a steep, wide staircase. Looking down it, I sense many people waiting in a large space below. The light is dimmer still than on the level I am on, but though I can't make out faces or bodies, I see, here and there, faint gleams of metal. It dawns on me that I belong down there, with the milling people. I'm in the wrong place still.

§

I take the coffee to the armchair by the window. Pick up *Around Toogood Pond* from the table where I left it, intending to spend the day inside reading it. Not going out, not even answering the door unless someone pounds without let-up. It will be the first day in months—the first in this window certainly—that I don't venture out of the apartment.

It's in the nature of a self-prescription, and a warning. *Home rest if not bed rest. Your act won't travel today.*

First, though, leaving the book in my lap, I tell myself again why I'm not following through with last night's vow to deliver "Christmas Music" to the police and the newspapers first thing this morning. Try to scrape off lies and evasions from the change in plans, see if anything's left standing.

Coming home last night, the four USBs in hand, there was no question of the next step. Three simple words: *Take them down.* Max and anyone in on it with him. Helping him, enjoying his product. The fact, first, that a girl might be sitting in his chair this morning. Thursday a business day after all. And the scene, intensely pleasurable, of cops brushing past Gwen, wrenching Max's arms behind his back to cuff him.

Take them down. Drain the Wyvern swamp.

Still the plan. Still what has to happen. Only—

Something I need to do first, before the cops swarm in and take over. *Like what?*

Cops too hasty. They adjust the obvious, so their adjustments never go far enough. I want more. *What?* I want to— yes, of course, blast him to hell, he's made for the place, but beyond that... *What?* Not sure yet. Something.

Once the cops swarm the scene, it's their show totally. The adjustment over.

And photo-play will be suspended after yesterday's disruptions, at least for a while. Eyes on them. Someone shaking their tree. That much they're sure of.

Sipping the coffee, leaning over to watch the traffic building on Eglinton.

More than one lifetime needed to catch yourself lying to yourself. To know for certain.

Sure, unless you're a terminal weakling or moron, you become a better self-interrogator. But the guy across the table in the little room has been practising too. Every minute of every day.

And no liar more dangerous than the one who believes his lies. Truth so toxic to him he never has to pretend.

I pick up *Around Toogood Pond*, by Wun Wing.

Flip through it first to get the gist of it, to situate it in the world of books.

A slim volume. At eighty-two pages, almost chap-book-sized. Something about the modest production values and the sparse colophon page says vanity publication, but with small presses struggling to survive alongside digital productions, it's getting harder to tell.

Glue-bound in signatures. Nice simple cover, pleasingly stark. Cream paper with a pebbly texture, title and author lettering in a plain black font. Between them, a small borderless photo, in blurred gray tones, of a close-up of a late-season dandelion with half its filaments detached. A single drop of water near the top of its thin, curving stem.

Plain back cover, no blurbs defacing it. Also very welcome.

Inside the back, a brief author bio without a photo. *Wun Wing has published fiction and non-fiction in a variety of Canadian and international journals. He lives in Toronto.*

Below, the press's Mission Statement, announced with equal brevity. *Wun Wing Press is dedicated to publishing quality works of fiction and non-fiction that explore issues related to caregiving, disability, health, and recovery.* Around Toogood Pond *is its inaugural title.*

Strange. The press having the same name as the author. As if author and press are identical. Which would seem to confirm the book as a vanity production. Except it doesn't—since the vanity author would take care not to give that away. Would take care to invent a professional-sounding alias for his cheque book and local printer.

A subtitle on the title page. *Around Toogood Pond: A Caregiver's Journal.*

Closing the book over my thumb, I watch as the pieces assemble easily. Wun Wing. Maude's single butterfly wing in its frame. Autumnal cover shot, like the autumn plants behind Maude in the photo taken by her caregiver at Toogood Pond. *A Caregiver's Journal*. Notebook ruminations in the Queen's Arms.

Sometimes even a bipolar detective gets handed a no-brainer, Sandor.

§

It begins with a series of quotations forming their own section. Nothing unusual in that. Except that the section, culled from an impressively wide range of sources, is ten pages long. Ten pages out of eighty-two. And the section has its own title, an interesting one—"Blazes, Cairns, Painted Stones"—and starts off with a little vignette, or parable, about the uses of quotation.

Blazes, Cairns, Painted Stones

...and pleasanter than never getting lost is to be lost for a time, and then, as you grope about blindly, to come upon a pale scar on a tree, a tumble of stones on flat rock, paint flecks peeping through moss—and realize that someone, perhaps long ago, has come this way and troubled to leave these rough signs.

I flip through the pages of quotations, letting my eye settle where it will.

Why not be totally changed into fire? (Merton, *The Wisdom of the Desert*)

Please—a little less love, and a little more common decency. (Kurt Vonnegut Jr., *Slapstick*)

...we must nurture everything that assists the descent. (Jung, *Psychological Reflections*)

We hate the people who try to make us form the connexions we do not want to form. (Weil, *Gravity and Grace*)

I saw to what extent the people among whom I lived could be trusted as good neighbours and friends; that their friendship was for summer weather only; that they did not greatly propose to do right...(Thoreau, "Civil Disobedience")

How do I know that in hating death I am not like an orphan who left home in youth and no longer knows the way back? (Zhuangzi)

Ten pages out of eighty-two. One-eighth of the book. But the bigger surprise—sipping my first Luck Yu—the impression of the author suggested by the quotations. Someone not in a hurry. Someone searching. Seeking. Patiently. Willing to work and wait for it.

Patience. Diligence. Humility? None of them qualities I would have associated with Sandor. Who, for all his troubled charm, which even I wasn't entirely immune to, still struck me mainly as a spoiled and lazy rich man's son. Indulging appetites until they overwhelmed him. Capable of compassion for another—from Danika's indications, which I trust implicitly—but far more inclined to pity himself. The fat life coming off him like vapours off a house pet.

And yet—

Evidence of another kind here in my hand.

As if a back wall in the Queen's Arms opened and I went through it to find him pacing beside a meditative pond. If not Walden, at least Toogood.

After the quotations section, the book is organized into a series of short entries, many less than a page long, each one titled and dated. I don't know if it matters whether I read them in order. Collage seems more the principle behind their arrangement. Each complete in itself, but gathering meaning by association with its neighbours. Nevertheless, I begin at the beginning. Read it straight through, quickly, then return to the start.

Out of simmering unease 31 May

Out of simmering unease, weeks of it, a plain question. So sudden it makes you gasp. *Where—who—would you be without someone to care for?* Anywhere? Anybody?

It arrives in the shower on a wretched morning. Depression is the occupying power now. Antidepression, a dispersed guerilla band, must resort to ambush.

Talking—so long ago—with other boys about Robinson Crusoe. *How* he survived all their absorption—healthily. While your puzzlement, your amazement even, veered already to *why*. Alone and pointless on the island. Why not a sharp clamshell and out? A secret to keep—this question. You knew in the moment of thinking it.

"Don't listen too closely to exhaustion," L says. "It will speak in a hundred voices, say a thousand things. But it only ever has one message: 'Rest.'" A wise, good woman.

Still, as evening and soft rain fall, the question lingers. Lingers and reverberates. A shot across the bow. Hardly the first.

But closer. Closer each time.

Let's get smashed 1 June

Let's get smashed.

·His statement of intent at cocktail hour. Sometimes with a grin. A fist pump. Or just, on occasion, matter-of-factly. An alcohol athlete's quiet discipline.

How I miss him sometimes! Fiercely, in sudden attacks or spells that leave me weak afterwards. Often for the same things I feared him for all my life.

The gestures and words that fell me with longing are the same ones that gave me the constant jitters in his presence.

Remembered presence pierces a screen, an overgrowth, a shell—cracks a hole, through which the past blazes. And is not past.

Weakness, afterwards. A frailness, dream-like-ness, about what I am about.

It is so terribly hard to believe in death.

§

A bang on the door startles me out of reverie. No need to ask who it is. Only one person announces himself that way: one thud of a closed fist. As if any gentler or more prolonged summons would injure his dignity.

Beside the Owner stands another, younger Owner. A possible purchaser of the building interested in taking a look around. It's the first I've heard of it—but then, why would I be informed? Despite having different facial features, they might be carbon copies. Suits of slightly different cut and colour assert the same level of class, of membership. As do the quality hair-cuts: one a rich white, the other silver and black—but the same careful shaping twice a month. Though I see him only once or twice a year, my Owner changes remarkably little. Aging coddles him, leading him by pinsteps to a handsome viewing.

"This is the Super," he says. As a farmer would say to another inspecting his land: This is my scarecrow. Knock him down, or keep him, when the field is yours. In the mean-time, patchy as he is, he scares some birds. Adding to me, "Someone's made a mess on the wall beside the garage." I nod, to show how his wind makes my head sway, activating my button eyes and my grim, stitched mouth.

And, after a few more words to the other, he leaves.

Showing the potential buyer around the five floors, then the basement garage and utilities room, I make sure he sees, while pretending to hide, some of the sixty-year-old building's defects. Crumbling plaster mouldings in the underlit hallways. Patches of bubbling paint from insidious damp. Gouges and scratches and scuff marks in the halls and stairwells, clustered from waist to shoulder height, legacies of many hasty departures. The many windows—the middle three apartments on each floor—facing into the wall of the Favorite or the Latimer—with only the end units offering a view of Eglinton or houses with treed yards. The undersized water heater, rust spots at its base. The bumpy, pitted garage floor, its concrete eroded by overhead dripping and flash floods down the entrance slope.

I could show him more, of course. And should. His eager investor's face is fading—its brightness dimming, glumness overtaking it—and I should do everything in my power to hasten its collapse. If a new Owner installs a new scarecrow, where in the city will I live on eight hundred a month? Under Snag's bench? In Mrs. Rasmussen's laundry room?

But I can't rise to the practical matter of looking after myself. This deep into an adjustment, this far into a window, the future is too unreal. Even at the best of times, it's only a few prudent hedges against disaster. Keeping clear of glass as lightning approaches, quickening your steps ahead of an oncoming truck—these hardly qualify as long-term planning. Basic battenings of hatches, so as not to seduce catastrophe: that's the level of my care.

"Christmas Music" blots my mind to Owner finagling. So do the dead and living mingling underground, shuffling around stairs that lead yet further down.

And so, too, does *Around Toogood Pond*. Musing about the voice in it—the book turned over in my lap—when the Owner's rude bang fetched me back from a long way away.

A different voice. Different from any I've heard. At least in this adjustment. Someone in crisis and looking, looking actively, for help. Pleading for it. With courage, but also with humility. *Humility*. Probably the last word I'd associate with the Wyverns. Not even with Judy, who crumbles inside a shell of defensive arrogance—who is condemned to make others ghostly, crepuscular, in order to deal with them at all.

The slickster in his Rolex-running office. Digging in people's mouths. Trapping them in his camera.

The burly baby in the bar. Black fishpond eyes. Ladykiller. Scribe on the side.

Surprises, new views, all around.

Still… a difference here. Here in this voice. *What?*

Something not yet spoiled.

§

Mid-afternoon, I head out. Breaking my resolve to stay put all day, I make an absurdly early supper, jazz ticking away. A quiet composition for just bass and drums, throbs on a couple of notes while sticks tick rapidly against the kit rims. Double-time of a heart fused to detonate. Melt the broth block, warm it to bubbling, add the baggie of chopped vegetables. Boil the ramen, rinse. Add them. Watching it all, thoughtlessly. Thrums and ticking.

A long drive that also contravenes management protocol. Two hours of here and there, up and down. Wasting gas in the service of no errand, no search. Just to get to dark.

Dusk finally settling, I pull up near Woodbine Beach. Walk the empty boardwalk, deserted save for a couple of power walkers pumping wrist weights. Strike out past the beach volleyball poles, across an expanse of sand and damp flats sprigged with grass. Climb the hill into the trees and curving asphalt pathways.

Opposite the inlet with the moored boats, a shoreline tumble of squarish boulders, like giant play blocks. Nearly always deserted, and is so now. Settle low among the night-cool rocks, back to one, a waiting throne. Sighting south across the giant, wave-chopped lake.

Night arrives.

Freighter far out, hung with lights. Plume of whitish smoke thins quickly in the wind, detaches from the ship. Wisp after wisp. Brief, fading signals. Dandelion filaments, departing one by one.

Curious how the book ends abruptly. A last entry, nothing special about it, and turn to a blank page. No closure, summation, conclusion, epilogue. Even treating the book as a collage—returning again and again to bits that glitter out at me—I was expecting a more definitive wrap-up.

And many of the last scenes peaceful. Placid almost to the point of complacency. Especially after the desperation early on. A short description of riding with his mother around Unionville. November. The pond walk too cold. The colours Maude loved done. And her increasing difficulty staying upright, even with the walker. Motor skills going, balance going. She prefers to drive around looking at the big, well-kept homes.

"These are likable houses," she remarks at one point. And the author comments on the strangeness of the words she recalls as well as forgets. Her sudden surprising eloquences, dotting aphasic stretches like reeds in a spreading desert. Like her "profound" on another day.

But reading—reading over his shoulder, so to speak, for who else will see these reflections delivered to the bank's charity bin?—you wonder if the author hasn't missed something more than accidental eloquence.

These are likable houses.

What you say maybe if you're thinking of houses—homes—that aren't likable. Never could be. And not necessarily her present home either. After all, she was looking at what most people would consider dream homes—solid, spacious. Brightly painted and decorated, landscaped impeccably. Like the one she raised her children in probably. But *likable.*

Making my way back, across and down the grassy rise, leaving the paths to cut between pines and spruce trees. Their needles fragrant in the dark. Startled sounds from clumps of bushes, scuttlings in close-knit groves. Sparks from cigarette ends, from a small furtive fire. Clank of bottles, an urgent whisper as I near. Silence as I pass. And then the reassured giggles, a male voice cracking wise, reclaiming the dark den with its females.

Every sound a spark. Spotted flares I wend through to stay dark.

The beach, palely glowing without moonlight, a great scorched plain. *Likable houses.* The more I think of it, the more it gives me a chill. Like the chill I felt looking at "Christmas Music"—a chill that seemed to come not from the pictures into me, but from my bones out, seeping to meet it. But along with the chill, battling it, someone trying to stay warm in a meat locker. For days I've thought of the Wyverns in terms of rot. Bad smells. Stains. Crawling things. *But isn't cold the true sense you get from them?* Like breaths from an open refrigerator when you stand near it. Cold of something missing. Nothing colder than a vacuum. Maude under her blanket, Judy placing her crossing talismans. Fuel for the ferry over frigid black.

Cold. Corrupt. Crypt. In crypt. Encrypt. All terms meet.

How you know an adjustment is brewing.

§

I park the car in my spot in the garage, pause on the lobby stairs and head back out. Still not ready to rise to the eyrie I said I wouldn't leave today. I set out on a twenty-minute walk, the big lopsided rectangle up Chaplin, across Roselawn and down Latimer to the short bar of Eglinton. Midway along Roselawn, however, where the streetlights fail outside the Jewish cemetery, I change routes and cut down the path, gravestones behind wrought iron to either side, that ends at North Preparatory Junior Public School.

Where election cards tell me I'd vote, if I voted. With difficulty I scale the fence, locked at sundown against vandals who topple stones, deface them. Hebrew squiggles and bars on a sign above—just shapes to me. *Good. Signs among graves should be inscrutable.*

A path, a ribbon, through the sleeping dead. Where two trees arch darkly over the exit gate, playground equipment on asphalt beyond, I pause. All day the dream that woke me before dawn has returned in vivid slivers, taking on a title in my mind as if it were a book I'd read: *Dream of the Exquisite Fetters*. Once again, it comes back—the people shuffling and mingling in the dim grainy light, me trying to cut the elaborate metal sleeves from their wrists, snipping off Maude's finger instead—but this time it returns with a difference, a way of seeing it so altered it stops me in my tracks.

Fetters, I called the patterned metal sleeves. It was the word they came with in the dream. But fetters are to bind, to restrain, and Maude and her husband moved their arms freely. And *fetters*? Rusty iron shackles in old movies, or, in modern ones, serviceable steel. Not chased and filigreed bands of precious metals. Not *exquisite*.

Where would you find such things? On the arms of ancient warriors, in their tombs.

No one in those underground rooms asked me, not by word or sign, to remove the metal sleeves. I went to work with my shears—shears that left welts and lopped-off parts—because I thought the need for release was understood. Was it, though?

They could be saying, with their precious metal sleeves, not *Release me*, but *See. This much I gained. This much I won.* They could be saying that.

That or another message. Or many messages. Or none. None fathomable to me.

And yet your answer is to mangle the precious bands? Lop off a finger? Stopped between the graves and swing set, barred from both, I feel, as if they are tangible things standing with me, solitude and strangeness. And recognize too, as if it is my oldest friend, my infinite capacity to be a fool. A fool whose folly it is to descend into darknesses I don't understand and wrestle there with powers I'm not remotely equipped to reckon with. Only to blunder about in hobnail boots, breaking, breaking...

As the adjustment builds to what it must...

11

I MEET THE EMPRESS on the second level down.

After a first steep flight, the stairs become more shallow and begin a gentle curve. They are wider too. She is sitting in a niche in the wall near the bottom. Sitting in a high-backed chair—tiny as she is, and straight-spined, she looks enthroned, which must be why *The Empress* flies into my mind. Peering down to find my footing in the gloom, I almost miss her.

She shows her face in shadowed profile. A half, two-thirds of it perhaps, with a somewhat flattened aspect, like that of a playing card, which may be a function of the dim, grainy light that robs things of dimension. White wispy hair straggles to her shoulders on the side facing me, bare scalp shining through it. Her skin finely wrinkled like tissue paper folded and unfolded innumerable times—but then smoother where it crosses the bridge of her nose and where her forehead merges with shadow. Her hair too—unless I am mistaken—begins to change on the far side, becoming thicker, yellow mixing with the sickly white. But I can only see the start of this.

She wears a simple white shift, high-collared, which falls past her feet. She is very tiny. If I used all my strength, and made a plate of my outstretched palms, I think she could sit or stand upon it.

The single eye turned to me regards me with a terrible intensity. No expression in it I can read. Just a pure, fixed, unwavering gaze.

My eyes flinch from it, rove up and down the stairs. But the movements, the restless shiftings above and below, have stopped. The people I met above, and the ones I sensed below, have moved further into the shadows and gone still. They are afraid of her, I realize. She emanates a power that clears spaces around her. I feel it keenly myself, along with an urge to climb up or down, to put more distance between us. But I can't move. *I'm stuck here with her.*

With the thought comes the realization that she is trying to turn. There is a quivering tension in her chin and delicate jawbone, a straining. It is partly this concentration of effort that gives such implacable intensity to her eye, vacated by everything but the will to turn.

Yet, as my eyes adjust a little to the gloom, I see what makes her struggle impossible. The far side of her partially turned chair and body are fused with the stone. She is part of the niche, grown into it. What I am seeing is the part that still remains free, trying with an unceasing effort to break loose or at least resist the pull toward greater incorporation.

§

A butterfly wing 29 July

"My inspiration," she used to call it. "My," she still says fondly, "my"—but can't retrieve a word as long as *inspiration*. Nor does she add the explanation she used to, especially in the hard days (hard years!) at

Rosewell. "If that little thing can fly all that way and back again, then surely I can get through my..."—trailing off without specifying what it was she had to get through.

It sits on her bedside table at Vivera. The piece of her I most want to keep when she is gone. Though sometimes—not very often—I will find it stuffed in a bureau drawer, socks and used Kleenex pulled over it. Next visit it will be out again.

She must have been in her sixties when she found it, lying on the ground at the cottage. A single monarch butterfly wing. A mark of her, to pick up and preserve it. Who else would have?

L framed it perfectly, in a four-by-four-inch shadow box with a border of dark wood. The single, orange-and-black-veined wing, floating behind glass. A thing detached, alone, and yet not senseless. A remnant of flight. An emblem of it. And of fragile beauty preserved.

And, too, "my butterfly" is the name she hit on long ago for J. "Always flitting, always restless. Touching down... and then off she goes again."

The nickname angered J in younger years, though it might not now, when she is trying to come to terms with the inner furies that whirl her from place to place, situation to situation. Coming to terms? Or just growing quieter, worn out by the long fight?

"She knew," J says one day, completely lucidly. "A mother always knows."

I'm not so sure of that. In fact I have no opinion about it, either way. And no way of ever knowing, now.

I only know Mom used the name "butterfly" for the daughter her husband had wronged so deeply. The daughter who left home one morning at age fifteen. And should have left, or been taken, at least a dozen years earlier. *What a catastrophe!* friends said, honest well-wishers, when she was diagnosed. But catastrophes come also as blessings to the crimes they disguise.

The daughter who shows up now at unexpected times, journeying from the remote places where she lives, to be the other child that visits.

Sleepwalker 20 August

You should write a book on caregiving. I've been thinking a lot about it. You're the one to do it, I'm sure of it... etc. L says it many different ways.

The tickle of flattery—smart start-up publisher asking you to write a book!—soon swamped by preposterousness.

Write about it while I'm still living it? If I'm riding the train to burnout, that sounds like the Express.

Yet something in the idea, far-fetched as it is, sticks to me, won't quite let me go. It comes back to me at intervals. I question it to make it go away.

Does L not know what this is like? (No, think of the losses in her early life. Her grinding struggles still.) Is she trying to buck me up, keep me in the game? (No, she brings it up too often—suggesting angles, frames of reference... real help. She really is thinking about it.)

Finally, around the summer solstice—feeling a half year out of sync with the dazzling early dawn, the long humid sunset—I give it a whirl. Whirl exactly the wrong word. I just relapse into what everyday life has become—caregiving from any and all directions—and take notes on whatever occurs.

At first I do it to put the idea to rest. To be able to tell L honestly, *well I tried*, and get her—and me—off the subject.

And then the first surprise: not only do I have things to say on the subject and the energy to say them with, but saying them makes me feel better, lighter somehow.

Two months later, I'm still going. Feeling a little stronger, a little lighter—though nothing else has changed, just this new job added. But *my* job. Really? Is that it?

Feeling skeptical. Grateful. Cautiously amazed.

Spending cash I didn't know I had. Waiting for notice of the overdraft.

I turned 52 five days ago, but I feel like a boy trying to wake up to the truth of his life.

Is that my brand of insomnia? A sleepwalker caught wandering between bed and waking?

Anything can happen to such a person. (Anything except rest.)

§

A help or hindrance? Am I deluding myself to think that reading these entries brings me somehow closer to the secrets of the Wyvern freezer? And does it matter either way? Deluded or not, helped or hindered—*Take them down.*

Though who to take down (besides the obvious), and how...

The Sandor I meet in these pages. Like the self-confessing, sparring guzzler I met in the Queen's Arms—yet different. Spruced up, cleaned up—chaos laid bare, but given a shave and a haircut, a new suit of clothes. Like people in wedding pictures—presented almost beyond themselves. You recognize them, but...

And the L he keeps mentioning. His publisher, from the last entry. But also the one who framed the butterfly wing. A counsellor, an advisor. An all-purpose person in his life.

Dangerous to know too well someone you might have to adjust. There's that too. Like a surgeon chatting up the patient in pre-op, getting his life story. Not done on principle.

Hard and sharp—what a knife needs to be. *Firm*—the hand guiding it.

§

Outside Ukiyo-e, Nicholas and Simone, looking and behaving pretty much as they were last Saturday on the construction site. Senseless irate voices, pushing and shoving. Oblivious of any audience and yet at the same time theatrical—the drama that moves inside and never closes. Same weird impression of a gender swap. Tall, leathery, toothless Simone in her greasy black suit, shoving with real malice. Meek and pudgy Nicholas, a head shorter, hunching inside his plaid jacket, pushing back half-heartedly, an open palm at her chest for every two or three hard, well-timed cuffs. Pedestrians scoot to the curb around them, like they did with Birdy's birds.

They give no sign of recognizing me. Step aside to let me through, then resume their hassling. Do they know or care they've just been bounced? A young Japanese guy standing by the door, looking uncomfortable. The chest and shoulders for bouncing, but not the appetite for trouble the job requires. Ukiyo-e for high-end, intimate dining—two-hundred-dollar sushi sequences, with the parking ticket on the Benz just another item on the bill. A waiter probably. Or a sous-chef, from his apron.

Two young men, Malaysian or Filipino perhaps, leaning against the glass of Obsession next door, playing with their cellphones. Too engrossed to take notice of this minor ruckus. They look like gym and fashion nuts. Silk shirts in pastel colours clinging to sculpted torsos, crisply pleated dark pants tight in the crotch. A purple-gowned mannequin behind glass between them.

Inside, my helpful reservation bird is taking a scolding from a suited man on the far side of the restaurant. Hair half-hiding her lowered face, his cheeks flushed. A busboy, also blushing, is filling in at reception. He greets me with a blank stare. Beyond him, two boys busy cleaning a booth, an assistant manager with his jacket off supervising, hands on hips. Third guy down on his knees, sweeping up with a dustpan and little brush. Obviously, Nicholas and Simone made the most of their half hour. Over on the right, in the raised section, Max and Vivian have been moved to a table for two next to the wall. While the busboy peers confusedly at the reservation book, I head on up.

White shirt and tie materializes instantly. *Mess after mess, Christ what a night.* "Sir?" he says to Max. While I'm pulling up a chair from the next table.

"It's all right, Takeshi," Max says. "He's only staying a minute. Could you bring us another cup, though?"

Max has decided to play it cool, at least to start that way. Vivian doesn't have to play. Her charcoal eyes disconcerting in their almond settings. Cinders surrounded by the flames of striking beauty. Neither is surprised to see me. *Judy's friend—the Face in the chair—Wednesday's underclass barrage—now Nicholas and Simone…* it doesn't take a Holmes.

Two ceramic saké flasks on the table, patterned with cranes and leaves. One on the house probably for the debacle in the booth. A waiter brings my cup. When Max reaches to pour, I reach across his arm for his water glass. Take a deep gulp, set it down beside me.

Brief flares behind his porthole lenses, but a weary smile beneath. Has coached himself, or been coached, to except some crap along established lines.

Max wearing a Clash T-shirt, earring back in his right lobe. Forest Hill Peter Pan. Grubbing out in ripped jeans and Nevermind on the weekends, telling himself he's still hip, still a rebel. Vivian far less confused. Soft cream sweater with lozenge peephole below her throat, silver band necklace, matching bangles on one wrist. Knows who she is, where she is, what she is. Rare in these parts.

"Nice place," I say, looking around the half-filled room. Diners focused a little too resolutely on their plates. "Classy. Though myself, I'd ditch the dinner jazz and put on some Christmas music."

No future in poker for Max. None at all. He maintains basic composure, but little tells flicker randomly over his face, like pings on a radar screen. Vivian, though, she'd take every hand. Turning her saké cup slowly between sips, pearl nails light on the rim, cocking a polite bored ear at the men's conversation. *In it all the way. Player and producer.*

"It's a little early for 'Jingle Bells'," Max says. "We haven't even made it to Hallowe'en."

"Never too early for old standards, Doctor. No timetable at all for some pleasures. Fortunes built on the fact."

"Are you a carols tycoon?" Max manages it lightly, cocking an eyebrow. Feeling his way onto familiar ground. Nothing these people imagine unbuyable. *How they'll come down.* "And here I thought you were just a poor man with crumbling teeth."

A mental case like my sister, he hardly needs to add.

"Tycoon? You underestimate the religious impulse, Doctor. I'm a man of conviction. Hymns to the Almighty are not for sale. Even if I had a catalogue of them, I'd still be forced to give them away."

"Charitable impulses. Admirable."

I shrug. "Like they say, it begins at home. These old tunes, they go from hand to hand naturally. Always have. Me, I'd just be giving them a larger push. Widening the circle, so to speak."

Vivian's stopped turning her tumbler. Looks up at me. Then, longer, at Max. Who's sitting with his spine pulled tighter, sipping too rapidly at his saké. Crumbles in the crunch, she should know. Why be with him otherwise?

"You know what it means, don't you? Ukiyo-e?"

Max raises a palm. "Good food? High prices? You got me."

"Close. It means 'Floating World.' It's what you live in. What you've always lived in. And it's time you came down to Earth."

Now I pour myself a cup of saké. Raise and hold it in my hands, warming it, but take care not to bring it to my lips. *Level time, just now. No stairs. No sights beyond this room.*

Max drains his cup, sets it down with a little clunk. "Disregarding this preamble about Christmas carols—"

"Christmas music."

"Christmas whatever. Which I confess is going right over my head. But I'd have to be an absolute idiot not to recognize that ever since you popped up in my sister's life—the day my mother died, no less—you've dedicated yourself to pulling weird stunts in mine. Only once in person, acting the fool in my chair, but it's pretty obvious which petty disturbances you've been behind, right up to half an hour ago. You have—I'm sure I'm not the first to say it—a certain signature. The thing I'm still fuzzy on is why. What you want."

"I've noticed you never call Judy by her name. It's always 'my sister.' Why is that?"

"What is it you need exactly? Or think you've got coming to you, perhaps?"

Thinking he already knows the answer. *One of my sister's people—broke, crack-brained, desperate.* Exhaling it on a pillow beside Vivian. Though she wouldn't be so sure.

"It's very simple, Doctor. I don't like people who hurt other people. It makes me want to hurt them."

A pause. Max *is* cold, but doesn't *do* cold convincingly. "Maybe they'll hurt you too."

"Maybe they will. They've had lots of practice. But here's the thing about pain. The pain I cause them will be fresh pain. Pain they're not accustomed to. With me it will just be scar tissue."

"Who would you be showing your Christmas music to?" Vivian says.

"I could show it to your wife," I say to Max. "She might be interested."

"I'm not married. I'm divorced."

"Even better. I don't imagine your alimony cheques have improved relations."

"Gwen? It'll just mean she can skip her Metamucil that day." From anyone else it would come out as a cruel joke, punctuated with a dismissive snort. But Vivian just stops her saké cup mid-turn and delivers it flatly, fingers poised on the rim.

Gwen? Really, *Gwen*? I'm thinking busily, while trying to keep all signs of it behind my face. Max's old lady *that* old lady. Cast off but still working his desk—in lieu of alimony? Sent down to the street to chase off sign carriers, get her picture tweeted. Chase off Snag and Sammy, spray Glade in their wake. Reserve a table for his current squeeze?

"It's an amicable arrangement, whatever you may be thinking. Not everyone is as bad at moving on as you seem to be," Max says, obviously twigging to some of the face behind the Face. Good at faces. Spends his days an inch from them. And has to be, to know which ones to make into Christmas Music.

"Maybe not. But I wonder if she knows about all her ex's hobbies."

"Spoken like a lifelong bachelor," Max says, a little too lightly. "After almost twenty years, a husband doesn't have *any* secrets."

"Well, we'll see I guess. If she's not interested, I'm sure someone else will be. Just look at the grief they're giving our mayor for his private life."

"Cut the shit," Vivian says. Ignoring a sharp look from Max. "How much do you want?"

Gotcha! A hard thought to think while returning her dead eye for dead eye. *A lack of normal motivations—pound for pound, my best tool as an adjuster.* Guaranteed to wrongfoot the target, stick him from an angle he least expects. I'm so elated I tell them the simple truth, sure that they'll mistake it for a bargaining manoeuver.

"I just want to take you down. There's nothing else I want to see happen."

"Yeah, right," says Vivian. How many men have mistaken the disdainful curl to her lip as a seduction tool, unable to believe she honestly despises them? Max just looks blank, a little deflated, the nonchalance he's put across all used up, waiting for new lines.

"Thanks for the drink," I say, draining his water glass.

At the door I look back and see Max with his saké cup suctioned to his face, Vivian busy on her cellphone.

§

Ten minutes later, I'm ready when the buzz comes from the lobby. A mumbled "...delivery for...," garble fore and aft. Amateurs. "Come see me first, Apartment 501," I call down gruffly, handing them a chuckle over a conscientious old clown.

Through the peephole thirty seconds later, the bovine young faces of the two cellphone loiterers outside Obsession. Called in by Vivian at the Nicholas-and-Simone show, standing by until she found out more. The taller one in a pale peach shirt. His partner in pale lemon.

I open the door a crack—"What's this about?" Let them shove it wide and me with it, backing me against the little shelf I use for mail and keys. Lemon shuts the door behind him.

"Okay, old man," Peach, the tall one, says. "It's really simple, okay? You've got something that belongs to our sister and her friend. We'll take it, plus any copies you've made. Then we're out of here. You see how simple—"

Crack! The finishing hammer raps him low in the fore-head, right between the eyes. The short handle and small head don't allow for a swing with much power, but you can swing it even with sore fingers and bang exactly where you mean to. In this case, the sweet spot where a calf would catch the bolt. He opens his mouth as if to say something, takes a pinstep towards me, and sits down.

"Simple enough?" I say, and turn to Lemon.

Stunned for a moment, his mouth open, as if the blow caught him too, he recovers now and gets his hands up, trying to look fierce. The left in a fist and the right open in front of it, ready to parry or grab the hammer while throwing a punch behind it.

Except it isn't a hammer that's coming. I drop it on the floor, reach behind me for the cutter, and swipe it across his forward hand. He yells and presses the other hand over the wound, hunching over them. Red seeps between the knuckles of his left hand. I slash more deliberately across the cheek that's turned to me. A dark seam for a moment, and then the blood wells thickly. He howls again, louder this time. Drops to his knees. Puts his left hand up over the new wound, blood dripping from face and hand to the floor.

"My face... my face... you fucking cut me...," he moans, rocking back and forth, as if he can't believe it.

"Take your hand away and let me see."

"No fucking way. You'll just do it again."

A moan from behind us. Peach is trying to get to his feet. I pick up the hammer and rap again on the red spot above his nose. He falls back and lies flat, arms outstretched.

When I turn back, Lemon has inched into the corner and is cowering there, making whimpering sounds, blood dripping from the palm he's holding above the floor and from the wrist bone of the hand over his cheek. The side of his face a red smear now. Looking down, I see the tip of the cutter blade has snapped off. I push out more blade with the button on the handle. At the *snick* his eyes go wide.

"I think you're wearing some of my blade. Take away your hand so I can see."

Shakes his head. He's crying now. Tears rolling down into the blood. But lifts his hand off enough that I see a small gray fin jutting from the red. His eyes rolling down at it to see, but he can't.

"Take your hand away."

"No… no…"

"Suit yourself." A short kick in the hand drives the lodged point down to bone and pierces the hand as well.

His scream high-pitched this time, frantic. "You're… you're…," he gets out between sobs, but can't decide what I am. While he's thinking about it, I duck into the kitchen and grab a bottle of Fantastik and a roll of paper towels from under the sink.

Get down on my knees beside him, spraying and wiping at the blood. "You filthy thing. You have no idea how the Owner feels about his parquet floors." I tilt the nozzle up and spray a puff at the cut face and hand, some of it catching his eye. His yowl becomes a string of curses—"Fuckfuckfuckfuckfuck-fuck*FUCK*"—as the chemicals burn. The hit eye closed so tight it's just wrinkles below his eyebrow. I aim the nozzle at the other eye. Shutting it just as tight, he cranks his head away.

When I turn to check on his brother, he scrambles up and out the door behind me. Blood smears on the jamb and knob from his fumbling with two sliced hands.

One down. One to go.

A few anxious minutes as Peach doesn't stir. Out cold—I hope. *Did they follow me down the street or know the address already? From whom?* Finally his eyes roll open. Close again. Then start opening and closing slowly, long long blinks. While he makes small movements with his arms and legs, bending and unbending the ends of them, like a baby in a crib acquainting himself with his limbs.

An idea comes to me. I see it, like a scene in a movie I'm going to shoot and have already watched. Everything I need is under the kitchen sink, where I got the Fantastik.

He doesn't react when I lift his legs and slide the long plastic leaf bag up over them to his hips. I know he's not paralyzed, but could he be brain damaged? I tried to keep them short, sharp raps on bone—stunners, not stoppers. *But the brain more complicated than a finishing nail.* That scrawny, rat-faced boy in lock-up who kept beating up on iron pumpers, putting one in a wheelchair. Shrugged when I asked him his secret: *Street muscle versus gym muscle. Use beats show ever' time.* Not a helpful reminder.

I fold his arms across his chest, hands at his waist. When I bind his wrists together, wrapping loops of tape around them, it's the shearing sound of the tape coming off the roll that brings him fully awake, like ice water splashed in his face. Like the *snick* that jolted his brother.

"What are you doing?" he says as I push up under his waist to get the bag over his hands. Barely slurring, but still not moving. He looks like a male model decorating a tomb.

"Taking out the trash. I'm the super here."

"You're insane." Wide-eyed with it.

"Just a bit of a neat freak. I'll cop to that." Tugging the bag up higher.

Suddenly, as if a key's turned in his brain, he's all action. A mad flurry of it. Kicking at the bag to get clear of it, pumping his bound hands in the air, then rolling to push with them off the floor. Dancing inside the bag, stamping to get it off. Scrabbling at the knob with taped hands, he can't get it to turn. Kicking at the bottom of the door. "Hey!" he yells through it. "HEY! HEEEEYYYY!!!"

"Here. I'll get that for you."

And he's through the crack so fast he bangs his shoulder on the jamb. Staggers with bound hands, kicking the bag from one foot, toward the red Exit sign. Straight-arms the door and is gone.

Three of the other four doors open, faces peering out. As the steps die away, they look down the hallway at me.

A bouncer in Hamilton, where I lived for six months, had a saying at closing time. *Motel time, people!* he'd call out, *Motel time!* But I can't say that to these people. They live here.

"Hard to convince some people No Vacancy means just that. You didn't really want him as a neighbour, did you?"

The doors close, one by one. After the last click, I close mine.

Who says it's hard to make new friends?

§

Around midnight, I unroll the sleeping bag in Big Empty. Not remotely tired, but knowing it's time to simplify the sleeping quarters. Bed to couch. Couch to floor. There's a schedule for meeting what's coming towards you. A time to wait and let it approach, a time to meet it halfway.

Thoughts like fireflies in my head, a swarm of them, random blips and veers of light, here, there, dead black, then another—though at some point I must drift off, because I'm on the stone steps again, descending to the level of the Empress. Am I imagining that she's managed to turn ever so slightly in my direction, a minuscule inching by sheer force of will, that shows me a fraction more smooth skin, a touch more streaming yellow hair? The lashes of the far eye?

The little mouth thin and set with determination in the wizened profile facing me.

Like a loop in a movie, I keep going down, keep finding myself halted at her niche.

The descent happens swiftly, as if I'm gliding on a rail, but also in a kind of slow-motion, a step-by-step slog downward. The impressions alternate, overlap. It hardly seems possible that such incompatible motions could be occurring simultaneously.

TAL in my mailbox six days ago. Six days that feel like six months.

Thinking clear waking thoughts even in a dream…

And seeing Maude's shadowy things. The dark gray, flickering window.

And the Empress straining in her niche.

Eyes open… closed…

Doesn't seem to make a bit of difference.

Sometime in the middle of the night I put one of the sticks 303 copied inside a Ziploc baggie which I put inside one of the vegetable bags in the fridge, shaking gai lan, bok choy, and carrots all around it. Push it two thirds of the way back among the other bags. I can't see Peach and Lemon coming back, but Max—or Vivian more likely—might upgrade to more capable models.

12

NOT MUCH TO clean up in the lobby. No broken bottles, no vomit. Just a couple of chip bags crumpled by the garbage can and three jumbo Coke bottles lined up on the ledge in front of the mailboxes. It could almost be an art installation: *Finale, Friday Night*. I've never seen this crew, but to choose this shabby little lobby two steps up from the street for their party room—they have to be very young.

Halfway up the stairs, a spot of red on the wall. Coin-sized, bright. Two steps above it, a bigger splotch right in front of my feet. Harder to see against the flecked tile—still, I don't know how I missed it. I made a thorough pass last night, down and then back up, stopping on each step with Fantastik and a rag. Lemon leaked like a haemophiliac. But the intermittent sprays of dots suggested mental disturbance more than clotting problems. Pressing a hand to the oozing cheek, flinging it out in dismay.

Watch yourself today. Not firing on all cylinders. Shredded nights below ground coming home to roost.

I have to read over my note to Ken a dozen times. So simple it's hard to screw up, but not trusting myself not to get a detail wrong. When the content doesn't wobble on repeated readings, I feel more confident it's stable, no matter how wobbly the writer.

Ken, unless you hear back from me within a week, could you mail the enclosed? ExpressPost packages pre-paid and addressed. Just drop them in any mailbox. Thanks.

Poor Ken. Sitting at his desk, staring at padded envelopes addressed to the police and the *Toronto Star*. Catching not a whiff of interest rates or portfolio diversification from either of them. The coffee in his mug growing cold, the screen saver of grandkids evicting his pie chart.

Yet he's the only person who entered my mind as certain backup. Interprets the role of financial advisor broadly, willing to accent the advisor part. Maybe a little bored after thirty years of bond yields. And just a good guy, basically.

Sorry, Ken, I murmur silently, sealing envelopes and note in one of the large banking envelopes he gave me. *I walked two hundred grand through your door, but it came with some weird carrying charges. Par for the course, I hope.*

Up the street, the suited rep who accepts the package for their inter-branch courier service tries to convince me of the large misdeed I'm committing in not opening a line of credit in addition to my savings account. It must have been seeing *Financial Services Advisor* below Ken's name that got him thinking I might be receptive. I have a brownie and a tea from his Welcome table while he lays it out.

§

Phone light blinking green. A familiar voice with a new message, proposing a meet.

Bad cops didn't pan out, now they're trying with the good. Trouble is, their bad cops were a couple of cadets and their good cop is an aging desk sergeant. They definitely need to do some new hiring.

And you definitely need to be ready when they do.

§

I've learned to set up early, even at a public meet, so I'm at the corner of Yonge and Chaplin Crescent by 10:30, an hour ahead of schedule. Spend a few minutes under the overhanging roof by Avis, scoping out the four corners of the intersection. Davisville Station, IDA Pharmacy, Timmie's on my side and Starbucks right across. I'm not expecting Peach and Lemon—they're on couches with ice bags on their faces—but there's no sign of their replacements either. Just a smattering of sleepy Davisville types, yawning as they make a croissant and caffeine run.

Inside the Starbucks, I take a tea to a back table where I can see the room. Take out *Around Toogood Pond* from the lower jacket pocket. I'm re-reading by intuition, hopping back and forth between entries. Trying to spot something I might have missed. An angle in.

Photograph 10 August

An early Christmas. J in her dress, M and I flanking her in suits and bowties. The shining drizzles, which must be tinsel reflecting the flash, make for an effect of blackness rent by ragged silver. Darkness raked by talons of light. Or snail trails of light sliding down a black windowpane—

Poetic memory lane definitely my least favourite of Sandor's modes. It feels like stalling. What he does when he wants to avoid facing something while assuring himself he's tackling it head on.

A lucky girl 20 July

Yesterday in the Food Court. Her wide-eyed pleasure in the (now) always-new: "This is a *good* drink!"—KFC's iced tea to go with her snack pack of popcorn chicken and fries. She eats with the pincer-picking slowness of a child, selecting a piece of chicken or a fry like a chocolate from an assorted box—learning food, marvelling at it, as she eats it.

A sense that she is looking *up* and out at the world. She has shrunk, and walks hunched over her walker, but it's more than that. As if she is seeing bright things from deep inside a well, or as a child again.

Back in her room, 7:20 p.m. "I'm a lucky girl." Something she says often these days.

When I arrived she was up on the secure floor, a place I've never found her before. I squeezed in back of a crowd of residents listening to John play his rambunctious piano—jazz, blues, show tunes—"I know six hundred songs," he said, and never missed on a request. I watched her a while before showing myself. Sitting on a chair near the front, twisting her fingers in a nervous gesture, though her feet were tapping. Huge, pop-eyed smile when she saw me. I sat behind her, singing along—"Roll Out the Barrel," "Mairsie Doats and Doesie Doats," "Bye Bye Blackbird."

"I wasn't sure you'd show up." Gwen sets down her coffee, then a stack of library books. Alice Munro, Maeve Binchy, Peter Robinson, *New Yorker* issues—an assortment for long evenings.

"A reader," I say. "An endangered species, I hear."

She colours slightly. "My library life. Load up on Saturdays. Sometimes mid-week too. There's an e-reader book club I'm thinking of giving a try. I guess you'll laugh at that."

"Nothing funny in it."

"Well, you're full of surprises," she says primly. Primly and tartly—any casting director would grab her for the homeroom teacher. A tremor in her hands—slight but continuous. "But this is the first pleasant one that I'm aware of."

Touché, Gwen. Sent out to clean up messes—though seldom fully briefed about the nature or extent of the spills. Certainly not this time. Barring Maude, who is dead, I like her better than anyone I've met on this adjustment—at least on the Wyvern side.

She sips her coffee, clears her throat, and gets right down to it.

"Dr. Wyvern says you've got some information that belongs to him. Not very important information, he says, but you're trying to hold it over his head. He says that's what's behind all the... unpleasantness you've been causing."

"If I held something over your ex-husband's head, it wouldn't be anything as soft as information."

She smiles wanly. "My husband's no saint. After eighteen years and no kids to distract me, I'd be the last to claim that. But he's no devil either. Not the kind you seem to believe he is. All in all, he's just like his father. I saw that long before we were married. I was just too young to pay attention at the time."

Meaning—what, exactly? You're fine with diddling your computer while your ex and his psychopathic girlfriend drug and pose women you bill for the privilege? Or you're honestly so out of it—pining or duty-bound or just habitual and lonely beyond words—that you've bought whatever venial sins he's confessed to cover up his cardinal ones? Tapping and mousing and recording phone messages, with nary a wonder why some dental procedures, especially with nubile women, require a closed door. Totally complicit or oblivious beyond belief—either way, it's going to be a challenge to keep liking you.

"You can tell him that I'm ready to give him what he wants. But I need to visit him at home. I want to see him where he lives."

"Oh, that's not possible. Max—Dr. Wyvern—only takes appointments in his office. But if you want, I can—"

"You're not going to do that. Not really, are you?"

"Do what?"

"Bar the master's door, protect whatever he's got going behind it. Fetch when he says fetch. For what, old time's sake? For a Davisville apartment? Which you'd have coming to you for enduring him eighteen days, let alone years."

"Are you done?"

I take a sip of tea.

"You don't know anything about me. About him. About us. Judy's filled your head with one of her wild fantasies, and now you're off on this... tear."

No fear, no anger—no strong feeling of any kind coming from behind her glasses. Just shrewd appraisal. Sipping her coffee. Her hands steadier now. Though she keeps them around her cup. A gripper of things.

A long silence, the two of us sipping our drinks. Nothing unpleasant in it.

"I don't hate Vivian," she says at last. "I guess you'll laugh at that too."

"You keep wanting me to laugh at you. But you'll have to say something funny first."

"It'd be hard to hate someone I've known since she was a little girl. Helped her with her homework. And getting over crushes on boys. Which started pretty early in her case— and really, it was generally the boys who needed more help getting over her."

Gwen in a mood to talk. And me certainly in one to listen. We seem to have begun our own library club in the corner of Starbucks.

Vivian a child refugee from the Mount Pinatubo eruption in 1991. Superheated ash buried her parents, who managed to pull her underneath them in the instants before they died. Four years old, she stayed alive three days under their bodies. Rescue workers heard mewing sounds, like a cat. Dr. and Mrs. Wyvern sponsored their move to Canada. Vivian, her sister Betty, and their aunt Paula. Dr. Wyvern had been retired a few years, a little at loose ends even with his real estate hobby, so he was able to devote a lot of time to getting them settled. Their own kids were long out of the house—the boys done university and settled in careers. Judy long gone too, of course—in a different way. The aunt, Paula, they hired as a live-in housekeeper. Betty, who was fourteen or fifteen, and Vivian they set up in a nearby apartment. Betty worked at the home on Paula's day off, and other times they needed her. But Dr. Wyvern was a stickler about school coming first. He made sure they got a proper education.

The Sandman. "What did you mean when you said Max took after his father?"

"I didn't say 'took after,' I said he was like him. I don't know what I meant exactly. Don't most children resemble their parents in lots of ways? Some obvious, some more subtle. Different people, but from the same stock. Anyway, I've already said more than I intended too. Too much probably, for someone sent to deliver a simple message."

"Well, the trouble was, your message wasn't simple enough and my reply was too clear."

"I'm not sure I follow…"

"They told you—"

"*He* told me."

"He told you I had something he wanted back. I already know that, so that isn't a message. The real message was to make me give it back, but he didn't tell you that or how to do it. He doesn't know himself, so he sent you out to fish a bit while he thinks of something. And I told you I'll give it back, but only in a meeting at Max's home. So that's how we got onto other topics so quickly. You never asked what it is Max wants back so badly. But I guess handling files discreetly gets ingrained in a secretary. What happened to Paula and Betty?"

"Pardon me?"

"Vivian's sister and aunt. They've been in Canada twenty-two years now. What're they doing?"

The Venti cup goes up to her mouth and stays there through a couple of sips. Fewer people smoke all the time, but we have these big paper cups—to give our hands something to do, to hide parts of our faces behind.

"Paula just disappeared one day. Poof! Off like that. No notice, no anything. No one had a clue where she went, or why. Everyone thought it was incredibly ungrateful. Dr. Wyvern never used that word, but you could tell it hurt him a lot, for a long time. Betty was a sadder case, and in the end a mystery too. Towards the end of high school she started getting these moods. Then started drinking. Not just with friends, at a party, but on her own. At sixteen, seventeen. The Wyverns stuck by her, even got her some counselling, even after she was in their house obviously under the influence. And after a few things had disappeared, valuable things. Things got pretty tense and messy—and stayed that way a long time—but in her first year of college, she met a boy and moved away. Suddenly, just like her aunt. I don't think even Vivian's heard from her since. It's an off-limit topic."

"Sounds like they went back to being refugees. Or else never stopped."

Gwen puckers her mouth. "That's a queer way of putting it."

A small mouth, even unpuckered, with fine age lines radiating around her lips. They make her mouth look more, not less, attractive—like cross-hatching, they add dimension. Like her slight overbite, they make her believable. An actual body. A lived-in person. When did that become something to notice, if not exactly rare? Early Saturday, an errand to a known freak, but she's put on pale pink lipstick, washed and brushed her cap of salt-and-pepper hair.

"And her brothers?"

"Brothers? I never said she had brothers."

"No, you didn't. I heard it from someone else."

She looks blank for a second, then laughs suddenly. A real laugh, showing crooked teeth she puts her hand up to cover. "Oh my God, I haven't thought of this for years, but she had this trick she discovered in high school, maybe even middle school, of keeping a jealous boyfriend in the dark by referring to her ex-boyfriends as her 'brothers.' They went to different schools—already she was pulling them in from a distance—so they weren't likely to find out the truth. 'And who knows,' she said to me once, 'if I keep them in the family, maybe they'll be around when I need them.' At that age. What a little fox."

"You admire her."

Her face serious as a judge's, just as suddenly. "I can appreciate qualities I've never had, even if I'd never want them."

"It's none of my business, but do you really need this particular job, or is it just a way of keeping close to him? Hanging on to whatever's left of your place in his life."

"You're right, it's none of your business."

But then, a minute later, she says, musing to a space beside my shoulder, "I do worry about Max. He's too intense. Like his father. And he's never learned healthy ways to release the pressure of his work. A Type A, but without any—"

I cut through the pop-psych blather. I have to, I can't help myself when it starts.

"Other than with some Christmas music, you mean?"

A look of utter confusion—or is it panic?—in her face. She stiffens, draws back a distance behind her skin.

"You don't know what I mean. Or what I want."

This is how it happens. Especially late in an adjustment, especially in a closing window. Things trigger me and I go off. And I see it for a moment—like a lightning flash—and keep going off, as if self-knowledge were no more than a storm in the distance.

"Yes I do. You want to gossip, trade jargon. Maybe dance a pinstep this way, a pinstep back. Consider each person's 'unique journey' through a picture window. Whereas me, I want to learn what's what and act on it."

"So you can do what? Barge around and break things? Hurt people?"

Maybe. "You need to stop drinking decaf. Or start drinking it, I don't know what's in your cup. The bulls are already loose in the china shop. I'm trying to put them down."

"That sounds plain crazy. I'm sorry to put it that way, but it does. Max warned me to expect a rant. Asked me to hear it out. But I've heard enough."

She stands up. When I reach out and put a hand on her arm, I feel the trembling all the way up to her elbow. I don't think it's just from my touch.

"There's one more thing." She's not looking at me, she's facing the barristas working like four-handed monkeys to serve the waiting line. "Nothing to do with you, I promise. Ever since I re-entered the Wyvern fold, there are two things I've heard more than any other. 'You don't know anything' and 'You're insane.' Crazy, lunatic. Whatever. You said them yourself in our visit here."

"Yes?"

"You tell Max and anyone else that's listening that in both cases it's pure wishful thinking."

Big purse in one hand, library books against her chest, she frees a couple of fingers to carry her cup to the garbage, push it through the recycle hole. I like her still and wonder why. Half wish I didn't. It seldom helps in an adjustment.

§

After she leaves, I stay a while longer. Treat myself to a Venti chai latte. Spicy-sweet, whipped milk froth—more than the price of two dinners. *Not every loonie can go to the homeless, Ken. A few of them have to find their way home.*

Islands 23 July

Getting into the car, she told me she wanted to talk about something. Fearing by her serious expression it would be her desire to leave—"to go home… back to the farm"—I distracted her with other topics and she didn't find her way back to it. *Using* Alzheimer's—when I have to.

The usual calming, pleasant time at Toogood Pond, splitting an oatmeal-fruit cookie, her beloved mocha frappuccinos. Her intense interest in all the birds as one big family, blurring their species differences into variations within one category. The geese… "the smaller ones" (ducks)… "the little one, so white!" (seagull). She sees bird-ness, in all its forms. But she still knows the robin, Robin Redbreast, the first one learned the last to go. She kept thanking me for staying "so long… all day"—two and a half hours—and expressing her love of nature, the breeze "heavenly."

The closed snack shop with the blue window coverings across the pond. It hasn't changed since our first visit in April, though there are plenty of strollers to sell ice cream or pop and hot dogs to. Something in transition? "They closed that house. No one lives there now. They're closing up every home around here."

She can't walk far now. To the first bench—then, after a while, to the next—back. Her knees. But also, she often presses her hand to a pain under her ribs—the right side today.

As I'm reversing out of our spot, she says beside me, "You like making them… All those ones…" She can't find the words. A look both sly and desolate on her face.

"Shh," I say, "shh." Using Alzheimer's again. No, worse. *Praying* for it.

Like father, like son. Gwen's words more or less. Vivian's aunt and sister going away, going off the rails. Judy gone at fifteen. Vivian posing, helping to pose. How far back did the Wyvern rot start?

Don't laugh 30 July

Went with her into Harmony Nook. A place we've never sat before—we always had Toogood Pond. High white fence. White bench under an apple tree, birds visiting a bath and feeders. A burnt-red Japanese maple opposite us, other parts unlandscaped yet. Mick's "work in progress." Mom liked it, but perhaps found the fenced enclosure eerie, kept asking "Who is that? What are those voices?" of people passing on the walk beyond. A refuge only peaceful if you understand it as such. She does better in open places where she can see who's coming and going.

After a time, she took her walker and circled the space with a quizzical expression, then crossed a patch of grass to the white fence slats and murmured, then called, to the people beyond. Bent over, eye to the crack. She looked like a madwoman peering from a cage.

Back in her room, Ivy came in to invite her to the social. She was reluctant to leave "Max," though I reassured her I'd just water her plants and follow right behind. But she halted beyond the door every few steps, looking back. Then she moved in an extraordinary way. She hurried with small steps, almost a run (though she hasn't been capable of one in years), towards me in her doorway. "Max... are you coming?"

I felt myself smiling. "I'm your son, Mom. Sandor." Usually that's enough.

But disquiet darkened her face. And something else—something wrong etched deep that wouldn't come out.

"Don't laugh," a staff member standing by said to me. Not sharply, but firmly. A large woman, pleasant face. No name, but I've seen her before.

Was I laughing? I must've been. Must've looked like I was.

I was only trying to jolly us back to recognition. I've done it often enough before.

Today was different, though. She seemed disturbed when I left her in the bistro. Said of the runny peanut butter on her fruit plate: "It looks like what I find in my underwear."

And now, a few hours later, the rebuke hits home and stings.

Don't laugh.

I did laugh, damn it. A craven social reflex to defuse a tense situation. Helplessness no excuse. Laughed at someone losing the ability to tell son from son, son from husband, keep her nearest and dearest straight.

§

Someone vacates a nearby table, leaving newspapers behind. On my way out I check the *Globe* and *Post* obituaries. Nothing in either of them. Only the *Star*'s sports section is in the pile, but the *Star* wouldn't be the Wyverns' paper anyway. They'd hold their noses and vote for Hizzoner, but not follow the scat trail of his takedown.

Nothing to justify your paranoia, Judy. No slighting mention, not this time. No mention of anybody.

Could've been in another day, of course. Though Saturday the standard—the most-read—especially for a society family. Writer another question mark. Max obviously with his hands (and eyes) too full. Judy—ah, Judy... Sandor the family scribe, her POA through the years. But writing takes real writers longer—they respect the work. And with the beer, the post-breakdown blanks, *flesh into smoke* tar pits... He might be a while getting it done.

Assuming it's to be written at all. You disappear someone who commits the booboo of stepping in front of a car—vanish her so successfully the neighbours have trouble recalling where she went. Do you want to reanimate her when she commits the bigger booboo of dying alone?

§

Mrs. Rasmussen knows how to bar a door. Not that I would have expected anything less from her. "Judy's not available. She's having a bad day." Arms folded, standing on the steps.

So that's that.

I don't hate everyone who blocks me, I'm thinking as I three-point on Selkirk. *Depends on why they're doing it as much as how*.

Strange, the court of self. When and where it convenes, when and where it calls a recess. Spells in the waiting room. Bawling clerks suddenly calling you back in to testify, prosecute, defend, pass judgement, sentence... in proceedings that never end.

§

Cantonese Chow Mein at Shanghai Food Gallery shouldn't really taste that different from my veggie-noodle bowl.

They're variations on the same simple theme. Theirs has more meat, though—shrimp, pork, beef—and slices of chicken, not shreds. More tasty grease, and much less water. And then, too—the main thing—occasionally you just need a break from your own cooking.

"Is the old man cooking tonight?" I ask the boy at the till. "Can I see him for a second?"

The boy says something in Chinese into the kitchen behind him, gets something shouted back. The old man sticks his face out of the steam, sees me, and mutters at the boy. Disappears.

"It'll be ready in a few minutes," the boy says, cancelling the order.

Compensation on completion, unless the adjustment is ongoing. As with Jared and Lucius and Lucy. A principle to adhere to, I think, sitting on a stool by the front window beside two girls showing each other pictures on their iPhones.

Two years ago, the old man was overjoyed to have his granddaughter's boyfriend adjusted out of her life—"gangster boy... no good, NO GOOD," with sideways cleaver motions—and bowed with gratitude at the modesty of the terms. Now, though, as the adjustment recedes, fixing me a free dinner once every month or two has begun to seem onerous.

It's while I'm looking out at the street that she returns. Not a dream, not a hallucination, not even a waking vision. More like an overlay. I don't stop seeing the street—still bright, it's not even 5:00 yet. I don't stop hearing the girls, the cooking sounds behind me.

But I also see what I saw intermittently all night long. That unrelenting struggle to free her face from the stone it's glued to or grown to be a part of. *Turning to me*, I thought at first—but maybe I'm just the one standing in the same direction as freedom. And she's succeeding, too. The wizened, wispy-haired half of the face now has almost a quarter of the plump, golden-haired side forced round... the profile getting on toward three-quarter view.

Such energy in the eyes! The eyeball rolled into the crevice of the far one shooting beams of intent where it means to go—but also in the outward one, sunk in veiny wrinkled folds. Shining out of both of them, a baby's clear, implacable determination to move from where it is.

"Order ready!"

The three of us turn. He points at the two girls, then at me.

"Yours almost."

13

DRIVING UP THE 404, I feel the engine sticking again. Like it's revving through wet sand. Do open stretches, higher speeds bring it on? But it was tooling down Kennedy when I first felt it, the Saturday Maude died, when I mentioned it to Lucius. Something that comes and goes?

Or you do? Mind on, then off. Aware, then in the dark. Present and accounted for, then AWOL.

§

Toogood Pond the nicest park I've found in the city. And Unionville's Main Street the perfect lead-up to it. Cafés, shops and restaurants, pubs, even an ice-cream shack (closed in October), hanging flower baskets—gracious old homes, Maude's "likable houses," down the side streets. Worth well over a million each, no doubt, but the owners in agreement—for property values if not for good taste—to keep an old-time, small-town vibe. Like Niagara-on-the-Lake in a way. But doing a much better job of keeping it real.

The parking lot full on a Sunday. I get the last spot and start up the dirt-and-gravel path on the left-hand side of the pond.

Big willows overhanging the water. Trees on the grassy slope further to my left, screening the road above. Quiet. Fall colours. Wine reds, golds, straw yellows. Browns in all shades coming forward, green dropping away. Dissolving like a scrim.

Strollers, joggers. Couples, kids, families. Old people, alone or with a middle-aged child, usually a daughter. A bench now and then, someone resting on it. Most people offering a greeting, unless too deep in the iWorld.

Midway up the side, I step into a patch of strong déjà vu. Like I've stepped into a painting I know, or a scene from a movie I've watched countless times. *Been-hereness.* My head swims woozily, and I have to sit down on the bench to get my bearings.

As soon as I do, it comes clear and I can account for it.

An oval of grass, a stubby curving peninsula. Willows to either side, but a clear view across the pond. Right in front of me, by the water, the long irregular clump of thistles, milkweed, tall grasses and wildflowers Maude stood in front of. The sun that's warming the back of my neck the sun that was shining on her face, glinting off her glasses. I don't have the photo with me today, but I don't need it. *This is the spot.*

They would have stopped here, for a rest. Shared the cookies or sandwiches often mentioned in the book, the mocha frappuccinos. The photographer—who else but Sandor?—maybe staying on the bench, zooming in on her. Or, more likely—her unsteady walking—leading her out by the flowers and backing off a few paces for the shot.

It's eerie to be sitting where they sat, and to know it for certain. And to see other things not in the photo but in the book, like peering around the glossy borders of the frame.

The closed-up snack shop with blue tarps over the windows on the other side, overhanging the water. To Maude it was another shuttered home. The birds dotting the water, dozens of them—geese, ducks, cormorants, gulls. Gliding. Flapping in short flights. What she thought of as one big family of bird, coming in different sizes and colours.

One glowing success as a writer, Sandor—if you'll take it. Your subject more vivid than her describer. The dead more present than the living.

The son's reflections and recriminations fall away, detaching like the dandelion filaments, leaving just pure glimpses of the gone.

For a few moments it's just Maude sitting beside me on the bench. Staring out at plants and sky. Same as we did from Vivera's window a week ago.

§

I move on. A full circuit of the pond is a kilometer, I hear one power walker inform another. Already a few have lapped me a couple of times.

A sign with pictures and the names of fish species living in the lake. A log covered with sunning turtles. Heron stalking the weedy shallows behind them. Then the path ducks into trees, comes out on a wooden bridge over a swamp dense with bulrushes. Flattened path through them, muskrat probably, leading to some splashing amid waving stalks.

A shady section then over the stream that feeds the pond. Cool and covert-seeming. Trees interlacing overhead to form a tunnel, it must be nearly opposite the end I came in. Leafmeal, stick bits, swirling along. Fall rains lately, the water rising.

Leaning against the bridge railing the spot to pull out the book, let it open where it will.

Little birds 31 July

Something I forgot about yesterday. Mom kept coming back to a part of the Chinese lunch they'd had. "Little birds," they'd been served, she said. How big? She made a circle the size of a toonie with her thumb and forefinger.

They couldn't have been that small, I said with a chuckle, trying, again, to jolly it away. I seemed to have been trying to do that all day.

"These little birds," she insisted. Thumb and forefinger again. They'd cooked them. She couldn't get over it. She seemed partly admiring and partly horrified at the ingenuity of it.

"Noisy to eat." Crunchy? I suggested. "Yes, crunchy. With little bones."

She always had transformative vision. Leaves that formed families and whispered their histories, insects that carried on quirky arguments, a corner of unstained board that protested its neglect. She was a wonderful mimic, and when someone took root in her brain, she magnified them into a caricature that surpassed the original, becoming, like a Dickens character, something strange and indelible. Under her gaze, everything alive and interacting—how it delighted us as kids. (Dad laughing along, chiding when she "went too far." His boundaries to the real not too elastic—just ask J.)

People with imaginations lose their minds differently than people without imaginations. I think

they suffer more. Whatever got added to sane con-
templation—depth, layers, richness, intricacy—now
gets added to insane obsession. Fancies, whimsies,
gorgeous visions now turn vicious, ugly, cruel, gro-
tesque—horror's gallery. It gives me a preview of
myself with dementia.

Maybe, Sandor. And maybe not. It's not just strength of
imagination. It's also how outward-facing it is. For all your
sympathy for Maude—who seems to have brought out the
best in you, no question—you seem pretty stuck on yourself. *I know, I know. I may be underestimating you.* I heard you
in the bar.

High thresholds 1 August

*These were (these are?) my family, and yet I can't easily
imagine anyone else, even strangers, hearing me call out in
distress so loudly and so often without offering some aid.
In them I sense what I have always sensed and feared: a
cold it is dangerous to stand close to.*

    What you thought, J? Mother? As you cut your-
self with blades? Offered your body to a car?

    What crimes have I conspired in? How far, how
deep, do they go?

"Beauty and gentleness." Where did I read that? That
no matter what someone's cognitive ability is, they
still respond to beauty and gentleness. What further
guide is needed?

    Mom submitting herself to Dr. Spira's treatment
table, meekly and somehow happily. Another sacrifice. She looked small lying there. Her feet dangled

off sideways until I shifted them in line with her body. "Thank you, dear."

No sign of pain, even in her eyes, when Dr. Spira injected the freezing in her upper lip, then cut the wedge out of her filtrum and seared the spot with several blasts of liquid nitrogen. She lay still as a statue, hands folded across her stomach.

"A high threshold," Dad used to say of her. "The highest pain threshold I've ever seen." Which meant something coming from an anaesthetist. But a strange thing to say—I thought so even as a child—about your wife. An odd compliment to keep repeating.

When her leg veins became varicose—she would have been in her late thirties, all of her children born—they used to go over to the ER in the evening so he could "strip her veins." They made the procedure sound minor—though how could it be, the stripping of veins? She would come back bandaged from thigh to ankle, limping and joking about her "elephant legs."

An online site tells me now that vein stripping—when it is still done—is done under general or spinal anaesthesia. Yet they were gone and back in an hour.

A high threshold.

Now I'm the one who feels cold—the cold I've felt before with the Wyverns. Cold to give you the queasy shivers. It drives me out of the silent shade and into the populated sun. Two Chinese men sitting on lawn chairs under a willow, fishing poles planted, bobbers out where the stream widens through rushes into the pond. Seeing them like emerging from a deserted subway into a city square at noon.

The more I read, the more light is shed, the more darkness is discovered.

Sandor's growing sorrow and pity, multiplied by guilt, remorse. Exhaustion. Burnout. Which broke him, surely, I have no trouble believing that part. But why did contrition never make it up into atonement? Giving up on visiting Maude eventually, downing pints with his friends the night after her death. Doing nothing—nothing I can see—to help Judy, his sister and a windblown moaning ghost these four-and-a-half decades. Like a confession record stuck on *bad I'm sorry bad I'm sorry*... Can't unstick to *make it better... make a start.*

No wonder you needed a high threshold.

From the deck of the disused snack shop, I see us looking back from the bench across the pond.

Maude and I. Snack bags in our laps.

No trace of fucking Sandor.

There's a stone bridge at the other end of the pond, near the parking lot, with a sluice gate under it controlling the waterfall that drops down fifteen feet or so and runs on in a fast, narrow stream curving past willow banks. The volume of water coming through tells how much water the lazy-looking stream at the other end brings in through the deadfall and bulrushes. Leaning against the railing, looking up occasionally at the dark clump of trees at the other end where I was, I open the book again. People pass behind me, saying *"Excuse* me" to squeeze a stroller or walker past.

Sunflower 21 August

I feel guilty for snapping at her, and alone in that feeling too. The special loneliness of being with someone with dementia is to be alone with your understanding. To be singly responsible for the total survey of two people and their situation. But the wrong in that is that it places too much emphasis on companionship of the mind. I pack up the lunch and we go on. Slower and slower she moves, hunching further over the walker. She shows no sign of unhappiness. Only an endless puzzlement and curiosity about the now always new-to-her. "What is that orange?" "The worker's vest on the next property." "What's that sound?" "A cicada." "Bzzz. Humming. Humming brr, hummer brr…" "A humming bird?" "Yes, that one."

And then one of those astounding moments. As we pass the window of her room, which she usually can't recognize from outside or another direction, I say, "There's your sunflower." "Yes," she says. "Facing east. Is that right?" Peering up at me. "Yes, it is. *Exactly*."

Driving home, more of the visit comes back to me, as often happens. Driving a kind of processing. When I arrived, she talked of what a wonderful place Vivera is, how kind the people are to her, how "lucky" she feels— beaming with unfeigned gratitude. As if she needs to believe, and has succeeded in believing, that she is in the best and safest of all possible situations. In her smiles and wide-eyed exclamations I saw a terrifying vulnerability.

The same terrifying vulnerability that prompted her anaesthetist husband to pack her away after her suicide attempt? The hassle—the endless hassles—of dealing with people not asleep. The Sandman seems to hover behind these pages, a source of unspecified darkness. *Stripping veins. The daughter he wronged.*

I button the book in my lower jacket pocket and resume walking around the pond. I do the whole circuit on the path. Once, twice, three times. Then a fourth—quickening my pace each time. Like a power walker—one who passes me, in spandex and wrist weights, beams solidarity—though I'm chasing a totally different kind of fitness. In fact, each lap brings more stabs and throbs from all the fracture and dislocation sites. All the ones I remember—from fights, from accidents, from stupid stunts—and all the ones I sense but can't remember, since they happened outside of conscious memory. *Damaged goods.*

Stop… ease up for chrissakes! Anyone seeing my increasingly distorted limp, the grimaces I can't suppress at particularly sharp jolts, would tell me that. But the pain is just what I'm after. It stokes the cold fury I need stoked.

Infants gumming grins from strollers. Seniors from walkers or wheelchairs. Middle-aged man matching the slow advance of a younger companion between canes. The able-bodied, the disabled. Young, old. Singles. Couples. Even teenagers breaking out of mutual engrossment to say hello. The whole human family at its warmest is greeting me with a smile of welcome. It's almost unbearable—like a travel brochure in the hole. It makes me walk faster, but the faster I walk, the faster it comes towards me.

Family. Belonging.

Why do—how can Max and Sandor prefer their hamster wheels of piss-smelling pints and porn shots in a dental bib?

Especially when Sandor knows better. Or knew, at least. *Around Toogood Pond* proves it. He saw a better path—walked it for a long time—and then stopped. Gave up. His "breakdown." Fair enough. But *breakdowns come and breakdowns go—what're you going to do about it, that's what I'd like to know.* *Graceland* Lois's favourite album—and the songs sank into me too. Before my all-jazz era.

It's Sandor I feel the greatest rage for. Probably because he's not all bad, far from it—and the not-bad part goads me like a key just out of reach. Max a clearer case. His royalties for Christmas Music are coming to him, coming soon. No need to think further on it. But Sandor? Comes from a family that, behind a glossy veneer, operates like a drug cartel: the strong reaping the family winnings, the weak tossed to the side of the road. Judy. Maude. And Sandor himself? Nobody said this breakdown was his first. But somewhere along the way, he did the hard and tricky work of escaping from the family freezer, stepping into the sun. Maybe just partway, maybe not for long—few escapes are permanent.

There's just now, now. Lois's mantra.

Every goodness in the world owing fidelity to that. And every evil to its flouting.

A plump Jehovah's Witness with thinning hair has set up where the path meets the parking lot. You can't retrieve your car without bumping into him. The woman ahead of me pushes through his outstretched arm like a turnstile. I stop momentarily, long enough to glance at what's placed in my hand. Usual atrocious art—a couple from behind, her head on his shoulder, staring at a fading wall of photographs of a girl. *Can the dead live again?*

"Of course they can," I say. "Who else do we spend our days with?"

Push the pamphlet back at his chest and move on without clocking his reaction.

§

Sandor's at the long table in the front room of the Queen's Arms. With his group from a week ago. Some of them anyway. There's the blonde's refined husband, nodding intelligently at something Sandor's saying, but no sign of the blonde. One of the younger faces I seem to recall, but another couple are new. And a pudgy, middle-aged pair with round, cheerful faces I've never seen before. Sandor's in the center, explaining something with hand gestures.

Can a breakdown actually enrich a social life? From what I'm seeing, maybe yes.

At my entrance, all three Kims go for the phone behind the bar, each anxious to make the call. Ella gets there first. Father watches her while Mother keeps an eye on me. I won't be staying long enough to meet the cops.

"Ah, my evil twin!" Sandor says, raising his glass as I approach the table.

It stops me for a moment. My mind goes blank. Which Sandor obviously relishes, peeking at me over the rim as he guzzles.

Then he wrong-foots me again, when I start to tug his book from my pocket. "Are you going to sit down and join us? We're always hungry for new members."

"Goody!" says the round-faced man, rubbing his hands together theatrically. "Another quorum-booster in our claws!"

Among the glasses of beer on the table are notebooks and loose pages, a couple of paperbacks. I was so intent on Sandor I hadn't noticed them. More proof I'm not his bipolar gumshoe.

"It's not a judgemental group at all," says the long-nosed girl with orange hair. "Believe me, I've been in other groups that were."

"Fresh meat, fresh meat," chants the boy beside her.

"Don't listen to him," she says. "You share whatever you want, whenever you want. I didn't bring anything my first few weeks. Which was fine. And you can say before you do what kind of feedback you're looking for. Hard-nosed. Encouraging. Or just some ears, no comments required. If someone's not constructive, they don't stay long."

Sandor eyeing me over the rim of his glass, obviously enjoying himself.

"Actually," I say, "I'm a fan, not a writer. I just came in to collect an autograph."

The sight of the book I set down brings the dark thing up in his eyes.

The young man beside him slaps him on the back. "You see, Sandor," says the blonde's husband, "We told you it wasn't a vanity publication."

"Depends on whether he paid for it," says the author.

"I did. Two bucks." Chuckles here and there, quickly suppressed. "But it was second-hand."

"Still. Wait'll Lynette hears," says a voice.

"Lynette?" *TAL Lynette? I don't know another by that name.* "His publisher."

The blonde, I think. It has to be. The swirl of déjà vu I've felt around her. The tug of familiarity that made me try to stare through her Infinite Tunnel. But try as I might, I can't fit that slumped, dun-braided farm girl from the ward—TAL-consoled one night, then back in the dumpster at breakfast—with this svelte, high-maintenance blonde.

"Well, I like her style. As a publisher anyway."

Sandor looks up at me with a weary, tapped-out expression, the red veins in his eyes prominent. A shape-changer, I can't get hold of him. I see a gamester, drinker, charmer, some kind of victim—at least in his own mind. A quitter but also a fighter, a convalescent in need of constant R&R… but also the author of the passages I've been living with, walking around with, coming back to. All the sides are there but not quite meeting. Like overlays that don't quite match up when you try to stack them. The only line that makes sense to me is the one that has him saying goodbye definitively to something in his past, closing the door on it firmly—maybe at someone else's behest, maybe feeling it was the only way to save himself. And good advice perhaps. But I keep scratching at the door, knocking on it, prying.

He picks up a pen. "You know me by two names now," he says. "Which signature do you want?"

"Whichever one wrote the book."

A frown at the inscription to Grace—he flips the page quickly to prevent the others seeing it—and then he signs: *Wun Wing*. Closes the book and hands it back to me. I turn to go.

"Wait. Wait." The orange-haired girl. "What about some feedback? You didn't even say if you liked it."

"I sought out the author for his autograph."

The faces expectant, fearful. Writers. Except Sandor. He just looks blank.

"It was a revelation," I say. And the faces begin to smile, but tensely. The artistic ego: used to the set-up before the smash. "Seriously," I add. I didn't get to ask him about Christmas Music—what he knows, if he knows—but maybe I'm not leaving entirely empty-handed.

§

A cop getting out of the patrol car at the curb, his partner inside at the wheel. They must have been close by. A bounce at the Arms hardly an urgent call.

"We got a call about a disturbing patron," he says after the usual head-to-toe. "But it looks like you found your own way to the door."

I turn towards Avenue Road, start walking. "Hey. The army jacket. Are you a veteran?"

"Soldier of fortune," I call back, not giving a damn whether he hears me or not.

After a few steps, I hear the car door close behind me. *Walking away*, along with *not answering*, two black marks in a cop's book. But maybe, it being a slow night, they want to keep it that way.

The Face has got me in a lot of trouble with the law, no question. But it's saved me some, too.

§

"I thought we were done. I thought that was the deal."

With a sigh, 303 lets me in. Similar-looking alien frozen on his big screen. Attacking this time—not splattering yet.

"It was. We are. This is just a bit of overtime. There's a little research I need your help with. I could do it at the library, but not Sunday—"

A bony hand in my face. Too close, but let it go. "You can stop there. I know what you're looking for. And it just happens I've already got it."

And he does. There are a few drugs that might have been used by the producer of Christmas Music, but 303 has hit on one as the most likely. Has the name and specs written out on a torn half-sheet of paper. *Midazolam. A short-acting drug in the benzodiazepine class. Skeletal muscle relaxant. Sedative properties. Used for inducing sedation and amnesia before medical procedures.*

"Why'd you underline that part?"

"Wouldn't you have? I quoted the next parts exactly too."

"'*Drawbacks include adverse events such as cognitive impairment and sedation. Used in executions by lethal injection in the USA in combination with other drugs.*'"

"You just Googled this?"

He winces, a twinge briefly wrinkling his face like I've zapped him lightly in the balls. "It wasn't a *random* search. I didn't just barge into chatrooms saying, Hey, any you freaks know a good date rape drug for knocking women out in a dentist's chair? I used some parameters."

"Parameters."

"I narrowed it down. I was pretty sure what I was looking for even before I found it."

"Really? Why was that?"

303 just stares at me. My eyes flick to the alien forever charging. Emerald green with a yellow cowlick, red eyes, black talons and white fangs. The pastime looks incredibly stupid, but colourful. "You think I'm just your resident drug dealer, don't you?" 303 says.

"Any reason I shouldn't?"

"Believe it or not, I actually had another life before I became your IT man."

"Tell me. I'm interested."

And he does. And I am, mildly. It's not as uncommon as he seems to think. A scholarship student in Natural Sciences at U of T. Good grades, but not good enough for med school. The competition unreal against "Asians who study twelve hours straight for fun. Sixteen when they get serious." Settled for Pharmacy, but quit after a year. Too much rote memory, which he found boring as well as insulting. Got in with a group developing game ideas, moving a little dope to support their own use. Then the gaming business—"insanely competitive" as well—fell away, and pot got moved in more substantial quantities.

"Until you became my resident drug dealer."

A bigger zap in the balls, a bigger twinge. This one warps his face for half a second.

"You're welcome. Now fuck off, thank you."

I owe him that much. As I'm leaving, though, something occurs to me. I put a hand on the door he's closing, stick my head back in.

"You had this information but you didn't tell me? Didn't think to slide it under my door? How long were you going to wait?"

"Not very long. I was thinking of coming up tonight. But how did I know you weren't the guy taking the pictures? Or a friend of the guy who does?"

It stops me briefly.

"That doesn't make any sense. Why would I expose myself by showing them to you? Why would I think they were music, not pictures?"

"I don't know, man. You're an actor? You're a psycho? A lot of what you say and do makes no sense to me."

I consider it a moment. "That might be why we're still on speaking terms."

"What is?"

"Mutual incomprehension. It can be a social aid."

"Whatever, man. Look, are we done now? For real? Quits, I mean."

I consider that a moment too. "I'd like to tell you yes. I think so. But you and I, we're"—I search for the right image—"we're like two leeches fastened to each other. Neither of us is getting anything very nutritious, but until something else swims by, we're hanging on."

That image is so unappealing that he shoves the door shut, locks it, and gets back to his charging alien.

14

GREEN LIGHT BLINKING on the phone machine when I come back upstairs. First I wash the plaster and white paint off my hands. For the moment, the couple in 405 have an intact ceiling again—until the next heavy rain knocks the plug out in soggy chunks and they're forced to catch the dripping water in a roasting pan in their living room. When the season of freeze-and-thaw sets in next month, the dripping will accelerate and patches will be impossible until May. The couple, who seem intelligent, have never withheld a rent cheque, though they've lived here ten years, for eight of which their ceiling has leaked, and they should know that until he feels the sting of absent funds the Owner will play patch-and-pray rather than hire a roofer to find the leak and fix it. He calls them his "best tenants ever" and shakes the husband's hand on the rare occasions they meet.

"Ken, I'm sorry about the mystery packages," I say when he picks up the phone. His voice in my machine was ominously solemn, asking me to call him at my *earliest convenience*. "Let's move up the timetable a bit. If you hang on to the envelopes two more days, you can return them to me using the inter-branch service. Or else just drop them in a mailbox yourself."

Since I may not be able to pick them—or anything—up myself, is what I mean by making my voice lean towards option number two as the best one for both of us. Silence from the other end. I can see the two envelopes with my handwriting on his desk, his hands beside them—as clearly as if I've crawled down the line and taken up a perch behind Ken's eyes.

"I assume the contents of these envelopes are… dangerous somehow. A risk to someone."

"That's true."

"Otherwise," Ken goes on as if I haven't said anything, as if he's talking to himself, "they wouldn't be in my hands for safekeeping. Of course, what are the chances of an anonymous package addressed to the police being utterly harmless?"

"Also true, Ken. And again—"

"Remember how things ended last time," he breaks in. Which last time? I'm wondering. A lot of adjustments have ended messily, and of course they all end with Stone. Though Ken doesn't know about Stone—not in specific detail, and not by that name. What *have* I told him? I'm tripping over my own loose history. Fugue states and episodic amnesia no help in a long-term relationship. But in any case, *Remember-how* advisories at this stage are like *Mind your step* to a parachutist who's left the plane. Still, Ken needs some reassurance. And deserves it.

"I know it's an imposition, Ken. But it's for something that matters to me. Matters a lot. A question of clearing house."

"Whose house?"

I see, in rapid succession, Maude lying dead on her side in bed, Judy sipping cocoa on the porch on Selkirk Street, faces and other body parts of nameless girls and women in Max's chair, the Empress straining to break her tiny face free from stone, and, for some reason, Jared. They flip through my head like cards in a riffled deck.

"Your house. My house. Everybody's house." Too late, I realize I've gone too far. "It's always my house, Ken. Ultimately, that's what it comes down to."

"That's my thought too, " Ken says. Heavy-voiced, like a father laying down a *Sorry son, but* line. "That's why I'm sending them back via the inter-branch courier. You can pick them up where you sent them from. Tomorrow, or Wednesday at the latest."

"I should've asked you first, Ken. But you're involved now. They're in your hands."

"Yes, they are. And yes, I am. So the best I can do is limit my involvement. After I put them in this morning's out-box, I can truthfully say—to whoever asks—that I received packages from a client without having a clue what was in them, that since the client's instructions fell outside my area of service I didn't want to keep them, that I notified the client of that, and returned them immediately via the same route by which they arrived."

I hang up feeling like I've just played a game of speed chess against Garry Kasparov. Reminded that any game between the two of us could only *be* speed. Ken's moves as crisp and prudent as you could wish from an experienced banker. But with a hint of ice in his voice I've never heard before.

Damage control now. Best spin possible? The package stays at the branch up the street until you pick it up. A safe drop box. Almost a safety deposit box. *And if you don't show up to claim it? If you can't?*

After a while someone at the branch phones Ken. *Your client never...*

And Ken—a good citizen, a good guy—calls me all the names I've earned and delivers a police matter to the police. Probably in-person, so he can explain in full his involvement.

Sorry, Ken.

§

Gwen's voice in my ear: "Dr. Wyvern can meet you tonight at 9 p.m..."—with an address and unit number on Bayview. The condos at Bayview and Sheppard, I'm guessing.

And my voice back in hers: "Hello, Gwen. I asked for a home meet but you didn't give me that, did you? You didn't mention home at all. Which was cute. But we both know that thirty years of 'Family & Cosmetic Dentistry' buys you more than a balcony overlooking Loblaws. Or even the penthouse facing south." *And of course Sandor helped me to that, telling me of the family's condo-flipping proclivities—but better you assume I'm a master of deduction.* "So I'll think about going to this meeting, which is not the one I asked for. But in the meantime—Gwen—could you please quit dicking me around?"

And—when she's brought her tremulous hands under enough control to move on to the next message—there, instead of matters dental, I am again: "You know, Gwen, up till now I've been trying to hold to the idea that you're some-how clueless about what's going on. What's been going on a long time. Which, when the shit hits the fan—very soon now—would be the only way, if there is a way, you'd avoid going down with the others. But you've got me wondering. When you pretend you can't hear a simple message—I have to visit him at home, I said—then I'm tempted to bump you up to the fully knowing and willing category. Which is a different brand of coffee altogether. Have a nice day."

§

And since you're yammering to people about complicity, how about the complicity of seeing Christmas Music Wednesday and on Monday its makers are still running free? Normal office hours again today. Assuming they restrict themselves to office hours.

With a wrench of her stem-like neck, the Empress jerks her furthest fraction free yet. Muscular effort passes like a shiver through her shadowed far side. More smooth skin, yellow hair. And welling blood. *Blood?*

She can't wrench free and stay whole, both. It's fused or damaged. *Either or.*

§

the birds in the bone dungeon walk about looking for food they are always moving since they are always hungry there are no seeds and no farmers pellets and no kernels of corn the dungeon is a starvation chamber as the birds

"Can you remind me what they look like? Sometimes that's a good—"

which are hollow and have no necks and big heads walk around looking for food they break some of the bones by pecking at them and trying to squeeze through them this makes pathways that other prisoners can follow most of the paths are very narrow only the size of one bird but sometimes a path gets wider where several birds have been pecking and moving around in a circle

"Do they also get wider if they fly? Do they break bones by flapping their wings?"

the birds can't fly they are flightless birds like an ostrich but with big heads and no necks they have little wings but even if their wings were bigger they couldn't fly because they have no feathers instead the bone dungeon birds have little dark stubs sticking out like broken pencils

"Broken pencils?"

as everybody knows when pencils break off there are dirty little ends that are dark and shiny the hollow birds have these dirty stubs poking out all over through their skin when the birds peck at a bone that has become clear sometimes it breaks off if it is a thin bone and they peck hard enough inside a clear bone are drops of liquid that the birds catch in their beaks and swallow this is how they stay alive even though there is nothing else to eat they suck on the broken clear bone to get all the drops out one time one of the smartest birds pushed his body under the broken bone so that it would pierce his skin and all the drops would run into him after they saw that all the birds copied him even though some of them only did it once because it hurt too much the birds still peck at the old yellow bones not just at the clear ones even though the old yellow bones don't have any nourishing drops in them the hollow birds have very small brains when they swallow the drops they don't get smarter but their dirty skin stubs start turning soft and white and fluffy

"Are they turning into feathers?"

these are flightless birds so they don't need feathers also their wings are too small to fly even with feathers also there is no room to fly in the bone dungeon this is their home and they have lived there forever there is no reason for any bird to escape and no bird

wants to they peck to collect drops for nourishment but they are
glad when the dirty stubs turn white and soft the white is very
white and there is no other thing that is white in the bone dungeon
since the bones are yellow or sometimes clear and the walls of the
dungeon are gray and the hollow birds are pinkish brown so white
is a very nice colour to be and the birds are very glad

§

"Is this going to hurt?" Max says, looking in the direction of my voice.

"It shouldn't. Not really." I pause, the headphones in my hand. "There'll be some discomfort involved, but it won't last long and the freezing will block any stronger sensations. Isn't that what you tell them, a dozen times a day?"

"Who?"

"Your patients."

"I guess so. Something like that. But we're not in my office."

"No, we're not. We're in mine. Still, it's the truth. You'll experience some unpleasantness, but not for very long, and it won't be nearly as unpleasant as it would be for a normal person."

"I'm normal," he says.

Which can't help but sound odd coming from someone wearing safety goggles smeared with Vaseline, and oven mitts with which he's awkwardly holding open a book of poetry. He keeps shifting the big padded thumbs along the edges of the paperback, trying to get a better grip. It must feel constantly as if the slim book is sliding shut or about to fall, since he can't feel it clearly through the mitts. He moves his head about in a bird-like way—which I don't think he's aware of, since it would offend his vanity to show me this—trying to get a clear view of me through the unsmeared, or less smeared, slivers in the goggles. Like shards in a kaleidoscope, but worse, since almost every bit is blurred, and they don't repeat in any regular pattern.

Without answering his claim of normalcy, I put the headphones on him. 303 wouldn't lend me his iPod and ear buds, but I didn't want anything so sleek and contemporary anyway. He rummaged in his clothing piles and came up with an older-model player, slightly clunky-looking, and these big headphones that make the ears disappear completely and block out all outside sound. Perfect, I told him. I start the first of the two songs he downloaded for me.

Max starts tapping his foot at the sound of Stiv Bators's "Evil Boy." It's partly pure relief, no doubt, at finding something familiar in the sea of strangeness I've concocted for him. That sense of safe ground will vanish when I crank the volume to a painful screech—then abruptly drop it to a whisper like dead leaves—twiddling the wheel either way. Still, I realize I chose the wrong music. The Soft Boys' "I Wanna Destroy You" follows "Evil Boy." Max would have heard both songs in his early twenties, just as I did. And a return to punk rock sentiments, at any volume, is bound to stabilize him—any original venom long leached out to the man in the Clash shirt sampling Ukiyo-e sushi. It was stupid to think otherwise. I let myself be seduced by lyrical content—trying too much to make a poem of the scene, forgetting that the essence of successful rock is to devolve quickly to a danceable beat, minimizing all elements that distract from the groove. "Bitches Brew," my other choice, would have been perfect. Those random honks and squirts of disconnected sound, the ominous drums like geiger counters—what was I thinking? Miles might have composed that fearsome weirdness expressly for this smug white dude.

I thumb the volume up to maximum. Max squints at the pain in his ears. I can't see his eyes through the Vaseline, but deep creases appear below the goggle arms, his cheeks rising into his temples, his lips wide around clenched teeth. His hands come up to remove the headphones. I grab one wrist, reminding him of our deal. But I turn the volume back to midway—I can still hear it crackling from around the headphones—and then down to a mumble, a nasal mosquito whine only Max can hear.

And then off. A test.

"When does it start?" says the man in the cane back chair beside me. He's lifted the headphone away from one ear. He looks silly and helpless, and, with his shoulders slumping from humiliation and vulnerability, small. Much smaller, with an almost-sixty's inevitable pot belly that was not visible on the tall, trim-figured man I've seen till now. He received my condition of a little demonstration coldly—"a demand before the demand," he managed to sneer. But the altered and unpredictable state of his perceptions have sucked all the haughtiness out of him, reducing him to nervous dependency in less than a minute. Just as the book promised.

"Start reading when you hear the music come back on. Read the title and keep reading till you reach the end. Then we're done. This part anyway."

He sits there, waiting. Thinking it's not a bad idea to prolong his apprehension, I review the elements of the perception-skewing interventions recommended by the author of *More Than Memory*. An empathy-enhancing exercise, he called it, a way for caregivers and other loved ones to experience, safely and briefly, something of the totality of Alzheimer's. Max is beyond empathy, of course, but parallel experience falls within the realm of what I can arrange.

Blurred and narrowed vision—a "dimming tunnel, startled by strange sights." Check. Loss of motor control, dimming of peripheral sensations. Check. Auditory instability—abrupt bangs and crashes, weird whisperings—making noise of normal sounds. Check.

No way to mimic the sheer number and randomness of perceptual distortions actually comprising dementia, all exacerbated by diminishing powers of focus and attention, not to mention the cognitive inability to transform the incoming chaos into an even rudimentary order—but a start. *A window, however unsatisfactory, into the other's lived experience.* Check.

I look around the condo's main room. Dining alcove, where we're sitting. Kitchen. Small square living room with a window south—the CN tower off to the right.

§

"The Ship" the nickname people gave this condo, even before it was fully built, based on the artist's renderings mounted on the construction hoardings. The company probably encouraged the identification on its website. It looked most like a ship before it was finished—a hull with many of its glass plates missing and a skeletal, scaffold-draped superstructure, dotted inside and out with tiny workers—rising out of a messy, half-invisible berth in dry dock, poised on the crest of a concrete wave set to plunge down Bayview through the ripple of the 401. Its likeness to a ship is pretty rudimentary: slim, longer than it is wide or high, with a built-up section near the "bow" descending in stages to the "stern." Still, most times I pass it, driving up Bayview or along Sheppard in either direction, I think, obediently, *ship*. Not a cruise ship or even a freighter, but some kind of stubby glass tug. It's more imaginative and better executed, at least, than its older condo cousins clustered a little east across from the Bayview Village entrance. Those are ghastly. Bland, almost instantly shabby towers surmounted by pseudo-art-deco topknots that look like forty-foot-high hood ornaments—cold, bleak monuments to expensively senseless living. Still, they answered a question about fifteen years ago, when, for a couple of years, my roamings took me around North York. At that time, nearing the century's end, Bayview Village was a mall visibly in decline. Empty shops vacated by high-end tenants, Book Sales with remaindered paperpacks stacked on trestle tables spilling out of temporarily rented spaces, black holes like missing teeth between basic outlets like Timothy's Coffee and Shoppers. Shrinking numbers of people wandering around looking for bargains or having a donut on a bench beside an unwatered tree. The whole Village flapping like scrap plastic after the carnival's departed. And then—it happened within eighteen months—a turnaround began. Chapters moved in to peg down one end, construction started on a giant Loblaws at the other. A big new LCBO. Glittery women's fashion and shoe boutiques. A brightly-lit Asian restaurant. An Oliver and Bonaccini. And on the streets nearby—where the condos would go—bungalows dotted with Real Estate faces, and fenced off when sold, at prices that quickly encouraged their neighbours to follow suit. It was like watching a documentary film on urban development and the wages of inside knowledge. For a time, the decay and renovation happened simultaneously, proving that not everyone was seeing the same future, or at the same rate. Small retailers, made skittish by ignorance, saw a mall on its last legs making spasmodic efforts to revive itself, and continued to desert it, helpfully depressing prices for the speculators. But the sureness with which the largest bettors acted made the truth clear. Somebody—some people—knew things. Money in envelopes—or e-transfers by then—had changed hands. The fix was in.

Inside, Max's unit hews to basic condo design. A little lighter and airier thanks to more generous windows— the glass of the hull. And with a good view, since it's two floors below the penthouse. Otherwise, the standard cube of living room with kitchen and dining alcove extension. And the strange cramped sensation produced by eliminating corridors. No wasted space of halls at all—just a door in one wall to the bathroom, a door in the other to the bedroom. You realize the function of hallways when they're gone. Without them, you're always more or less stationary. Doing everything in one spot, right beside anyone else who occupies it.

At least it made it easy to check that we were alone. As did the sparse furnishings—which seem almost mandatory in a modern condo, totally unlike those richly cluttered and dusty New York apartments in old movies. Nowadays, any clutter is electronics or fashion-related. No overfilled bookcases or dishevelled stacks of magazines. No linen-draped tables crammed with tiered miscellanies of inherited antiques and knickknacks. From where I sit, I can see every object in the room, which, with its monochromes of glass (clear and frosted), polished metal, white pressed-wood and black leather, could serve as the developer's display unit or a contemporary, high-end hotel room awaiting its first guest. Even the two table accents— the jewellery, mostly silver, in a glass dish on the coffee table; and the artificial ikebana on the dining table where we sit, purple and yellow synthetic blooms spiked in a shallow black porcelain bowl—qualify as standard grace notes by a competent home stager.

The bathroom and bedroom show more signs of life. The former from the sheer number of tubes and bottles and jars of personal hygiene and beauty products, and the number of fluffy white towels hanging and stacked—small as the space is, it seems the warmest, most inviting room in the residence. The bedroom has outfits in dry-cleaning cellophane lying on the bed, and, behind a sliding door, a closet stuffed with clothing and footwear options. Multiple reflections in ceiling and wall mirrors make the space seem antic, if not as lived-in as the bathroom.

A minute's tour assures me Max is alone. There's nowhere for anyone to hide. Not unless they can fold up to gnome size and slide into the cupboards above the microwave, or curl inside the washer-dryer wombs stacked in the closet beside the entrance.

§

I push Play and thumb the volume wheel to midway. Max starts reading after twenty seconds or so, first moving his head about in that bird-like way, trying to find a crack of less-smeary goggle plastic, then, when he's got it, keeping his head at that tilt, like a robin listening for a worm under the earth, probably keeping his other eye closed to tighten the focus on the sliver of relative clarity. A smart guy. Quick on the uptake, and resourceful in a pinch.

> "To Waken an Old Lady
>
> Old ape… Old *age*… is…
>   a fright of small"

He waited a second before the second line, making sure he had it, then delivered it in a rush. Already realizing, after the mistake in the first line, that a quick run at the line gives him better odds against the blurs and the noise. He makes another mistake—an interesting one, like the one he caught, reading "flight" as "fright"—but I don't stop him. I thumb the volume to three-quarters. He squints against it, holding the focus-tilt he's found, but delivers the next line inaudibly, moving his lips but unable to hear himself over the din in his ears. I stop the player, and lift a headphone clear.

"What? You said one read-through. One read-through to the end." He says this without altering his head-tilt, which is away from me, as if he's objecting to a shape near the bottom of the door I came in.

"One *correct* read-through is what I said. Mangling doesn't count." *Disable yourself with these artificial impairments and try to perform adequately an everyday task, reading an address or telephone number, for example, or completing some simple arithmetic.* "Here's what we'll do. One tap on your arm will mean you've got a word wrong. Go back a couple of words and try again. Two taps will mean I can't hear you. Repeat it louder."

"Whatever."

And we get through it that way, with Max shouting to get over the screaming in his head, or when it falls away to mumbling before he can adjust. And shouting when he has to repeat something he thinks he got right the first time. And, increasingly, shouting whenever I touch his arm, for whatever reason. The effect is that of William Carlos Williams, the old man in straw hat and glasses on the cover of the book, becoming enraged as he declaims his quiet and beautiful poem at a complacent audience, screaming it finally into their stupidly nodding faces.

270

"To Waken an Old… TO WAKEN AN OLD LADY"

Old age is
a flight of small
cheering… chirping… CHEEPING BIRDS
skimming
bare bees… TREES
alone… ABOVE… a snow grave… A SNOW GLAZE.
Draining and flailing… GAINING AND FAILING!
they are buffets
by a park…
THEY ARE BUFF-E-**TED**
BY A **DARK** WIND—
But what?… WHAT?
On hard beef… ON HARSH WEED-**STALKS**
the shock… FLOCK has rested,
the snow… THE SNOW
is coored… CORED… COWERED… **COVERED!**
WITH! BROKEN!
SEED HUSKS
and the wind… AND! THE! **WIND!** PEPPERED!
PEEPERED! **TEMPERED!**
BY A SHAWL!… KRILL!… SHILL!…
BY!!! A!!! SHRILL!!!
PIP!!!!—ING!!!! OF!!!! PLEN!!!!—TY!!!!!!!"

§

A knock at the door. I answer it, Max throwing his gear off
behind me. A guy in a Nickelback shirt, braces on his teeth
though he's in his thirties.

"Whoa, listen man, I know it's only nine o'clock, but…"
Peeking around me. "Is everything all right?"

"Absolutely." I lean out and down, lower my voice. "A poetry lover. Got a little carried away. Sorry about that. Won't happen again."

"Whoa. Sure. Thanks, man." With a couple of slow blinks he shrugs off. A new kind of screaming from his occasional neighbour.

Max fixing his hair where the headphones flattened it, his fingertips hovering, air sculpting until a uniform soft hemisphere meets them. He's balder than I realized. It takes skilful sessions with a blow dryer and light gel to train outposts of fluff into that golden halo. Rings around his eyes left by the tight-fitting goggles are slowly fading. He adjusts his round glasses, which still sit slightly askew, one wire arm bent a little. Despite his dishevelment, he looks defiant. Or perhaps just businesslike and alert. A little impatient. Anxious to get on with it.

"I hope that's brought us back to where we left it Friday night," he says. "You keep returning us to the starting line, underlining it with heavier and heavier strokes. You can make my life inconvenient, even miserable—all right, you've made that clear repeatedly. Why do you think I agreed to your so-called 'exercise'? There was no need to display your box cutter. I'm quite aware—very aware—of what you're capable of doing to people. I get it. Okay? And it's quite beside the point when we both know you've got something I need and that I'll have to do what you ask—if I can—to get it back. You know what I want. But we're still waiting to hear what you want. And when, and how, we make the exchange."

His chatter like his haircut: skilful and elaborate, to cover up bald spots. But what if the bald spot's in me, not him? What makes him most nervous—makes him fear something he'll have no idea how to deal with—is the possibility that I don't want anything rational. Nothing a normal person might want, nothing that can be reasonably accommodated. Or accommodated at all. *A friend of Judy's.*

Vivian comes in. She closes the door behind her and sets down Loblaws bags. With a brief, incurious glance at the two of us—which must take in the headphones, goggles, oven mitts, paperback, CD player, and the Shoppers bag it all came in—she goes into the kitchen and starts unpacking the bags. Max doesn't watch her and they don't exchange a word. Not for the first time, I'm struck by the aura of telepathy that cellphones give people, especially couples, who use them habitually. Appearing and disappearing at prearranged times, performing scripted actions, speaking or not speaking on cue—all from a sequence of short calls and texts, invisible to the one not in the loop. It must be one of the technology's major attractions.

"I want," I say—and realize I have no way to finish the sentence I've started. What do I want? And how can I be asking that now, at this point, at this table? Have I forgotten what I planned, or was there no plan to forget? Either possibility is frightening. *Dangerous to begin an adjustment late in a window.* Yes, Stone, yes.

What I want. To acquaint Max with pain, *bring him the world*—which I've done only in minor ways, hassles he'd put in the category of nuisances, maybe even the "price of doing business." And beyond that—way beyond, it should've been—*take him down. Them* down. Off the street, out of business. Bringing in the cops would do both, and right away: close down Christmas Music and bring them all the world they can stand. World without end, amen.

Vivian crosses the room and enters the bathroom. I half-expect her to emerge with a weapon, a gun she keeps behind her face creams. Part of me hopes she does. But there's a click as she locks the door, and almost right away, the sound of the water running in the shower.

Max is right. I'm a guy at a starting line. Stamping his feet to show he's there.

Show who?

Rapidly, with a lucidity more frightening than any nightmare, a voice inside me ticks off a checklist of mental disintegration. *Catnapping two, three hours a night. Merging of sleep and waking, neither complete. Disruptive, obsessive images. Focus slipping, forgetting. Judgement—reeling. You're a day or two, a few at most, from total collapse. From Stone.*

And with a whirling sensation behind my forehead, a kind of cosmic cashier turns to me and looks up, I can almost see her face, her startled eyes—

Was there something else?

§

It is the Empress who gives me an answer to Max, lets me finish what I've started saying. She doesn't speak a word herself. Her thin lips have never once moved on my visits—she won't do anything that lessens her struggle even for an instant. But I find myself beside her on the dim stairs. Pinned in her raised niche, she is at eye level as I stand on the step. I don't lose the sensation of my hands flat against the cool glass of Vivian's table, or the sight, a background I can easily bring into sharper focus, of Max's impatiently waiting face. She has wrested herself further around. There is blood flowing from the far side of her face, which shows, beyond a curve of plump cheek, chewed-up skin flecked with grit. Like the cheek of a motorcyclist after a spill on gravel. Some of the blood flows down her neck into the shadows, becomes a dark line before it disappears. A thinner, brighter thread trickles out under her chin and down her thin neck, staining the high collar of her white shift. It is a bright, fresh red despite the grainy light.

Seeing it, seeing her, puts words in my throat. I think them as I hear them.

"I want," I say, "Judy taken care of. Taken care of for life. You'll set up a trust fund of two hundred thousand dollars. We both know that isn't much to live on, for however long she lives. But she's used to making do, and it will be enough. You'll invest it with a man I'll put you in contact with. He'll see that it returns at least five percent annually, maybe a bit more on average. That will give her eight hundred dollars a month. Together with her disability benefits, plus old age security in a few years, she'll have enough for what she needs. A small apartment, even. Maybe shared. We'll see. There's a lot to work out, including a reliable POA. But your part is the two hundred thousand, set up in a legal trust fund with all the necessary papers."

Max shaking his head slowly back and forth, starting from the first mention of Judy.

"You don't know what you're asking," he says. "It's not possible."

"I know exactly what I'm asking, and it's dead easy."

"Now, if you were to ask what I assumed you were going to ask," he goes on, as if I haven't said anything, "I could make out a cheque directly to you. Not for that amount, obviously, but for whatever figure we arrive at."

"Nothing's coming to me. And I've just told you what's coming to Judy."

The bathroom door opens. Vivian, dressed again, drying her hair with a towel, crosses the short distance to the bedroom, closes the door behind her. Max doesn't turn.

Again I expect her to emerge pointing something at me. Instead, I hear the thunks of drawers opening and closing, the chings of hangers on rods. Sounds of a woman changing her clothes.

"You don't know anything," Max says.

That sentence again. Old Faithful. "I know that two hundred grand is chump change to you. A rock bottom rate for Christmas Music. It wouldn't even add up to Judy's share of the estate, though I'm sure there's nothing coming to her there. The family's done too good a job at keeping her from money all her life to mess up now. So consider it a piece of her share, which went to you instead. Or take it out of your own petty cash. Streams from dentistry, from real estate, from other investments, from God know's what—and now, some huge chunk from your mother. C'mon, Max. It's coins under seat cushions to you. You won't even miss it."

Shaking his head again. His lips set. "That's off the table. We'll have to come to another arrangement."

"You're out of arrangements," I say, getting up. "That's the thing you people can never believe. That there isn't another option to click. If that's off the table, I'm off the table. And out the door."

I scoop the gear into the Shoppers bag. "I did what you asked," Max says. "Crazy as it—"

"You didn't do shit. I said your home, not your fuckpad."

Silence for a moment from the bedroom, then the dressing noises resume.

"What is this *obsession* with where I live?"

"I don't trust what I see anywhere else. With anyone that's true, but especially with you. I have to see home base, or else I don't see anything. What are you out here anyway? Credit card trails, fine dining experiences. Your *professional life*. Parking garages, ready-to-flips, fuckpads. Put it all together and it's nothing but smokescreen, squid's ink. I need to see the rock you flatten under at night, the crack you peer out from, before I can even believe in you."

"That doesn't make any sense. It sounds—"

"Insane. I know."

"All right. We'll do it at my place, if that's what it takes." Saying it in a tired voice, but sitting up straighter, as if energized by the thought of another round. In some ways I've underestimated him. He's like a slim reed. Easy to bend over, bend double. Hard to break.

"No, Max. We already did it—you did it—right here. The package is on its way."

"You lied to me."

"And you lied to the girls in your chair. They thought they were getting their teeth cleaned, not starring in your wank gallery."

"But… but…"

"You do a pretty good stalled engine. Keep practising it while you wait for the knock on your door."

§

Stupid. Stupid, as I'm going down in the elevator. You surrender any leverage you had without getting anything in return. Vivian your best hope now. Vivian and Max together. Unwilling to believe they've really run out of rope. It'll take a flash argument, followed by meandery seeping debates, but they'll get to where it's just my latest move, my starkest-seeming yet, the supposed last straw that announces the start of the endgame of real negotiation. *They have to, they have no choice.*

And have just about convinced myself when the elevator reaches the lobby.

A huge pale guy is filling the small couch opposite the security desk, a cellphone to his ear. He's enormous—*the biggest brother*. Somewhere between lineman and sumo-in-training. The phone a canapé in his palm. I sit down in the armchair kitty-corner to him.

"Uh huh," he says, after listening for a minute. Then says it a few times in succession, with pauses in between, as if confirming a series of instructions. "Uh huh… uh huh… okay… uh huh…" Midway through, he becomes aware that I'm just sitting here looking at him, and he stares back at me, his expression darkening.

After another long silence, he begins repeating things for the person on the other end, speaking slowly and louder than normal, as if to someone elderly.

"Red peppers… zucchini… kale… no, the other kind, I got it… mixed beans… brown sugar… Dad, hang on a second, will you?" Holds the phone out from his head, like a rock he's going to throw. "Excuse me," he says to me. "Do you have a problem I can help you with?"

"No, I don't. I thought I did, but it's gone. Have a nice evening."

15

SITTING IN THE graveyard with my back to a headstone, waiting for them to stop breaking things. The air strangely mild for the end of October, almost sultry, as if summer has forgotten its window closed five weeks ago and we're halfway to winter. Still. The closed-down way things get during scrambled interludes, when animals large and small stay hunkered in the nest, wary of pleasant conditions that make no sense. No stars at all, though the clouds are sparse and thin. Just thick layers of whitish mist that the streetlights turn in places to glowing cotton.

The heavy dew brings a chill. Quickly soaking my jeans and coat, releasing mould and caramel apple smells from the fallen leaves. Forming little clear beads on polished marble.

How long to wait? Till dawn would be prudent, let night's predators sign off—but my bones and joints are aching, muscles stiffening and cramping around the old injury sites. Shifting about, I can't get comfortable in any position for more than a few minutes at a time.

Upgrades to Peach and Lemon will wait a while, maybe quite a while, for me to return. But not as long as they should—which is as long as it takes. ADHD endemic to the breed.

It's the sluggard and the fool who counts the enemy's failings and calls that strategy.

Still, it's far from daylight, the slide and swing set just gloomy shapes beyond the gate, when I get up stiffly and start limping along Roselawn and down Latimer home.

Halfway down the first floor hallway, Mrs. Xue is standing outside 103, washing her door. Her door and the frame and a precise-looking foot of wall around the frame. She's fully dressed, although it's dark outside, her kerchief knotted under her chin. Bending to rinse her wash rag in a bucket of soapy water, standing much closer to the door than most people would.

Lucius is standing behind her, at the correct distance to indicate support without crowding her beyond endurance. He gives me a helpless shrug, drops his eyes. Behind him, Lucy's sticking her head out of the far stairwell. At the sight of me, she disappears.

Mrs. Xue and her husband are the most profoundly withdrawn people I know. I don't know how they could have met and married. Schizophrenic, or autistic, or some other combination of syllables that closes like a shell far above them. In their fifties—though, like all extreme introverts, they can look ancient or almost babyish at times—they live in absolute silence behind an embossed metal plaque whose meaning has always eluded me. It shows, in reds and golds, what look like two toddlers, a boy and a girl, but dressed in ceremonial adult robes, smiling as they embrace each other playfully. Mr. Xue will be as far behind that door as he can get, if not in a closet or in bed with the sheets pulled over him. I've rarely seen him. On the rare occasions when communication is unavoidable, Mrs. Xue handles it, usually in writing: propping an envelope with twelve post-dated cheques against my door once a year, waiting just long enough to make sure I answer her mouse-like tap. Sliding a request for a repair under the door, vacating the apartment while I complete it. When speech is unavoidable, her voice is quiet but clear and precise, to avoid the need for repetition or elaboration, and she flinches visibly from the effect of my voice in her ears. They shop at night, at one of the 24-hour groceries, and return by bus laden with bags. If anyone else is entering or leaving, they shrink against the wall until they pass, becoming slender silhouettes of negligible dimension.

A stranger seeing Mrs. Xue now might see a woman working so intently that she's oblivious of the two men in the hallway with her. Yet our presence is so intolerable, even at the distances we're observing, that she's quivering all over with the strain of keeping at her task. She's somewhere deep inside herself, atom-sized, cowering in a safe black space preserved beneath her rattling paper skin.

To relieve her, Lucius comes up by the entrance to talk to me. "They went up and down every floor, banged on everyone's door. Don't say anything, just banging a couple of times. Loud. A few people sleep right through. But most people wake up. Come out into the hall, see who's banging, maybe a fire or something. Some people got scared when they don't see anyone. We knocked on your door but there's no answer."

"I was out."

Lucius nods. He's speaking softly, barely looking at me. An honest man's mild rebuke. "Lucy and I get them settled down, tell them it's just kids, no problem. But Mrs. Xue..."

"Trying to wash them off her door." Now I'm the one nodding. Lucius is just looking at the floor. "What did they look like?"

"Big guys. Two of them. They were at the end of the hall." Flicks a glance up at me. "Your door," he says. "You want me to come up with you?"

"Thanks, but no. Go to bed. I've got it."

My guys. My problem.

I brought them here to soil Mrs. Xue's door. Brought them to where people were sleeping.

Time to put this adjustment to bed.

§

Upstairs, the door hangs crookedly, the jamb splintered above and below the knob.

Piss stains on the wall by the balcony door. Side by side, yellowish-gray, almost dry. Puddle beneath them. Reassuring somehow—hardly the seal of craftsmen.

Fridge and freezer doors standing open. The contents scattered in a circle, some dumped or smashed. Two veggie bags ripped open, bok choy and gai lan flung about. But not *the* bag. It's with some others in a puddle of milk and coffee grounds, the stick inside dry and intact.

Two blocks of chicken broth dumped out and thawing. Just two again. Two out of perhaps a dozen. These wall-pissers didn't want to get their hands too dirty. But no point in tossing a place unless you toss it all.

Wyvern hiring—Wyvern outsourcing—to the rescue again.

A shambles, all the same. The bedroom first up, and hardest hit. Bed and bedding thrown around, mattress and box spring knifed open. Curtains yanked down. Closet box of keepsakes and papers dumped and flung about. I close the door on it.

The Ikea sofa—lumpy and stained for twenty years—finally done. Lying on its back with short legs in the air, the frame and cushions sliced open wildly. Half-empty cushions thrown around, gobbets of stuffing like gray sponge cake. Coffee table upended, a leg kicked skew. Only the armchair strangely intact, lying on its side by the window.

Big Empty's talismans sent skidding around the floor. Too much space, and not enough things, for them to do much with. They found the USB when they tore the lid off "Precious Things." Before the kitchen, probably—it helped make them lazy. The original *and* any copies would have been stressed—but see their faces: stupidly pleased, leering at snagging the prize.

The butterfly wing frame smashed against the window ledge. Glass pieces and twisted wood beneath it, square of matboard. And—what's this?

Over in the corner, lying on its side, the single wing. A faded orange and black—it seemed brighter under glass. But whole. Not of interest to them.

Just as she found it. Northern rock. Scarred parquet floor. Still voyaging.

I stare at it a while, lost below thought. Then retrieve a sheet of paper from the bedroom mess and make a crude envelope, slide it in gently. Fold over the top.

One last place.

The empty inside Big Empty. Its empty heart.

Nothing for them to do in there. Yet fearful just the same. Knowing they swung hands with knives, kicked apish feet. *Knowing—*

I switch off the light before approaching the open closet. Sky brightening now. No light normally reaches it, not beyond what leaks under the door.

Move my hand through timidly. A pass across. Up and down. The nothing they found. It couldn't have detained them long. Moments, no more.

It's the one place air has substance to my hands. A solid shape it takes under my fingers, just for an instant, before vanishing. Like thinnest ice—melting at the first touch.

Close the door quietly.

§

It takes a couple hours just to put things in basic order. Decide what can be salvaged—not much. Start taking the rest in loads down to the garbage room. Bags of the smaller stuff for the bins, which are almost full. Tonight the garbage goes out to the curb for morning pickup. Their timing was perfect, that way. The wrecked furniture leaned in the niche for odd items and exchanges, an alcove of leftover space beside the garbage room at the bottom of the stairs.

Someone has left a mattress there. Not too old or stained, still fairly firm. I take it back upstairs and set it down on the bedroom floor, once I've swept and mopped it and let it dry again. I don't need it at the moment. The bag in Big Empty's fine for whatever sleeping's left in this window. But once the window closes I could be spending a lot of time on it. *Time you may not remember. But it'll go by all the same.*

I stand in the doorway, taking it in. The padded rectangle the only furnishing in an otherwise clean, bare room with white walls. It looks like a display, a piece of art—some kind of simplified statement in a museum—rather than anything normally meant by the word "bedroom." And I can't decide if it's beautiful or hideously ugly. A meaning in it hovers just beyond my reach.

The whole apartment's that way. Radically reduced. Aside from the appliances, just two pieces of sizable furniture remain: the mattress, and the armchair by the window. The rest had to be pitched.

What looked like the spare essentials of a management monk seem, in memory, almost cluttered. What would simple actually look like? Where—how—would you find it?

Maybe to answer that—to get closer to the answer—I bag all the keepsakes and old papers and journals from the closet box, even those not ripped up, and take them down to the garbage. The small bookcase in which I kept library books and magazines, and a couple of other small tables for setting things on—these go down to the exchange space, for anyone who wants them.

I wash the wall by the balcony. Then refill the bucket with soapy water and wash any other smudges. Sweep all the floors and mop them afterwards with Mr. Clean and hot water.

An armchair and a mattress. That takes care of sitting or lying. If you're not doing those, you're standing or walking—and plenty of unobstructed space for that.

Sleeping bag in Big Empty, for a guest.

Which is you at the moment.

I phone the guy I use for doors. A surprising number of them get smashed: thieves occasionally, more often going-away gifts or break-ups. He can't fit me in until next Thursday, he's too busy. For an extra hundred bucks, he offers an expedited service, but Ken's funds are already overstrained. And, obviously, the Owner is nowhere in the picture.

"Just the regular. Thursday's fine." And, after a trip to the hardware store up the street, I get the door fastened well enough with a staple and hasp and padlock, screwing them in above the splintered section around the knob. A hinge is jiggling loose, but that can wait.

If someone wants to smash through this, they'll have earned a used mattress, a twenty-five-year-old chair, and two weeks' of chicken soup.

The USB of Christmas Music goes in one of my top coat pockets. *Where it should've been all along?* Can't remember, at the moment, why I decided that was a bad idea.

§

Before heading out, I undertake a few repairs from my list. Partly because I'm in a maintenance groove, and partly to show the tenants I'm back on the job, that their super is no longer AWOL. From their dubious looks and sourly mumbled thanks, they're not buying it. Why should they? Where was I, after all, when assholes were pounding around the premises?

I knock softly on the Xues' door but get no answer. I wasn't expecting one. Putting my ear to the door, I hear—or imagine—glidings, sub-whisperings. Twin absences that graze the threshold of communion, silences rubbing against one another in endless consolation.

After a visit to the No Frills off St. Clair, where I restock what's needed to keep my meal plan going, I drive over to Mount Pleasant, south to Bloor, and then east over the viaduct. The anti-suicide mesh creates an effect of taut, stretched sails—but sails you can see through. The Luminous Veil, it's called—a name which, like my denuded bedroom, is either delicately beautiful or brutally callous, depending on my mood. Sometimes I see it both ways, like a coin spinning above me in a toss. A veil, luminous or otherwise, exists to screen something off from clear view. But what is being screened? Suicide? A life without suicide? Everything about the barrier has been ambiguous from the start. An editorial citing the moral necessity of suicide prevention, especially since most attempters, if stopped, do not make a successful attempt later—but the well-reasoned paragraphs concluded by adding that falling bodies often endangered motorists on the DVP below, traumatizing them if seldom hurting them more directly, and holding up traffic on an already notoriously congested roadway. Before the barrier, the Bloor Viaduct had more fatalities than any other elevated structure in North America after the Golden Gate Bridge. After the Luminous Veil was in place, suicides from that spot all but ceased. Yet the number of suicides by jumping from other structures in Toronto didn't change…

Mrs. Rasmussen is raking the yard on Selkirk Street. There are no trees on the lawn, but the wind has blown a few leaves and paper scraps onto the narrow strips of grass on either side of the walkway. More than necessary landscaping, it looks like an excuse to get out, get some fresh air, a little exercise. One of the residents is also standing with a rake, close to the edge of the property. He's just holding the rake loosely, staring down at the ground.

When she sees me coming, Mrs. Rasmussen comes down the walk. She holds the rake straight up and out from her side, like a soldier in a movie about the old aristocracy might hold a staff. She looks tired—beyond tired, burdened to the end of weariness. Her heavy shoulders slump in her cardigan. Like she's carrying the viaduct on them. *Oh no*, I think.

"She's gone," she says. We're close to each other, but still moving.

I stop walking. "When?"

Now she stops too. "Oh, no," she says. "No, no, no." She puts a hand into the space between us, as if to touch my arm or chest, though it doesn't make it all the way. For a moment, before she drops it to her side, I see it hanging in the air between us, like a third party that has floated in to take its part, not attached to either of us—this smooth, pinkish hand, which could almost be a girl's, though with dirt under its lacquered nails. "I mean, she's not here. She's left."

"When? Left for good, you mean?"

"I don't think so. She's always found her way back before. She went to bed early, just after curfew. But she wasn't here at count this morning." Mrs. Rasmussen looks back at the young man, who hasn't changed his posture. She turns back to me. "She does this sometimes. Goes off her meds. We don't see her for a while."

"Does she say where she's been when she gets back?"

"Sometimes. Not usually. We assume she's back on the streets. Turning tricks, at least part of the time. She often comes back banged up, though her weight's about the same."

"What do you do then?"

She looks surprised at the question. Perked up by it somehow, standing straighter, as if it's shifted some of the load off of her. "What else? Get her back on program."

Sun breaks through the clouds over the house behind her. Full sun still, a couple of hours till setting, it lights up her pink ears, makes them glow, purple veins in their tops, curly hair like thin silver wires around them. I feel it on my face. Clear, golden autumn. Except there are grains in the air—everywhere I look. Not as fine as dust, not as coarse as black pepper—like soot, maybe. They dim the light, float like a veil between my eyes and what they see. It's the same light I see on the stairs, in the rooms underground. It's the sun that makes it obvious. Light that should be clear.

§

Driving back through the city. Judy's home at the moment. A big home. Big and small.

Taking major streets—Bloor, Church, Yonge—for the same reason others avoid them at rush hour: because they're slow. The car a good place to be, to sit in, to see and think about things while barely moving.

Today, though, I feel tension driving. A strange kind of tension—maybe tension isn't the word. It's not a feeling of being strained, stretched hard or tight. It's more like fizzings, or pricklings—many small movements, in many directions at once, that have a sickening sense, something faintly nauseating, about them. I'm a while locating the feeling—it keeps running away from my attention, like beads of dropped mercury—and then I realize it's coming from my chest. My heart, the area around it. Or over it, more precisely. The pocket in my coat.

The USB.

It doesn't feel like what it is: a thin stick of metals and plastics, whatever carefully machined products they compress into this elongated wafer to store digital information. It feels like something primeval. Something nasty and unpredictable. Like a bunch of big red centipedes, the hairy kind with pronounced pincers, scurrying, writhing, trying to get out.

A boy in a schoolyard once set fire to the bottom of a big nest of tent caterpillars in the fork of a sapling. As the flames spread in the cottony lower layers of the whitish, semi-transparent nest, the ball of dark worm-like shapes separated and started to wriggle outward and upward, looking for escape from a structure they'd designed to have none. As the fire broke the nest open, burned bodies dropped to the ground, writhing and twitching. Using whatever legs remained to inch lopsidedly away. Caterpillars from the upper part of the ball, insulated from the flames by the burned bodies of the others, scattered like pinata prizes, scrambling away on small rushing feet. We stamped on them gleefully, turning them to green-black smears.

Nasty, veering sensations. They tell me the other reason I wouldn't carry the sticks with me before. Hid them in the fridge, hid them in the mail to Ken. *Even if someone takes you down, rumbles your pockets, they'll survive.* True—but not the whole truth.

It's also having the images against my chest, next to my heart. Faces and parts of the girls and women come faster to mind, seeping directly through the skin into the bloodstream. Stirring a soup of nasty feelings, of guilt, of dirty dealings, of fear. Faces, bodies, parts of bodies. I see them all, except for the images of Vivian—*why?* In Christmas Music she appears more often, and more nakedly, than any other woman. Its leading lady, in a way. But you've seen her as a person, cold and calculating, damaged and damaging who knows how—but whole. Not just a flesh bit, captured in a hole with a shutter click.

Things happen quickly once you know they have to happen. *Nothing to it but to do it.*

I buy another ExpressPost packet at a postal outlet I've never used before. In the line-up, I look up the postal code for the *Globe and Mail*'s address on Front Street, so the clerk can enter the charge. The *Globe*'s been lagging far behind the *Star* in the investigative journalism department—analyzing the skulduggery others have uncovered, and editorializing about political morality and public accountability, even the media's (their own) role, while the *Star* keeps on piling up juicy chunks from Hizzoner's dismal ruckus. Give the *Globe* a fighting chance to lead for a change, though I doubt they'll take it.

Pick up the two packages returned by Ken, which are waiting at the other branch. A new branch, it's still open nearing 5:00—showing the Avenue Road crowd it stands behind its banner pledge "to set a new standard for customized financial services." I don't even have to show any ID— the Face, once seen, is not forgotten. It could be a sight gag in a comedy about the world's worst undercover cop. The manager, still standing by the coffee urn and some picked-over muffins, gives me a half-hearted smile but doesn't offer me a cup and a nibble. His memory is perfect too, clocking me as a low-roller and a future-phobe.

Back at home, I slit the taped flaps of the addressed envelopes, just to check that the USBs haven't been damaged or exchanged for others in transit. Any trip through a chain of hands is a descent into Wonderland, with every kind of distortion and substitution possible. Nested inside their folded paper and bubble pack, however, the sticks look perfect, shiny and damning. Dollarama self-adhesive labels in the centers, Max's name and office address printed on them.

I re-seal the *Star*'s, and then, as I'm about to do the same to the one to the police, inspiration strikes. Take that stick and transfer it to the new envelope, the one going to the *Globe*. For the one to the police, I'll use the stick that's been giving me heart trouble—the one crawling with nasty centipedes. And I've got a better address label than the Dollarama white sticker.

A few minutes later, it's ready. Max's gold-and-black address label from the envelope with his Mother's Day card. Sliced off carefully from the corner where Gwen attached it, centered under clear tape on the third stick.

At 6 p.m., when I'm sure the last pickup has come and gone, I drop the three envelopes in the mailbox outside Shoppers. ExpressPost delivery is next-day within the city, so starting from tomorrow morning, I've got till Thursday to make something happen with Max. That seems unlikely, though, and at the moment I haven't a clue as to how I might proceed. It's peaceful, all the same, to watch the red mouth swallow the three packets and close with a metallic gulp.

Goodbye, Judy's brother.

§

The white dog isn't there, but a glance at the railing where he gets tied reminds me that Sandor is my next stop. He checks in at the Queen's Arms in less than half an hour. Hard to believe it's been a week since our last tête-à-tête. Seems like yesterday, seems like a year ago. Time in a closing window behaves like Silly Putty, stretching and squishing. Like an Eglinton Avenue mini-verse, Big-Banging out, Big-Crunching back.

After only a couple of blocks, though, I slow and then turn back. I don't have a plan with Sandor. What's more, I suspect—it's been dawning on me all along—that, while he's more interesting than the principal players, in terms of this adjustment, he's peripheral.

All the questions I had for him fall out of my head. Leave swirling vacuum behind.

§

Time in Big Empty is nasty tonight. Wrapped in the sleeping bag, I know I'm not asleep, and know equally I'm not really awake—and not being either place a human being is supposed to live, and knowing it, feels horrible. I sit up at times to give my state a cause, but it doesn't work. Sitting helps explain why I'm not asleep, but it doesn't explain why I can't wake up.

Even worse, I'm utterly alone for the first time in a while. No matter how still I lie, breathing deeply with my eyes closed, I can't meet the milling people, dead and alive, on the first floor down. Much less the Empress in her niche on the stairs below. Or the shyer, unseen shapes sensed even deeper. I can't find any stairs at all, or any means of descent. Not even an Ugly Dream.

I might as well be a flagpole sitter, perched above my life.

To escape it, I head out again. It's just after one. Closing Time. My feet take me towards the Queen's Arms without a plan or even the ghost of one. Empty Mind—nirvana, supposedly, if you're trained for it. Chinese water torture if you're not.

Follow him if he's on foot. Get a fix on one more Wyvern, at least.

But there's no fix on their kind of refrigerator, I realize on another mental track. On any refrigerator. It's either open, displaying what's spoiling slowly, puffing cold breaths out at you... or closed and sealed, a smooth white humming. Spotting it in a corner tells you jack.

Leaning against the wall of the Petro-Can across the street, I see Sandor emerge at 1:25. Right behind him, the blonde and her husband. That's a surprise, on a Tuesday. Don't any of these people have to get up for work? None of the other writing group members emerge, it was a mini-session. One of the groups within the group—the core one, I'm gathering.

As they pause outside the door, the blonde links arms with the men on either side of her. The streetlight catches her upturned face as she laughs at something Sandor says, leans her head briefly against his shoulder, her husband smiling along. Lynette? TAL Lynette? Even allowing for plastic surgery and diets and gyms and whatever other transformations twenty years can permit, there's no way I can make it work. Can't match this stunner tossing her hair with my chronic ward weeper.

I follow them as they cross Avenue and stroll west on Eglinton. No sign of a car. *A local job. Local at every turn.*

No sign of the white dog either. Whole families might subsist, and probably do, on dog-sitting wages in this neighbourhood.

I keep well back and on the other side of the street. The Face perched on six and a half bony feet draped in shabby commando—an illustration for Do Not in the undercover manual.

When they turn up Castle Knock, I have to cross over, but I stay at least two blocks back. They're engrossed in conversation. Have been every time I've seen them.

They turn left on Crestview, and just when I reach the corner to pick them up again, they stop. Brief hugs from Sandor, who heads off right up Shields Avenue toward Roselawn. The couple keep going west on Crestview. Holding hands now, which they weren't before.

On impulse, I decide to follow them instead. Telling myself I can always find a drunk—but really, it's because it's the first clear impulse I've had in hours, and it's a joy just to obey.

The blonde has a narrow waist and generous hips below her short plaid jacket. A languid rocking in her gait. Following her, I am suddenly somewhere else. Sometime else. Padding in sock feet after wide slow hips in a plaid housecoat as she shuffles in fluffy slippers down a corridor smelling of overnight disinfectant to the breakfast room. My eyes on her hips lust's fading silhouette, seeking solid flesh to become body again, to live on Earth. Lynette no more than the nearest, faintest chance.

Somewhere in the afterlife of crazy, Brad is doing a Putin riff to celebrate.

And then—just as suddenly—I'm back. Tracking two strangers down an empty autumn street smelling of cinnamon and damp. Knowing there's no meaning in the vision that just snared me—used to strange news from my head, especially in a closing window. But worn out from just that: the meaninglessness. Being in a blender that whirls and whirls, making nothing. It's why crazy at sixty feels like ninety.

They don't go far. Two streets on, at Castlewood, they take a right, following a parallel path to Sandor's, up a gentle rise toward Roselawn. *Castle* and *Rose* parts of a lot of place names in the neighbourhood—in a lot of wealthy neighbourhoods, I imagine. *Shields* fits in there too somehow.

They stop on the sidewalk in front of a house a few down from Roselawn. A trim brick bungalow with Tudor-ish mullioned windows that would set you back, with agents' fees, a million dollars. *But why stopping?* Why not heading in?

I get close to the side of a helpful maple, stand in its deeper shade, a hand on its cool bark.

They have what looks, from a block away, like one of those earnest couple palavers which are necessary to decide how many people are going to go down the driveway and in the front door. Without hearing a word, the negotiations are as clear to me as if I'm taking part in them.

The comfortable closeness of their bodies, combined with a certain weariness in their postures, a slumping seriousness I associate with health food stores and passport offices, tells me this is not a new couple debating, with fear and excitement, whether to go through the door for the first time, but an old couple deciding, in spite of history, whether to go through it yet again.

In a short time, without any sign of anger or protest from the guy, they hug and kiss, mostly air, and he goes to his car parked a little way up, gets in and drives away. She waves from the front step as he leaves, then enters her, perhaps formerly their, home.

I stay a little longer by the maple, liking it there. Spying what we called *good climbers* just above my head—stout horizontal boughs arranged in comfortable rungs—and wishing I had the spryness to ascend.

Wrapping my head around the fact—which feels like unsettling confirmation more than news—that I'm less than a five-minute walk from where I was twenty-four hours ago, sitting with my back to a gravestone—and about the same distance from home.

16

8:30. **GREEN LIGHT** blinking when I come in from the balcony. Chill hours out there felt endless. No sleep, no stairs. Dawn finally grudging a view of Latimer brick, the brown-orange of a scab. The firehouse door, the sun finding it from over Shoppers, the bright red that wells when the scab's torn off. But not flowing—halted instantly at the moment of trauma's gush. No scabbing, healing over, scarring—just an ever-fresh picture of bleeding. Never opening, not once through the long night. No sirens. I plug in and listen.

"Dr. Wyvern will see you at his home at—"

"No, Gwen, fucking hell, not this—" The voice continuing imperturbably through my outburst. I'm growling at a machine. I play it back again, holding the receiver out from my face, the woman's voice issuing from the top bulb. End it, and jab the first six numbers of the office, before I stop and slam the phone into the cradle. Bang—plastic hurting plastic.

Dunbar Road. The address fits. A bit rich maybe for a normal dentist, even a busy one, but not for one flipping condos since his twenties, and with who knows what family money on top of that. An inheritance from his father, gifts before...

Normally, one might think, the husband of a woman institutionalized with a chronic condition would leave all the funds for her unforeseeable care costs, let the children wait and split what's left when she passes. But "normal" goes out the window when the husband's willing to pack his wife away after a suicide attempt. A man like that—good at putting awkward things out of sight, paying for quality locks to keep them there—might just decide her care was worth exactly so much, set it aside for Max and Sandor to mind, and let the kids play with the rest.

Not the kids. The boys. Judy was packed away long ago.

The Wyverns, through their mouthpiece Gwen, sending me down another false, if more plausible, trail? I decide not. It feels right. Sweet Rosedale scent. Ivy-coddled brick and cocktails on leather loveseats. Lois's roots. And a neighbourhood I got to know so well in the first couple of years alone, creeping up and down its streets on my searches, sensing she and Megan would heal awhile in the family nest before venturing further, that I half-believed I lived there. A sense of borrowed home even last week, stopped on one of those leafy streets for the first time in ages.

A city of neighbourhoods. More than an empty civic slogan once you know Toronto. Forest Hill, Davisville, Rosedale, Riverdale, The Beaches. Regent Park, St. James Town, Chinatown, The Annex. Yorkville, Koreatown, High Park, Bloor West, Corso Italia—just a smattering, and you haven't even left Old Toronto. Etobicoke, Scarborough, York, North York and beyond… all subdivided into their own enclaves, each with its characteristic look and feel, customs, ethnic make-up, architectural styles, street life or lack thereof, languages, codes of conduct, levels of income and aspiration. Fitted close together, some as small as a few blocks long and wide—a few steps and you're in a new zone, no passport needed.

Except—you're always stamped with where you really belong. You can visit anywhere, but any neighbourhood not closely resembling your own will clock you as an outsider. No passport is asked for because you're wearing it, speaking it, doing it. Displaying it with every move you make and don't make.

No job is truly local. All adjustments occur on foreign ground.

§

Snag's in a place I've never found him before, the corner of Dundas and Ossington. I'm a while tracking him down, following some false steers from other vagrants. He's sitting with his legs outstretched with his back against the wall of the TD branch across from St. Christopher House. People have to step around or over him, but he hasn't got his baseball cap or coin can out. His gaze looks glazed and muddy, his thick hair matted and greasy. Snag goes through long periods where someone meeting him might well ask why he has to be homeless. No one would ask that today. Beside him, Sammy is curled but not tightly, ears pricked, hardly shivering. A plump woman with rosacea covering her face and patches of her bare, goose-bumped arms is sitting beside them. Close enough that I assume they're together, though they don't exchange a look or word while I'm there. She's sitting cross-legged, the crotch of her gray sweat pants stretched to make a little triangular table. On it she's fiddling with a key chain, trying to fix it maybe.

"Judy?" Snag says. Seeming to come to my question, to me, from a long way off. "You mean Sandy? There's a Sandy who does hand and mouth in the park sometimes."

Sandy? The only connection I can make is with The Sandman, Judy's anaesthetist father. But why would Judy, who barely inhabits one name, need another?

"When I say small, I mean tiny. Four foot eleven maybe. Ninety pounds. If that. Quiet little voice, whispery—when she does speak—and almost never any expression. Moves like a ghost, sort of gliding. Spooky."

"Yeah, I heard you the first time," Snag says. "And spooky covers a lot of people. Including you."

No light in his eyes, neither of hostility nor humour, and no hint of smile or challenge in his mouth, which moves like a puppet's. Dead man and straight man worlds apart.

"Strange dresses. Too long or too short." Snag's mouth moves around the words as if he's chewing them. As if he can't quite feel his lips. "And loads of make-up. Heavy."

"Maybe, yeah." *In certain phases*. "It sounds like it could be."

Snag shakes his head heavily, like it's filled with sand. "Don't think so, man. Your girl hasn't showed up."

A bank employee opens the glass door and approaches, timidly but with obvious intent. I don't stay to watch.

§

Lucius knocks on my door at 6:00, just as I'm about to go down and ask if we can move Jared's session up a bit in view of my appointment at 8:00. *The car*, I think when I open the door, but Lucius looks too uncomfortable.

"Jared doesn't feel well. Maybe getting a bit sick. He says they give him a lot of homework today. So maybe better skip tonight. Okay?"

Unpracticed at lying, Lucius gives me both excuses he and Lucy considered, forgetting to run with just one. But the glances he flicks at the splintered jamb tell me the real reason he and Lucy would rather keep Jared at home and away from me. *Only yesterday you let creeps in to harass people and break things*. Time plays ever more fantastic tricks when you stop sleeping. Everything happens in the same instant, an instant that can last eternities. Yesterday morning, later tonight, finding Maude and Judy eleven days ago—these don't stretch out on a string in sequence, but jumble and compress into something more like an atom, elementary particles zipping and jumping shells, trading places and energies, popping into and out of existence in a mostly empty zone of forces and probabilities.

§

Leaving just after 7:00, I find Jared waiting for me on the third-floor landing. Lucy is doing the laundry down the hall. Jared pretends he was just doing his homework while waiting to help her fold. He's a demon folder, able to turn fabrics of any size and shape into perfect rectangles.

"Don't you want to know how a prisoner escapes?" With his squinting frown, as if *I* cancelled the lesson.

"Of course. Have you figured out a way?"

"I *always* knew the way. I created the dungeon."

He hands me his writing book and pencil and we finish "The Bone Dungeon" that way, sitting side by side on the top stair. This time, I refrain from asking questions until the end.

if you follow the trails made by the birds long enough you will hear a strange scrunching sound it is a very strange sound of quiet munching and also soft slithering like a snake but much slower and heavier like something very big and wet moving slowly over the floor you may also notice that the floor of the cave is wet and sticky with a kind of slimy clear glue under your feet this is from the snail who you will now meet he is in a clearing with many broken bones he is very large about the size of a lion or small bear he looks like a normal snail with horns and little eyes and stripes on his neck but what is very peculiar is that he has no shell his back is the same as the rest of him the snail lives on tiny green lichen that grows everywhere on the walls and floor of the bone dungeon the lichen is microscopic that is why everyone just sees bare stone and is starving or else breaking clear bones to drink drops of nourishment it is also why everyone is trying to escape but the snail has never tried to escape and has lived there forever when he hears you approach he will stop feeding and ask you one question do you eat other animals if you say yes he will lower his head and start feeding again and you will wander forever and never leave the cave if you say no he will show you the way out and you can return to where you live

"Are you going to give some more details about the escape? How the prisoner gets out? Where he has to go or what he has to do?"

Jared looks pained. He always does, more or less, even when he's smiling, but certain questions seem to intensify his suffering. *Disabled*, or *learning disabled*, is a strange term to apply to him—a crude approximation at best—when his difficulty seems more like one of translation, not just of words but of thoughts and feelings. Of constantly meeting people from another world, or many other worlds, and struggling to find crude signs and gestures that will allow some sort of rudimentary exchange.

"Getting out is easy," he says. "There is nothing hard or interesting about it. The only difficult thing is answering the snail's question."

§

On Elm, half a block before Dunbar, the Honda quits on me. There's no warning, no sluggish churning, the engine just stops and I coast to a spot at the curb. I try several times but can't restart it. There's a brief buzzing sound the first time I try, and then no sound at all, just a click as I turn the key in its slot. I sit there, sighting down a double colonnade of old shade trees, their massy tops halfway to meeting above the street. Streetlights peeping companionably through them, like the warm yellow eyes of animals through ivy and sculpted shrubbery.

Peaceful. Nobody on the street. Occasional surf of cars from Sherbourne behind me.

What do I want? What can I get? Sitting in the dead car, I try to arrange the answers in my head. But they keep sliding out of sight—I'll think I have a firm plan and then it will slither into shadow, its edges running.

On the one hand, Wyvern money. Lots of it. On the other, the family's determination not to let Judy get her hands on any of it. The family, or just Max? He's the one with women problems—stick-fuls proving that. His balk at the figure of two hundred thousand—more than bargaining incredulity, it seemed. Would rather go to jail than enrich his sister. Of course, he doesn't know jail. Still…

Fifty thousand, I think finally. A cheque to Judy tonight, which I put in an account for her tomorrow. Salt it away before he's in stir. But how does Judy keep it—*or you keep your freedom*—when Max, with nothing more to lose, starts howling extortion? Unknown. *But if you can…*

Set it up with Ken so she draws down two hundred and fifty a month, say. Not much, but a lot to Judy. Better food, some treats. *How does a ghost treat herself?* Or maybe siphon off a bit of the principal, enough to kick it up to five hundred—until her OAS starts, five years or so from now.

Maybe—the best idea yet—get it in your name and parcel it out to her. Regular cash gifts. Keep it from queering her benefits. Avoid mad splurges. *How does a ghost splurge?*

Which means you keep on looking after her. An adjustment that keeps on adjusting. Commitment, people call it. Relationship.

There's a thought.

§

Flagstone walk—worn, with grass-moss strips anchoring the irregular shapes, like lead in stained glass—between neat hedges and flower beds. That warm yellow light flowing out from behind curtains through diamond-mullioned panes. Dark beams in stucco facing. The roof's low-slung, generous overhang completes the home's secluded, cottagey feel. Classy but understated. Cosy. I could be arriving for scones with Bilbo Baggins, rather than to shake down a perverted dentist who drugs young women and poses them in freak-porn shots.

I ring the bell beside the blond oak door.

"Dr. Wyvern?"

"No other," says the very tall, very old man with his hand on the jamb. Thin, distinguished-looking: dark slacks, cream shirt, gray cardigan. No glasses, despite his age.

"That's funny. You're the second one I've met this week."

"Max Junior is a *dentist*."

"Someone should tell him. He's got *Dr.* on his office door, *Dr.* on his business cards. *Dr.* on his bills, no doubt."

A long stare of appraisal ends in a thin smile. "Come in. I think we might be able to reach an understanding."

"I'm sure of it."

We're involved in a courtly dance from the start. Max Senior is a charmer, he makes it seem natural. Knows the steps and knows how to lead without insisting. Without any feeling of oddness or displacement, I find myself being welcomed by a man I never suspected was alive until a minute ago. Shrugging out of my coat, which I seldom remove outside No Name, watching him hang it in the front closet. Removing my shoes and sliding my feet into a pair of soft slippers waiting in a row of different sizes. When I straighten, he's eyeing me somewhat quizzically, with what may only be the mild puzzlement the wealthy sometimes feel in the presence of the poor. He's extremely tall. It's rare for eyes to meet mine straight on, unless they belong to a professional basketball player. I'm sure it's never happened with someone in his mid-nineties. Without apparent effort, he stands erect, shoulders back, no stooping. A Nordic face. Long and lean as the rest of him. Max von Sydow in *Three Days of the Condor*, except Max Wyvern Sr. still has a full head of hair, blond gone white, with platinum gleams in places, combed back with water. He doesn't look like any of his three children. Max Jr. would come closest, but besides having a more powerful build, the old man has stronger features, dominated by a Roman nose that would do a senator's marble bust proud.

"Follow me," he says. "There's really only one room in the place I occupy. Two, if you count the bedroom. I might as well be living in an apartment."

Which brings a dose of déjà vu. Jordan's eternal battle with Melanie to exempt the scruffy room he called his "cave" from her relentless home improvements. Insisting, with a kind of reverse snobbery, that even the grandest mansion needed one room that looked "lived-in."

Following the tall old man, his gait as steady as his posture, through the formal outer rooms of heavy furnishings, untouched except by the hands that clean and polish them. Into a small room at the back of the house, where a low wood fire burns within a hearth of smoke-darkened brick. Deep cream carpet, heavy brown drapes. Matching maroon leather armchairs and hassocks, scuffed and cracked with use, set diagonally before the fire. Photographs and diplomas on the dark-panelled walls.

"Well, now," he says after I'm seated. "You'll take a drop of Scotch, surely? I realize our business isn't entirely pleasant, but that doesn't mean it has to be entirely *un*pleasant, does it?" His smile stiff but gracious, under clear gray eyes tinged faintly with blue, like circles of spring ice reflecting sky. I like him, at least a little, and wish I didn't at all. He's sure his sons—most people maybe—are feckless wimps who can't hold a candle to their old man, and I'm sure he's right.

"Yes," I say without a moment's thought. And then have time while he's occupied at the sideboard to wonder at my answer.

Management monk's rule thrown overboard after twenty years, with what? Half a dozen lapses in them? Here? With him? With Maude's old X-face come to life?

A pseudo-mystery, since the answers come as promptly as my acceptance of the drink. I won't see what I'm afraid of seeing tonight—how I'm sure of that I don't know, but I am—and what I'll see I'm not afraid of. And, too: *This is the last adjustment.* The thought arrives from nowhere, a pebble dislodged from a wall I can't see, but it rolls to a stop in my mind and sits there, tiny and solid. Astounding. Not surprising.

"Look around if you want," says the man with his back to me, tilting a crystal decanter carefully, its stopper in his other hand. "An old man's not a nimble bartender. He makes a good drink, not a quick one."

The pictures on the wall arranged artfully. A group with complementary subjects or tones, then blank wall before another cluster, higher or lower. Some pictures set off to stand alone. Using space, symmetry and asymmetry, to guide the eye in focusing, help it wander fruitfully. What you want but seldom see in professional galleries, which mostly shun the adventure of looking to deliver safe display.

The subjects of the pictures are more typical: family life and cottage splendour. The latter celebrated not just in dock and picnic shots, but in scattered prints and watercolours. Muskoka Art. The same loon and sunset you can see for yourself, but here on your wall they remind you—and inform others—that you own them. Renters don't display them, no more than the childless put up baby shots.

Dinners, at home and in restaurants. Graduations. His retirement party. Non-cottage vacations: sun trips to various islands, hiking in mountains, a cruise with icebergs beyond the railing. Some pictures with handwritten captions—event, place, date. You have to know the family a bit to see how much editing and selection is in the seemingly comprehensive display. How much is left out to control the theme of the good and happy life. Like the principles of exclusion I saw operating in Maude's room at Vivera, though far more strictly here.

No picture of Judy alone, and none past what looks like her Grade Eight graduation, a frilly white dress with a pink bow between Mom and Dad in the garden. None of the boys past their thirties, the most recent probably the retirement dinner a quarter century ago, waiter-taken in a fancy restaurant. Lots of Maude—in bathing suits, in dresses before going out, in work clothes in her garden. But none past age sixty or so. And none of her early life—she enters the wall in a courtship picture with another couple, though Max is represented as a boy, a serviceman in uniform, a med student clowning with chums in a lab. And, in his life beyond Maude, as the esteemed and wealthy retired doctor and professor and current real estate speculator. Tall and lean, straight-spined. The wave of lush white hair trained back from the proud angular face. The clear gray eyes. Haughtiness, tempered by courtly restraint, gives him an aura of suffering dignity. Of burdens bravely and stoically borne. Two photos were taken beside pools. In the first he's alone, with four medals around his neck above a caption in ceremonial script, like that on a diploma: *Hart House Swimming Club Freestyle Champion, Senior Division, 2009–2012.* His expression and posture send a double message. The wry, self-deprecating grin: *Yeah, not bad for an old fart, I guess.* The crossed arms and lifted chin: *Don't forget, Seniors starts at seventy, and over ninety I still whip 'em all.* The other poolside photo is at a resort, also sometime in the last few years. A speedo bathing suit concedes the minimum to age. Flesh sagging where it must but without fat. Nothing but sinewy strings of self-preservation. More fat on the brown-skinned woman on the chaise beside his, though most of it in the right places: plump breasts and thighs in a bikini that should be wrong for a forty-something, but she pulls it off with a languid sexiness.

The stringy tanned man reminds me of magazine photos of Ramses's mummy. It's partly Judy's *Sandman.* But it's also the sense, uncanny, of extreme power still managing to project itself through extreme dessication.

Four walls of pure egotism. Undiluted vanity and self-absorption, whose overall title might be: The Ascendance and Continued Ascendancy of Maxwell Wyvern, MD. The profusion of other people blurs the theme at first, then underlines it. They enter and exit the stage according to how well they support its main business. Three little kids in Christmas cracker hats grinning as Father carves the bird and Mother points slyly at his crooked crown. The same kids in life jackets, a bit older, at the back of a big wooden boat, Father and a male friend water-skiing behind, knees bent as they prepare to jump the wake. Max and Sandor welcome even in their challenging primes, tall and fit young men in their early twenties and late teens, both with long hair then. The sixty-year-old standing between them at the end of the dock —all three dripping and grinning, the lake behind them—shows the origin of their swimmers' builds, though he stands a head taller and may have just won or certainly made interesting the impromptu race to the point.

The devil raped me. She always said it matter-of-factly. Never insisting, never with any emotion at all. It might be news to you, but to her it was an everyday fact of life. *The devil raped me.* Is this Judy's devil? One of them anyway?

News in a closing window comes unbidden. Or more unbidden, since all true information is gathering out ahead of you, waiting for you to pick it up. Words. Pictures. When the window's almost shut, they arrive as confirmations from remote places, instants of sudden light that tell of cataclysms eons ago.

"Drinks are served. If you've had enough of my rogues' gallery, come have a seat."

Neither of us ventures a toast, but we clink glasses. The first sip. He closes his eyes a moment to savour it. So do I. Like a warm storm unrolling across the sky.

"Good, isn't it? Lagavulin. With just a sprinkle of water to open it up."

"It's wonderful. Like sipping a campfire."

His eyebrows rise and he nods appreciatively. I might be a resident who surprised with a shrewd observation. "Exactly. But in all Max told me about you—quite a bit, as you can imagine—he never mentioned a poetic streak."

"Max doesn't bring it out in me."

Another nod, a rueful smile. *My son, the disappointment.*

The second sip, rolling it in my mouth, brings a vivid picture. Jordan's face over a brandy snifter, telling one of his stories. In that brief phase when I was being inducted into the family, into a promised life, he and I repaired after dinner to a nook like this, muted talk and giggles from Lois and Melanie doing the dishes nearby. They must—when they got to the stage when they could mention my name at all—they must have asked each other how I could have turned my back on such a life. The honest perplexity the privileged feel in the face of misfortune, since a large part of their own good fortune is the delusion that choices and talent and effort were its chief architects. Why would Snag—why would anyone—choose to live on the street? In a cell? Why would they *choose* not to?

"You have a nice house here. What I've seen of it anyway."

"Thank you. I'll take credit for the purchase and a little of the decorating. But I haven't done a stitch of housekeeping in years. And not a lot before that, I'll admit. Oh, I'll pull up my sheets in the morning and microwave some soup if someone else makes it. Even rinse my bowl and put it in the dishwasher. Men get lazier as they age. Women too perhaps, but not as quickly or as drastically. At least, that's my experience."

I look around me. At the bits of a couple of rooms I can see through the door. Up at the ceiling.

"I gave Iris the night off. She's gone to visit a relative in Mississauga."

"Well, now," he says, setting down his glass and placing his hands on his knees. Hands that show all their years: you can't do laps for hands. "I think it's time to move past niceties. I've never been slow, nor do you strike me as slow, to get down to the business at hand. And it's hardly home appreciation that brought us here."

Actually it was precisely that. But no way to explain that to him, and anyway, I agree it's time to move out of his charmed circle. I extend my hands in a *Go on* gesture.

"Poker faces don't fool me, even expert ones. So I know you weren't surprised when I answered the door instead of my son. And yet we've never met. A small point maybe, but I'm curious."

No way to tell him about the transmissions in a window, especially a closing one. The swiftness and sureness with which you catch up to what you already know, to what part of you has travelled to and understood ahead of the rest. Or even the acquired sense of deepening Wyvern dirt, always another layer of crawling things hidden below what you think is the last. It had never occurred to me—not consciously—that the patriarch might still be alive. But a sense of forces pushing people around, a compelling demon or demons—that's hovered behind every Wyvern I've met, including Maude. It came off Judy twenty years ago on Ward 4A. Like a shadow I could see, with the eyes I had then, behind and above one of her shoulders, then the other.

"I'm used to getting the runaround from your family when I ask for a home visit. This is just the latest twist. Gwen gives me the message, but it's someone else giving me the business."

"Poor Gwen. She's never quite accepted that she's not part of the family anymore. Though truth to tell, she never really was."

"You underestimate her. She knows exactly where she stands. And you can hardly blame her for not being able to compete with Vivian. How many women could?"

A flash of something in the gray eyes at Vivian's name. For a second, they look molten. Something Max Junior has that Max Senior likes? Or liked. Something he wants to have. Have again? *Hit this guy with surprises. Knock him off the podium he likes speechifying from.*

"The other trend I'm getting used to is Max and Vivian using cheap help, then, when that craps out, getting something a little better. They're sloppy employers, sloppy workers. Instead of picking the right tool straight off, they blunder their way up to it."

A pause as he takes two long sips. Getting himself under control, I think, though he does a good job of imitating a man merely savouring a single malt. Cups the tumbler in his palm. Exhales in a long sigh.

"My children. I love them dearly, but they are... disappointments. Good people. Some of them." Sucking a cheek, nodding in concession. Could play a retired judge. "But weak. Mentally. Morally. Both, sometimes."

"*Dearly*. Now there's a red flag word."

"Excuse me?"

"Forget it. Go on."

"I heard you."

"I know you did."

For two seconds the gray eyes harden into rivets, pinning me fast.

He sniffs, a long inhalation while he lifts his head. "They're duds, to put it crudely."

"How so?"

"You've met them, haven't you?" He holds up a spotted hand, ticks off the defectives on his fingers. "Judy, my first. Troubled—a serious medical condition, no question—but she did nothing to help herself. Did one thing after another to make things worse. Drugs. A parade of men. Shutting my door to my own daughter was the hardest thing I ever did, and I did it years too late. I don't know how many times I tried—"

"But after that dud you got a doctor," I say cheerfully. "One for two isn't bad."

The gray rivets again. Not someone used to being interrupted. Not by sleeping patients, not by scared residents, not by real estate agents hungry for his business.

"Max is a *dentist*." A dry, mirthless chuckle. "Medical school was a bit *too* challenging. Particularly when you've been caught buying an exam your second year."

For an eyeblink I feel pity for Max. For anybody bringing their case before this hanging judge. "Sandor, then," I say. I hold up three fingers of my own. Ticks to tick him off. "English teacher. Published author. And he took good care of his mother. For a long time."

"Phh. Every glass he raises—and he raises many, as I'm sure you know—should be to the teachers' union. What other profession lets you stumble around, teaching the young between 'breakdowns,' and then puts you out to pasture with a lifetime salary when it all becomes just too much?" He pauses, looks through the air in front of him at something faraway. "Maude. Yes, he was good to Maude. I'll grant him that. Good to her. For a long time." Then the judge returns to the courtroom, and the hardness with him. "But not long enough. That's Sandor in a nutshell. A well-meaning sprinter, forgetting life's a marathon. He always gave up too soon. He wasn't a runner, but he was the same in tennis and football, as I recall." Swirl of the brown liquid in his glass, then he downs it. "Truth to tell, I haven't seen my youngest son in years. I gather he held his mother against me. Phh. As if I were master of her neurons. But weak men cling to grudges."

Old man or no, my hands start to curl into fists. Past time to change the subject. But he does first.

"Listen"—with that thin smile not without charm, a more than professional warmth. "We can anatomize my fallen children all night long, but believe it or not, I invited you here tonight to help them. Help them from you, quite frankly. You seem to have stirred them up a lot."

"Pay me to stop stirring?" I say.

He doesn't flinch from the word. "You don't strike me as too rich to… compensate. Or too stupid, either. Why don't I refresh our drinks and we'll put this on another footing?"

17

A LONG, MEANDERING conversation follows, that visits many topics yet does not feel disjointed. More like water flowing down a slope, finding the cracks and gullies it needs to make its way to the bottom. It feels relaxed, even convivial at times—sensations too pleasant to kick against more than feebly. An atmosphere of permission reigns in which, it seems, anything might be said, partly because we are speaking outside of time. Clock time has disappeared, or been paralyzed, and we can ooze like droplets of oil through the gears of its stopped mechanism.

It's partly the Scotch, of course. Not making me sleepy, not taking me anywhere near sleep yet, but tucking me back into my body where sleep is at least a possibility, and where I dream with open eyes. I see no pictures: I live them instead. Smoke in the glass is smoke in the fireplace, the warm bloom in my chest is the orange ember in the grate, and fibers of hazy silk enfold me irresistably, building the rich shielded dark in which every transformation is possible. In which, second by second, you change utterly, from something you can't remember into something you've never imagined.

Our formal business, the purpose that brought me here, is quickly finished. That helps to set us free. "Under other circumstances," Dr. Wyvern allows, he might well have written me a cheque. "To spare my son another disaster. Disasters brought on, always, by his own self-indulgence. I've kept him from taking his lumps before, I'd be ashamed to tell you how many times." But a cheque to *me*, not to his daughter. You see, he could never be sure money given to me would not find its way to her, and that he refuses categorically. She saw her last nickel from him long ago.

I bring up the peculiarity of Wyvern nomenclature that I've noticed before. Referring to one another not by their names but by their family roles: father, brother, sister, mother. They might be talking about positions in a company too large or too impersonal to go beyond functions: the VP, the secretary, the janitor… Dr. Wyvern listens, head tilted, fingers laced under his chin, as if to an interesting digression in a lecture. Nodding, he says that undoubtedly some families have to develop ways of calling each other that go beyond given names, names that appear on birth certificates and driver's licences, names that anyone on the street might use. Especially families bound together by shared sorrows. Families trauma has pushed too close together, while keeping irrecoverably apart.

"And Judy was the worst sorrow? The worst trauma?"

"First, and worst. It shattered us, he says, looking into the fire. Shattered our family. It came at the worst time or the best time, I've never been able to decide. There's no right time for catastrophe. You're always equipped in some ways, unequipped in others. I'd just turned fifty, was entering the peak of my career. My wife wasn't forty yet, with a son just starting high school and another still wetting his bed."

"And your daughter was diagnosed with schizophrenia."

My voice sounds strange to me as it says this, ultra-distinct but distant, like an airport announcement. Dr. Wyvern's voice when he replies is just the opposite: hushed and intimate, like an insect whispering in my ear canal.

"Schizophrenia. There's a disease with the perfect name, for once. A poet might have named it, someone like yourself. Schizophrenia. It sounds like mumbling in a foreign language. An alien language. Which is exactly right. The person you knew is gone, vanished before your eyes, though she still looks much the same—at least at first. Leaving this alien mumbler, whisperer... screamer. But the illness itself wasn't what hurt us most. We were a medical family, after all. And I consulted my colleagues in psychiatry. Not a specialty I'd ever had much use for, but I respected them more—a little more—when I saw what they were up against. It was all the things my daughter did to me, did to us, that hurt the most. That finally forced me to give up on her and bar the door. Running away from home one morning. Not a note, not a word for my wife. Taking up with boys, men—God, squadrons of them. Abortions courtesy of our new socialist health care system. Drugs. Street drugs she took, and prescribed drugs she didn't. Hateful letters, phone calls. Visits at two in the morning. And then just when you're ready to give up the ghost—our daughter is gone, she's died, we tell ourselves in the middle of the night, we have to accept that—she's at the door, she's turned the corner. Clean clothes, clean hair. A new resolve. Back in she moves. For a few weeks, a month or two. Usually just long enough to decide what to steal from us. Her mother's jewellery was a favourite. Small. And her mother willing to look the other way far longer than I was. You see—I knew her. And by certain looks I'd catch, which my wife could never believe, I knew that if the illness was using her, destroying

317

her, there were times, not infrequently, when she was using it. When she'd do exactly as she pleased and call it sickness. Of course, soon enough, it would be. And I never knew which was worse: sickness through and through, or sickness as a robe you wear."

A long sip, a long look into the fire. "It broke our hearts. She broke our hearts."

There is no communication between the compartments of the mind. People will say anything, and seldom are they lying.

"But you can't be a stranger to this yourself, can you?" says the close, whispery voice. "To these kinds of matters? My son didn't supply many details, but I know you knew my daughter from the hospital."

"Not a stranger, no," booms the voice in empty space. Empty space that, I notice now, is pierced by a visual tunnel, at the end of which sits Dr. Wyvern, a small shape in a telescope ring, surrounded by velvety shadow trailing veil-like shapes across him. *Closing window stuff. But coming on fast. The Scotch a drastically bad idea.*

"And forgive me, but since we're speaking frankly— besides your facial disfigurements, your movements are quite stiff, even for a man of late middle age. I saw it briefly in your gait, I see it even in the way you sit, raise your drink. A stiffness in your neck and shoulders. How you carry yourself. Pronounced swelling around your knuckles. Your little finger. Advanced osteoarthritis—from repeated traumas, I'm guessing. Yet I'm also willing to bet you don't see a doctor for any of your conditions. Am I wrong?"

"I have a low opinion of doctors, it's true. But then, by their words and actions, they've had an even lower one of me. Ask Max."

"My son's not a doctor, he's a dentist. We've been over that."

"There's a doctor in front of his name, same as yours."

Dr. Wyvern sniffs. "There's one in front of a professor of Art History too."

The Empress staring at me with one unblinking eye and the corner of another. Blood streaming from the mangled flesh of her face. It's not seeing, it's a memory of seeing. There's no mistaking the two. And is it that distance, the space that memory allows, that makes me wonder if she's tearing herself loose at such cost not just to be free but to warn me? To be with me somehow. On the stairs. And Gwen's voice saying: *He's just like his father.* To warn me too?

Hard to imagine two more unalike. Yet not strange— not at all—to find them here together. Acting in concert. *Why not strange?* The question flits and vanishes, a moth.

Wake up, they say. *Wake up and tear the cocoon before it dries.*

"Was it only dealing with unconscious people that perverted you?" I say to the old man slumping with half-closed eyes beyond the tunnel, our knees almost touching. Forming the question feels like stages in a grammar exam as I assemble it, deliver it, and start working on the next: three phases that extend in time like a complex construction project. "Or was it perversion that made you want to only deal with people who couldn't deal with you back?"

He sits up straighter in his chair. Obviously he feels the Scotch far less than I do. *If it's just Scotch.* Keen and ageless as a gray-eyed hawk, he looks poised to swoop down upon a field mouse or sit a final exam.

"I'm an organized person. Careful. Always have been. You should try it."

"I know you are," I say, and find an adrenaline surge of fluency. "Your photo wall can tell me the day and even the hour you summited Kilimanjaro. The day the College of Physicians and Surgeons awarded you your specialist's degree. I know another wall, probably in the kitchen, can tell me where you're eating Christmas dinner, catching your next flight to the Caymans. Yet Maude's got—Maude had—a calendar two months out of date on her wall."

The old man covers his face with his hands and hunches over. Overcome by emotion? Or by the need for a private place to work at seeming so? No way to tell. Griever and actor identical behind the screen of hands. Long, laboured-sounding breaths, but no tear trickles down a seam in his sunken cheeks. Eventually, he lowers his hands to prayer position, chin behind fingertips, and murmurs of his wife's long struggle, his despair at witnessing her decline. "You see, she was a depressed person, deeply depressed and for many years. I'm afraid I wasn't always the help I should have been. Out of my depth with psychological ailments, and too busy and tired, wanting a cocktail and my supper when I finally got home and not understanding if they weren't waiting for me. Selfish. All ambitious people are. But she was a brave person, my wife. Possibly the bravest person I've known. The day her dementia was confirmed, she told me in a way she felt relieved. She'd known there was something wrong with her mind for years, something besides her 'dark pits' as she called them, and she thought she was going crazy. Like Judy, she didn't need to add."

It's a strange story to listen to while remembering Danika's account of Maude being sent away after her suicide attempt, long before her diagnosis of Alzheimer's, which she heard with Danika and discussed with her over lunch. Like watching two films of the same event. There's no doubt which one I trust, but it's a question of vividness. The one I trust is a memory in my head, a memory of a conversation with pictures I supplied, and the one I know is false is acted by a real man showing the devoutness of remembered pain right in front of me, full colour, full sound, I could reach out and touch him if I wanted to.

Dr. Max Wyvern Sr., emoting on the stage of his illustrious life. Judy and her secret dramas in which you play a role in her time, according to her needs. Something deeply alike binding father and daughter, for all the deep and terrible differences dividing them.

After a bit more in the same vein, his voice trails off and he lets his hands fall into his lap. Closes his eyes and seems to go to sleep. His thin lips parted. His chest beneath the cardigan rising and falling slowly. Like a baby after it has cried itself completely out.

Like looking at a death mask, except for the slow breaths. The throat wattles, the liver-spotted skin, waxy beige beneath the snow-white hair. Flesh all but melted away, just a stretching of wrinkled parchment over the surfacing juts of brow, nose, cheeks, and chin.

The sight jolts me into speech, though the voice I hear is thin and slurred.

"Wakey, wakey, Sandman. Time to come down off Bullshit Mountain."

Opens his eyes slowly. Like an owl summoned at the wrong time of day.

"I wasn't sleeping, I assure you. There's a world of difference between sleeping and pondering."

"What was your great brain pondering this time?"

"Where I'm going to put you. This house, spacious as it is, is already crowded. Fifty years of life in it. Most of the nooks and crannies have long been filled up. Including the extras I had to create myself. And you're... bulky. Not broad, certainly, but very tall. An inconvenient length, let's say. You'll be forcing me back to basic anatomy. Never my favourite subject, I'm afraid. And many long years between me and the lab."

"You talk too much. And we both know you've stayed in constant practice with anatomy. It's what your skinny ass has lived for."

Aluminum. The colour of his eyes. The faint blue shine it gets when buffed.

"Come to me, boy," says the mouth below them. "It's time you saw a doctor."

Boy. Yet I do. I try to. A feeling of pouring sand in my head when I lean forward. Slush where my legs were when I try to stand. The leather seat cushion puffs—*haa!*—when I sink back into it.

"Midazolam." My voice a reedy blur, all boom and distance gone.

Shakes his head tolerantly. "You keep confusing me with a dentist. An anaesthetist has a few more resources than someone who pulls teeth."

My brain sends signals to my legs—Stand! Run! Kick!—but nothing happens. Not even a muscle twitch. Just the slush where my legs were, a cold jelly, rising.

The pouring faster in my head. Sand pouring through it, or my head pouring through sand. Grit swirl across vast spaces behind my eyes, the bright narrowing tunnel in front of them, like a tube sharpening focus as it closes. Dr. Wyvern at the end of it: hands clasped, fingers interlaced, his face all pious absorption as he observes the stages. So familiar, yet so individual—no two cases alike. Cold jelly below my neck.

Getting what you came for, after all.

§

A click. Clicks. Faraway.

Checks his watch. "That'll be Iris, I expect. Later than usual, but she almost always forgets something essential, even for an overnight. Back she drives with her sister to pick it up." A searching look from the end of the tube, quizzical. All the intake docs I've met in the peering eyes, furrowed brow. "She's discreet, always. Lets herself in and out. I don't think you'll have a voice, or much of one, but go ahead and try if you want."

A lie. But why bother now? Muffled sounds from the next room. Someone moving. Drawer, cupboard. Wooden slides and knocks. *No Peach and Lemon this high up. Qualified fruit only.*

It's the last clear thought I have. After that I'm all eye.

An eye watching a film, or many films, with fizzing white between them. Either I'm losing consciousness at times, or else my mind simply blanks, balks white, at what it's taking in.

Seeing Judy, red and white, glide into the room and up behind her father. She doesn't rush, yet he gives no sign of registering her presence. Hand on his forehead, a small priest's blessing, and then something very long going back and forth, back and forth, under his chin. A long, long carving knife with a bone handle. She saws but doesn't strain, he must keep it sharp. She might be bowing a violin.

I close my eyes and greet a sickly jubilance in the dark. TAL rides again. Judy taking it further than you ever dared. Who else? Lynette nearby, connected somehow. Oh Brad, if you could see us. I feel a falling sensation, an all-over plummet inwards from the cliff of my skin. I open my eyes to make it stop. Judy still sawing unhurriedly. Back and forth. Back and forth.

Blood sheets the front of him, drenching his shirt and cardigan. Sprays when she hits the artery. One jet hits my knee, another the floor between us. Then they fall closer to him. He makes a brief high sound, a whistling hiss. The blood pours down, pooling in the leather triangle between his thighs, soaking into his slacks.

An interval of fizzing white, the longest yet it seems, but beyond it Judy still tilting his head and sawing again, or starting, time is looping on us. Dull white gleams through the red as she exposes the knobs of his spinal cord.

Watching, I am frozen in stone. *You are the Empress. This is where you live.*

His head lolls back on a rind of skin. Perpendicular to his body, it perches on the top of the chair like a thing set there, staring up at the ceiling, blood running along the leather and away down the chair back.

Judy gives the head a gentle push—or he moves it a last time, to hide his terrible wound—and it flops forward to hang at another impossible angle on his chest, dangling from its skin shred, his features lost in gore.

It's over.

I never saw his eyes, the expression in them. They were tilted up at Judy.

His hands rose just once, halfway, then dropped back into his lap. As if to say, *All right then.*

The blood on the knife the same red as her jumper. She doesn't seem to notice it trickling past the guard and down the bone onto her hand. Her white frilled blouse again, filmy scallops swirling around her chin. Antic now with spatters and mad red polka dots.

She's peering intently to my left, as if someone or something a little taller than herself is standing there. Smiling shyly, almost demurely, as if what she sees is nodding approval. She holds the knife aloft, awaiting further instruction.

No idea how many men are on her list, or should be.

Close your eyes.

§

Open them again, she's sitting in a straight-backed wooden chair, a dining-room chair it looks like, between her father's body and the door. She sits slightly behind and to the side of him, as if they're taking a car ride together. She is sitting up straight, her patent leather shoes close together, her bloody hands in her lap. *First day of school.* Still staring upwards at that spot beside me. There's no movement in her body, no expression on her face. Her marble self. There's no sign of the carving knife, but she holds my finishing hammer in her lap, one small red hand around the grip, the other on the shaft.

An instant. That's all that's passed, I think at first. Like drifting off in a movie and waking up a second later, the scene slightly advanced.

Except that can't be. It's wrong. Too many things have happened. She took the knife someplace. Found my hammer in my coat pocket. Brought in the chair. The blood drenching the corpse slumped opposite me's sticky-looking where it isn't dry. Dull, not shiny.

And the fire dead. Gray ash, black chunks of wood. My neck stiff and sore, spiky jabs and aches, when I turn to take it in. Cricked from hanging straight down on his drugs.

An hour? Hours maybe. The lamps in either corner still on, but the room darker without the flickering flames.

On them still. Armies in my head. His sand swirling, stoked kiln of closing. Fusing to murky glass. Struggling to climb up, see straight.

Judy stands up smartly, as if at a teacher's command. The hammer in one hand, the other smoothing the hem of her dress. Blood splotched and smeared all over her now—dress, blouse, arms, swipes on her face. Anywhere she's touched with her gore gloves. Her white legs bare and skinny, scabbed in places, above her white socks. She takes a step toward her father and hits him on the back of the head with the hammer. Not a blow of anger or undue force. Just the smart crack you give something out of whack. A dull sound, between a thud and knock. The head moves slightly. She sits back down as if returning from the blackboard.

A new game. Neck, knife, hammer, head. Knife beats neck. Hammer beats head.

Watching me now to see what I'll do, her eyes averted. *Ward watch.* What you learn in stir never leaves you, not even when you want it to.

Not knowing my play or wanting to, I close my eyes.

Sand beats flame.

§

Gone.

I listen, but I'm sure. Elapsed time hangs around me like a fluid. *Something dark that is your element, breathing where others drown.* Straight-backed chair gone with her.

I get up, cautiously. The room veers. I bend over the chair, holding on to it, taking deep breaths. Things slow to a wobble.

Fizzing weakness in my legs. Like I've run a marathon and been transfused with ginger ale. My arms too. Bubbles fizzing up and down my body.

But I take a step, and stay upright. The next step better. Move my arms. *Get your blood working. Disperse his shit.*

It will take a while. *Which you haven't got.* You need to leave now. *But you need to do some things first.*

A glance at my wrist, my watch gone. Since when? Don't remember it all night. Part the curtains. Still dark beyond.

Move as fast as you can.

No faster.

A trail of blood spots, getting smaller and more widely spaced until they stop, leads through the kitchen to the dining room. The center drawer of the sideboard pulled out. The carving case in it, but the bloody knife left outside the case, laid between it and the front of the drawer.

Locations always approximate with Judy. Or micron-accurate, by her measures.

Turn and see her table setting. Partial… or complete. Dining paraphernalia, mismatched in kind and number. Two stacks of dinner plates, different patterns of china. Smaller one of side plates, also various. One bowl. Two drinking glasses. A wine glass. Teacups, saucers. Many mugs. Pieces of cutlery blocking out a couple of rectangles. Scattered elsewhere. Napkins in rings, folded, crumpled and strewn. *Banquet in Bedlam.*

Time to start thinking. My head clearing, but not quickly enough.

Smears and splotches all around. *Her prints, not yours.*

I take a linen napkin from the open sideboard drawer. Retracing my steps to the door, I try to remember what I touched. Not much. The Sandman took my coat, led me straight to my cage. *Careful*, he called himself.

The front door's ajar, cold air sidling through it. *You shut the door on her, Sandman, but you forgot to take back the key.* Probably couldn't imagine her having the nerve to let herself in. How on earth did she keep it all these years? Hang on to it, cyclone after cyclone?

I shut the door, first wiping the knobs on either side and the edge of the frame. None of which I remember touching, but could've. *The bell outside.* I open the door again and wipe it. Jump at the ring inside the dead house. Keeping the napkin around my hand, I open the closet, take my coat off the hook. Put it on, pat the pockets. The hammer back in its place, crusty with blood.

Judy. Such a strange, wrecked creature.

Still wearing the slippers, careful not to step in any of the blood, I take three plastic bags from a dispenser under the kitchen sink. Drop the napkin in one of them, put the other two over my hands, huge white fingerless gloves. Grab a new napkin. Go back into the room with the corpse collapsed in his gore, wipe down every part of the chair I could have touched. Bag the glass. The slippers will follow last, added outside the door.

Did I touch any of the pictures? Just stood before them, wondering. Amazed and appalled.

Just one more place to visit, and easy to find if I'm right. *An organized person. Careful.*

Yes, but old. And cunning. Knowing there's a point past which help is mandatory.

His office downstairs. The basement chilly but dry, no hint of must. I leave the stair and hall lights on to dispel some of the dark, but the shadowy pantry and the rooms beyond it still make my skin prickle. Dark mouths, things in them that want to rush out.

Sitting at his solid oak desk, in a straight-backed maroon leather chair matching the armchairs upstairs. On the desk two framed pictures. One with friends on a fishing trip: three old men, each grinning and straining to hold up a salmon by the gills. The other with the brown-skinned woman at a party with balloons, their heads leaning together, laughing.

The wall in front of me a curriculum vitae of sorts, its entries framed and under glass. His medical degree. Specialist's certificate, a duplicate of the one upstairs. Certificates of membership in physicians' colleges in Canada and the U.S. A testimonial of appreciation on his retirement from the hospital, colleagues' signatures in various inks at the bottom. A similar tribute on his retirement from U of T. Other honours and ceremonial expressions of gratitude.

What stops me longest is a metal nameplate set in brackets just above the desk. The metal painted black, the deeply-cut letters painted silver. **M.S. Wyvern, MD, FRCPC, ABA, Professor of Anaesthesiology**. I stare at it a long time, wondering what kind of man still wants— needs—to be reminded of his privileged office space twenty-five years after his retirement? Wants to see it each time he raises his eyes.

The kind that bleeds out in a leather chair, butchered by his daughter.

What I'm looking for is in the bottom right-hand drawer of the desk. Where I expected it to be, more or less. Where it had to be. It is a large rectangular packet of soft suede, the colour of yellowed ivory, much handled. Like an oversized wallet or undersized briefcase. **Last Will And Testament** and **To Be Opened By My Executor** are printed in black pen on white labels slid into plastic windows on the front. It has a button clasp of dark wood inside an elasticized loop. Inside are various soft and stiff compartments, the latter with documents in them, the former with articles of miscellaneous size.

All pretty much as you expected. As if you've been here in a dream, with only the details gone blurry. It has to be where

Max, the executor, who has seen it many times, will find it easily, so he can remove it on the first pass.

Holding the packet with one plastic-wrapped hand, I poke through the contents of the soft front pocket with the other. Two disks labelled "Christmas Music," in different pens. Other disks: "Holiday Favourites." "Easter Parade." "Valentine's Medley." Two envelopes of old prints, some of them Polaroids, predating the musical titles theme: "Fond Memories" and "Home Snaps." Either never digitized, or else kept in their first format anyway, originals too precious to destroy. The first image I flick to shows me Max Senior's disdain for Max Junior was justifed in one respect at least: in terms of sexual sadism, the son might have learned from the father but could only ever be a dabbler by comparison. In bringing home pictures the old man could no longer procure for himself, Max was doing more than ensuring for himself the lion's share of the inheritance. He was also propitiating the father who saw him as a failure, the dentist who couldn't cut it as a doctor. On some sick level, a little boy trying to keep Daddy happy if he can't make him proud.

Take in another couple, even more extreme and elaborate, thinking, *Where's the surgeon? The OR nurses? Is this blindness or collusion?*

Then close "Home Snaps" before I can see Judy. Or anyone else I recognize.

No need for another reason to get back on the wagon.

Rage clarifies. To a point. Past which it fogs and blurs. My mind's almost back to hyper-drive. Just the body lurching and fizzing a ways behind.

I riffle past the envelopes which start with the will and go on to various dated codicils. I can guess the contents in broad strokes, without needing to know the details. Dead Dr. Wyvern trying tirelessly to control people, even from beyond the grave. Bestowing or retracting this treat or that, according to how well and how recently someone had pleased him or the reverse. In some ways a brutally simple man, with a brutally simple code: Play by my rules, you get paid off. And with a wish of diamond simplicity yoking his personal and professional lives: that other human beings be reduced to pliable, unthinking flesh to serve his sovereign desires.

With legal means as well as drugs to accomplish this. An envelope marked **POA Maude**. Outlining, I assume, the Max / Sandor split. And behind it, from thirty years earlier, The Sandman's first foray into legal de-personing. In lawyerese it spells out that, beginning 12 November 1972, the power for all of Judy's decisions—financial, medical, choices of any kind—rests with her father. And this power never revoked. Handy. If she ever said or did something inconvenient, to be able to produce a document proving she hadn't been a legally responsible adult since age seventeen—in other words, ever. But he hadn't ever seriously feared waywardness from Judy, no more than waywardness from any other sentient being. He just preferred people supine and paralyzed, and knew ways beyond hypos and IVs to achieve this. It puts Judy's migrations between group homes and alleys in a new light. She might have been choosing the safest, even wisest, course she could—retaining the only powers of self-determination left open to her.

And here, ah, yes—an addendum from 1989: Sandor, in his twenties, named Judy's alternate POA. In case the patriarch's immortality ever proved to be a myth. Maude left out of it even then.

I fold the document and put it in my pocket. Only to realize, a second later, that that changes nothing. Another copy sits in a lawyer's office. Probably in a safety deposit box as well. No matter. I want to have it.

In some way, reading it brings a bitter relief. A kind of vindication even. It demonstrates, in the only slightly faded black ink of a 1972 typewriter, what I have always known and understood perfectly. Judy forfeited her right to family membership by becoming mentally ill. She forfeited her right to citizenship by the same mistake.

Upstairs, looking down again at the dead man, a surge of the bad rage, the fogging kind.

You got off too damn easy. Maude losing her mind slowly, in a series of institutions. Like being eaten alive by ants. Likewise Judy, starting long before. Max and Vivian, who deserve no pity, facing a long battle to keep their sanity in a prison cell, after a long and costly battle to stay out of one. And Sandor—as always the question mark, the one I can't decide about. His role in all this? The grieving eyes above the glass say victim more than perp to me—though no law says you can't be both. Either way, wherever he finds himself, he'll go on being swamped. Will break down and rally, break down and rally. What did he call it? *Death by a thousand paper cuts.* One of the many entries where Maude's plight segues quickly into his own. Whereas you, the author of so much harm—what happened to you? No perp walk, no public vilification, no class action hatred, no cell rot. You went on doing exactly as you pleased, exactly as you'd done for ninety-four years, right up to the moment your daughter slit your throat.

Your carefully curated public self will be smashed to pieces posthumously, but you won't be around to see the demolition.

I drop the satchel in his lap, wishing, too late, I could slip Judy's POA papers back in. It might help in her defense: how can a non-person consciously kill a person? It would keep her in the kind of facility she's used to instead of prison.

And then remember, again, it doesn't matter. There are other copies, in all the right places.

Not thinking straight, still. His drugs as good as his word. Time to go.

A last look back from the door. The curled figure sunk further into the chair, a wet pulpy outgrowth of its leather and brass buttons. Stained a deep red, looking small, almost fetal. Cradling his satchel.

Another voice in the Wyvern chorus. Their mix tape from hell.

§

A brief stop to try the Honda. Not a cough or sputter. I wonder what he planned to do about my car. He would have had it covered.

As it is, it will be towed away soon after 10 a.m. The parking regs odd on Elm. You can park all night and most of the day, but not between 8 and 10 a.m. But parking regs tell a story, if you listen. In this case, no hassle for lines of friends at dinners and other do's running late into the night. And no hassle for busy people needing lots of road to wheel big cars to work.

Someone will be on the blower by 10:01.

And that, with luck, will be before Iris returns from Mississauga. And before the police open their mail, and Max, panicking, starts calling Home Office.

Who—*you hope*—amidst all the kerfuffle to come, will recall the junker briefly disrupting the melody of a Rosedale morning?

I won't be picking it up anytime soon, if ever.

Walking. The pre-dawn air cool, not cold. Making my slow way home on drugged and battered bones. Stopping for frequent rests on curbs, benches.

4:10 by the clock tower on UCC, staring from atop its column down Avenue.

When and how did the watch disappear? Image now of it on my wrist, glancing at it soon after I arrived. It can only have been Judy. Odd to think of her close to me, unclasping and removing it. An oddly delicate action amid the night's carnage. But no bloodstains on my wrist. I stand under a streetlight checking. Another unanswerable adjustment mystery. *Closing windows thick with them.*

Scary thought: Judy the sanest, least spooky member of her top-end crazy, top-end spooky family.

Sane enough to get out for good.

No, not scary. Nothing is that clears your head. That lets you breathe.

Wherever Judy is gliding in the city, I know that in some sense she is right here beside me and always has been. In our very different ways, through twenty years apart, we've always been on the same unending path: ignoring red lights to cross deserted streets in the middle of the night.

18

HALLOWE'EN IS THE usual lumpish modern affair, limping remnant of a rite that must once have had real verve. I set up around 5:00 on the landing at the top of the stairs. Half blocking the buzz-in pad—visitors have to reach awkwardly around me, or I key them in—but there's nowhere else to sit without blocking the door. Dusk has barely begun, twelve steps down people are passing back and forth from work and shopping, but this is the time of highest traffic in a neighbourhood of young couples, who walk the little ones around between school and suppertime.

Most of my gear borrowed. Lucy's kitchen chair. Her largest mixing bowl, with the assortment of Shoppers candy bought from the tenants' donation box, topped up by Ken's almost-empty fund. My Mayor Mask came from 303, who bought it for a party but decided to stay home and game instead. It's hot inside the cheap latex. And it doesn't bear much actual resemblance to His Worship—just a hairless, jowly orb that could belong to any old, fat man who eats and drinks incessantly. It's a glutton's version of the Face, I realize, minus the scarring and perched bizarrely atop an anorexic body. Not many kids brave the trip up to it. They hesitate on the threshold, peering up at the vision, elongated further by their low-angle perspective, of impossible stretch topped by a blob of sickly white. Parents murmur them back, but they're already retreating. Would more, or fewer, make the climb if I took it off?

It's mostly teens who empty the bowl. Later on, when the little kids are done and the ritual is all but concluded. Costumeless, elbow-dared by a friend, one mounts the steps, attempting some sort of hard but wheedling face, grabs a fistful of candies and jumps back down to guffaws. Part of the joke seems to be that I don't move or speak at all. Wax dummy.

§

Nichols' Variety was about a mile's walk from my foster parents' home. My second or third set, I must've been about seven. It was a new subdivision, filled with vacant lots and houses under construction, with dirt mountains and excavated pits and concrete basements with rooms but no doors, perfect for fantasy explorings. Mr. Nichols was tall and bald, with sad eyes and a pot belly, the image of stern authority to a kid. His wife was a mass in a flowered dress filling an armchair in the shadows while he worked the counter. Big glass jars of candy along a board in front: jujubes, gummi worms, raspberry dollars, lemon chips, licorice strings, black balls, peppermints, sour balls—three picks for a penny. It changed the way you walked, ignoring what's ahead to inspect the curb and gutter for glints of copper. The day before Hallowe'en, I snuck out of the house after dark and broke the windows in Nichols' with a metal rod from one of the homes-in-progress. Climbed through and smashed the candy jars, after filling my pockets with a few handfuls. Sat on the curb in front of the store, ringing rhythms on the road with the bar.

"Don't you like Mr. Nichols? Did he do something to make you angry?" I can't really remember the cop except for an impression of solemnity and weariness, mostly from his voice. My foster parents, faceless, standing behind him— one very still, one shifting nervously.

"I like him. He's a nice man."

No shock like the truth. Not a phrase yet, but a fact flaring in the old cop's eyes.

Grounded on Hallowe'en, which I'd planned to skip anyway. Few adults, then or later, able to guess what might actually constitute punishment to me. They'd have to be bent themselves.

§

Dr. Wyvern stares up from my lap, having pushed the Big Man off the front page for the first time this month. The *Star* and the *Sun* both used the same photograph. Not one from his self-tribute gallery and not one he would have approved. He's smiling blandly, a little vacantly, perhaps on a public panel. He's in his sixties, no doubt at the height of his influence at the university and hospital, his opinions sought and courted. The *Globe* went with one more suitably sombre, but with his mouth partway open, as if a question has stumped him or he's been caught between expressions. All are obviously photos on file for a public figure, rather than a shot selected by a family who has more than enough on its hands today.

ROSEDALE RAMPAGE! screams the *Sun*. The *Star* only slightly more subdued: **Rosedale Slaying Shocks Community**. The subheadings differ slightly, but use variants of the same key words: "prominent," "respected," "doctor," "professor," "dead," "murder." No sign of "victim," curiously. Is it only for the poor?

These are the late afternoon editions. It was still just the Big Man on my first trip to Shoppers. Either because the body hadn't been discovered yet, or because the police were giving themselves time, before an official announcement, to search for the "person of interest" both articles refer to.

Run, Judy, I think. Though it's not really how I imagine her—not as a person fleeing, a fugitive. More as a force pervading the city, a wild but diffuse radical element, beyond pursuit or capture. Bizarre as she is, she might seem hard to miss, an easy target for trained detectives, but they won't find her quickly, she lives too far underground. Learned invisibility is the deepest disguise. A cicada is a big, odd-looking insect, but when it burrows under the earth for its seventeen-year sleep, no one scouring the surface has a chance of seeing it.

Other than the fact of a homicide, and its characterization, perhaps by a junior officer caught off guard, as "gruesome," the focus of this first coverage is on the status and achievements of the deceased, and the shock and dismay of his neighbours, granted disproportionately lengthy quotes. The paucity of detail, along with the scant mention of the rest of the family, gives me hope that the murder has already been folded into a wider investigation, with multiple arrests made or forthcoming.

Eventually including—to dig a little more greedily in the candy jar—others from the same social echelon who enjoy the Wyvern holiday classics. Connoisseurs willing to pay for special, hard-to-get bootlegs from a special, hard-to-locate source. Without ever having seen them or any evidence of them, I sense these others, a complexity in the Wyvern aroma, a deepening of its stink.

It starts, I assume—this special new smell—with a change in Max's status with the police. Summoned, the shell-shocked son, sometime between this morning's lattes and lunch, from his routine Thursday office to the scene on Dunbar Road. Standing near where Judy and I sat, staring with a white and frozen face at the bloody ruins of his father. The Sandman by then a curled small castle, locked in rigor, red paint thrown down its walls.

Max standing in that special cleared space granted the bereaved, from custom if not respect, and, especially in the case of cops, to see what he'll do in it. A space, a little stage on which to do and say wrong things, while cop eyes note the flicker of false gestures and expressions from the wings. *Family kill each other, every day. Don't look far until you have to.*

Is Sandor there?

No, not yet. Max at the top of every list the cops turned up: Executor in the suede packet in the corpse's lap, first name on the list beside the phone, in the Contacts book. The name the funeral home card in the deceased's wallet has on file. Max has to get there first, remove the pictures, pictures, pictures. *Yes, Dad, yes...*

So, a little disconcerted, eyes flicking from the thought-tumble behind them, when he's stopped from reaching for the blood-soaked suede packet. "...my father's will... I'm his..." "I'm sorry, sir, but that was found with your father's body. It's evidence at a crime scene at this point." "Of course, I understand. I'm sorry, it's just all so..."

Is that when it first flutters into Max's big brain that I might, for the moment, have my uses? He sent me to the old man—like a weak teacher referring an incorrigible student to the principal—to get disappeared. Which still has to happen. My eviction from Planet Wyvern is long overdue. Meanwhile, though, if I was greedy dolt enough to abscond with all the family pics, well, at least that's one way of keeping them from the cops.

If he could just X-ray through the suede and confirm they're missing. Relief tingling as conviction gains, delicate tendrils twining around dread, that I wouldn't have left without grabbing the extra leverage. All my threats of disdaining a payoff and sending Christmas Music to the cops just self-righteous shtick and bluff. Holier-than-thou crapola from a classic friend of Judy's. Embarrassing, really, these clowns she hooks up with. Just as he and Vivian decided the other night, after the poetry-and-dementia farce.

Vivian. God, he'd like to see her—*needs* to see her—now, and from the gurgling in his stomach it's got to be past one—but you don't check your watch or take a sec to call your girlfriend, not with your father bled out three feet in front of you. Not with several pairs of cop eyes fastened to you, none of them even pretending to roam.

Steadily, the scene becomes more crowded.

Forensics. Tech guys, photogs. Funeral home people, called by someone, told they aren't needed yet. Print dusters. Juniors outside to secure the scene, fend off neighbours, media as they twig.

Several tries to reach Sandor, his phone ringing off the hook. Finally a constable is sent to rouse and inform him. Reports back. A weeping wreck. Drinking all night, looks like.

Another constable sent to inform the sister. Who has no telephone of her own? A mentally unstable person, very fragile, Max informs them solemnly. Back now, alone. Apparently she's AWOL, the landlady at her group home hasn't seen her in two days.

Oh, really? A person of interest.

And Max, overhearing while a cop with slow handwriting asks him questions he's already answered, feels relief like elation, these little gas bubbles collecting on the inside of his chest, hollowed like a drum by fear. *See, Viv,* he imagines telling her later, *the nut jobs do have their uses occasionally. My sister a placeholder for her friend. Until we get what's ours. And then he can get what's his.* Feeling more than a little giddy—freaked-out giddy—at how they might just have walked right to the edge of a crumbling cliff and still jumped back in time.

And later, back home finally, giddiness persisting—though mellowed a bit, wine and a pinch of something harder with Viv—when a rap on the door startles. Trick or Treat? Not even gray yet.

Two men. Big. Suits. They'd have got here sooner, except the brass insisted on mapping out a careful approach, given the reputations of the people involved and the possibility, a hunch gaining in some minds, of a large, far-reaching investigation. And, too, a few of the usual turf squabbles between Sex Crimes and Homicide, even though Homicide has priority until their part is down. There was that, as usual, too.

"We have a few questions we'd like to ask you, Dr. Wyvern."

"Questions? I think I answered every possible… It's been a terribly long and difficult day, as I'm sure…" It's upsetting how thoughts trail off and die in front of the butcher's block faces. "Um… here?"

"Unless there's somewhere else you'd like to talk?"

It's pleasant not to have a clue how things went down, when any way they might have gone down is pleasant.

And when even clueless speculation stops you thinking how your own day's gone down. And down…

I woke up a couple of hours after returning home, cored. Not from real sleep, but from a mud-like stupor that was only partly a madman's chemicals seeping slowly out of me. I lay on the mattress a long time, staring at the ceiling.

Eyes open or closed, I saw no stairs. No Empress. I couldn't reach them, or her. I felt unspeakably alone. As if the planet had been blasted into dust and I'd been left behind as its janitor to sweep it up.

This is the last adjustment, said the voice, the one I'd heard last night. *But it has to finish first.* And I had a premonition I've never had before, not just of an adjustment that isn't finished but of an adjustment that won't ever finish, it can't. It brought me to the point of shaking all over. My hands, my arms, my feet, my legs, my chest, my back, my head, my neck—all of me. Like leaves in a wind that won't stop. Except I had no trunk or branches. Just leaves.

And still now, replaying the day as I sit on Lucy's chair and dole out Smarties and plastic-wrapped suckers, every moment I find again in memory feels stale and unreal—like loops of waking dream I sleepwalk through, and sleepwalk through again remembering. Until, at last, I find the only place—I reach it—that's dark enough to wake, and know myself awake, in.

Gwen's voice when I call, around noon: "Hello, you've reached the office of…" No change.

But when I call again, a couple of hours later, a new voice, young and crisp: "We are sorry but the dental office is closed due to urgent family circumstances. We apologize for any inconvenience. The office will reopen at a date yet to be determined. Patients with issues of urgent concern are advised to…"

The Wyvern dismantling underway.

No sense of triumph, not even of satisfaction.

Don't feel anything.

It all—the whole adjustment—feels like something that happened a long time ago, helped along by hands unrelated to my own. Something that had nothing to do with me.

"I have something to atone for," I say to Stone. Standing in Big Empty, my shirt off. Hearing the formality, a ceremoniousness, that always comes into my voice when a window's almost closed and our meeting is drawing near.

You need to pay, says Stone, who never lies. *Yes you do.*

Using the fine-tipped X-Acto, which has the sharpest blade, I score a series of parallel horizontal lines in my chest, beginning just below my shoulders and ending just above my navel. Six lines in all, about an inch-and-a-half apart.

Through them I score vertical lines, top to bottom, four of them, about two inches apart.

For a brief time, as the lines go bright red and, dabbing with the shirt, I can keep up with the bleeding, my chest is a crimson checkerboard. But the flow increases and, even blotting quickly, it becomes a general smear.

Later, when it has stopped and crusted over, I clean up the boxes with water and alcohol as best I can. But I can't get too close to the lines without reopening them. So the grid effect is crude, and bumpy. Rust-coloured now, too. Not bright anymore.

Staring down at it, I feel a clammy kinship, almost an identity, with the blood-soaked old ghoul curled in his chair—as if Judy's bone-handled carving knife, as weirdly magic as the rest of her, operates in two dimensions and at two different speeds, opening one man's throat as I watched, and now, a half day later more or less, completing the job remotely, slicing the chest of his doppel-target... wound without end, amen.

Mid-afternoon, I pick up *Around Toogood Pond* and read some passages from near the end.

It's no longer possible to tell myself I'm reading it because it's part of an adjustment. Or because it tells me things—suggestions, hints—about a man who interests me, who is a mystery I can't resolve.

I'm reading it for company. To preserve my connection to a human shore I'm leaving, swept on a current that was always there but which is quickening, surging for open water.

Faces 23 August

Yesterday a quiet day. It felt as if we were out walking on a long thin peninsula, narrowing as it went, far away from the long shoreline of her life. She asked me questions that were—I was going to say terrible in their extremity; but that is not how they felt. A sweetness suffuses anything so utter.

"Was this my husband?" She had moved the photo of their wedding dinner to her bedside table. She seems to rotate her pictures according to what needs to be brought forward, brought back—taking the best care she can of her diminishing stores of recollection. "And is that the same man?" Of a photo taken a few years later. "Uh… huh," she says when I show her one of a family dinner. That strains credulity, the middle-aged men and the elderly married couple.

Once, early on in Vivera, she turned to me, and with a curious shy courtesy, said, "You've always lived very alone, I guess. Tell me, did you have any help from your mother and father?" "You're my mother," I said. And she looked startled, and covered it with a laugh. But she knew what had happened—in that moment she did. In fact she said, "That's what's happening to me. I forgot for a moment you're my son. I thought you were just a nice gentleman. Helping me."

I felt challenged more than saddened. For fifty-two years she has given me abundant notice of my identity. It's time now to be a nice gentleman.

Guide lines 16 December

What I say, carefully, wanting to get it right for myself too: "The thought I'm guided by is that this lady has been disrespected enough. However late in the day it is, it's not too late to give her the treatment she deserves. The buck stops here."

That seems to satisfy L. She nods. And it satisfies me too, I realize. It's a guideline to try to hold to.

Vivid dream again last night of trying to kill him. With a long knife, flashing in the sun, as we splashed and floundered in a stream of variable depth.

After hearing me talk of the sudden waves and longer spells of dislocation, of dream-likeness—leading to disorientation: *Where am I? How did I get here? What am I doing now and what am I supposed to do next?*—Dr. P gives me a name for it (which helps). "It's called de-realization."

It can be a consequence of anxiety, apparently, often related to post-traumatic stress.

And I told a story about a man I'd known who discovered, in his mid-twenties, that he'd been adopted. That his parents, with whom he'd had and continued to have a warm relationship, were not his blood parents. He felt, he told me, the ground shift and dissolve under his feet. So that even elements of ordinary reality became dubious, became things he couldn't be sure of: chair, table, wall. Who he was. Who the person next to him was.

Hours later I realized—it seeped into my awareness—that there was no such man in my real life. He was a figure slid in from dream: more true than real, more honest than a lie.

A curious book, Sandor's. *Curiouser and curiouser* each time I read it.

Sipping Luck Yu on the balcony, staring above Latimer brick, I consider it. Chill cobalt, with low, shouldering gray clouds. No witches on broomsticks sailing before them yet.

A man caring for his mother. Suffering with her, devoted to her. Then not.

A man flailing, while analyzing his flailing.

Different men, not quite matchable. Slides that don't quite overlay, not exactly. *Do anyone's?* More or less. You can be scattered but still of a piece, sort of. Glob of mercury dropped, running off in tiny beads. But this guy—this *author*—with loud leviathan in the bar, trouble cresting from his deeps?

Is this what writing means, Lois?

To stop no pain, but comment on it sensitively?

To be a dolt, but deftly.

Atrocious pastime. And nothing in it to declare—only to strongly hint, to tantalize—that he knew anything about the mayhem in the family vaults. All that induced paralysis and rape. Did they, too, speak to the poem?

And L—Lynette, as I gather now—the one he confides in, is consoled by. And? What more? Listening to his trials, does she tell him of her own on a locked ward? Tell him of Judy? Me? TAL? *How could she?* How could she not?

Close my eyes. Shift my hands to grasp new, cooler sections of the railing.

Breathe. Slowly. *In, out.* In, out.

A kind of gray. A shadow world... but without features.

No stairs. No Empress.

No nothing.

Mid-afternoon, I give up and enter the empty in Big Empty. Sit in the cool, back to the wall. Pull the door closed. Megan's closet. Her dark. Though it draws me like a lodestone through each window, I resist its pull as long as I can. Knowing that when I reach it, Stone waits just beyond.

It's all right to be here. You've waited long enough.

Desperation the price of admission. It's all she ever asked of you. Street sweeps, endless drives and walks in search of, circling, backtracking, peering—futile, yes, of course, but essential. Pointlessly crucial. *Need* more than a word. Not just four simple letters, a burped syllable.

More than that or nothing at all.

Reaching, moving my hands about, I feel them. Feel her colours.

Red. Green. Yellow. Orange. Blue. Purple.

Redyelloworange, crisscrossing slashes of flame. Her *far cors*. What she loved best.

347

Touch them, gently. Feel them. Sitting with your back against the wall, your knees drawn up. A small dark space. The only space in No Name with no name.

Closet does for strangers.

I found them one day with a flashlight, looking for something before I emptied it. I doubt if Lois ever saw them.

How did Megan find her way in here? And when?

Found a few moments when she could be alone and came in here. Reached up to shut the door behind her. Not afraid of the dark, wanting it. Needing it. Needing it to reach up—as high as she could, tiptoe—and slash upon it.

Feel them! Fiercer than any colours in sunlight could be. Burning to the touch.

Far cors!

Our fierce arguments that last fall. Fiercer than I realized as we were having them, since even war was giddy life. *She's Daddy's girl all right.* Lois sneering but afraid. Our child listless, sitting sunk for hours in torpor, her eyes dim and unfocused. Then, with Lois still murmuring suspicions of autism, clambering up to stand on a chair, waving her arms wildly, screaming with glee. Screaming herself hoarse. Lois with her hand over her mouth, eyes wide. She knows these things, lives with them. Mad ecstatic dances, trance-paralysis in caves. Daddy's girl.

Smashing the crayons into paper so hard they broke into bits. Racing the bits across paper and onto the floor.

Far cors!

Fire colours, honey?

Far cors!!

A magical place, even the air feels electric.

You can hear another voice, every other voice, sensible and friendly, saying, Just a child reaching up with short chubby arms and scrawling with her crayons. Random, the voices say.

Hear them and know, calmly, with no need to repudiate, that the marks are far more purposeful. Are a map. Uncanny. Precise.

Map to where she was. Is.

Map to where we are.

Colours burning in the dark.

§

Jared and his parents return around 9:00. It's the first time ever he's wanted to join Trick-or-Treat. Brave the streets when recess is everywhere. Lucy teared up when she told me. Tuesday's door-bangers aside, she still considers me her staunchest ally in strengthening Jared for a normal life. But our purposes, I know guiltily, diverge. I want to strengthen Jared for himself. Wherever that may lead. To people… or away from them.

He shows me his pillow case, half-full. They went everywhere. His plastic, head-to-toe outfit is expensive. Costly for Lucius and Lucy, even at Walmart. Alien superhero that will have a special name, special powers, but which to me looks utterly generic. Breastplate. Talons. Helmet with battery-powered blinking knobs. Cape. Gold. Red. Black. Blue belt with flashing red tips hanging from a yellow "weapons cache."

I nod, try to be glad for him. Get partway there.

More power in his lichen-munching snail than in warehouses of this dreck.

My days as his tutor may be numbered.

No Name's real Trick-or-Treat begins soon after, a farce of activity on the steps and sidewalk. 305's new couple pull up with their helpers, even though I warned them three times today—until I stopped answering their calls—that the cruise shippers had till midnight by law and would likely take every minute. They'd be better advised to wait until morning and move in leisurely.

"They can't take *all day*."

"They've *got* all day."

That deep furrowed silence from the other end—someone struggling to fathom that *what I want* and *what's coming to me* do not precisely coincide.

Sure enough, the minstrels start around 10:00 and take their surly time about it. Ferrying small armloads of practice amps and a shower curtain and an LCBO box with the bottom going and an unwashed cereal bowl teetering on top. One chubby girl passes carrying a music stand. More naïve or sentimental eyes, watching this, might surmise they're seeing the artistic temperament out of which creativity rises and for which allowances must be made. But I know I'm seeing the asshole temperament out of which nothing but bullshit rises and for which there is no excuse. Prolonging an eviction is the best number these birds have.

I stay on the kitchen chair, pig's head on a stick, eyeing them through black slits. Let three skinny guys lever a couch around me, almost losing it down the stairwell. A van pulls up around 11:00 beside their piles and they lean against it, yukking it up with the driver, jerking thumbs up at me. It's Hallowe'en, all right. Dull lethargic devils who know they've got till the stroke of 12:00 to harass and goad the townspeople, try to drive them blind with rage.

Meanwhile the new saints, more than halfway to rage when they arrived, fidget by their rented U-Haul, stalk five steps forward and back, huddle griping with their oversupply of helpers: two hired movers (leaning against their truck, smoking), three parents, a muscular friend or brother. They chatter, mope, cast unremarked glares at the dawdling minstrels.

Twice the guy opens the door and holds a wrist up at me, tapping a big watch. I tap my own bare wrist, no watch on it now. *Mid-night*, I growl down through my mask.

I keep expecting the cops to come through the glass doors below. Dressed like adults on their way to a party, their costumes perfect.

By now they've had several hours to sweat Max over the pictures. Several hours, when minutes is all it would take to have him squealing like Gainsborough's Blue Boy getting a hot lead enema. Vivian! he starts yelping. And she's there now, in another room. Though how it helps his case to have an accomplice he employs and fucks and poses and, apparently, drugs—it would take a panicking pampered dentist to fathom.

The Super! he squeals next—or first. I don't *know* his name. He never *told* me. The *Super*, is all. *The Super made me do it!* It makes no sense, of course. How did I make him do for years what they've got evidence of copied multiply: drugging women and girls in his dentist's chair, undressing and assaulting them, photographing them, passing the pics to his father and who knows who else? But he *can* say I tried to extort money from him and he sent me to his father to straighten me out—all true, so long as English walks a tightrope. He can put me at the scene of a murder, and maybe he thinks, with flailing logic, if he gives them a murderer they'll overlook, or go easy on, serial drugged sexual assaults.

Minutes stretch like days—the chair is hard, the light is harsh, the room is hot, his questioners smell and have yellow teeth—body and soul, he's in *pain*—and he can squeal and yelp a lot before his high-priced lawyer gets there and gives him the excellent advice he's paid for: shut the fuck up.

But the cops don't arrive. Just Darth Vaders, Batmans, X-whatevers, witches, "ladies," half-assed vampires in Dollarama fangs, zombies, and the inevitable ghost with ragged eyeholes.

No cops. Think.

The help Stone often gives in closing windows. Hints. Prompts. Cajolings. Coming faster as his time approaches. Hardly from a spirit of altruism. He wants me finished with my work, done with the adjustment, no hanging threads, when he takes receipt of me. A clean slate for him to scrawl things on. With every unobstructed minute of the shift he's got coming to him.

Spoiled, of course. Spoiled rotten. What in his life has prepared him to believe he could run out of options? That there's no safe tab to click. No card to swipe, insert, or tap.

So he clings to the hope that I haven't sent the pics. Or not the worst of them. Since the cops aren't saying yet. Tells himself I wouldn't give up my leverage without getting something in return.

Or?

Or?

Think.

Handing out Hallowe'en candy a strangely good way to do just that. Sitting behind a mask as another mask comes up the stairs and mutters Trick or Treat, or stands there saying nothing at all. And you fish absently for some goodies and drop them in the bag.

Or… he doesn't put me at his father's house because it wasn't him who sent me there. Wasn't him who saw, coolly and without passion, that things had got to that point.

Which point?

The point at which you jump a sinking ship.

One home, Grade Eight or so, had these two little brainiacs down the street, twins, their parents both theoretical something-or-others, and the mother used to call out the door as they trundled off with their lunch bags: Remember, think! Warbled it after them in a high, posh voice.

For a couple of top-grade browners—nerds not yet the default word—they got picked on surprisingly little. They had a knowingness about them, an irony about their special status—yes, they'd been cast as angels in this particular play, but in the next act they might be dolts —that seemed to take the air out of bullies. Apart from the usual hissed remarks, some trippings and shovings, they got off pretty lightly, even in gym.

Remember. Think.

Lucius comes down just after 12:00 to make sure change-over is going smoothly. It is. The cruisers have finally shoved off and the new team is working in quick-time, using a fireman's chain up to the elevator, an operator to shoot loads up and down, and a chain on the top floor down the hall and into the apartment. They've had all night to plan it.

I've moved inside to keep out of their way, which is where Lucius finds me. I was just about to come up and return the chair.

"Is okay. I'll take it up."

"Sorry about the noise, Lucius. 305 might be up all night, cleaning and unpacking."

He smiles. "Is okay. Last day of school week tomorrow."

And his own busiest day—lawns needing sprucing before the weekend dinner parties—but his sleep doesn't matter, only Jared's.

"Your car. I notice is gone all day. You take it in somewhere?"

"It stopped. I left it on the street."

"Just left?" Frowning, like his son. "Police gonna take it then. Impound. Probably they do already. And is expensive to get back. Parking fine. Towing. And something else—"

"It's okay, Lucius. I've been walking everywhere lately. I think I'll just keep doing that."

"Just walk?"

"Yeah. Take the TTC if it's too far."

I realize I'm still wearing the mask. You get used to it, despite the heat. But as soon as I take it off, cool air surrounds my head, even in the hallway. A sour chemical stink comes off the sweaty latex.

"Why you keep looking down the stairs? Is midnight. Is all done, right?"

"It is, you're right. Just don't want to miss anyone, I guess."

"Your chest." Lucius points at it. "Those guys again?"

I look down at myself. Blotches in places, dark burgundy on the light gray T-shirt. Some bandages on the checkerboard must have soaked through.

"No. Another guy. But it's minor, nothing to worry about. Get some sleep. I'll come up in a while to make sure 305 are keeping it down."

He nods, stands there a few more seconds before leaving. He's back to looking at me again, but with worry lines almost as fixed as his son's.

§

I stand in the living room a long while, like someone try-ing to remember or decide something important. Then go through the door onto the balcony. The tower blinking orange and blue—*no such thing as black lights*. All Saints' Day. The devils have had their due and now it's the turn of puri-fied souls. Hands on the cold railing, I cock my head and breathe slowly and deeply through my nose—as if I might hear some faint blessed rustling, the glidings of super-good-ness, or catch the sweet elusive scent of incorruptible will.

But nothing—nothing new—comes to ear or nostril.

I think the devils are just sleeping it off. A Venti Bold is all it will take to put them right back in the fray.

From halfway down the hall, I hear 305's move-in clam-our. Thud and slide of heavy boxes, shouts to each other about where to put things, water running, hammer bangs even. They'd howl to all the gods—they *will*—when their neighbours pull something like it. And yet I find it hard to get angry with these two. They seem too innocent, too unformed. Being their super will be like being their teacher. Like training an autistic élite to recognize and respond to others, to come a step closer to actually sharing the world with them.

I knock gently.

"Some of this *can't* wait till tomorrow. We wouldn't be doing *any* of it now if you'd given us a clean apartment instead of a pigsty."

"When was I supposed to clean it—between midnight and a minute past? I told you to wait till tomorrow. Till later today."

"Well, we didn't know those clowns would be using a stopwatch. I hope you kept their damage deposit at least."

"Show me the damage."

They do, the darlings.

"That's sweep-up stuff. Bag and drag. Some vacuuming—in the *morning*. Or Comet and a rag. If you want, I'll show you what damage looks like sometime."

"Thanks. I think we're seeing plenty."

Walking away, I feel light and clear when I shouldn't feel either, and I ask myself when I last really slept. A nap on the mattress after the cleanup Tuesday is all I remember. Closing my eyes and maybe drifting off a few minutes. Just that until Doc Wyvern's drug-daze.

Two and a half days ago. Catnaps in the days before that.

I feel the drag I should, the anchor pulling me down. The spots, dark grains, in front of my eyes. Like a black veil, swirling. Everything on fire, the air alive with soot.

And yet I'm bubbling still. Ready to set up 305's kitchen for them. Eager with it.

It's why a window closes. To put a stop to these absurdities. To end the contradictions.

Substantial and profound 19 October

A drive down Unionville streets, admiring the houses as she loves to do—"These houses are… substantial"— amazed at the word, at the sound of it in her mouth. "Yes, they are, that's exactly the word." I made a bit too much of my delight. Then, walking around Vivera, we came to a tree with very dark red leaves, an almost black burgundy, which she reached for, saying, "This colour is… profound." *Profound.* I wanted to weep, without knowing exactly what I would be weeping for.

If we met in an afterlife—which I don't believe in— what could she tell the absent ones of these years they've missed? (Say death reforms them, say they grow an appetite for others' news.) A handful of disjointed, contradictory phrases, scenes that change with every telling. They would be hungry for how it was with her, but she couldn't give them that. She has moments, some good—but not news. Not a story made of stories.

She turned to me yesterday. "Something so... wrong with my mind. I think I must be dying." And then, when I didn't say anything: "I should talk to a doctor. Is there anything they can do for me? Do you think?" She was looking right at me, her eyes wide and guileless. "I think everything that can be done is being done," I had to tell her.

A new idea comes to me. I feel excited thinking about it. *She wants visible damage. Like it is with her,* and smack my head with the obviousness of it. Why the checkerboard was no good. Bloody and determined, sure—but who's seeing it under your shirt?

Snapping off the X-Acto blade to get a fresh segment, I begin scoring lines in a ring around my eye. Like a sun's rays, up into forehead, down into cheek, out into temple and across the nose. It's important to apply a steady pressure to each line until it starts to coagulate, especially the upper rays, otherwise I'm blind from the trickling and can't continue.

Excited, *really on to something,* but I force myself to keep a steady hand and go slow.

Afterwards, sitting expectantly among the *far cors,* I know a disappointment so profound that it would bring me to weeping if I wasn't already so far below that.

I'd settled myself with such expectancy, my knees drawn up and trembling. Tried it with eyes open, closed—tried it both ways, not knowing which would work best. Which would delve me faster through the dark.

But no stairs came, and No One waiting on them.

A timeless, thoughtless daze. And then quickly, numbly, as if I'm exiting a room like any other, I leave that place and re-enter Big Empty and resume reading to be doing something, riffling back to near the end.

§

Black letters in a cone of light. How special they appeared, how different. Words you knew by heart, knew to clogging boredom, when you encountered them on a page by simple daylight, under soft lamplight. Now transposed to so much more, sometimes something altogether unconnected, trapped and transfigured in this zone, seared by this selective shining.

Move the source even slightly and the black all around responds like a living thing, lets fall pieces of itself into the radiant charged circle, squiggles that squirm and oscillate before finding their new, proper shapes.

Old, old memory. It comes from far away.

Fabrics, rough and smooth, above me. Touching my head, grazing my neck and back. A tent of bedclothes? Forbidden reading at night?

No. Nothing touching my legs. A hardness under me. But my left hand, reaching up, ripples cool uneven textures.

I pause a long moment, flashlight and book in hand, before entering. Not sure how she'll feel about it, *I've never carried anything in but myself.*

But it feels permissible. More, it feels right. Not reading yet, but she loved hearing stories. And talked non-stop, babbling like a tiny old drunk.

And fire slicing dark. Pouring pure white *far* upon the black squiggles.

That she would love.

It's the final entry I'll try. Sandor's non-conclusion, non-epilogue. Non-anything but end.

Undated

Some things can only be reported. In the four months since I agreed to lock her into the Memory Gardens, she has grown increasingly combative. Insults and threats to other residents. To staff. The reports reach me by phone, by monthly checklist with Comments box.

J visits now, according to Jade. Has all her life equipped her for this? Prepared her to be the one who accompanies her on this final, darkest leg, when no one else can?

Yesterday she had another old woman down on the floor, slapping her in the face and head. Was taken to ER for tests and observation. Results negative, as expected. Around 4 a.m. they phoned to advise me that they had given her Haldol and she was being returned by patient transport.

All the reasons she has had over eighty-two years to beat on someone—for whatever they did, whatever she knew. And yet she served dutifully. Only to now assault a sweet and balding old woman, as frail and lost as herself.

Ah, Sandor. Omissions are your signature, the secret of your mystery. You trail off sprinkling them like bread crumbs. Let the reader follow if he will. If he reaches the hut in the forest, you won't be home. Critical reflection all through on your care of her, hard questions put to yourself—only to clam up at the starkest juncture: *In the four months since I agreed to lock her into...* Judy visits now because forty-five years of wandering wards and alleys have "equipped" her for it? Maude's demented battery now an echo too late of real punishment due. *...for whatever they did, whatever she knew.* Casually mentioned, never followed up. Why allude to what you won't explain? In a purely private journal, yes...

Writing: a wily weakness. Seducer, pander, dodger—will-o'-the-wisp. Confess on a cross to duck the resurrection entirely. To do your bit, to be seen doing it, to have done with it...

I'll meet you, Sandor. We're not done yet.

And on the day goes, endless and instantaneous.

Through cuttings, re-readings, cuttings. Aimless drifting spells. Vigils among the *far cors.*

Fire trucks go out sometimes, not as many as usual and not for long. They come back soon, the helmeted men looking bored as they halt traffic while the driver backs in. The angels must be keeping ashtrays closer, elements more distant.

The honking from below swells to a minor frenzy and levels off.

And then I see a tall man standing in the window looking back at me, and know it's night.

19

...SOMETHING YOU FORGOT... *something you've forgotten...*
All night long, in whispers, instead of sleep.

Saturday morning, early. Sitting in the armchair by the window, the streetlights still on. Back it comes. Two weeks ago, sweeping up the night's trash in the lobby. Paper peeping from the mailbox. An address and three letters. TAL.

An acronym, an old joke. *A thread dropped. An itch you forgot to scratch.*

From Judy, you told yourself, before you forgot to ask. But when did Judy ever leave a message someone else could understand? From a location they could reach? And how, and when? Judy in bed beside her dead and cooling mother.

You chase through an adjustment to find out how it starts.

A mother's voice, decades ago. Grateful, confiding. Speaking to the window mesh so your face won't make her lie. *All girls sob, hug stuffed animals. It's that darn Scribbler I worry about. Scribble, scribble, scribble. Who knows what comes out of that?*

But you don't say. Still a long way, most days, from speaking.

Memories: addresses from the future. Smells from rooms you'll live in, to help you settle in.

Strange reversal, sorcery of a process unwinding. My head getting clearer, drop by drop, like a bone in Jared's dungeon, when it's got no business doing anything but raving or sleeping.

Dark lightens, more gray seeping in. Fire door an ember filmed by ash. Whispering why the adjustment that should be over, isn't. Why the window so ready to close—can't quite bang shut.

Still some people to see. One, two. Two at least.

Clarity. It comes sometimes as a window closes. Like a circle that needs to find its start to seal itself. To be complete so it can end.

Comes from *how* a window closes. Not by sliding down, across—not that kind of window. By fogging over, and then the fog goes dark. But rub a patch of the fog, you might catch a detail skipped past when you were busy scoping a larger scene. Scanning to find an adjustment which soon swept you away, until its closing almost-end, when you glimpse the thing skipped past again, and know.

Know who wound you up and sent you ticking after Wyverns. Know where they live.

Even have a glimmer of why.

§

Shoppers not open for another hour, 9:00 on Saturdays. I buy the *Star* at the Convenience on the corner. A place I usually avoid, for the surly eyeballings the Asian owner gives the Face. A mixture of truculence and suspicion, as if he wants to give it a preemptive whack. Which makes me want to give him one. Which is just too many mental beatings for a paper or a litre of milk.

But he opens early. Closes late. Sleeps who knows when, if at all. Maybe we're just too much alike.

Walking up the street, I scan a front page that's all-Wyvern. For the time being, the Big Man and his Brother are banished to Local, strictly small-time sleaze. They'll have to ramp up their act past crack, lies, and denigration if they want back in the limelight.

The dead man's photo still central, as befits a murdered king. But around him have sprouted pictures of Judy, Max, Vivian—*daughter, son, foster-daughter*. As if the family is growing in death, giving birth to itself in posthumous scandal.

There's no mother for the brood—no photo of Maude, thankfully. Nor one of Sandor, yet. Just a quote near his name, asking the media for "privacy during a difficult time... dealing with difficult issues." Instead of a mother, there are broken white lines, interrupted by white question marks, connecting the dead ruler with his offspring and foster-offspring. The white lines, nicely stark on black, remind me of Creation graphics in mythology books. All of these children springing from the head of Zeus, with roles and relations yet to be defined. Happily, the *Star* has included wavy lines to blank white boxes with black question marks inside them—their graphics department has obviously had a blast with this—to signify suspected but still-to-be-identified peers and partners. These are the boxes I hope to see proliferate and fill in.

It's the nest I've envisioned all along. A hive with secret chambers and cells, various humid tunnels connecting them.

The headlines evoke the same excitement and uncertainty. **TRAGIC PLOT THICKENS. Sex Crimes Investigation Joins Murder Inquiry. A Family's Woes Multiply.** Sadness and intrigue vying for precedence—with disgust pacing in the wings, awaiting its cue.

"Alleged" and "allegedly" sprinkled throughout, fairy dust to keep the lawyers happy and let the readers know it's all true.

Judy, picked up early yesterday while I was cutting myself and reading by flashlight, hasn't yet been formally charged. Like Max and Vivian, she's being "held for questioning... no further comment at this time." It was just wishful thinking to hope she'd ghost past the police. Apparitions are their business, after all.

And I don't seem to be their business whatsoever. No uniforms in sight. No spinning lights on cars. Not even a green light blinking on my phone.

Max not fingering me? Vivian not fingering me? And Judy not—well, only Judy's no surprise. Assuming she thought of me at all, they'd have as much luck getting a statue of Kali to come clean. I saw her on the ward. The shrinks, nurses, social workers, occupational therapists—all the professional talk-jocks that took cracks at us... when it came to Judy, they looked like big flies trapped in a room, batting themselves against a tiny pane of glass.

Along with puzzled relief, I feel a twinge of disappointment. Part of me was ready to head back to the small room and wire-mesh window. Head home, set up camp, and take stock from there.

They've got one nut. One nut coming home. Maybe that's all they need.

Sitting on the steps of Shoppers, I spread the paper open to follow the stories to the inside pages, forcing the line-up to swerve grumbling around me. But my eyes focus poorly through the swirling grains, I can't take in more than isolated words and phrases. It's just too late in the window. Or past it, more like: window overtime.

I flip to Births and Deaths, where side-by-side photos of Max and Maude—in smiling middle age, on vacation maybe—warn me to expect an incongruous obituary, with no connection to their obliterated family on Page One.

Near the end of **A Family's Woes Multiply**, a fragment pops out at me, Maude's name in a wistful windup: "...perhaps a blessing that she died too soon to know..."

Which is a question—how deep the hell of her marriage?—for despair and kindly oblivion to debate to an eternal standoff. Though the driver of a car on Bloor, slamming to a stop at a sickening thump, will always give the nod to despair.

The doors unlock, the line shoves in, a voice says, "Next time find a Starbucks for that."

I look up into the stupid eyes and immaculate coats of two large black poodles, chained to the wheelchair ramp railing. Their thighs and groins and rumps have been shaved, accentuating their calf muffs and fluffy erect tails and the curly matted hair covering their backs and faces. They stand alert, blocking the ramp entirely. I return their spoiled black stares, wishing an obese paraplegic with a power cart would flatten them.

When that doesn't happen, I take their meaning and move on.

§

Lynette's kitchen is cosy, light-filled. Varnished pine-slat table in a glassed-in eating nook, cushioned banquettes on three sides around it. Trays of herbs and flowers inside the windows, a more ambitious rock garden in the small back-yard. High, narrow bookcases built into brick walls, dividing the nook's airy spareness from the cluttered kitchen where she's fixing our teas.

This is the other side of Forest Hill, the side I tend to forget exists. The Good Life, gracious and tranquil. It may be only the more discreet and thoughtful sibling of Fuck-You-I-Got-Mine—but discretion and thoughtfulness count. Especially when, apart from miscellaneous outposts like No Name, they seem to be the only two residency options available.

Watching her pick loose leaf from a jar, fill the kettle, get down mugs from hooks—I have the strange sense I've lived here a long time. It's nothing like anywhere I've actually lived, and bears no relation to my present state of mind or circumstances. Yet the illusion persists even when I close my eyes to dispel it. Is joined, in fact, by an equally disconcerting, equally pleasant feeling of heaviness all through my body—as if I could actually fall asleep, if I let myself.

Milk? Cream? Some honey? I hear faintly, like wavelets lapping deep inside myself.

So much to say, we don't say anything for a while. Just sit and sip our teas, a little too regularly, on either side of the pine table, uncertain where to begin. "You look good," I say finally, repeating what I said at her door.

She colours a little, murmurs, "Well…" She can hardly repeat her own first words: "Oh, dear." Which popped out of her when she saw my eye, the fresh cuts rayed around it, but seemed to mean more than that or than the Face in general or the beat-up body attached to it. Maybe just the fact of these physical things she'd passed so often finally being on her front step, ringing her doorbell. Though she had to have been expecting that, sooner or later.

Her eyes, now that they've broken out of the Infinite Tunnel to meet mine, are hazel. And familiar. They're a deeper green-gold now, and seem bigger in her thinner face, but they're the eyes I remember from the ward. In almost every other way, she's changed. Slim and self-contained, deft in her movements; not farmgirl-plump and clumsy, hugging her flannel-nightgowned body, knocking things over. Chic blonde bob; not wheat-brown braids she did herself and sucked or chewed when upset. Strong cheekbones, chin, a speedwalker's spring and slimness. Her breasts smaller but sitting higher—they sagged back then. Anyone looking at her would see miraculous transformation, all for the better. A metamorphosis from lumpish depression to mature beauty. So why on earth do I feel something has been lost?

Twenty years ago, Judy and I were nearing forty, confirmed in our insanities. Lynette was twenty-three? twenty-four?—on the cusp, basically unformed, in a bad way but still capable of becoming anything, including something very different from what she'd been up till then. *Are you regretting she had to become anything definite at all?*

She raises her hands and holds them flat above the table, as if to rescue me from my dilemma or to confirm her identity. They shake. A fine constant tremor, not so far from Judy's.

"Still?"

"There's no Botox for bad nerves. No surgery either."

"I'm surprised you didn't find me sooner. I thought TAL would be a dead giveaway. I mean, how many people could it be, right? And back then, I don't know, I guess I thought of you as someone with special powers, sort of." She says it around her mug, blushing a bit. "I needed to think there could be someone like that, especially there. You were older too. I might've had a bit of a crush. Back then. And when I started seeing you around the neighbourhood, and hearing some stories—it came back a bit, I think. I mean that sense that you were someone who knew things other people didn't—almost that you could see through walls. It sounds so silly to say. Little Lynette. But I've been afraid for two weeks you'd knock on my door, walking around on pins and needles. It's a relief you're here finally. Really."

"Why afraid? You left the note."

"I did. But I was desperate. When you got the idea to give that awful nurse all those pills, did you have any idea what they might do to him?"

"Not a clue. None of us did."

"True. But we were basically just following your lead. You sounded so sure of things. And like I say, you've got kind of a reputation now, whether you know it or not. People tell stories. You may not hear them."

"You know about Brad?"

"Yes, I heard it from someone. Very sad."

I sip my tea, trying to piece it out. Just two weeks ago, but it might as well be two years, and it's hard to get back to anywhere near the beginning of the adjustment, see where I might have dropped the thread. Even to remember what happened, in the order it happened. What I was thinking, or might have been.

"You're right," I say after a bit. "It should've been obvious. You gave me all I needed. But I got distracted. These Wyverns…" She nods, but that blush comes into her cheek again, a teenage tell she hasn't lost. "I told myself it had to be Judy."

"Judy!"

"I know. Leaving a note I could understand? With an address I could get to?"

"Besides, Judy was up with her mom. All night that night." She plays with her spoon in the mug. "I'm saying too much probably. But you know I know Sandor. You've seen us in the writing group. And maybe you know I published his book. He told me he signed your copy."

I let the part about Sandor go for now. It's coming back to me, my thinking that first day. Blurry but I can make it out, like pieces of a wreck I'm seeing underwater. "It was a choice between you and Judy, in my mind. But—" Trying to get it straight for myself. "Judy and I are lifers. Different kinds, but lifers. That adjustment wasn't my first—I realized that on the ward—and later, over time, adjustments became a pattern. And Judy has adjustments too, her own kind. By whatever rules go on in her head. You? I thought of you as passing through the ward, Lynette. I assumed—I hoped—you'd moved on, like from a bad dream. So I didn't think you'd remember it."

"TAL? You don't forget the things that kept you alive."

"Did it really?"

"*Did it? Am I talking a bunch of shit?*" She tilts her head and asks it in a different voice. Like a drill, a reality check, she's learned, or been taught, to put herself through. "Yes. Yes, it did. For five hundred and forty days."

"You counted them?"

"Afterwards I did."

"That was a short-stay unit. Where'd you get sent for a year and a half?"

"Oh, home. But I kept getting re-admitted. And coming back for ECT series. Drug trials. One way or another, I was on more than off." She pauses, and the drill person, the word checker, comes back, her face goes stern with it. "I don't like the word *lifer*. It's too negative. Defeatist." And then the checker, having done her job, leaves the room and her face relaxes again. "But I was pretty full-time for a while, back then. And still, even now"—she holds up her quivering hands—"I might be full-time. Like you."

Like you. Not like you and Judy.

"Full-time? Everything a manic-depressive does is part-time. Or rather, double-time and stop-time. Maybe that averages out to full-time. It's a nice thought anyway."

"Manic-depressive," says the drillmaster, frowning. "You accept that label?"

I shrug. "I've got my own." Though we'll leave *windows* out of it. "People can put anything they want on the treatment package. It doesn't matter if I'm not buying it."

"You're not in any treatment? You haven't been?" She says it with a hint of awe, as if the special person from the ward just flew back into the room with his cape and all his powers.

"Just my own. But that takes in a lot."

"How 'bout some coffee cake?" she says. "Apple. I made it last night. And it looks like we could both use more tea."

And I hear myself answer yes, in a quiet murmur not quite my own voice, an underwater voice from the dream life I sensed before in the nook. *Life that might have been.*

She stops, hands on our mugs, about to rise with them. Rolls her eyes up to a place above my head. Trying to remember something, place something, her face blank with it. Then smiling as it starts to come to her. "You had *someone*, though. Not a therapist, not a doctor. But someone… this person, I'm trying to remember what you called him—"

"My case officer." *Stone.*

"That was it!" Her eyes alight with it. "Your case officer. Like a secret agent has. Do you still report to him?" She says it teasingly. Probing for the joke or what a joke might cover.

"I do." *Any day now.* "I have to. He runs me."

A joke? Standing now, fingers crooked through the mug handles, she looks down at me a long moment, trying to decide. Or trying to decide if she should follow if it isn't. Then comes down one way, tips into it in an instant, hazel eyes laughing above, and just ahead of, her mouth. Pale pink lip gloss. Nice white teeth.

§

Busy then in her kitchen, getting cake and making tea. While I sink into the nook life, so strange and familiar, feeling that pleasant tiredness take me down peacefully, swaying and lilting, thick coiling weed. Some cross-currents I fight, not very hard. *No one leaves the ward.* Not if they belong on it in the first place. What the mental health chatter tries to hide. The treatment porn. You close the ward, blow it up—Brad—or find a way to go on living on it. All kinds of ways. Judy's. Mine. Lynette's, with aspen-leaf hands and Botox and boob lifts and the Infinite Tunnel. And talk another way. Legends neither true nor untrue, signposts from a trail of losts. My wife and daughter? (In the bars, those first months, before I gave them up and called Ken.) Dead—both of them. One of them. From suicide. From murder-suicide. From accident. In coma from a failed attempt. Or simply gone without a trace. No notice even, no note? Yes, a note, but… Death an easier tale to tell. Except that—legends lead to intimacy. Trading them tugs you close, leans heads together. Freckled girl, big breasts, a gap between her teeth. Listening intently. *She loved me, believed in me despite knowing all she knew—and I felt the same about her— we lived every day wanting nothing but the best for each other. Every day—including the day she told me my craziness had burned her out. She couldn't take it anymore. Love wasn't enough. It wasn't all we* needed. *It never is—for anyone.* Freckled girl: I'd hate to believe that. Things always happen for a reason. Otherwise there'd be nothing to fix. No way to learn. *Things happen for a reason and they happen for no reason. None you'll ever discover anyway. That's what you learn. And knowing it does fix something.* Fixed, at least, the question of us going home together. And brought me, alone, a pinstep closer to sober and to Ken.

Quiet in the nook. Lynette's small clatterings might come from two doors over, through walls. Backyard so still, it might be painted on the glass.

"Where's your dog?"

"Gracie? David, that's my ex, he takes her on weekends. Sometimes during the week too. Believe it or not, she was the biggest sticking point in our separation agreement. Still easier than a kid, my lawyer said. My second ex, I should say. No kids with either one. I've had better luck meeting men than keeping them."

"Most of us are better met than kept."

"See, that sounds like you. It's partly why I kept my distance, especially after I saw you didn't recognize me."

"But you recognized me."

"Well…" She colours again. Awkward Lynette from the ward comes back into view.

"It's all right. I wouldn't forget me either."

Talking so much easier when you're doing something. *Almost a rule: the more you're doing, the more gets said.* It's a wonder we try it any other way. Setting up the face to face, insisting on it, when we'd be better off painting fences together, speaking out of the sides of our mouths over brush slaps. But fences to paint seem harder and harder to find. Like gold. Diamonds if you're talking dual jobs, side by side. Find one and you're doing well, one and a bit. Lynette slicing fruit for a salad—"Heck, we might as well make it a light brunch"—while I send feelers around the nook. Brush it with soft antennae. Out it comes that way, easily.

"Sandor got the call first. Early. 4 a.m., 4:30. POA, he's first on the list. Judy's there, yes, Maude's daughter, but she's not *really* there. That's harsh, I know. But it's true, isn't it? Five minutes later—five minutes after Vivera notified him—he's at my door. Which isn't what you're thinking. Oh, we had our moment— Sandor and I—had a few of them. But that's ancient history. It's something different now. Friendship. Writing. I know you don't like him. He's told me and I've seen it. I can feel it coming off you right now, without even turning my head. You judge him too harshly. Just my opinion. Funnily enough, he doesn't mind *you*. Fine. Boys will be boys. The point is how desperate he was that morning. Desperate. Not just from grief. He knew his mom was sick and old, you've read his book. *Desperate.* If you could've heard that knocking. Like someone trying to get out of a cage. It's not even light outside."

"Desperate about what?"

"It's hard to explain unless you know the family a bit. I don't know them well, mostly just what Sandor's told me. But something he said once stuck with me. He said, My family's good at a lot of things, great even, some of them—but what they're best at is smoothing. Making wrinkles disappear... reality wrinkles. He sat at my table two weeks ago, the day his mom died, sat where you're sitting, not drunk, stone sober, but shaking all over. Crying a bit. But mostly too upset to cry, if you know what I mean. Closing and unclosing his fists. Not making a lot of sense. He just kept talking about how quickly they were going to make things disappear, make his mom and everything go away... and then he started in about being asleep himself, how he'd always felt asleep in the family, like he was a dream he was having or someone else was having... and if things wrapped up too smoothly, he'd never wake up. He needed time, not necessarily to do anything, but at least to think. But thinking's what his family never had time for. They're just do-ers, do-ers and talkers..."

"I've read the papers, Lynette. So have you. Everybody has."

"Sandor didn't know anything about *that*. He's devastated by it. He's been locked inside his house since Thursday afternoon. Won't answer his phone, won't answer his door. Think about it. He's lost everybody in two weeks. And lost his good memories of them too. Lost his whole past."

"So what he didn't want smoothed over, whisked away—"

"It wasn't anything that specific. More like a sense he's had, maybe always had. A sense of something bad. Something creepy in the house. Something haunted, if you want to get gothic about it. And all these busy people, talking and doing, keeping the bad thing out of sight, driving the ghosts away. And I think it just hit him all at once—hit him when Maude was gone—that soon there'd be no one but the smoothers left. That they'd almost wiped the board clear."

"And you remembered an un-smoother you once knew. A wrinkle-restorer. Someone who might lift a clamped lid, poke a stick in and try to stir the pot. Disturb the sleepers with his racket."

"Yes, but... you make it sound a lot more thought-out than it was. Someone I knew, someone I cared about, was in trouble. He needed—"

"Shock therapy?"

"He needed *something*. Sandor didn't know anything about it. He was settling finally under a blanket on my couch, two of my sleeping pills taking effect, when I took Gracie for her early-morning walk."

"How did you know where I lived?"

"Everyone knows you're the super of that building. The one between the Latimer and the Favorite. Across from the fire station."

§

Great fruit salad: mango chunks, blueberries, raspberries, blackberries, melon, peaches. All the out-of-season things jets and MasterCard can bring you. And great coffee cake too, which is more seasonal and all Lynette's, with bits of dates and walnuts mixed in with the apple, and a crumbly brown sugar topping, not too sweet. We savour it together, sipping Earl Grey, but the nook magic is dissolving. It needed both of us in it to seem real, and started to wobble while I sat in it alone, looking at Lynette's collection of good books, quite a few of which I've read.

"You wrote it, didn't you, Lynette?" I say as she's refilling our cups.

She doesn't do a dumb *Wrote what?* and for a moment the nook shimmers back into view.

"Parts of it. Sandor had notes, and I stuck close to them."

"Notes?"

"Detailed notes. And a good plan for where he was going with them." Her smile a little cruel, a side of her not born yet on the ward. "But yes, all right, in the high court of literature, I suppose I might be convicted of heavy editing."

"Hence 'Wun Wing'."

"No. I mean, Sandor wanted some distance from it from the start. That was part of his vision of it: sort of anonymous dispatches from the front lines of caregiving. But yes, for that too… the co-writing process that evolved… we decided to bring it out under the press's name. And to honour his mom. She had this… well, you've read it. It's just a fragment, really, *Around Toogood Pond*. But what did you think?"

"It's good. It surprised me how good it is. I wouldn't have thought Sandor had it in him. But it's not as good as it could or should be. That's why you went ahead and published it on the quick, isn't it? Sandor was never going to slug it out and finish. You thought if he got a taste of writing he might actually write. But don't you see he can't?"

"He might if you accept that someone can be fragile *and* have substance." Narrowing her eyes and pressing her lips tight together, like an intake interviewer.

"You're trying to wake this guy up. You see signs of life and get encouraged. But it's only sleepwalking. What's more, I think you realize that. Some people you can't ever wake up. If they can't stand the light of day or the dark of night, they can only go on snoring."

She starts crying as I remember her crying. Big plump tears rolling off sharp cheekbones where plump cheeks used to be. Eyes wide and unblinking, unashamed of the sadness springing out of them. In the day room, sitting on the edge of her bed, standing beside a window in the corridor—I came upon her many times a day like that.

"You love him, don't you?"

She laughs hollowly, tears still flowing. "There's a guy question. A woman's crying, so it must be for another man." She sighs, wipes her eyes and cheeks with the backs of her hands.

"You were different on the ward. I thought you might just do something like what you did to Fresca. Stir things up a bit. Jolt people awake."

"That's stupid, Lynette." She stiffens, flattens her nostrils. "I was in a confined space on the ward. I was years, decades younger. And Fresca was aggravating people, not drugging and raping them."

"I told you, Sandor didn't know—"

"Not letting them rot alone for years because they had the bad manners to become ill. For decades in Judy's case. Like tossing mouldy fruit in a bin."

"I believe him. Most people aren't good liars. Not when you know them."

"On TV shows maybe. Otherwise they'd never catch anyone in half an hour. In real life, we're perfect."

"That's a horrible thing to believe."

"Yes."

After a time, she says, "Not just years younger. Years more… approachable. Gentler too. Why is it people always think hardness means you're learning? Gaining *experience*?"

Good question.

"Lynette, I was hard when you met me. Had a sheet of things I'd done"—*to people, to things, to animals*—"longer than you'd been alive."

"I'm not talking about armour. I'm talking about the man inside it."

As an Island shimmers into view…

"Good peaches. Juicy. Do you always peel them?"

"I don't like the skins. The little fuzzy hairs."

"They can be chewy sometimes. But they don't come off easily. I tug at corners with a paring knife, but chunks come off. You end up with a plum-sized peach."

"You scald them first. Two minutes in boiling water. The skin slides right off, sometimes in one piece."

§

"Tell me something, will you? What did Sandor do when he found out the truth?"

She exhales noisily. "You're going to believe what you want to—"

"I mean *any* truth. One even. Maude's, let's say. Father shuts his wife away so he can bang young immigrants without a depressive cramping his style. Pays number one son to handle the bills so not even an invoice distracts him. Number one son visits occasionally at first—probably to make sure costs are in line—then not at all. Father's consistent from the start. Away's away."

·"It's childish to believe in monsters, isn't it? Ultimately, we're all people."

"I am a child."

She looks so long at something out the window, to the side of my face, that I turn to see what's there. A line of green hedge, virid in the sun. A walkway I can't quite see down to the street. She answers me without taking her eyes from the view.

"Well, he just about went crazy. Or did go crazy for a while. You read the book. He thought he was living inside a dream, a nightmare. He said he knew he was an alcoholic, but he was afraid of what he might see if he got sober. He thought that if he could just..."

"What did he *do*?" I say again, quietly.

Her eyes come back to me: flat, hard buttons. Her lips set in a thin bitter line. Is there any good way to get older?

"Lynette, there are two types of people in a crisis. Lots of types in other situations, but just two in a crisis. One rolls up his sleeves and gets to work. Gets whoever he can to safety, calls for help, and so forth. The other type doesn't.

"One of the things that mars Sandor's writing—that keeps his book from being the book it could be—is his constant need to tell himself he's the first kind of person when he's really the second. That's why he doesn't put the blame where it belongs. Because if he did, some of it would have to fall on him."

That new—to me—capacity for cruelty, and taste for it, spreads over her face like an ash cloud—

"Which would qualify you to complete the book, I guess."

—and lands me smack dab in the nook again, snug in searing light and space.

"I could do some heavy editing. No question."

Post-mirage, deserts are hotter. Dryer and more lifeless. Nothing burns like the memory of hope.

She isn't surprised or flustered when I ask for Sandor's address. She refuses politely, citing her promise to help protect his privacy. What surprises her is that I don't press.

I stand up to go. "It's a small neighbourhood. I'll poke around."

Awkwardness at the door, on both sides. Lynette breaks the silence.

"Well, maybe now that we've met... Met again, I mean."

With that girlish blush. *Teen to crone to angel on a tombstone.*

I look down the street at the maple where I stood a few nights ago, watching her draw the line with her ex. The tree's almost bare. A few red-orange leaves cling to it like flares. Like the tips of milkweed stalks set on fire with Bics stolen from foster parents, just catching or just sputtering out.

I turn back to her. "Lynette. You come into Sandor's book fairly often. He always calls you 'L.' But an 'L' also framed the butterfly wing. The 'one wing.' I can't see you working as a framer anytime recently."

"That was Lois," she says, wincing a little. But it aches rather than stabs, like a thump on an old bruise. "She worked at Loomis for a while. The art store at Yonge and Eg?" *Back where we met. And the one place on earth I'd never have looked.* "We talked a bit, not much. Enough to establish we both knew you."

"And my daughter? Megan?"

"We never talked about kids. I'm sorry. It was quite a while, maybe ten years ago, and she left not long after. She did ask if you were well."

"And?"

"I said I really didn't know."

Silence behind me as I'm heading toward the street. Then quick steps. She runs after me, grabs my wrist when I'm almost at the sidewalk.

"Don't hurt him. If you do find him, I mean. He doesn't know any better. Nobody's taught him how. He's damaged and doesn't know how badly. Or how to heal himself."

I look at Lynette. Sniffling girl, sniffling old woman. Identity gone spiralling in the sun.

"Past a certain age, past childhood, that's not an excuse. It's an accusation."

20

SANDOR. WITHIN A few blocks, I know, from following them the
other night. But the neighbourhood bristling with Castles
and Shields. A local job, but Forest Hill. *Steep, dark woods.*

A few doors down Roselawn, on the north side, a guy
standing on the sidewalk with a metal box in his hand.
Thirty-something, glasses, buzzcut. Fleshy arms and calves
coming out of his T-shirt and cutoffs. An ex-soldier or an
office wannabe, cadets in high school. His right hand on
a lever on the box, making small movements with it while
he stares into space. I stop a few feet from him, look where
he's looking. Finally see a small helicopter hovering over
his lawn. Neat as a dragonfly, maybe triple the size. "Excuse
me," I say. He doesn't move his hand from the box or take
his eyes off the copter. "Excuse me?" No reaction.

"Happy toggles, gearbox."

A little farther on the same side, an old man mowing his
lawn. His steps a bit tottery, even with the mower support-
ing him. He seems to be using it as a kind of walker —but
with electric, whirring blades? I stand where he can see me
on his next turn. He shuts off the machine.

"Excuse me, sir. A friend of mine, Sandor Wyvern? I guess you know his family trouble. Everybody does by now. And he called me to come over and talk a bit. But—it's stupid—I can't remember his house number since the last time I visited. I guess the news has really got me rattled," I say, shaking my head with it.

The old man's neck lengthens under his Blue Jays cap, like a turtle's extending from its shell.

"It *is* stupid," he says. "Someone who doesn't know where you live, yet you call him in your hour of need."

"Look, sir. I'm not with the media. Does this look like a face for television?"

The neck lengthens further. Wily old snapper, well-fed in the mud.

"Don't need much of a face for radio. Don't need any face. Or for newspapers or the Internet either."

"All right, old man. Have a nice day."

Across the street from the grass-cutter, two houses over, a flash of white in the backyard. Go closer, Daisy with her nose pressed against the mesh fence.

Ah, Lynette. Stand by your man.

§

No answer at the front door. None expected. Go round back and get over the fence. Daisy walks at me, growling. I raise the hammer to her and she slinks off. Curls near a bush, licking herself.

I approach the house. Behind the sliding door, Sandor is sitting at a round wooden table, drinking. I have to cup my hands around my eyes to see him clearly. Lots of cans in front of him. He's got his head down, not looking my way.

I try the door. Locked. At the sound, he lifts his head. Peers blearily in my direction, raises his middle finger. I raise the hammer, cock it at the glass. Slowly, pushing off the table with his hands, he gets up, can in hand, and lets me in.

"Back at work, I see. Busy on the grieving process."

Bare feet, jeans. Untucked plaid shirt falling to his thighs. Days of black stubble, eyes sunk in whiskers and greasy curls. A rank smell. He speaks with his back to me, returning to his corner seat. "Come in, get lost, sit down, stand up. Have a drink, don't, I don't *give* a shit."

"I know you don't, Sandor. That's what we're here to discuss."

"My tête-a-tête with the avenging angel. The perfect end to the perfect week. I wonder what I ever did to deserve you. It must've been something horrible."

He drains the can he's on, head way back to catch it all. "Have a beer if you want. But I've got nothing to say to you now. I never did really. And I don't think you've got anything more to say to me."

"There's where you're wrong. But I'll take that beer."

He reaches into the nest of cans, knocks a couple of empties over, and pulls out a full one for himself.

A weird assortment of beers, hectic. Maybe a dozen brands among the twenty or so cans on the table—Budweiser, Canadian, Heineken, Tuborg, Blue, Coors, Grolsch, Kronenbourg… It would fit a bunch of kids learning to drink, mixing and puking. Or someone in desperate straits and searching confusedly for the right drug, the one that might work. Even so, I can't make this grab bag fit a long-time drinker, who knows his brand as well as all the others.

I select a Coors Lite, thinking to start cautiously, but at the first sip my thoughts reel, as if a socket wrench has been

fitted over my brain and torqued violently. As if I'm on my
fifth can, not my first. Stone: *Last call.*

*Judy hitting his head with the hammer. The head shifting
a little, hand and hammer bouncing back.* That picture more
sickening, somehow, than her carving of the Sunday roast.

The Wyverns swept clean. Or nearly so—Sandor could
be the janitor left behind to close up the building. Five of
them at the start. Or six, with Vivian. Eight, counting her
vanished sisters? Who knows how many the hive contained
finally, swallowing up adjacent colonies, carrying back cap-
tive strays? Now, one dead of natural causes. One dispatched
by the daughter he abused. Three in lock-up: one for a short
time, I hope, before she rejoins her life in homes for the
mad, back behind the pharmaceutical bars she knows. The
other two for years and years. For forever, I hope. And the
last, bloated in front of me, deluged by the family problems,
bailing the flooded ship as best he can. Bailing its bilge back
into himself. The women not of Wyvern blood knocked
down too. Vivian, used and using, talking as fast as she can
in a little room to cut a deal. Gwen, popping Tums like
never before, gnawing her nails between calls to her lawyer.
Lynette—well, who knows about Lynette? The only thing
you can say about a lifelong depressive is that, whatever's
happening, she's probably depressed and anxious about it.

So sick of all of them.

Sick enough that the questions I had about them, mys-
teries that assailed and whipped me on, seem pointless now.
I feel them falling out of my head, grains from a smashed
hourglass. Did Maude know about her husband's secret life?
How deep a hell *was* her marriage? Deep enough that she
welcomed—a part of her did—the oblivion of Alzheimer's?
Keeping Christmas Music when she was put away, shoving
it down under old nylons—an attempt at leverage? A trump

to hold over the old prick? Lost when she didn't use it in time. *Which means you've been working for her on this adjustment all along.* Pleasant thought. The dead make the best clients, the only truly satisfying ones. The most exacting, and the most in need.

Or someone else buried it there? Hid it to find?

No, you're done with them. Done with this.

"Ten minutes ago, I thought it was crucial to find you. Now that I have, I've got no idea why I'm sitting here, drinking your beer at eleven in the morning."

"That makes two of us."

"A last-ditch effort, I thought, to get you to take care of Judy. To try being her brother. To start. You've got the power and the money, or you will have. What would it take? But that's the one thing I've never been able to get from any of you Wyverns. Looking after Judy in even the most basic fashion. It's a deal-breaker, as they say. I don't think I could force you with a blow torch and pliers."

"She's mentally ill."

"Unlike you and me."

He gives me a sickly, plastered smile. Idiot leer the bare truth summons—sniffing a con, utterly unable to take you at face value. Count on one hand the people who've asked me, Really? You think everyone's batshit crazy? And never got as far as defending it as the most humane assumption, true or not. Assuming universal insanity helps you deal with people properly. The ones with dangerous conditions you avoid or handle with wary ruthlessness, as you would vipers or scorpions. The harmlessly batty you treat with compassion. The rest you approach alertly and with an open mind, ready for anything. *Ward world.* Locked and unlocked, teeming.

"Just kidding, of course. There's a puppeteer works my face. A ventriloquist says odd things through my lips."

"No secret there," he says. "Hard to miss when they're standing right behind you."

And so we find ourselves back on familiar ground. *What we've found together. All we could find.* Bantering in a pub. Challenging to escape challenge. *Candour a flag truth hides behind. Whip and chair to back it into its cage.* Saying anything, since saying has no price.

"The last time we met, you were a fan seeking an autograph."

"I was a reader. One of the few. And a devoted one. Though the theme of the martyred caregiver got a bit thick."

"Which tells me you've never done much of it."

"You're addicted to the idea of yourself as a gentle giant. But there's no such thing. Not in a crisis anyway. Then you're either a giant, wielding a giant's might... or else a cruel dwarf."

"And that's how you see yourself?"

"Which?"

"A gentle giant?"

"No. Not gentle. And definitely not a giant."

"I don't know what you're talking about. I seldom do. Strangely enough, it keeps me listening."

The room is oddly unfurnished. Undecided maybe. The table we're sitting at, and the chairs around it, seem to belong in a kitchen, but the kitchen's over there, across a large space. The appliances gleaming new, the counters covered with dirty dishes and glasses, takeout cartons and bags, liquor bottles and beer cans. Empty alcove at the end of it where this table should go. Instead, it's pulled over into this corner by the sliding door, sitting on rust-coloured shag. Most of the large, L-shaped room beyond us is empty. A gas fireplace in the brick wall at the other end. Large-screen TV, a black rectangle, mounted on the wall beside it. A little way out from the TV, a U-shaped sectional couch in pale leather, like a sand spit with more cans and cartons, clothes and a quilt, washed up on and bobbing around it. No lamps, no overhead I can see. From this brightness by the door the room recedes into dim, the couch a shadowy whale rolling at dusk, then brightens again at the short end of the L, presumably from windows at the front. It looks like an animal's den. Except for all the evidence of feedings, and the absence of boxes, it could be the lair of someone just moving in or just moving out—or, more likely, the debris field of a bad divorce, with the remaining partner failing utterly to pick himself up and regroup.

"You're too late," he says thickly, the can resting on his bottom lip tilting up as soon as the words are out. He's hard to see, a bulk with pale gleams. He's got himself tucked into the corner by the drapes, out of the direct light which falls on me, but it's also the grains in my eyes, swirling more thickly now, enveloping him in sooty smoke. "For whatever you were after. Which none of us were ever sure of. Opinions varied. Judy's friend was all we knew for sure."

Which us? What opinions? Lynette, most likely. The other members of the writing group perhaps. They saw you in the Queen's Arms, would have talked it up. You always assumed Sandor was outside Max and Vivian's thing, the old man's thing when he surfaced—on the outside of everything, planetoid orbiting the rim of the family solar system, assigned the lowliest jobs of caring for the deranged. Such a man knows very little, as little as needed. It still seems true. *But question it. No disguise like that of the total fuck-up.* Hard, though, with the window closed or closing fast, each sip of Coors like a full can chugged.

"It's hard to explain what drives me," I hear my voice saying. And see a neighbour man, a long way back, I was helping clear his eaves of wasp nests. Him up on a step-ladder, rearing back fearfully as he sprayed Raid into the opening of the cone, the yellow bodies falling out covered with poison foam, me stamping on them as they wriggled on the ground, impressing him with my zeal. He doused the largest one with barbecue starter and lit it up, a blackly smoking torch, me standing by with the hose in case the house caught. But when I pressed to hunt for more, he got a strange look in his eyes and sent me home. *Go on, now. You were a big help, but it's time you got on home.*

"I came over here to get the truth of your involvement in this, and to get a promise from you that Judy would be cared for, but you're too far gone to work with. Your trouble is you always take the easy way out. Even when you think you're being hard on yourself, you're really going easy. You spoil yourself rotten."

"Involvement in what?" he says, sounding several degrees more sober. And there it is again: the weird sense I've had with him, from first meeting on, that we have port-holes into each other's heads. But I don't know—and it's an effort to remember this—what Sandor knows and has done, just as he doesn't know the same about me. Couldn't imagine that I spent his father's last moments with him, our knees almost touching. Or what those moments were. Or how merciful they were compared to the prison cell and public zero-ing he had coming to him.

"I read the papers," I say, hoping that enough of **Sex Crimes Investigation** has been aired.

"Do you?" he says, with a hard look that reaches me out of his murk. Not his Toogood Pond thing surfacing, it's per-manently up and wallowing, his eyes black gleams off its back. "I was beginning to wonder. I thought you might just be an avenging angel that swoops day and night around the skies, touching down where you're needed." As a picture of the adjustment life, it comes close to accurate, if way too exalted. But self-pity comes to the rescue, as it does so often when human conversations threaten to become acute. He uncaps another can, takes half of it down, and hangs his bushy head. *"Fuck. It.* I lost my entire family in the last two weeks. Mom first. Then the rest of them in the last three days."

"You lost them long ago. And never sent out a search party. Why, I wonder."

"I don't follow you. You're not making sense."

"You follow fine and I'm making perfect sense. You're just a terrible listener. All your family are. Your ears work perfectly, but you take in what you want and flush the rest."

"My family's ruined," he says, slurring now, fingers lost and roving in his curls. "Everything's fallen to shit."

"So start building."

"Build what? Where?"

"Start with Judy. She's going to need your help. She always has."

He looks up at me without raising his head, blinking, as if I've said something utterly outlandish. *Judy again? Still?*

"Or demolish it. Finish the job. Sometimes you've got to smash things. When the house is rotten all the way through, there's nothing to be salvaged—you've got to take the wrecking ball to it and then dig up the foundation. A clean hole is all you can expect to work with."

Stillness from his side, the fingers stopped, peering with glazed eyes above the cans and below my face. Jab him with something new. *No, it's too late for this guy.*

"Where's your can? I've got to take a leak."

Barely moving, the black eyes indicate a short hall past the kitchen.

§

"…a look'n your way pas'," burbles the voice behind me. Is he putting this on? Sober and sparring one moment, near coma the next? No, a veteran drunk, drowning the cells, turning them to pure alcohol, while the mind teeter-treads above, floundering and sinking, then riding a clean board high above the churn. It hasn't been *that* long. Hell, is happening on half a Coors.

This morning's *Globe* on the corner of the kitchen counter, open to the obituaries.

Head and shoulder shots, staring up: the officer in dress uniform, the bride in white. *What you saw that first day at Vivera, the missing heads.* But two hours ago, the poolside pensioners smiling from the *Star*? Two sets of obit pics? Or are you that far along? Past distortion phase, on to full hallucinations?

I can't read well, even worse than earlier. I just pick out scraps, fuzzed space between them. Enough to confirm the usual malarkey, in the usual proportions. The great man's childhood, schooling, service to his country, medical career, service to the community, *honoured by… presented with… proud to.* Maude's name flitting in and out, her two main appearances near the start—*met the love of his life*—and two-thirds through—*devoted mother to their three children.* And, near the end, before it reverts to him: *courageous battle with…* Like watching a movie with the sound off: just count when people come on, how long they're on for.

Endings matter. Force yourself to focus.

I turn back to Sandor. He looks smaller, slumped behind his moat of cans, me looking down at him.

"'He died at home, surrounded by his family.' You added that last line, I guess, as some kind of payback. A joke on him."

"No, he did, believe it or not. He wrote their obituaries and filed them with the funeral home years ago. Tinkered with them probably, like his will. Had individual ones, if they died far apart. And this joint production, with Mom slotted in around him. He always thought he could control everything, even his own end. I think it had something to do with putting people to sleep for forty years. But I left the line in. No, not quite as payback." He muses, seeming to go somewhere distant and come partway back. "But I guess to show how wrong I think he was."

"Wrong about?"

"Always knew something was off—wrong—about my father. Something about women. People in general, but especially women."

True enough, but I don't trust Sandor's fleeting epiphanies. He lacks the guts—the cornered need, if there's a difference—to stick with anything, even a valuable truth he's discovered. *The baby of the family. Arriving late on the scene. Overlooked. Spoiled.*

Standing there, sighting through swirling grains, I see yet another version of the dark bulk in the gloom. It comes over me in an instant, a new account of those turbid, roiling eyes. Not grief, not guilt and shame—not just—but something more like embarrassment. Embarrassment and lifelong pique. He sicced me on his older brother and father, or acquiesced in Lynette doing so—not to avenge his discarded mother, not for money (which Max will hardly be able to spend, or at least control so well, from jail)—but to get out from under their thumbs. To stop being the baby, the overlooked one. Even Judy more respected in a weird way, at least for her power to disrupt. The thing surfacing in his eyes: the look of sly guilt and fright in a little boy who lights matches and then sees the flames spreading beyond his control. Panic of mischief gone amok.

Past childhood, an accusation not an excuse.

Time to find the bathroom and finish this.

§

During the flush, I open the cupboard under the sink. Find, on one side, Comet and Drano, about twenty bars of Dove from some sale. Next to them—hello. A stash like I found in another brother's pad. But concentrated here, two small half shelves in the dark, not spread out as in the official home. Nothing to contradict—at least not to eyes not too prying—the filthy razor and hair-laced soap bar on the sink.

Bag of cotton puffs. Curling iron, cord twist-tied. Make-up case. Mirror. Creams and ointments. Lancôme in gold letters on a little mauve obelisk. Other swishy names.

One ship going down, jump to another? Or keep passage booked on both of them—who knows what the high seas will bring? Or just—a periodic return to home port? The old man's "disappointment" in his youngest, their long estrangement. Sandor a lazy athlete, he sneered. But not so lazy as a ladies' man. Unless finding your first at home counts as sloth.

The thoughts trail off, I can't follow them long. It's not just closing window fatigue. More like built-up toxicity from prolonged exposure to the Wyverns. Their cold congealed sleaze—like staring at a plate of yesterday's spaghetti crawling with roaches. I've never felt it on an adjustment before. Disabling exhaustion, sure, many times, the last steps performed as if underwater.

But not this sheer disgust swamping me, oozing like cold black gel between me and the targets.

Adjustments have ended badly for lots of reasons. Never by out-repulsing me.

I close the cupboard door and rise on creaking knees to check the medicine cabinet.

Pills. A lot of them. Bottles and bottles. I flush the toilet again, run the water while I bring them out of the cabinet. Antidepressants, a couple of kinds, doctors' names on the newer ones with drugstore labels. Sedatives, various benzo-diazepines. Scrips with lots of latitude: 1-3 pills at bedtime, enough for three months, a couple of repeats. Older pills, or at least older bottles, behind them. No labels, or scurf of labels torn away. Pink pills. Yellow pills. Orange pills. Beige ones. No names on any of them. *Lots of obliging doctors. Two less now though.* I peer at one pill, then another. They're just colours.

No way to tell, really. I take what I think I'll need.

§

Go back in, take my seat. Sandor doesn't look surprised when I set the pill bottle on the table in front of me. Take my cutter out of my pocket, open the blade with a *snick*. He doesn't look remotely drunk either. He watches me alertly from his corner, his mouth looking like it wants to smile. The eyes black and baleful, far past grief.

"Is this the part where you use your knife, make me swallow a bottle of my own pills? Force me to tell you what you think I know. Make me do something. Sign something. *Take care of Judy*," he says mincingly.

"No, you goddam pussy. This is where I show you the easy way out and see if you follow form and take it."

"Ah, right. Follow my goddam family down. People would believe it."

A caving in my head. Like an anthill collapsing, sand and tiny scrambling bodies. Except it keeps going on. *Not an event. The way it is.*

I swallow the first handful of pills to stop seeing it. Uncap the bottle and tap half a dozen into my palm, swallow them with what's left of the Coors. Open another can.

"What the fuck?"

Shake another handful into my palm. Pause. Cock my head, trying to catch up to what's happening. There was something else, another plan, I'm sure of it, but whatever it was, if it was, it's whooshing into the past like a bullet train and I can't catch it now. The new thing that replaced it is waiting, just ahead, for me to catch up to it. When I do, my lips will move and sound will come out of them.

I swallow the pills with a long chug of Coors.

"Stop! That's enough! We can talk. I'm not gonna let you do this." But he doesn't get up, doesn't move except to raise his hands. This dance is paralyzing him.

I shake out another handful.

"HOLD IT! You can't do this here!"

"Lynette and your book have got me half-believing you've got a heart. The start of one anyway. Now we're going to see if you've got any balls to go with it. A heart without balls is nothing but a curse in this world. You're Exhibit A on that score."

I still don't know what I'm doing, can't go fast enough to catch up to it. I barely hear what I'm saying, though

I follow it and it sounds like me. What I know: I *am* the adjustment.

Down go the pills. Fifteen or more in me now.

"Now *listen*. We can talk. We can go somewhere, talk to someone. This is *not* happening. You can't just come in here and off yourself. It's too fucking crazy. Way too fucking crazy. You're crazy if you think—"

"Of course I am. So is Judy. You're so busy cataloguing your own blues, you can't see conditions that make yours look like hiccups. Not even when they're right in front of your face. You think you've come close to the edge? Touched the void? You haven't gone near it."

My voice high in my ears, climbing toward shrill near the end.

Not my voice. Crazy for real.

I ready the next handful, take a gulp of beer and a deep breath before swallowing them. I want to get the next part out clearly while I can. Make sure he gets it all.

"You've got two choices. You can let me die here, which will take me out of your hair for good but will also give you something difficult to explain. At a time when your family's doing nothing but explaining. How did a man happen to O.D. in your home, in front of your eyes, without you stopping him? Or you can do the safe thing—call it in—which is going to keep me in your life, knowing the secrets of your filthy family, badgering you to take care of Judy. I'm betting you'll pick safe, for all its aggravations, but you're weak enough and privileged enough, with just enough dumb cunning, to feel you might just want to take a chance and clear the slate. But understand this: if I wake up, I'm hounding you until Judy gets her due. You know me enough to know I won't stop. If I'm here tomorrow I'm on your case."

He sits there, shocked. Mouth and eyes sex-doll wide. I swallow the handful. Then two fistfuls after it, enough to make me gag a bit, even sloshing down beer.

The bottle's empty.

Sit there, waiting. For the second time in three days, I feel myself beginning to go numb, my head emptying and coldly fizzing from Wyvern drugs, while a Wyvern watches me quizzically. *Not the drugs, not yet. Though it means the drugs will work even faster.* Christ, how I hate their faces: Max, Vivian, Sandor, that ancient ghoul… Judy too. Just for ridding me of the sight of them, death will be a blessing.

Not here. Another plan forming. Still catching up to it.

I stand up.

"What're you doing? What's going on?" Sounding panicked, boyish. *Hey, guys, wait up. Gu-ys!*

"I'm leaving. I need to get home."

"Wait." He reaches the door as I do, grabs my wrist. I stare down at the hand encircling me. It's enormous: these massive fingers, black wires coiling from them. He removes it.

I slide the door open. Step out into cool air, sunlight. Turn back.

Sandor in smudgy dark. This huge mess, staring back at me. Petrified.

"Do you eat other animals?" I say, and slide the door closed.

§

"Good girl," I say to Daisy, still hunkered in the shade. Something I don't recall ever saying before, I'm not a dog person. Not a pet person in any sense. Cage creatures for cuddling? If she comes at me I have my blade ready.

§

Walking down Shields. Walking slower than I should. My legs rubbery, not quite there. Gliding a hair above the sidewalk. Faraway dark oblongs make slow-motion leaps across the cracks, land fizzing on the square beyond. That long moving walkway they used to have at Spadina, transferring people from one line to another. Some strode beside it, impatient: when they matched its pace you both stopped moving and just hung there, side by side. Some people walked on the belt, adding muscle to machine, brief superheroes. But most just let themselves be carried along. Moving without moving. Horizontal balloons. Sailing...

Right at Crestview. Then the jog, past which the sidewalk disappears. Curb and grass. Crossing Castlewood. Lynette up there. Crying. Phoning. Doing the dishes to distract herself. Giving up, hammering on his door. Crying.

All just the same. Exactly equivalent ways of doing exactly the same thing.

Things look large and wonderful. *En*larged. Their outlines sharp, their colours rich and so deep.

Also faraway. Behind something. Like things coated in clear plastic. *Paperweights. Souvenirs.*

A maple key. A yellow leaf. A black ant, stopped on the sidewalk encased in clear.

Except the people. Raking lawns. Shooting baskets on the driveway. Coming up Latimer with their bags. These stay free of the clear, it can't coat them. Because they're moving? No, this old man too—planted in a lawn chair, striped blanket over his lap. He too has scratchy, shifting edges—duller, hard-to-make-out colours. He and what he touches: chair, blanket, newspaper under his hands.

His zone. His human sphere.

Closing window permit. Before all clarity disappears, allowed to step for a moment outside the room you've been so busy in, and there, in thickening mist, rub a circle with your fist on the pane and peer inside, understanding the mess and order you see within the room, the patterns of the person living in it, what set him going and what accelerated him to fever pitch.

Or—*since likeness is a queen that must lay eggs*—say you tinker with a watch that's breaking down. It keeps bad time and soon will stop altogether. Opening the face, picking gingerly at the gears, you find, in tiny letters scratched inside the cover, the initials of the watchmaker, and know—a calm recognition—who first wound the mechanism and set it going.

Back up. Old man's eyes widen in fear as I come up his lawn, but it's not him I'm after. It's what stares up from his lap. Vivian's head. What I glimpsed, floating past. Her face covering the front of the *Sun*.

She's banged up bad. Eyes just slits in blue-black mounds. Puffy blue on one cheek near her jaw, scrape down the other like she's been dragged. No make-up. Her hair limp, unwashed.

A brother did her up right. Just right. Lots of colour and ugly, but no cuts to leave scars.

Homolka's gambit, with her raccoon eyes. The same exit strategy. What, twenty years ago? How many will remember in the Age of Amnesia?

Sun-blared caption at the bottom: **FACE OF A VICTIM**.

Old man's eyes staring up. Wide, watery, unblinking. No, I'm not Death yet. Enjoy the autumn light a little longer.

Moving off, I think I may have to exempt Vivian from my Wyvern hate-on. Reserve a special place for her.

Vigil under the scorched and decomposing parents. Airlift to the land o' plenty. Glitterville. Where aunts and sisters vanish. Where brown-skinned dolls get passed from lap to lap, playthings for old men and teenage heirs.

Just keep crawling out from under. Out and over and up. Out.

§

At Eglinton, by Tuscany Cleaners. Stopped near the corner, leaning against the wall of the Latimer. The brick cool against the back of my head, a strip of shade. A cool hand, almost.

Looking straight across at the red door. Sign beside it: 641. High, wide doors, big trucks blurry behind the glass. *The old brick fire station.* Brand new EMS down right, pie-slice corner of Chaplin. You take it in, but your eyes come back.

Red door. 641. Loaded trucks, bulging behind glass. Fire Station 135. These things, they have a meaning—*something to tell*—but you can't make it out. Can't see, can't hear, clearly enough.

More than help. But what more is you can't decide.

And then I do know, for an instant anyway. Staring at the red door, I see the facts behind it. The truth visits me like a lonely comet from deep space, crosses my sky for a few seconds, and carries on towards some distant star.

Vivian. She set up my meet with Dr. Wyvern. Max knew nothing of it. Wouldn't have the stomach for where it would go, and anyway, wouldn't want to cry for help from daddy yet again. For a serious threat, all right—but not for "Judy's friend." Not yet. But Vivian knows people. Has had to learn to read them since squirming out from under her parents' broiled bodies. She made the call—or had Gwen make it. Dear old Gwen, half-mad with loneliness and dyke-mom yearning for this "fox" she's always "admired."

And then the helpless call to her other lovelorn guardian. Her sponsor. Her foster-father. Who had the run of her girl's body all his late watch, sweet ripening years of retirement. Maybe she had to seal the deal with a nostalgic hand job. Or maybe just her voice with the right note of promissory pleading and gratitude was as good as a tug through flannel. Who knows what it took to move him? The mention that this annoying person was a particular friend of Judy's?

Maybe, not having bodies delivered to him on stretchers anymore, the mere thought of a live one walking in his door unsuspecting was enough.

Vivian would have told him what he needed to hear. And would have been prepared for how it went, either way. Not many left Dr. Wyvern unscathed—as she had cause to know. Still, ninety-four being ninety-four, if someone did get the drop on him—well, in a world with one less father, she'd be that much better equipped to handle things her own way. Take the next step needed, do what she required—all she'd asked from life, from earliest memory.

I see it all, so clear, and then it's gone. The big red truck goes wailing down the street without the red door ever opening.

§

Moving farther down. The end of the Latimer. Moving even slower, step by step slower, though I know I should speed up.

Looking up at the balcony. 501. Straight above. Fear plunge. My insides lurch with it. No one's at the railing, looking down. He's inside, arrived already, I see him moving from room to room, uncertain where he should be. Where he should sit or lie. Mattress? Armchair? Floor in Big Empty? Among the *far cors*?

No place seems right, seems his, and so he paces between them guiltily.

You've checked out.

Get inside.

But no. I don't. So goddamn stubborn, even now. Picking my way down the short bumpy slope to parking. The garage door standing open for some reason. Only Lucius and I key it open, air it out. No rain for days.

Tagger's kraken just as it was. Thrusting black bulbs, thrashing tail and jaws. Never came back to add to it, though I kept expecting him to. No Owner-ordered gray goo either. Stasis. Status quo.

Stalemate. And both know it.

Why not send Judy too? Cosy threesome. Throw her into the mix like an unguided missile. Primed with a tale of Dad and Super chumming up, making deals? Nonsense may prevail—better than even odds with Judy, always. On the other hand… only blood and good can come of it.

Vivian the survivor.

I stick two fingers as far as I can down my throat. Retch up a brown froth flecked with grit. Not much left of all Sandor's pills.

Too late. Behind the play on Wyvern dope, again.

§

Stepping inside. Stepping gingerly. Sensation from below all but gone now. The concrete gouged and pitted. Lunar lot.

Cars in their spots. One to twenty-one. Two between each pair of pillars.

Mine in number six. Beside Lucius's pickup.

Mine?

Step closer.

No, not mine. Close, though. Another Honda, gray. Even older. Rust around the wheel wells. Punch-size pockets, scalings along the side panel. The licence dirty, road-bleared.

Stoop to read it better.

How—

White in the corner of my eye. Bandaged face, stepping to me from behind the pillar.

Big backswing, greedy for it. Get my hand up to catch some of it.

Crack! Fingers break, my head rocks back with it.

The hand falls, a shot bird, swoop down after it.

Whump! Small of the back, the other side. Pain roars up my neck and down my legs, rockets around my head trying to get out. Sink to my knees, then all the way.

Tucking, curling weakly, trying to keep an arm over my head, but it doesn't matter, they're not looking for an open spot, just blasting away, pounding like apes with clubs.

Amateurs.

Their bats descend like rain.

Gray swirls, darkening.

Mud red.

Black.

§

Waiting for me on the stairs. Just sitting there with her hands in her lap. First kid at school before the bell.

No memory of coming down. Just got here.

Wasn't then was.

Am.

Inside's out now. Facing me. Long cornsilk hair. Bandage where the blood was, shining white. Big bandage on little face: temple to chin, cheek to ear. Some of her hair shaved for it. Stub of nose poking out.

Doesn't smile. Or else just faintly, with her eyes. Reaches up her hand. I have to bend to take it. Cool and firm, makes me think of a fish. But dry. Like talcum.

She leads me further down.

One flight. Turn. Another. Our feet padding on the stone. I look down. Mine bare too.

Nobody in the lower rooms. *They only roamed when she was pinned.*

She got free, wrenched herself unstuck, to bring you here.

Three flights down, she stops. Looks away. The back of her head, corner of the bandage.

Doesn't say anything, she can't, but I understand.

This is as far as she can go. As far as she can take me.

A step or two myself. Slowly. Pricklings in my gut.

Quick pattering. Turn, and she's running up the stairs. Tiny figure in a white shift fleeing, hard to see already.

The ground shaking up above me, where she's gone. Dark slidings, back and forth. Except it isn't ground. *Is your body, being hit. You just can't feel it anymore.*

Peer down into the gloom, thicker now. Or seems so, since I know how deep I am.

One step at a time, descend. A long way down but no more turnings. And no sound—none not my own. Soft footfalls.

Until I reach the bottom.

Rooms lead off, black. Black openings in stone. Jelly-like, bulging.

Four, five, six... lots of them.

A bad smell. Old toilet smell.

Going back. *Can't go back.*

Keep going. I look up but can't see her. I've never heard her voice before. Didn't know she had one. She must save it for emergencies.

Gray fluttering in a room to my right. Not there before, or else my eyes have changed.

I follow it. The light gains feebly, shows what's glimmering in silver-grays.

Which changes once, abruptly, as I near.

Looking up. Way, way up. Big man, big lady—sky faces—looking down. Smiling.

Laughing! Mouths wide with it.

Looking down then, and in. At a scene with three, not two. The picture a dark box. I am the light that opens it. Man sitting cross-legged, woman kneeling beside him. Good-looking people. Man raw and rangy, daredevil smile, dark suit and tie. Woman softly pretty in a tight gray skirt and black sweater, string of pearls. Meek worried eyes.

On his lap, behind his crossed arms, the little blob in white. Eyes in a flesh slit, mouth hole. Feet in sockettes.

But the rest white. Bandages. Windings of them around the face, over the head in a skull cap. And plaster casts—two arms, one leg. Little white mummy. Stiff white arms and legs sticking straight out above and below the man's arms.

Who took this?

Strange squiggles behind them, between them and above their heads. Bright drizzling gray. Smidges of molten silver, melting, twisting down black velvet. *Siver nakes.*

Tinsel. Tree.

Murmurings, tense shiftings, in the space beyond this.

The stairs go on beyond. This is just an alcove, though the deepest yet. Beyond leads further down.

Stone waiting, close. Impatient for his start. Eaten into, delayed.

Close up, close up! My turn now.

You'll get yours, Stone. You always do.

Just now, for a few seconds more, I have to stare at what I've found. Stare and stare, not knowing how long it may last.

A charmed circle. No one here gets in or out.

I don't know these people, I've never seen them before. Yet who else can they possibly be?

?.11.13
—
21.12.13

21

NOTHING.

Nothing I trust from the hospital. Confetti glimpses, dreamless sleeps.

Just—*there*. Then—*back, somehow*.

Seeing a world in bits. Thing-bits. Body-bits.

Voice-over by Stone.

Clanks, running water. *Someone washing the dishes*.

Bundling sounds, foul smells. *Seeing to the garbage*.

Chair by window.

Bringing a coffee. Blur of face, fall of hair as she bends. Hands—warm, rough—steadying mine around the mug. Smooth and warmer still.

Hands, hands, coffee. *Russian doll*.

"Sandor?" says a voice. Dead leaf swirl in my throat.

"No, no Sandor. Is…" But speech too fast.

Down here they blur. Rustle and dissolve. Move too fast to see. Freeze in statue shapes. Only the dead move credibly. Speak words that reach the ears.

Been here before. And returned from it. And will again. Eventually. No clock time here. Where you rest. And learn. And pay. Where adjustments come from—and go to.

§

Memory scraps, scissored from—this morning? A day ago? A week? Water running, steam. Bathroom. Hands holding me to strip off stinking clothes. Step out of the rank pile. Four hands—two holding up, two popping buttons, tugging down pants. Strong hands. Women's.

Slivers in mirror mist: puffy, blue-black, scabbed. Hello Dead Eyes.

I can't see her well. *Them?* After a time I can look up, find a woman-shape across the room. Fuzzy oblong at the stove, the sink. I can't see more than that. When she comes close, to give me food or drink, take my cup and plate and wipe my face and hands, she disappears. Just bits of her. Tendril of gray-black hair. Chapped red finger. Cracked nail. Corner of an eye, like a clamshell closing. It helps me start to talk. This blur, nearby.

"Devils." It fills my mouth and then I hear it.

"Devils, sure." Close, above. "Always lots of devils in the world. One for every angel. And I think you have an angel with you when you need. They find you here, upstairs… with what you have inside you? But no, they wait in the basement. Somewhere someone going to find. Devils? I say you have an angel. Very good angel by your side."

"Money." Another time. A question, though it flatlines.

She laughs. "Why? You want to give me some? Mebbe fire me? Well, you know what? You're not my boss. You no hire, you can't fire. You want to, talk to the boss." She laughs, a deep sound. "So eat your soup."

Later. Window dimming to dark. Nighttime? Same chair. Somehow a day has passed without anything happening. Without my seeing, feeling—without my being in it.

No matter.

Beside me again. Her coat on. Putting paper, warm in my hands.

Cookie on a napkin. A star, five-pointed. White icing, pink.

"...come to you... ready for bed." Sounds start, then I understand, catching the last.

People climbing down to me on ladders. Warn them what is here.

Warnings are useless.

You see—so can't be warned. Don't see—can't be harmed.

Hand brings star to mouth. Sweet glaze, soft warm crumbling. Good, says Judas mouth. Bits fall on my lap. Drool drops, black between brown stars.

For a moment I see her face. Her mouth at least. Smiling. Teeth, not too white. Real.

Strong hand on my shoulder. *Leave it there forever.*

"Is Christmas coming," says the voice above. "Isn't it?"

§

Two visitors, a long way in. Christmas closer from her stars and bells. Santa Claus with red and white icing. Green tree with sparkles. I hate Christmas, like cookies—nothing's right to say.

Knocking, firm. Low words at the door, and she goes. Her footsteps clicking away.

Tall shapes, they bring over the chairs she keeps by the stove. Sits on one, puts her feet on the other. Set them by this chair by the window.

Keeping a little space between us, not crowding too much.

Cops all the same.

Close, I see them a little better. The gray fog eats at them, but in between, I catch bits of not-old faces, a suit, a skirt and blouse.

"I'm Detective-Sergeant Beverly... is Detective-Constable Frank." Coming in with lots of static, but I get the main bits. The names would slide on out again, except the man's is Beverly and the woman's Frank. The oddity a signal boost. "We're from the Integrated Crimes Unit. Have you heard of that?"

Heavy feeling when I shake my head. Delicate, too. Broken parts, sloshing.

"It pretty much explains itself. Most bad actors keep it simple. One bad thing, one department to deal with them. But some bad actors do so many bad things they cross borders. Departments crawl over each other to get at them. Homicide, sex crimes, fraud, drugs, cybercrime, immigration..." He runs out of fingers and just holds them up, ten fat wrinkled worms—sliding in and out of fog—while he muses at the uncountable kinds of bad acting. And expects me to, I guess.

I go back to looking at the low gray through the glass. Half-forget they're there.

"You don't remember us, do you?" The woman. Frank.

Don't shake again. That sloshing's bad.

"We visited you three times. Twice at the hospital, once right after your admission and once a couple of weeks later.

The first time you weren't conscious. The second time you were, off and on, but couldn't speak." Her voice not unkind, for a cop's. Taking it slow, but not so slow it's mean. It takes out some of the static, brings her through clearer. "The third time was a week ago. Your injuries are healing, and the doctors don't feel there'll be permanent brain damage—otherwise they wouldn't have discharged you. But you couldn't give us any answers. Didn't seem to quite see or hear us, was my impression."

The guy shifting, beside her. Wants to take this harder and faster. No need to look at him to feel it.

"But that wasn't—*this* isn't—just your injuries. The beating you took. The, uh, pills you'd taken. This is… your condition. Am I right?"

That's a go, says Stone. *Give 'em something so they don't amp up.*

I nod, heavily.

"Listen, *sir*"—if Beverly heard what Frank just said, he didn't understand it—"we're not asking for much. Just a few simple questions and answers, details we're trying to clear up. We ask, you answer. You don't even need to get out of your chair. You wouldn't be back home if you couldn't do that much. And I think we've been very—"

"How about *this*?" An edge in her voice as she cuts over him. She may be junior, but Beverly out of his depth here. "I don't know how much you remember, or how much anyone might be telling you. I assume you're not reading the newspapers or listening to the radio. So why don't we do it this way? I'll tell you some things we know, or think we know. Show you some pictures. If I've got it right, you don't need to say or do anything. If I'm out on something, you can shake your head. Correct me if you can. I won't ask a question unless I need to. And then you can answer… or not. All right?"

It is, so I do nothing. She maybe smiles. Seam of white anyway.

"We know you know Ms. Villanueva."

Slides a photo, a newspaper blow-up, into my hands. A Vivian I've never seen before. Grainy news grays, but more than that. Hair back under a hairband, no make-up. Wide, earnest eyes. Blazer over high-collar blouse—what it shows of her clothes. A microphone in front of her. If you could shower the vamp and cunning from a fox. *A de-sex spa...*

"It's hard for her, really hard. But she's been making some public appearances. Radio a couple of times. TV, once. Trying to get other victims to come forward. We know who some of them are, but unless they're willing to make a statement... Cross-examiner in a courtroom—well, that's a whole other thing. But by working with us, she's also trying to work with them. Leading by example."

Hello, Ms. Villanueva.

"We know you saw her quite a lot in a short time. Met her several times, those two weeks in October. At Dr. Wyvern's dental office where she worked. At the restaurant up the street"—she flips a pad—"Ukiyo-e, where she was having dinner with Dr. Wyvern. You visited her at her home, too. Her condo at Bayview and Sheppard. Again with Dr. Wyvern. All that's established. Sign-in books, security cams, witnesses if we needed them. You're not denying any of that, I take it."

I'm not.

"The fuzzy area—the gap between versions—is why. According to Dr. Wyvern, the visits were escalating harassments in aid of extortion. He named the sums discussed. There's no disagreement there. But according to Ms. Villanueva, you were attempting to obtain the money for

Judy Wyvern, now in custody, charged with her father's murder. I'm sorry if I'm telling you things you already know, that you may have trouble following, I'm not sure. But we need to get this clear." Grit in her voice when she needs it. "In Dr. Wyvern's version, your concern for his sister was just a front, a scam, to get the money for yourself. To keep on getting it, probably, as long as you held on to evidence that incriminated him. What else would you expect—Ms. Villanueva's view—from a serial sex predator? Someone who, like his father, drugged and sexually violated women in his medical practice? What other kind of motive would such a man understand? Her words, more or less. And a view I'm strongly tempted to accept, absent other evidence. As I suspect most women—most people—would be."

Making Max eat the whole thing. Not that he doesn't deserve to choke on it.

"Your car. Your Honda." Beverly, snappish. It's not just his junior taking all the play. It's interviewing someone with my file, my Face—the Face done double, super-Face—and having to mince along like this. No talkee, no speakee. Kid gloves all the way. "It was impounded after being towed for a parking infraction two blocks from a murder scene. The morning *of* the murder. Or the morning just after. Several hours later, say."

I have to talk to make him disappear. Performing way out somewhere beyond myself. Subway busker in Carnegie Hall. "My ex-in-laws. They live nearby. I go back sometimes."

"Nostalgia?"

"The car died."

Worth it, despite the effort. The words hauled up like rocks. He sinks back in his chair, fog closes over him. Like a gray blanket. Like a head slipping under the waves.

Frank leans forward. I don't mind that. Her. "We're not interested in you for the murder. Not really. We've got Judy's confession, freely given. Which for all her… challenges… hasn't changed since the first time she gave it. For motive, there's all we need in the victim's photograph collection. Which should go a long way towards reducing her sentence. Some sort of special custody, obviously, given the nature of the crime. But… Even that will seem too harsh to the people who'd like to see her walk. You wouldn't know, I guess, but there's a groundswell for that already. Blogs, editorials, Facebook groups. Ms. Villanueva gets asked about it in her interviews. She doesn't tip her hand, but it's pretty obvious she'd lean to leniency, too. I can't say I disagree."

Shiftings in the fog shroud beside her. Beverly unhappy in his bag.

I'm taking in too much. Static mostly gone, radio almost clear. It's dangerous—wrong in post-window time, Stone's time—and it scares me. I've climbed up way beyond myself, up into regions I've no business being in. Like a fish taking a stroll on deck, gazing at stars. Gopher lounging beside the burrow—sky full of hawks.

Stone not saying a goddamn word. Which scares me too. He should be howling foul.

"Just a couple more things today. Then we'll let you rest. We've made a good start. You know these men."

Glossy colour photo. Peach and Lemon in a doorway, pastel shirts and crotch-kissing pants, heads leaned together grinning. Heading out for a night at the club, it looks like.

"This is a more recent shot."

Ms. Villanueva doesn't issue pink slips. The slips are pulps of red, white and gray where the heads were. Strangely little of it on the shirts, just flecks on the pressed collars. Someone strong and swift. And, too, they're hanging off a couch, most of them still up on it. A natural drainage position, the pool going out of the frame.

Bye bye, bros.

"A lot of blood on the bats, as you can imagine," Frank says. Something soothing in the way she talks. Not hard, not gentle—just quiet and direct. "Most of it theirs, of course. But a little of it yours. Traces, down in the cracks. You were in our system... and the match came up."

"Which means the guys who did you got done too. Exact same way," Beverly growls from inside his bag. Pointing out the obvious for any morons in the room. It's torture for most men to sit silent while a woman does the talking. It eats like acid, all over.

A little more gets said. Not much, but most of it I miss as I descend back into the element where I'm supposed to be. Feel Stone waiting below, fuming.

Just a few more things I catch.

I hear them go to the door, call the woman back in. Hear her chuckle at something said as she returns to the kitchen. A strange sound to hear, that chuckle. I can't place it up there where I was for a few moments, can't place it down here where I'm heading.

Detective-Constable Frank comes back for a moment. A gray skirt flecked with black, a fine plaid, in front of me, the start of legs below.

"Something you may be wondering. It just occurred to me," says her voice, clear but thinning as I drop. "Something you may be in the dark about. It was Ms. Villanueva who hired your caregivers. Round the clock at first. Then just for daytime. She said she wanted to come and thank you personally, and plans to. But for now this was the least she could do. For helping her get out of a trap she couldn't get out of herself."

A pause. I nod in it. Something, someone, tells me to.

"I think Sandor Wyvern might have chipped in too. Maybe even some strangers. Like I say, there's something of a groundswell. It's touched off something, this case. And you... you've got some fans out there."

Hand comes out, stops in time. Smart lady.

Out there.

She comes back one more time. *You could like her... if you were here.*

"Something I forgot to ask. Everyone in ICU's been scratching their heads on it. A couple of office bets, even. Where'd you find the Christmas Music shots? How'd you get your hands on them initially? From Judy?"

I need a voice again and find one, finally.

"Old... Maude's keepsake...," it says. Rust-thick, fading. .

"Maude... Wyvern?"

A nod towards a nod. A single wing in flight.

§

Bombed backward after they go. Like the time after TAL, like every time since. Ruins, blacker than before. Rubble chunks, dangling wires. Not even a sign of smoke. Dresden '45.

Stone needs his time. He takes it. If he grants a window, he exacts its full equivalent in stir. Any unsanctioned movement back to operations, any unwarranted life in the world—he yanks the chain back, hard.

Like this episode with the officers. I didn't ask for it, they came to me. Still, it's a premature flit upward. A flap into adjustment territory—into life. Which isn't due to happen for weeks. Months maybe. An exchange with anyone, however passive and piecemeal, is reaching over my head. Living off the ranch. It's got to be countermanded by a spell in the depths.

Super-subtle in some ways, Stone's a brutalist in others. He keeps strict books.

Shut-down is shut-down. Closed means closed.

§

Vivian out there. Vivian and—who? Doing things. Making plays.

The thoughts come singly, far apart. Long sticky spaces between them. Reaching one feels like breaking free from tough elastic webbing—some determined insect, all mandibles. And a shiver of *wanna act*, itching of wing muscles slime-coated and pinned, meeting clean air.

Followed immediately by a Stone advisory.

Not your beat, son. That's window talk. We're post-window now. This is mine.

Work to be done.

Course there is. Always. But not till we're done.

Not till I say.

Stone's voice lazy, apt to drawl, when he knows he's got the floor.

And then almost gently at times, crooning as to a restless child. *You know how it works. Window's open, then it's boarded up. Settle into dark. Shh. We'll get there soon enough.*

And webbing, soft sticky gauze, comes back in. Heavy and thick, like the first days. Soft, dark, impenetrable cocoon.

Woman—women?—there again. There longer, there all the time it seems. Sometimes, opening my eyes in the dark, I see her reading in a chair pushed up against the kitchen counter, little lamp over her shoulder. She? They? I can't see to tell them apart. Just fuzzy blobs.

Close my eyes.

Waiting for a sign.

It comes from Stone—who else?—from the zone he runs and summons to. And who else would be speaking now? It's Stone's watch. Stone's time.

Except—it doesn't sound like Stone. Not quite. Stone-inflected. Stone-plus?

Waiting for a sign.

§

Rain at first. Just rain. *Soft sleepytime.*

A hard pattering. Skittering sounds, mice scurrying on glass. Seeds, grains thrown in fistfuls. Drifting in and out, lulled by the sound. In the chair, a blanket over me.

Harder now. Frozen pellets, slashing. Oozing thickly down, hardening in spots to glaze. Aquarium. Freezing over.

Ice storm.

Longest day. She said that earlier. Start of winter.

Calendar time. Clock time. Not yours. Not ready yet.

Stone's voice… but fading. His meter ticking too.

Awake again. The window ice glowing. That thick. Feel my forehead. Warm, not burning. Carefully, I stand. Get next to the glass. Hands and forehead on it, cool. The street bare. EMS, the Fire Station, wide open. All out. One car slewed up onto the sidewalk, clear-coated with ice. Toy dipped in plastic.

Hear it, behind the ice scatter. Tinkling, like a million chimes. Squinting, see them. The coated twigs, clear bells, jostling. The great trees leaning impossibly. Bulks straining to hold.

A long time. And then the first crash. A crack, a deep rending tear, long like a scream, and then the splintering rush. The thud. Immediately, the stoplights go out. Condo at the corner goes black.

Ice keeps coming down. Limbs, whole trees, sagging lower under the clear heavy hand. Strangled creaks and groans inside it. Lurches, then toppling, taking more blocks into black.

An area of darkness. And another. Joining to make a greater. Light streams trickling through, around. Another crash. Another chunk of darkness claimed.

The black, the dancing gleams.

And now, inside the striking chips, the tinkling and the crashes, a warmer, fainter sound. Drifting high wail of sirens, from faraway, from all around.

Singing of adjustments without end.

Singing of the long climb back.

Acknowledgements

THANKS TO THE staff at Biblioasis, particularly Grant Munroe, Natalie Hamilton, and Chris Andrechek.

Special thanks to Dan Wells for his warm personal support and close, perceptive editing.

About the Author

MIKE BARNES, a dual Canadian-American citizen, has published eight previous books across a range of genres: poetry, short fiction, novels, and memoir. His poems have appeared in numerous anthologies, and his stories have appeared twice in *Best Canadian Stories* and three times in *The Journey Prize Anthology*. He has won a National Magazine Award Silver Medal in the short story category. His collection of poems, *Calm Jazz Sea*, was shortlisted for the Gerald Lampert Memorial Award; and *Aquarium*, his first collection of stories, won the Danuta Gleed Award. He has also published many essays, one of which, the photo-text collage "Asylum Walk", won the Edna Staebler Award. His last book, a collaboration with the artist Segbingway, was an illustrated book of fairy tales entitled *The Reasonable Ogre*. He works as a private English tutor and lives in Toronto.